ROLL HITLER!

BY
DANIEL BRUCE BROWN

INKWATER
PRESS

PORTLAND • OREGON
INKWATERPRESS.COM

Paperback
ISBN-13 978-1-59299-465-6 | ISBN-10 1-59299-465-2

Kindle
ISBN-13 978-1-59299-542-4 | ISBN-10 1-59299-542-X

Publisher: Inkwater Press | InkwaterPress.com

Printed in the U.S.A.
All paper is acid free and meets all ANSI standards for archival quality paper.

3 5 7 9 10 8 6 4

For Diane,
for everything

Many in my generation no longer feel like guests in anyone else's land. It is not enough for us, as it was for our grandparents and parents, that we be tolerated as a minority in a country where only the majority are first-class citizens. We insist on being treated as equals. We have no qualms about seeing a Goldberg, a Shapiro, or a Cohen run for governor or even president. We need not *sh'a shtill* (be quiet) as my grandmother constantly warned. We don't have to worry about *shanda fur de goyim* — fear of embarrassment in front of the gentiles — or being lightning rods for anti-Semitism if we are too visible or successful. Maybe we are overconfident. Maybe we are no more secure than the Jews of Germany thought they were in 1929.

— Alan M. Dershowitz, *CHUTZPAH*

Contents

THE CHOSEN PRESIDENT

1

It is D-Day. Debate Day. Do or Die Day. The press, indeed almost everyone who has followed this presidential campaign, has said this third debate will decide the outcome of the election. And I agree. I am fighting for my political life. After the Democratic convention in July, I led Sanders 52% to 42%. But following the Republican convention in August, the elephants charged and the donkeys retreated; suddenly I trailed by ten points. Since that time I have slowly clawed my way back up. The latest polls showed us dead even.

But there's no point in thinking about that now. What's done is done. History. Tonight is what matters. The moment is what matters. We are into the eleventh hour of the campaign. We have each taken our best shots. We're nearing the wire. Standing here, awaiting my chance to get in one more blow, the sweat continues to ooze and drip from under my arms. My brow feels moist, my upper lip wet. My God, I must look like Nixon did when he squared off against Kennedy, on the night his sweat glands, his five o'clock shadow and his shifty eyes sealed his fate. Fortunately I am neither hairy nor shifty-eyed. But will it matter? My Republican opponent, Robert E. Lee Sanders, clears his throat into his fist as the moderator invites him, as decided by an earlier coin toss, to make the first closing remarks. Sanders, though a bit weary-eyed, still looks fresh, patrician. I am sure he knows that we have fought to a draw. I am sure he will now try for a knockout punch. I wipe the sweat from my brow and upper lip with one finger in an attempt to be as inconspicuous, as casual, as possible. Then I notice something very odd. There are three times as many spotlights bearing down on me as there are on Sanders. So much for level playing fields. I should have expected something like this, this being Sanders' home turf. The first debate was on mine, the second on neutral territory. I remember going out of my way to be sure nothing like this happened when I was host, nothing that would give ammunition to my opponent. But what good did my sense of fair play do me? I look over at Sanders. He stands in a cool autumn light. What's more, his face and his salt-and-pepper hair are being massaged by the gentle breeze of a fan placed no more than six feet in front of his podium. There is no such fan for me. I stand in the Sahara at noon. During summer. In a heat wave. The air is oppressive and stagnant. I continue to drip and melt while Sanders drones on. His face bears a warm glow. I fear I must look like bleached-out bones. I grow angry. No, furious. But I am no longer feeling hot. My rage has become cool, calm, collected, like a sword freshly forged being plunged into water. I will be ready. I will be ready.

I am listening now to that terrible nasal drone of my illustrious opponent as he crisscrosses his way through the tangle of issues we have covered, trying valiantly to arrive at some intersection of wisdom, some bumper sticker line to graft to the fickle mind of the American electorate. I am not listening intently enough to know if he will succeed, because I am trying hard to formulate my own closing remarks. If he has nailed me at all tonight, it is on the pork barrel issue. Have I transgressed here? Of course I have. What senator hasn't made deals, reluctant compromises, bent over so far backwards that he could kiss his own ass? But have my transgressions been more visible than most? No. Maybe. Yes. Certainly the cigarette compromise applies here. Still, to single me out is a bit unfair, although I suspect fairness is not something my silver-tongued demagogue of an opponent has on his mind at this moment. But I must not let him get away with his cheap shots. I must strike back. And I will. I can tell now by the tone of his voice, decelerating from fourth gear to third to second to first, that Sanders is about to make that one final push. "And so, my fellow Americans, your choice is clear. A vote for Robert E. Lee Sanders, a man of principle. Or a vote for Myron S. Goldberg, the King of Pork."

There is a polite pitter-patter of applause but nothing like the thunder I had expected. And then it is my turn. I have a script, rehearsed well into the previous night, but it no longer seems to apply. A few seconds go by as I gather my thoughts and the crowd seems to grow anxious, uncomfortable with the silence. In the back of the room I see the blonde and gorgeous Ashley Jones, press director for the Committee to Elect Ron Goldberg, easily my sexiest traveling companion for the past eight months, waving a hand in the air and then puckering at me. It is now or never. For some reason, I begin to think about the debate sponsor, Oscar Meyer, then about ham, bacon, pork. Pork! Of course. Pork.

"Madame Moderator, honored guests, my fellow Americans. Thank you for giving me the opportunity to speak to you tonight. To share my views on a number of vital issues. To share my hopes and aspirations for this great and wonderful country of ours, the greatest damn country on the face of the planet." I remember being told by my old friend Candace Rowe, a career diplomat, that many foreign countries regard swearing in English as a sign of sincerity. So, given that this debate is being broadcast around the globe I decide to throw in some moderately salty language. "I will not bore you now by rehashing what has been said here on this worldly stage. Nor will I stoop to the level of personal attack as my opponent has. Mr. Sanders has called me the King of Pork. The flip-flopper. The consummate hypocritical dealmaker, willing to sell my soul to whatever devil crosses my path or my palm. Okay, he's had his say. You can believe him or not believe him. But let me first say this in my defense. You all know that I am a Jew. And what is a Jew? A loaded question. And one, I'm afraid, that would require a bit more time to answer than I have left here. But I will say this. As a Jew, I am obliged to honor not simply 10 but all 613 commandments, many of which you are familiar with already, though you may not realize it. One in particular is instructive here. And that is keeping kosher. The laws of *kashrut* tell me that, as a Jew, I must not eat shellfish. Or certain meats, most noticeably pork. Not for health reasons as commonly misconstrued. But, as it says in Leviticus, to be holy. 'For I am the Lord that brought you up out of the land of Egypt to be your God. You shall therefore be holy.' Holy. Please burn that thought into your mind and, at the same time, ask yourself who more than an authentic Jew could pledge what I am about to pledge to you, the great American people? Yes, I have made pork barrel deals as a congressman and a senator because that, my friends, is what we legislators do. Mr. Sanders knows this well and I can assure you that he doesn't practice what he preaches. Be that as it may, as a Jew and, I hope, as your next president, I now make this formal pledge." I pause for maximum effect. I look around the room, at Sanders, at the moderator, then right into the camera. I am dripping once again, but this time it is with sincerity. "NO MORE PORK!" I say. Then another pause. "NO MORE PORK!" I begin to pound the podium. "NO MORE PORK! NO MORE PORK! NO MORE PORK!" Suddenly the entire room joins in the chant. "NO MORE PORK! NO MORE PORK! NO MORE PORK!" I look over at Sanders. Despite the utter look of disgust on his face, I notice that his hand is involuntarily tapping his own podium in time with the chanting. "NO MORE PORK! NO MORE PORK! NO MORE PORK!" This goes on for another minute or so. All the while people are randomly jumping out of their seats, clapping their hands, stomping their feet. "NO MORE PORK! NO MORE PORK! NO MORE PORK!" Finally the moderator puts an end to all the commotion, though it refuses to die easily. My God, I think, I have really stumbled onto to something here. My pollster, John "Jack" Frost, who is standing next to Ashley Jones in the rear of the room, looks positively ecstatic. Woody Stone, my campaign director, is absolutely giddy. Ashley sends another pucker from those beautiful rosy lips of hers in my direction and nods with pride and approval. For the first time since the convention, I feel like I can actually win this thing. Ah, but can I give up pork?

❧

It is October 31st. One week before the election. The dust has long since settled on the final debate and I have taken a slim lead in the polls. Gallup shows me leading 50% to 46%; *The Wall Street Journal*, 51% to 44%; and my private poll, according to Jack Frost, shows me ahead 49% to 45%. Not exactly breathing room unless you're taking shallow breaths. But it is clear the call for NO MORE PORK has struck a responsive chord with the electorate.

We are in my senate office, deciding what to do for the final push. It is about 9:00 a.m. and we have already been pouring coffee down our throats for an hour or so. At the center of the circular conference table lies a large, ornate tray looking like a silver sun. Just a short while ago it had been piled high with pastries and donuts, a burial mound for healthy living, but it is now populated with only half a croissant and few crumbs. We are raw energy, emphasis on raw. We are ravenous for victory. Woody has said we must keep the heat on, make as many appearances as humanly possible during the last week of the campaign. Jack, an optimist with a sense of reality — a good blend for a pollster, I think — agrees.

"You've got the momentum, Ron," he says. "But momentum at this stage of the campaign is like virginity — easily lost and not something you can get back."

Ashley agrees, saying that maximum exposure is the key to victory. Calvin Foxx, my deputy campaign director, nods his approval as well. Only Phil Hurley, my political coordinator, seems out of synch with the rest of us.

"Phil?" I say. "You look like a fly in the ointment. What gives?"

Phil reaches into the inside pocket of his sport coat and ominously extracts a piece of paper. Slowly he begins to unfold it. Phil is a mousy looking man, balding, with a wispy gray mustache and a narrow face, who looks as if he's spent his entire adult life trapped behind a desk in some obscure federal facility ten floors under ground, going half blind from reviewing too many forms under a single light bulb dangling from the ceiling. He has a predilection toward being a Chicken Little. The sky is always falling. Phil's sky anyway. While working for the Whitney administration as a senior adviser, Phil had been indicted on charges of influence peddling, of selling his access to the president to various high-powered clients through a public relations business he ran in his spare time. The charges were eventually dropped but questions still remain. One of which was where the hell Phil was during the week before the hearings. He had been rumored dead, a suicide, and was later reported to be staying at a retreat, owned by a billionaire friend, on Lake Champlain in Vergennes, Vermont. On the day of the hearings, Phil suddenly materialized again, unwilling to say where he had been or to acknowledge that his disappearance made him look guiltier. Why do I have a Phil Hurley, a Whitney loyalist and life-long Republican, as part of my organization? Because the best way to beat them is to get them to join you. "Another raisin in the pudding, Ron," he says as he flattens the paper out on the table. Phil, a man who never uses profanity, calls rabbit turds raisins.

"So let's have it," I say.

"I just got word that Sanders is running a new commercial. It's going to break over the weekend."

"And that's it?" I say, referring to the paper.

"Yeah, that's it," says Phil, his voice muted but nevertheless unable to conceal his pride in being the bearer of this, for the moment anyway, fence-sitting news. "It starts out showing a clown walking across a white seamless background toward the camera. When his body is full frame, he reaches down, takes off his shoes and then exits the frame. The camera slowly zooms in on the shoes. The voice over says *Ron Goldberg has been making a lot of promises lately. He would like you to believe that he is a great man. And that Robert E. Lee Sanders could never fill his shoes. Well, we don't agree with the great part. But we do agree that only Ron Goldberg can fill his own shoes.* Cut to black. Super: Robert E. Lee Sanders for President. Voice over: *It's time to get serious.*"

"And you think that might be damaging?" I say flippantly.

"There is one other thing," says Phil.

"Yes?"

"The clown was wearing a yarmulke."

~

"So he thinks Jews are clowns, does he?"

"He thinks you're a clown," says Phil Hurley.

"And you think that's believable?"

Phil shrugs. "The American people have an amazing capacity to believe just about anything. As long as it's presented well. Hell, they got Schwarzenegger to do the voice over for chrissake. The guy's believable. Even if you hate him."

"I'd have to second that, Ron," says Ashley. "Presentation is everything."

"Ditto," says Woody.

"Jack?"

"I'd have to agree, Ron."

"So all of you really think we need to respond to this crap? To dignify it?"

"Respond, yes," says Phil. "Dignify, no."

"We can't just sit idly by," says pollster Jack Frost. "Remember what happened to Dukakis. That whole Willie Horton thing."

Ashley, smirking, uncrosses her shapely legs and rocks forward. Sometimes she has no use at all for Jack. She's always telling me she'd much rather create public opinion than blindly report it. "It wasn't Willie Horton that killed Dukakis. It was Dukakis himself riding on that tank with his official Army-issue helmet looking like fucking Snoopy.

8

Every goddamn TV station in the country ran that footage on the six o'clock news. People knew instantly that as commander-in-chief Dukakis would be a joke. The guy never had a prayer after that."

"A clown in a yarmulke isn't Dukakis in a tank," I say. "At least we know a clown in a yarmulke can fight."

Frost shakes his head. "Makes no difference, Ron. To the American people, Bozo with guts is still Bozo."

"I disagree. You can't be a clown and have courage, too. And as far as I'm concerned, if the American people want to believe all this garbage, they can have Sanders."

"I still think we gotta respond," says Phil.

"And I still say we don't."

We argued for another hour or so, sometimes raising our voices, sometimes trading insults, occasionally apologizing. But in the end I chose to stay with the hand I had. And when the morning papers hit the streets, it appeared that I have made a good decision. For once a prominent non-Jew has been crucified. The press has torn the Sanders commercial apart and urged him, in the name of decency and honor, to disavow it and to yank it off the air. *The Washington Post* went so far as to say it was blatantly anti-Semitic. At our status meeting later that morning, I drop the *Post* on the conference table and say, "It seems now, ladies and gentlemen, that the shoes are on the other feet."

❧

In a short while the polls will be closed and the projections will begin. I am at the Worcester Airport Suites Hotel standing in the middle of the living room of a mammoth penthouse suite with dimensions that would effortlessly inflate and corrupt an egotistical man, but only serve to make me feel smaller, embarrassed, queasy, Republican. I am surrounded by campaign workers and key staffers who apparently feel nothing of what I feel. Their posture is confident. Their mood festive, self-congratulatory. Two dozen or more flat screen TVs, mounted high in a continuous border on the otherwise stark walls, provide me with a 360-degree view of the macrocosmic frenzy in the ballroom on the main floor. Red, white and blue balloons are suspended in a net from the ceiling, poised for their ethereal victory dance. Red, white and blue banners, as if patriotic eyebrows, arch above the cathedral-like windows. Two bars, diagonally across the ballroom from one another, are hopping, the lines from each extending into the crowd like giant umbilical cords. Rock 'n' roll, disco and folk music, slicing across five decades, is blaring. Right now the Bee Gees are whining "Stayin' Alive." Before that the Stones belted out "Start Me Up." Before that, at the expense of someone's job perhaps, a smoky-voiced Gene Simmons growled out "Asshole." A lot of people are dancing, gyrating like serpents. Others are just mingling and yapping, creating an exuberant din. Secret Service agents, conspicuously sober-faced, guard the various ways in and out of the room and take everything in with eyes that move faster than those of an Evelyn Wood Speed Reading graduate. In the meantime, an arsenal of champagne stands by, waiting to be uncorked. I have refused to let even a single bottle of it be opened before I am projected the winner, if indeed that is what fate holds in store for me. The press may have largely been on my side in the waning hours of the campaign, but the reaction to Sanders' commercial was mixed. Indeed he actually seemed to pick up more support than he lost because of it. I am worried but hopeful. Scared but exhilarated.

"Excuse me," I say to my staffers, who keep chattering in a way that tells me I won't be missed, and go sit down on a couch between Sheila, my wife, and Ashley Jones. Sheila is a tall dark beauty with ebony hair. Her body is firm and shapely. It is hard to believe that she cares so little about sex these days. (Talk about false advertising.) Ashley, on the other hand, is petite and blonde, a woman who can't talk without using her hands. She is charged with sexual energy. Also huddled on chairs nearby are Woody Stone along with Phil Hurley, Jack Frost, Calvin Foxx and their spouses; the women combined haven't said more than twenty words all night, including "thank you" several times.

"I need to get out of here for a while," I say to Sheila. "Back to our room."

"Want me to come too?" Sheila says. She puts her hand on my knee, something she hardly ever does anymore.

"Not yet. I need to be alone for a while." I nod to Woody and Ashley, a gesture not lost on Sheila.

"Define alone," Sheila says knowingly.

"Being with less than five people at once."

Sheila smiles. I smile back. It feels good to be on the same wavelength with her. But then we always are at times like this. It's the day-to-day stuff that's so difficult sometimes.

Woody, Ashley and I enter the bedroom through a door with a small, slightly askew "Private" sign. The voluminous room is designed, very much like the presidency itself, to elicit passion (the wallpaper is bordello red, its fleur-de-lis pattern is gold), as well as to chase away loneliness. It's large enough to house two king-size beds, four night tables, a sofa and a loveseat, a coffee table, several stuffed chairs, an armoire and matching dresser, an entertainment center, and an oval conference table that seats eight. I grab my briefcase from atop the table and stretch out on one of the beds, propping myself up with a few pillows. Though I've been sitting most of the night, my feet throb. I kick off my shoes. "The polls will be closing in a few minutes," I say. "How about flipping on the TV?"

Woody obeys. "You sure you want to watch?"

"On second thought I think I should polish up my speech first."

"Which one?" says Ashley, deadpan. How could I not love this woman?

෴

The moment of truth is near. Peter Taylor, the ABC anchor, says he is about to project a winner. My bedroom has become wall-to-wall people. There must be ten of us squeezed onto my bed alone. I'm sitting on the edge of it, staring at the TV screen. Sheila is clutching my right hand. Ashley Jones is clinging to my left. "And this just in," says Peter Taylor, "we have a new president-elect. And he is the first Jewish president-elect in the history of the United States." Suddenly a whoop and a cheer erupt, so loud that I cannot even hear Peter Taylor say my name though I can read it on his lips. "...all the way from a city in Massachusetts called Worcester."

Political analyst Charles Andrews interrupts, "You know, Peter, Ron Goldberg once told me a joke about Worcester. He said that when he went to Worcester Academy, the boarding students used to say that Boston was the...well, actually Peter, I don't think I can say on the air what the president-elect told me."

Peter Taylor and Andrews politely chuckle. "Too bad," says Taylor. "Guess I'll have to wait for the commercial break. Which actually, yes, I'm getting the signal to cut to now. We'll be right back, America. Don't go away."

The bedroom is in a total frenzy. Everyone is hugging and kissing as if it were New Year's Eve. I have so many arms around me I don't know to whom they all belong. I squeeze and hug and kiss back indiscriminately. I am inadvertently touching shoulders, faces, bellies, buttocks, breasts. I wonder if ancient Rome was like this. No, I think not. After all, this is not an orgy of masters. This is a revolt of slaves. Here there is new-found freedom, blind joy, untainted optimism, love thy brother, love thy neighbor, swords into plowshares, no more suffering. Here there is a tomorrow, a glorious sunrise, a long overdue end to mourning in America. Suddenly there is a burst of laughter and fingers pointing at the TV. As all heads strain to see what's going on, I too turn just in time to catch the end of an Oscar Meyer commercial. "NO MORE PORK!" someone shouts. "NO MORE PORK!" the rest of the room begins to chant. Sweat is now pouring off my brow. "NO MORE PORK! NO MORE PORK! NO MORE PORK!" My face too is soaked, but I realize the drops on my cheeks are different from those on my brow. They are tears. "NO MORE PORK!" I find myself shouting over the shoulder of a woman whose body I am embracing. The body is Sheila's.

◈

I am at the podium in the main ballroom of the Worcester Airport Suites, wrapping up my victory speech, which I am sure practically no one has heard because of the constant cheering and clapping. Sheila is at my side. As are my daughters, Sam and Ray. Sam is nine and Ray is twelve. They are holding up pretty well, but I know they must be exhausted. I feel the same way. In fact, I almost feel faint. I can't remember that last time I ate something. Was it breakfast? Where was I for breakfast anyway? Atlanta? Dallas? New York? Chicago? Standing nearby are Woody, Phil, Ashley and Calvin. They're all beaming like Doctors Frankenstein proudly displaying their creation. A moment ago Ashley smiled impatiently at me and kissed the air.

"We have much to do as we go forth from this room. But before we do I would like to once again thank Robert E. Lee Sanders for waging a strong campaign." This is greeted by a chorus of loud boos. "But most of all I would like to thank every one of you for helping me snatch victory from the jaws of defeat. On to Washington! God bless you."

The applause is thunderous as I make my way through the crowd behind a wedge of Secret Service agents. Actually "wedgie" would be more accurate, given how constricted I feel. Occasionally there is a loud pop from a champagne bottle being uncorked, which causes the heads of the agents to jerk toward the noise. The flashes from cameras are blinding. I can't wait to get the hell out of here, even though I'm high as a kite from being the center of attention, the center of affection. With each step, the weakness in my limbs grows. I just want to make it to the private elevator. If I can do that I'll be okay. A path to the elevator doors has opened. We are only ten feet away. I am still shaking every hand that slithers through the web of Secret Service agents. Warm hands, cold hands, skinny hands, fat hands. Hands that have touched God knows what. Finally, we make it to the elevator, but not before one more champagne bottle pops like a gun. The doors close. I sigh. Next thing I know I'm being carried out of the elevator into my suite. The girls are sobbing. Sheila keeps telling them that everything is going to be all right, that Daddy just fainted, that he's been working much too hard.

"Cookie," I mutter.

"Cookie?" Sheila says, chuckling. "Ron, you gotta be kidding."

The girls giggle uncontrollably. "Oh, Daddy," Ray says.

"A cookie?" says Sam. "Daddy wants a cookie?"

"He scares us half to death," Sheila says. "And now he wants a cookie? Remind me to kill him when he feels better."

"Cookie," I manage to whisper once more.

"Why not pork?" says Sheila.

THE FIVE COMMANDMENTS

2

She says that if I take one of these I'll feel better. I am not so sure. She says that if I take one of these, I'll relax, sleep, just drift away. Of that I have no doubt. For how long is what I wonder. She would like it to be for a long, long time, I fear. I am a bother to her now, where I had initially been a novelty. I interrupt her card games, her talk of enemas and organs, her flirtations with young doctor Kildare. Besides, I think she's a Republican.

"Enough already, Mr. Goldberg. It's late," she says. And then, if I continue to complain as she puts it — to ask for more ice water, a copy of *Time* or *Newsweek*, whatever — she shouts, "Did you take your medicine, Mr. Goldberg?" "No, I didn't take my medicine, Nurse Ratched!" I whisper fiercely. Frankly, I've been putting the stuff, three doses worth, in the vase of flowers Sheila gave me. The flowers have been wilting ever since. Is it from the medicine, I wonder? Have you ever

16

seen roses on Valium? I can tell you it's not a pretty sight. "If you put it in the vase again —," I can hear her shout from the hallway before I can clamp my ears shut tight with my pillow. I wonder what's in it for her. Why does she care so much about me taking my medicine? Is her job at stake? Who is she really working for? Did she vote for Sanders? It's late, she says. After midnight, she says. Get some sleep, she says. The sun'll be up before you know it, she says. Nag, nag, nag.

I pick up the vase, which is on my bedside table, and throw the wilting, drugged-out flowers on the floor. They make a sickening splat. I look at them for a while, sadly, and then I put the vase to my parched lips and drink down the swampy water with a series of important gulps. The next thing I know Woody Stone is shaking me awake.

~

Woody Stone is no longer my campaign director. He is about to become my chief of staff. He's a nice kid. Graduated from Dartmouth in 2002. Yale Law in 2005. Woody may be something of a wolf in sheep's clothing, but he's a benign wolf. There is a boyish charm about him that is irrepressible. And there's a solid intellect behind all that charm, too. After graduating from law school, Woody clerked for Supreme Court Justice Anita Hill for a year, a position he had won in head-to-head competition with hundreds of candidates — a majority of them female and black — from the nation's top law schools. During that time, he occasionally crossed paths with Ed Drinkwater, a Mississippi Democrat out of the William Fulbright mold, currently the Senate majority leader, who back then chaired the Senate Judiciary Committee. Ed took an immediate liking to Woody, as most people do, and offered the young man a job on his staff when his term with Justice Hill ran out. Woody, whose love for politics borders on obsession, jumped at the chance to work for Ed, a political figure of mythic proportions. "You can teach a horse the ropes but you can't make him Drinkwater," the saying around town goes. But under Drinkwater's hefty yet gentle wing, Woody would do more than learn the ropes. He learned how to use them. Which is precisely why I hired him. "The kid knows Congress and the city," Drinkwater told me when I called him up for a reference, "and no PAC or individual holds a mortgage on him." What more could any presidential candidate want? A campaign director with major assets but no debits.

Woody hands me a cup of coffee, black, the way I don't like it. "Looks like you're out of a job, boy," I say.

"Looks like," Woody says. It is obvious that he couldn't care less about that. His horse has come in.

"Well, we'll just have to find you a new one." I say. "How's chief of staff sound?"

"That would suit me fine, Mr. President," Woody says.

"Elect," I say. "President-elect. Let's not go rushing things, Woody."

Woody is still all teeth. He's thirty-two years old but he looks maybe twenty-two. "Whatever you say," he says. He hands me *The Washington Post*.

The headline reads: GOLDBERG DEFEATS SANDERS BY NARROWEST MARGIN EVER. The sub-headline reads: 275 to 273 in Electoral Votes, 56,221 in Popular Vote.

"Can't get much closer than that," says Woody.

"A win is a win is a win," I say.

"Sanders is demanding a recount in Massachusetts. We only beat him by forty-five votes."

"That's his prerogative," I say.

Woody looks annoyed for the first time since he rocked me into consciousness. His pearly whites have vanished behind a frown. The sparkle has gone out of his eyes. "It's just an exercise in futility," he says.

"The man has a right," I say.

"The man ought to concede."

"Oh, he'll concede, Woody. He'll concede."

Two weeks later, after a painstaking hand counting of the Massachusetts ballots under the supervision of federal marshals, the verdict was in. Myron S. Goldberg has carried the state by not forty-five, but fifty-four votes. "He should have quit while he was losing," I say to Woody.

"Right," says Woody.

&

I was dead wrong about Robert E. Lee Sanders. He never did make a concession speech, not even after the Massachusetts recount. I suspect that means he feels he really didn't lose. During the next two-week period when the recount was in progress, the *Post* ran a headline that said: BOTH SIDES STILL CLAIMING VICTORY. This was followed by a subheadline that said: Sanders refuses to concede; Goldberg thanks America for mandate.

Sanders, to say the very least, was teed off by my statement, although I can assure you it was not intended to be inflammatory. For the next week or so, his people called my people and my people, with a courtesy I doubt his people would have reciprocated had he been in the lead, attempted to explain what everyone agreed was a minor faux pas. Let me say this in my defense. In the first place, I was not, as the Sanders camp professed, referring to the still-in-doubt election results. What I was referring to was a Gallup Poll that appeared in the *Post* two days after the election. The question put to the American people was this: How would you rate the job performance of President-Elect Goldberg since the November 7th election? Here are the results of that nationwide poll:

> 83% Doing A Good Job
> 10% Not Doing A Good Job
> 4% Too Soon To Say
> 3% Unaware of Election

Now I ask you, if that's not a mandate from the American people, what is?

∾

Another thing that got Sanders all in a huff was the fact that I had been taken to Walter Reed Hospital for treatment from "exhaustion." Neither he nor his people bought that explanation. He issued a statement at a press conference, again before the Massachusetts verdict, that "reliable sources" had told him that I really had been admitted because of a "nervous breakdown." Apparently, Sanders and his people felt that even if the recount did not go in his favor, he should be declared president-elect anyway, since "it is obvious that Goldberg is unfit, physically or mentally, to assume the reins of power." He went on to say that a president must be tough. He said a president must be impervious to pain. He said a president must have stamina. In the final weeks of the campaign, Sanders made a thirty-two day sweep of the Southern states and then called it quits. I, on the other hand, covered forty-two states in the last twenty-three days. I even made an unscheduled trip to Israel, though sentiments being what they were, I certainly didn't have to. Now I wasn't wearing an odometer, mind you, so I can't say exactly how many miles I covered, but I certainly covered more than my venerable and, I think, overly critical opponent. Enough, at any rate, to lay the "stamina" issue to rest.

As for the "nervous breakdown" accusation, let me say this about that. I am not a nervous person but, like everyone else from time to time, I do run out of gas. Is that such a crime?

In a few days I'll be out of here anyway, as good as new I am told. How could it be otherwise? After all, Mother has brought me her chicken soup. Sheila presented me with flowers for the first time in sixteen years of marriage. Ray and Sam have called every night. Tim Green dropped by with a pack of Wrigley's Spearmint Gum. And, of course, there's my "mandate." Suddenly I feel like anything is possible.

The only thing that's missing is Cookie Dunn.

&

You want to know what the real bug up Sanders' ass is? It has nothing to do with losing per se. I mean the guy has lost almost as many elections as he's won. He was elected to the House from Mississippi in 1970, lost in 1972 and 1974, made it back in 1976, ran for the Senate unsuccessfully in 1978, practiced law for the next six years in Jackson, defending white collar criminals who had committed "victimless" crimes, then ran for the Senate again in 1984, as a self-proclaimed "champion of the common man," and won. Since that time he's managed to keep getting himself reelected, thanks, in large part, to some Rovian "grassroots" fundraising, but as you can plainly see, he's no stranger to losing. The thing that's really making him crazy is that he lost to a Jew. Now, how can he show up at a KKK meeting with an albatross like that around his thick red neck?

There's something else about Robert E. Lee Sanders that brings his "champion of the common man" claim into question. While still maintaining his law practice, he managed to become a self-made millionaire as the owner of Robert E. Lee

Cutlery, a company known to pay employees rock-bottom wages and to provide only the benefits required by law. This austerity program aside, the company was largely unprofitable for its first ten years in existence, but then skyrocketed to fame, infamy really, and to the number one position in the industry when Sanders, in a move that led to the indignant resignation of more than a dozen key managers, introduced the O.J. Simpson Cutlery Collection. When blasted in the industry and the press for bad taste, Sanders struck back. "Now who all you boys tryin' to kid?" he said. "Ain't nuthin' more American than bad taste. And nuthin' that sells better neither."

❧

Dr. Bernard Cohen, my personal physician and a good friend, says that all my tests were negative and that I have absolutely nothing to worry about. I trust Bernie. We go back a long ways. He's also my mother's doctor and was my father's too. One of the many thoughtful things Bernie always remembers to do is to ask me how my dad is, even though he's been dead for ten years. I appreciate that as much as anything else he does for me.

"Nothing, Bernie?"

"Nothing, Ron. Physical anyway. I can't help you with the political stuff."

"Too bad."

"I'll check back with you tomorrow morning. I'm sure we'll be able to discharge you then." Bernie shakes my hand. "Take it easy. And don't forget to say hello to your dad for me next time you talk to him."

"Will do."

❧

It's 3:13 a.m. and I am having trouble sleeping. There is another patient down the hall who is screaming at the top of his lungs. The whole floor was supposed to be vacated for me but, due to overcrowding, the hospital was able to give me only half a floor. I am content with this arrangement, being only half a president at this point. But Woody Stone is not. Woody had suggested George Washington University Hospital or Bethesda Naval Hospital as alternatives, but apparently the same conditions exist there. So be it. I just wish they could gag that loudmouth SOB, so I could get some sleep.

"The hell with all you assholes! I ain't lettin' no goddamn Johnson cut me open. I told you I want the Jew. Get me the fucking Jew! Bernburg, Bernstein, Burnbomb, whatever his fucking name is. Just don't let him put any of their blood in me. Don't want no Heeb blood flowing through my veins. It'd probably kill me."

This ranting goes on for another fifteen minutes before the nurses and orderlies can pack up all the monitors and gadgets attached to the patient and move him to another floor.

"Get me the Jew! I want the Jew!" he screams as he's wheeled down the hall. "But no fucking blood! You got that? No fucking kike blood!"

A moment later a nurse pops her head into my room. "Sorry you had to hear that, Mr. Goldberg. I can assure you, it won't happen again."

"Not to worry, nurse," I say, "I've heard much worse. Besides, with all the people who've screamed for Jewish blood over the centuries, it's really quite refreshing to finally come across someone so dead set against it."

∾

The patient who was doing all the screaming is a retired

general named Thomas Ridgeway. He served in the Gulf War under Stormin' Norman Schwarzkopf and was seriously wounded during a Scud missile attack while he was stationed in Saudi Arabia. He is a distant cousin of the late four-star General Matthew Ridgeway, who led the U.S. 82nd Airborne Division against the Germans during World War II.

"What's wrong with the guy anyway?"

"He's in for a quadruple bypass. But we've had to delay it due to other complications," says the nurse.

"What complications?"

"Just this morning he developed a peculiar red rash around his neck."

"Hmmm."

"We don't know what caused it yet."

"Too bad. It's always the good ones, isn't it?"

❧

It's 6:42 a.m. and Bernie Cohen says I'm being discharged. He tells me that all I need to do to get my strength back is eat right, get some regular exercise and plenty of sleep. I do not know yet if any of these suggestions are compatible with being the President of the United States. But I will soon learn.

When Bernie leaves, my brain trust floods in. There is Ashley Jones, looking alert and beautiful as ever. There is Phil Hurley, looking furtive and nervous as ever. Woody Stone, in a navy blue pinstriped suit, seems calm, but wears his game face. And, finally, there's Calvin Foxx, the former 60s anti-war activist turned elder statesmen, sipping coffee from a Styrofoam cup, looking all the while like the cat that ate the canary.

We exchange handshakes and good-mornings. Then Woody pulls up a chair next to my bed and pulls out a piece of paper. Cal and Ashley sit on the end of my bed. Phil remains standing, pacing, straightening the pictures on the wall, his tie, the newspapers on my tray table. "Ron, we know you've had a rough day or so," says Woody, "but we really need to get things moving. Yesterday the four of us met and hammered out a plan of attack, including a list of responsibilities for each of us. If it's all right with you, Cal will advise you on domestic policy. Phil will be your senior advisor. Ashley, your press secretary. And of course I'll be your chief of staff, which we already discussed."

"Sounds like you've got all the bases covered. But what do I get to do?"

"He's such a card," Ashley says.

"The first thing we, you, have to do is pick a cabinet. We've already worked out a short list for each position."

"Fine. Let's just be sure we've got plenty of minority candidates."

"They're on the list."

"What about Abe? He on there? He's my first choice for Treasury you know."

"I know. And, yes, he is."

"Let me see the list."

I give the list a quick once-over. It looks like the guest list for the inaugural ball. I think it IS the guest list for the inaugural ball.

"Look okay?" Woody says.

"Look's great. Thanks." I hold the piece of paper above my head. "This, my friends, is gonna make me the best damn Jewish cabinet maker since Jesus."

⌘

I cannot blame Ashley for leaking my statement to the press. I thought it was pretty damn clever myself and deserved to be heard. Nor do I blame Ashley for my words being misquoted. In my home state of Massachusetts, the *Herald* ran this headline next to one of the many unflattering photos of me they have collected over the years: WILL HE PLEASE US MORE THAN JESUS? The *Washington Times* headline, though not as poetic, had the same basic message: PREZ-ELECT SAYS HE'S BETTER THAN JESUS. Robert E. Lee Sanders has called for my impeachment and the word is that he and his cronies are pouring through volumes of court cases trying to uncover a legal precedent. Has a president-elect ever been impeached?

"They're burning you in effigy all over the South and West, Ron," Ashley says. "Making bonfires out of our campaign posters. I'm really sorry. It's just like what happened when John Lennon said The Beatles were more popular than Jesus."

"I know you'll fix it," I say. "In the meantime, at least I'm in good company."

"You're approval rating is down to 28%," says Jack Frost.

"So it can only go up."

"I wish," says Phil Hurley.

"Of course, American voters do forgive and forget quickly," Jack adds. "Remember they're still reelecting incumbents 95% of the time. They're like battered women for chrissake. They know they should change, but the devil you know is better than the one you don't."

"The question is, Jack, which devil am I?"

⁓

Like I said, I don't blame Ashley for all the flak I'm now getting. Without Ashley I wouldn't even have the privilege of getting this much flak in the first place. I have learned a lot from her about how to handle the public, and what I have learned has served me well. It was Ashley, for example, who taught me the Five Commandments of political life.

One: always stick to the script. Assuming it's a halfway decent one, Ashley says, even a passable actor like myself can be convincing. Of course, on the night of the third debate I ignored this commandment and was damn lucky things worked out as well as they did.

Two: KISS, but don't tell. KISS is Ashley's favorite acronym, one she learned during her ten years in the advertising business. It stands for Keep It Simple, Stupid! Or, in other words, never explain too much. People get confused the more you say and the more confused they get, the less likely they are to vote for you. Whenever Ashley thinks I'm beginning to ramble, she just sends a pucker my way and I know what to do.

Three: Keep your mistakes complicated and your successes simple. This is sort of a corollary of Commandment Two, which Ashley developed from studying Republican strategy and campaign tactics. "What are the biggest mistakes the Republicans made over the last 40 years? Watergate, the S & L fiasco and Iran-Contra, right? Well, who, except for a very select few, really understands what the hell anybody did wrong? And then the Republicans turn around and nail Mondale for being 'Norwegian Wood,' Dukakis for being 'Zorba the Clerk' and Clinton for being a philanderer. Now that's kind of stuff people understand. And, believe me, it sticks."

Four: If you do make mistakes, don't make them near an election. Try to make them during the first two years of your four-year term. Conversely, save your biggest successes for the second part of your term. Like Jack Frost says, Americans have short memories.

Five: Don't peak too early. Greatness, Ashley always says, is a dish best served just a few weeks before an election.

I have done my darnedest to live by these commandments. And I will forever be indebted to Ashley Jones for teaching them to me.

⤳

About a month has passed since the election and, while I live in fear that my Jesus comment will be resurrected during the Christmas holiday season, I have been assured by Ashley that it would be far more appropriate for that to happen during Easter.

"Very funny," I say.

"If we can't laugh, where would we be?"

"Besides," says Jack, "people are already starting to forget. Your approval rating is up to 54%."

"How do you explain that?"

"Your press conference, for one. The passage of time, for another. The fact that this is the time of year people feel most charitable doesn't hurt either."

54%. Indeed things seem to be falling into place. I have made my cabinet selections and, by and large, they have been well received by Congress and the press. I expect that Senate confirmations will take place without a hitch. The only choices I made that caused any stir at all were the two I thought would be received most favorably. Live and learn. Max Berger, once a highly effective criminal trial lawyer and currently a well-respected justice on the U.S. Court of Appeals, came under severe criticism because of his opposition to the death penalty. In his defense, I held a press conference, reminding the country that I too am opposed the death penalty. "For me," I said, "the determining factor is accepting responsibility. If one cannot personally pull the trigger or throw the switch, one should not endorse the death of another human being." Since that statement was made, I have received about a thousand death threats, virtually all of which the Secret Service has classified as "very serious." I have been told that this is something of a record since the other presidents of the past three decades only received about 1500 serious death threats a year. Imagine that. And I used to think the American public was apathetic.

My other surprisingly controversial appointment was Abraham "Honest Abe" Rubin as secretary of the Treasury. An eminent Harvard-trained economist who has always been adamantly pro-business and a former chairman of the Fed noted for keeping a stranglehold on interest rates throughout his tenure, my good friend Abe seemed like a natural choice. Little did I know that the Christian right, with a poisonous string of totally unfounded accusations, would mount a counter-attack against Abe, dubbing him, of all things, "the secretary of usury" and "leader of the international conspiracy of Jewish bankers." The most radical members of the right said that, one way or another, Abe would not serve out his term. What did Abe have to say about all this nonsense? "Fuck 'em if they can't take a joke."

&

I have made one other appointment during the Whitney lame duck period that I know will serve me well. I have made my personal senate secretary, Rosalee Wilson, my personal presidential secretary. Fortunately, Rosalee will not have to go through Senate confirmation hearings because she has a tongue and a wit that would most certainly sabotage her appointment.

Rosalee, white-haired, in her late sixties, is kind of like a second mother to me. In some ways, I suppose, she's like the mother I never had. She is fiercely loyal and over-protective. She has the best darn built-in shit detector I have ever seen. In fact she has X-ray vision for bullshit and is not afraid to confront it, no matter who the source happens to be. Rosalee also happens to be a very big woman, built like a wrecking ball, probably close to 200 pounds. She commands respect.

One other thing that I really appreciate about Rosalee is her ability to remember names and recognize voices, neither of which I am particularly good at and which is definitely an occupational hazard. As a matter of fact, since Rosalee is so good at these things, I'm sure I've gotten worse at them over the years.

∽

"Candace Rowe on two," Rosalee says through the intercom. "She's using her important voice."

I pick up the phone. "Candace, hi, what's up?" Candace is my nominee for secretary of state. I also plan to put her in charge of the NSC in order to minimize foreign policy disputes within my administration. Hey, it worked for Nixon and Kissinger. Kissinger held both titles too.

"It's the Iraqis again."

"What's our good friend Diya Bakir up to now?"

"The CIA claims he's planning to assassinate Solomon Dayan."

"So what else is new?"

"They think he really means it this time. And that's not all."

"It never is."

"They say he's going to come after you."

"Let him come. You think 3,000 Secret Service agents can't protect me?"

Lines four and five begin to flash. "Look, Candace, I gotta go. We'll talk more about this later."

"Take it seriously, Ron. Bakir may be a crackpot. But he's a dangerous one."

"We'll talk."

I hang up and push the intercom. "Who we got, Rosalee?"

"Your wife on four. Bull Dozier on five."

"Get rid of Dozier. I'll talk to Sheila."

∽

"What's up, hun?"

"A slight problem."

"With one of the girls?"

"No. With the inauguration."

"What could be wrong?"

"January 20th. It's a Saturday."

"Yeah. And?"

"The Sabbath, Ron. It's the Sabbath."

"Hmmm," I say.

THE TEFILIN PRESIDENT

I'm telling you, Ronnie, it's gonna take an act of Congress to get them to change the inauguration to the 22nd.

So be it, Pop. Besides, they had no problem moving the observance of Lincoln's birthday. Or Veterans Day. Or Memorial Day. All we'll have to do is call it Inauguration Day observance. And then it will all be kosher.

This is nothing to joke about.

I wasn't joking.

You're getting off on the wrong foot, my son. Trust me on this.

You'd rather I take the oath on the Sabbath?

I'd rather, for your own sake, you start by making ripples, not waves.

I'm sorry, Pop. I really am. But that's the way it's got to be. Anyway, pebbles make ripples. And I'm a rock, not a pebble.

Rocks also sink.

I've made up my mind.

You'll piss them off.

What do you mean piss them off? I'm giving them another god-
damn three-day weekend. Pretty soon even Simchat Torah will be a
national holiday!

❧

My father was right. It did take an act of Congress to
move Inauguration Day from Saturday, January 20th to
Monday, January 22.

President Whitney vetoed the measure, but by some miracle, fomented, I believe, by a major outcry in the so-called
Jewish-dominated press, his veto was overridden.

"This is only the beginning," Maxwell Albright, a prominent leader of the Christian right said. "It's not enough their
women are pushy. Now their men are becoming just as bad.
A Jewish tide, my friends, sinks all boats. Beware. Prepare."

Bang, bang, Maxwell Silver Hammer.

❧

It is Monday, January 22, 2013. The rain is heavy, far
heavier than any I can recall since my arrival in Washington
some twelve years ago. Storm drains are overflowing. Many
streets, including some main thoroughfares, are now impass-
able. In the middle of Pennsylvania Avenue, I saw ducks
floating, their snowy bottoms periodically turned up toward
the clouds in heretical protest. Woody Stone says he heard
unofficial reports that fish are jumping on Virginia Avenue.

"Maybe it's an omen," I say to Woody.

Woody is watching the chief justice of the Supreme Court
adjust his tie. "Maybe," he says absently.

"Not since Noah, Woody," I say. "Not like this."

"Noah," Woody says. He is now adjusting his own tie.

When he is done, it is still crooked but I haven't the heart to tell him.

"I wish I could swim," I say. Then I laugh self-consciously. I imagine another Great Flood cleansing the world, washing everyone away, starting the whole foolish soap opera all over again.

"Me too," says Woody. "Wish you could swim."

"It's a good thing it's not snow," I say.

Woody cannot be reached for further comment. His eyes are riveted on the chief justice, who has just made his way to the podium. History, my fellow Americans, is about to be made.

⁓

I raise my right hand as if it is weightless. In fact my whole body feels weightless. Am I floating? If I am, no one seems to know, to care, or to think it's anything unusual. On Inauguration Day, presidents float. That's just the way it goes. A rule no one told me about. Happy to oblige, though. Unfortunately, as I lift my left hand to place it on the Bible, I suddenly crash to earth in a heap. But why? Have I flown too close to the sun on wings of wax? Have I shown up at the wrong address? Or at the right address but at the wrong time? Is that why this is happening now? Is that why underneath my left hand there is a Christian Bible, with its so-called New Testament? Held so innocently by the eighty-five-year-old chief justice of the Supreme Court, a Republican appointee, who surely remembers that I, a lifelong liberal Democrat, warned that the next president would get to replace him and, therefore, must not be another Republican. Yes, the New and Improved Testament, staring me down like a friendly pogrom, cocky about its pervasive status in America, as if the Hebrew Bible, or Old Testament as it is insidiously known, the basis for virtually all Western ethics and law, were somehow obsolete. My hand flinches backwards as if I have touched a hot stove. "I can't," I say.

"Sir?" says the chief justice.

"I can't take the oath with my hand on that. What good would it do? What would it prove? What value would it have?"

"But I thought...you were...my God, you're an atheist, too!"

"Too? No, I'm not an atheist. I'm a pious Jew." A Jew, anyway.

The chief justice looks baffled, bordering on horrified, but soon anger begins to ooze from the deep cracks of his prunish face. "Then what, sir, may I ask, is the problem?"

By now there is a murmur rising all around me, from the dignitaries at my back and from the immense undulating crowd at my feet. A murmur growing like a forest fire, like a rumor. "I want my Bible, damn it!" I whisper forcefully. And then, somewhat against my will, I add sarcastically, "You know, the Old Testament, the one our whole damn legal system is based on. I think you may be familiar with it."

"Oh." The poor old man is stunned. Looks pathetic. Defeated. Emasculated. His spinal curvature seems greater than it was just a moment ago. Clearly, this has never happened to him before. Certainly not in front of 100,000 people. Not to mention a TV audience in the tens of millions, perhaps billions. Shakily, he turns to soon-to-be ex-President Whitney and hands him the New Testament. "He wants the Old Testament."

"He wants the what?" says Whitney gruffly. One term was obviously not enough. Or maybe the festivities have him all stopped up.

"The *Old* Testament."

Whitney shakes his head and turns and hands the Bible to his wife. "He wants the *Old* Testament. Jerk."

Mrs. Whitney slowly lifts her hand to her cheek and turns and hands the Bible to Candace Rowe. "He wants the Old Testament. Oh dear."

Candace in turn hands the Bible to attorney general-designee Max Berger, who hands it to secretary of the treasury-designee Abraham "Honest Abe" Rubin, who hands it to someone else who hands it to someone else who hands it to someone else until it finally makes its way over the last row of spectators behind me, vanishing from sight like some piece of hapless cargo washed overboard in a storm. About fifteen minutes later, the whole process happens in reverse, the murmuring of the crowd growing louder and louder as the replacement book moves downward on a slide of human hands, finally being passed to the chief justice who then turns to me with a look of disgust and says, "Satisfied?"

I look at the cover. It says *The Hebrew Bible*. It is not our own family Bible, which has mysteriously disappeared, but it will do nicely. Or will it? For some reason I think of John Fitzgerald Kennedy's inaugural speech. *The torch has been passed to a new generation.* I smile reflectively, recalling how at bar and bat mitzvah ceremonies, the Torah is passed from grandparents to parents to the child to symbolize how this, the world's greatest and most influential document, "a tree of life to those who cling to it," is passed from one generation to the next.

"Mr. President-Elect?"

"No," I say. "I'm not."

"No?" says the chief justice, as if trying to decide whether to cry or explode.

"No. I want a Torah."

"A Torah?"

"Yes, a Torah."

"Dear God. You can't be serious."

Thirty-three minutes later, a Torah miraculously arrives by limo. A secret service agent, in mirror sunglasses and nondescript suit, steps out cradling the Torah in his arms. As he pushes his way through the crowd toward the podium, Jews reach out to touch the holy scroll with their hands or programs. When the agent reaches the steps of the Capitol he hands off the Torah to one dignitary who hands to another who hands it to another, and so on until it reaches Sheila.

"Now?" says the chief justice wearily, obviously fearing that I might choose to pile one more straw on his brittle, bent back.

"Yes, Mr. Chief Justice. Now."

The chief justice raises his right hand and instructs me to raise mine. I place my left hand on the Torah. Today I am a president, I think.

❧

"I, Myron S. Goldberg, do solemnly swear that I will faithfully execute the office of the President of the United States, and will, to the best of my ability, preserve, protect and defend the Constitution of the United States."

So said the first Jewish President of the United States, as forty-four presidents had said before him.

❧

Standing at the back of the Capitol, breathing in the exhaust fumes from the endless train of tour buses lining Jefferson Avenue and beyond, I realize that Washington is a spectator sport par excellence. I am well aware, too, how different this magnificent view is from what one sees entering the Capitol from the front. Those front stairs are forever filled with somber looking people, most sitting, some sprawled out on their backs, some solitary, some in groups, even some homeless people, all protesting something, many holding up placards or banners dripping with angry penmanship. I was always, and remain, a bit saddened by this daily scene, this wonderfully American portrait of democracy inaction, whereby anyone, provided he or she doesn't block access to the building or cause a disturbance, is welcome to be ignored.

But let's, for now anyway, return to the Capitol's backyard. As I look farther down Pennsylvania Avenue from this heady vantage point, I can see the Greco-Roman columns of the Treasury Building where the avenue bends. The Air & Space Museum is on my left, the National Gallery on my right. Yes, a very heady point of view indeed, tempered only by the stone image at the reflecting pool of Ulysses S. Grant on horseback, the general's noble steed facing the Lincoln Memorial. It is no accident, I think, that incoming presidents are forced to gaze upon the south end of a northbound horse. It keeps us humble. And with this in mind, I speak to America for the first time as president.

"I come here before you today, not so much as your leader, but as your ally. I come here today not to dictate how our streets will be made safer, how our economy will be made stronger, how world peace will be made firmer. I come here today not to dictate how disease will be cured, how education will be improved, or how the environment will be saved. Instead I come here today to ask for your help as a full partner in America's future. We have much to do and not a lot of time to do it. We must turn quickly to the job at hand, rise above petty and divisive politics, resist gridlock of the mind and spirit. For only then can we achieve what we, together, pledge here today to do. And so, my fellow Americans, ask not what your country can do for you or even what you can do for your country. Ask instead what we all can do together to achieve national and international harmony. The road may be long and hard but the American spirit is indomitable and immortal. We will not fail. We will not turn back. We will succeed. God bless you all. Thank you."

Suddenly there is thunderous applause and cheering. It goes on and on with no sign of abatement. All the while, people are waving white sheets of paper in the air —100,000 copies of the transliteration of *"Ein Keiloheinu,"* distributed before the ceremony, flapping in the breeze like the wings of eagles, ascending higher and higher. I had requested that the words of the traditional hymn not be translated, although they do nothing but praise the glory of God, and not in a uniquely Jewish way either. When the applause and cheering finally begins to wane, the orchestra begins playing. Most everyone joins in. They act as if they are singing "We Are The World," swaying slowly with the music. It is a high I will never come down from.

◦~◦

It is just prior to Rabbi Jim Simon's benediction and we are asked to pause for a moment of silent prayer.

I close my eyes, but instead of bowing my head, I tilt my face toward the sky. *Hey, Pop! Proud of me?*

A mishegoss that thing with the Torah, Ronnie. Especially after they were kind enough to reschedule the inauguration. Please listen to me. You would do well not to make them too angry too soon.

I gotta be me, Pop.

I know, I know. You were never much good at being anyone else.

I love you, Pop. Forgive me.

I love you too, my son. But forgiveness is for God to grant. I will, however, be happy to put in a good word for you.

Suddenly there is an out-of-synch chorus of amens.

Thanks, Pop.

&

After the inauguration, I am hustled into my limousine by Secret Service agents. They slam the door shut and jump into the limousine directly behind me. The third limousine in the fifteen-car motorcade carries the military aide responsible for the Black Box, which will always be kept within my reach just in case I get a sudden urge to start a nuclear war. Also in the third car is Calvin Foxx, to whom I have given the authority to make civilian-level decisions should something happen to incapacitate me — like a bullet through the brain. The Secret Service calls these three limousines "the Package" because we are never supposed to be separated. The Secret Service has a penchant for cute descriptives. Just the other day, while traveling to a speaking engagement in Chicago, I inadvertently learned that one agent had nicknamed my limousine "Greedy One." When I shared this with Abe Rubin, he, though not even sworn in yet, immediately had the head of the Secret Service replaced, the offending agent fired, and then personally changed my car's code name. Henceforth, it will be known as "Mazel Tov." I have also told Abe to make sure that no one ever refers to the Secret Service as the SS, for reasons that were obvious to him.

Next to me in the limo sits my wife, Sheila, who looks tired and upset. On my other side are Rachel and Samantha. They are being good sports about all this, too, considering that their lives will never be the same. The presidency is like a disease; it affects every member of the family.

On the seat opposite all of us sit Ashley Jones, Phil

Hurley and Woody Stone. Nobody says anything to anyone else. We're all bushed.

Finally, Woody says, "Nice speech, Mr. President."

"You wrote half of it," I say.

"I meant the half I didn't write," says Woody.

"Thanks," I say.

The motorcade splashes down Pennsylvania Avenue. Throngs of people, undaunted by the rain, line the street. They are all waving. They are happy. They act as if they have been witnesses to a miracle. Is this what it was like for another Jew two millennia ago? I wonder. There is an out-of-control character to their conduct, indeed a drunkenness, as the limousine of their newly anointed leader sends waves of muddy water lapping over their feet.

I don't quite feel their elation, though I smile and wave back. Do I know them? I wonder. Do they know me? We are all strangers. Smiling strangers. My father always told me, "Never smile at a strange dog, Ronnie. Show your teeth and he thinks you're going to attack. Likely to take your fool hand off." My smile begins to shrink, the way my body shrinks after making love. I think the honeymoon is over. I think how am I going to make this marriage work?

Joseph Zeiger of the *Post* has dubbed me the "tefilin president." No doubt Zeiger had Ronald Reagan on his mind when he did, since he had just published a 78-page biography of the beloved Teflon president called *Chips in the Teflon Coating: The Final Reagan Years, 1986-1988.*

Tefilin, or phylacteries, are leather boxes that contain pieces of parchment on which sections of the Bible are written. Leather straps are attached to the boxes so they can be fastened to the forehead and arm during prayer. In

Deuteronomy 6:8 and 11:18, we Jews are instructed to place a sign or symbol "on the hand and between the eyes" to serve as a reminder to obey God's commandments and also as reminder that God delivered us from Egyptian bondage. Having grown up in a reform synagogue, I have never worn tefilin. Nor do I feel a particular need to be reminded of God's moral presence or God's gift of freedom. These are not things a Jew takes for granted. In any case I have to say, while witty and germane to my faith, the label of the "tefilin president" is simply not accurate. Although, I suppose if I did wear tefilin, they'd help me to remember Ashley's commandments as well.

In addition to having the distinction of being the tefilin president, Carl Svenson, also of *The Washington Post*, has dubbed me "the Jewish Kennedy." My kingdom, he says, is "the kosher Camelot." Another paper, I forget which one, says that I'm "as Semitic as apple pie." The *Herald*, from my home state, has printed an editorial about me, headlined FUNNY, HE DOESN'T LOOK JEWISH.

I am taking all of this nonsense with a grain of salt. Yes, my hair is sandy brown and my eyes are blue and my nose is Roman, but I swear to you, on my father's grave, I am one hundred percent Jewish, or at least as Jewish as the next Jew. I refuse to let them take away the magnitude of my accomplishment by implying that I'm not really "one of them."

Also, for the record, I do not keep kosher. Although I have, of course, sworn off pork for the foreseeable future.

Regarding my genetic baggage, I can say with pride that

I have never checked it but always carried it with me. In fact, I can recall that, even as a boy growing up in a largely non-Jewish world, I had no difficulty saying that I was *Jewish*. Still, I cannot recall any time in my distant past when I identified myself as a *Jew*. That is a recent phenomenon for me. And one, I surmise, that pretty much sums up the meandering and surprisingly purposeful journey of my soul. I was once an adjective. Today I am a noun.

~

Ever since I came to Washington as a congressman in 2001, I have dreamed of this day. Frankly, I don't believe that there is any red-blooded American politician who comes to this magnificent city who does not, at some idle moment, have dreams of making it to the White House. The smell of power is everywhere. Yes, a garden of power, some of it sweet, some of it sour, some of it tangy, some of it nearly odorless yet beautiful to behold. I have cultivated every square inch of it. I have been labeled ruthless, tactless, charming, warm, cold, hard, soft, charismatic, bland, a black heart, a bleeding heart. My skin must be a foot thick by now.

The raindrops on the window of my limousine look like tears. They make blotchy shadows on all of us inside. We are now splashing our way still further down Pennsylvania Avenue, past the Justice Department, past the IRS, then turning left onto E Street. I can feel my body start to become rigid, anticipating the turn into the White House driveway. We are not, however, making that turn. Suddenly my body feels cheated. It does not understand what my mind already knows too well. My stomach churns. The people lining the White House sidewalk are as frenzied as the rest of the crowds that we have passed. They are not aware of my body's confusion.

"Maybe in 2017," says Sheila.

I say nothing. We have been through this before. We have, I should say, argued about it before. She blames me. I blame the Senate. On the night I found out about the whole thing, she could not be consoled. A fine how-do-you-do, she said. The First Lady treated like a bag lady, she said. She locked herself in the bathroom for an hour. If I tried to talk some sense into her, she turned on the shower or flushed the toilet to drown me out. What a water bill we'll have this month! When she was done with her tantrum, she got right into bed without saying another word. She didn't even turn on my side of the electric blanket. That's how angry she was. So now I say nothing. I play it safe. I think a little lovemaking tonight would do Myron S. Goldberg a world of good.

'Maybe never," Sheila says to my silence. It is as if the insult is hers and hers alone.

The limousine is now directly in front of the South Portico. Even with this gloomy gray day as a backdrop it looks festive, alive. It is bathed in artificial light. I look at it with longing and think, one of these days, Fleming Hodgetts, one of these days.

In the back row of the crowd, there is an awkward bunching movement, like a caterpillar experiencing a cramp. A sign on the White House fence is exposed to my view. Police are trying to keep the people away from the fence for some reason, and then I see why. The sign on the fence says, WET PAINT.

We splash by.

⁓

The man I have just spoken of, Fleming T. Hodgetts, is the Senate minority leader. He's a crusty old bird. Though

we practically never see eye to eye on anything, there is
something I like about him. Call it Southern charm, I don't
know. Fleming can make a racist remark seem like a compli-
ment. "My goodness, aren't you a pretty little nigger!" he
once said to the seven-year-old daughter of Booker T. Brown.
A big man, nearly three hundred pounds if he's an ounce,
with a jowly red face, Fleming has what people call "presence." What they mean is that no matter where he is, you
can't miss him.

Fleming is a powerful man, probably the most powerful
Republican in the country. Especially now, with the defeat of
Robert E. Lee Sanders. Fleming, on his first try, was elected to
the House from North Carolina in 1980 on Ronald Reagan's
broad coattails at the wet-behind-the-ears age of twenty-nine.
Six years later, he made it into the Senate, which is where he
has been ever since. In 2012, he won reelection with 78% of
the vote, whereas Sanders carried North Carolina this year
with a mere 52%. That's presence.

For the past eight years, Fleming Hodgetts has been the
chairman of the Senate Foreign Relations Committee. He's
a diehard anticommunist, who was unwilling to concede,
even with the fatal fracture of the Soviet Union more than
two decades ago, that the Red Menace would eventually
fade to pink. Of course now, with the resurgence of Russia
— bolstered by a combination of American post-Cold War
pampering and neglect, and fueled by a leader who is a chip
off the old Soviet Bloc — Fleming has become something
of a cult hero to non-hatchet-burying people everywhere.
Fleming is also, coming from North Carolina, a champion
of the born-again tobacco industry, dating back to the days
when it had become anathema and its addicted clientele
modern-day lepers, banished from all common areas. In fact,
the stroke of genius that helped to reestablish the noble status

of tobacco in the U.S. has been almost universally attributed to Fleming. (He himself denies it, though I suspect, knowing Fleming as I do, it's simply his way of capturing the spotlight.) Tim Green says that one cigarette company actually wanted to put Fleming's puffy face on its package. Presence is what it's all about.

Fleming Hodgetts is the reason I am not headed up the White House driveway today, on just the sort of day it would have been heaven to curl up with a book next to the fireplace in the library. Fleming, you see, is also the chairman of the Senate Redecorating Committee.

∾

About my one hundred percent Jewishness, I confess, I exaggerated a little. Forgive me. The pressure has been getting to me lately, as well you know by now.

The truth of the matter is, I have some non-Jewish blood flowing through my veins, as I suspect most every Jew does. For centuries our women have been the victims of rape, so how could it be otherwise? Still, we have attempted to be as homogeneous as possible, willingly allowing ourselves to be herded into ghettos, as much for our own protection as from persecution.

Mother said it happened sometime during the administration of James C. Buchanan, our fifteenth president, who, for those of you who have forgotten, was a Federalist later turned Democrat, of Scottish descent. I mention this Scottish descent not so much as a point of interest, but as a point of fact so far as my lineage is concerned. No, I am in no way related to our fifteenth president. But I am, so the story goes, a descendant of one of his humble brethren.

The story was handed down in my family from generation to generation like a basket of hot sticky buns at a holiday dinner, transferred from one set of cradling hands to another with loving care. And like those buns it grew tastier with anticipation, with the sweet caress of time. Part of it was myth, I am certain, but which part that was I could never tell; so I was compelled to believe it all. It went something like this.

Along about 1858, Sophie, my great-great-grandmother on my father's side, was coming home from a dinner party at a friend's house. It was around midnight and Great-Great-Grandmother was pretty tired, but she felt like walking anyway. When she walked through the middle of town, she stopped in front of a Wells Fargo office and there, tucked in the corner of a window, was a sign that was asking for people to join a wagon train headed for California. Sophie had seen trains before, but never a wagon train. The idea of a string of wagons parading down the train tracks for California fascinated her beyond belief.

My great-great-grandmother's full name was Sophie Morgenstern. She was born in Hungary in 1834 and came to New York City with her parents in 1846. The Morgensterns loved New York City, in spite of the hardships and discrimination it bestowed upon them, and so they made up their minds that they were going to die and be buried there. Sophie was happy to see her parents content, but this did not make her content. She wanted to visit strange new places and do strange new things. She had heard all about the California Gold Rush of 1849 and that there was gold in them thar hills, and she dreamed of being rich. She had little use for hardships, thinking nothing was really gained from suffering except debilitating cynicism or inane optimism. It was no surprise that she decided to join the wagon train and seek her fortune out west.

Sophie changed her name to Morgan because she thought

that, if people didn't know she was Jewish, she would be subjected to less abuse. What she forgot was that, in addition to being a Jew, she was a woman and, therefore, was destined to be subjected to all sorts of abuse anyway.

~

The second month out, when the wagon train was somewhere in Wyoming, Sophie wandered into the woods to relieve herself. When she was done and started to head back to her wagon, she was grabbed from behind and pulled to the ground. She screamed and kicked and scratched, but it did no good. The man who had pulled her down had his way with her. His name was Clarence Rob Roy MacGregor. He was a solemn-faced Scot whose life had cut a crooked swath across America for most of his thirty-five years. MacGregor was a Pony Express rider who just happened to cross paths with the wagon train on one of his runs to California.

When Sophie told the organizers of the wagon train what had happened, a group of the menfolk got together and chased after MacGregor. They caught him easily because he wasn't trying to get away. He hadn't thought he had done anything wrong, frontier law being practically no law at all, so when they caught up with him, he was just riding along at a trot, singing "Oh Susannah."

They took MacGregor into custody and delivered him into the hands of the sheriff of the nearest town. After Sophie fingered him, he was found guilty of rape. MacGregor was scared when he first heard the verdict, thinking that they were going to hang him on the spot. What he didn't know until later was that they only hung murderers and horse thieves. He got off with a five-year sentence.

MacGregor came very close to not serving any time at all. The wagon master made the suggestion to him that should he marry the "poor girl" and "make things right," all would be forgiven. Meanwhile, the other women on the wagon train urged Sophie to back the proposal, husbands being a scarce and fragile commodity out west, and MacGregor, with a bath and a shave, being not all that bad a catch. At least he had a steady job and wasn't a horse thief.

Neither Sophie nor MacGregor cared all that much for the wagon master's proposal, however, so MacGregor ended up doing his time anyway. Sophie was not so fortunate. Nine months later, in San Francisco, she died in childbirth. Her daughter, just two and one half pounds at birth, was given no chance to survive the day, let alone to adulthood. But survive she did. The doctor, being the closest thing the parentless child had for kin, named her Lena.

The doctor, a man named Walter Harrison, raised Lena. He was a widower with two young sons. The boys loved to roughhouse with Lena, so she grew up hard and fast, and she didn't stop growing until she reached one hundred and eighty-seven pounds. (This was the Victorian era, you must remember.) People said the lonely doctor overindulged Lena, trying to use her to replace his dead wife. That may well have been true. Yet none of his attention kept Lena from leaving when the time came. The wanderlust was in her genes.

～

When she was a young woman, Lena moved back east, first to New York, then to Philadelphia, and finally to Washington. There she met and, shortly after, married a butcher who had, some two decades earlier, come to America from Poland. His name was Moshe Polchuk. He was a Jew, though to Lena this meant nothing more than his being left-handed. Lena had been raised Protestant and, in fact, did not learn the whole story behind her not-so-delicate birth until she had reached her teenage years. Before Moshe Polchuk, her only other contact with a Jew came from reading *The Merchant of Venice*.

I have a great deal of admiration for Lena Harrison Polchuk. Imagine. Just two and one half pounds at birth at a time in American history when many a normal sized infant did not survive the first few years of life, and yet she lived to be one hundred and ten! She had already passed one hundred when I was born, but she still had all her marbles. She also had about a dozen thick brown whiskers on her chin, which made her look a bit like a circus freak, but they never actually repulsed me.

When she died in 1969, Lena left behind four children, fourteen grandchildren and twenty-two great-grandchildren. One of these great-grandchildren would one day grow up to be what every mother in America told her son he could be, if he was so inclined: President of the United States.

∽

As chairman of the Senate Redecorating Committee, Fleming Hodgetts was to oversee the renovation of every square inch of the White House over the next four years. In order to make sure that the amelioration project took place without a snag, the Senate, prodded by Hodgetts, voted 56 to 46 to have the new president set up residence for his four-year term in Blair House, the lovely historic mansion used as a guest house for top-ranking foreign dignitaries. However, when Hodgetts drew fire from Fergus Preston Helms, my illustrious, Republican-appointed ambassador to the United Nations, a man with a deep fondness for Arab causes and traditional Arab attire — as a young man he was frequently seen wearing a white sheet — the order was quickly rescinded. For my own good, I must add. "What with all those foreign dignitaries traipsin' around, creatin' a veritable four-story Tower of Babel, Mr. President, I think you and the first family would be much more comfortable somewhere else. Someplace where you wouldn't have to be on your toes all the time, weighin' your every gosh darn word as carefully as a butcher weighing meat at the deli counter. I know you know what I mean, sir." Having been to many a deli counter in my time I certainly did. So Blair House was not meant to be either, despite the fact that precedent would have been served, since the great Harry S. Truman lived there from 1948 to 1952 under similar circumstances. A modified bill and a new vote of 64 to 38 landed me in the Ridgeley Hotel instead.

Proponents of the bill hailed it as another milestone in U.S. history. For only the second time ever, they said, the entire White House could be refurbished all at once. Face-lifts, after all, they maintained, should never be done piecemeal. Far better to do nose, eyes, cheeks, chin, buttocks, whatever, all at once.

Carpet salesmen were, of course, delirious with the possibilities. Interior decorators were going out of their minds with joy. Sears offered to provide every drop of interior and exterior latex absolutely free. Then Reynolds topped that by offering to do the entire White House in aluminum siding, for free as well.

Most excited of all about the project was a young senator from Alabama whose name was Booker T. Brown. Jumping on the Hodgetts bandwagon, much to Fleming's chagrin, Brown put forth the idea that, since the White House was going to be renovated inside and out anyway, we take this "unprecedented opportunity to alter its lily white complexion." Continued Brown, "People of color have too long been excluded from presidential politics. Calling our chief executive's residence a white house only serves to perpetuate this deliberate exclusion and to provide refuge for the heinous myth of white supremacy." Brown then suggested that the exterior of the White House be painted something other than white — mauve perhaps, or taupe — and that it henceforth be referred to as the "Presidential Mansion." The Senate voted down the measure, 84 to 18.

Opponents of the renovation bill called it a disgrace. They saw no good reason why the president and his family could not enjoy the use of one part of the White House while the other parts were being renovated. Nor could they accept the thinly veiled reason behind the president's exclusion from Blair House. Secretly, they saw the vote as evidence that we in America had not come very far after all. "We'll let a Jew run the country," one said, off the record, "but we still won't allow him in our home."

No amount of eloquent oratory, private or public, changed the verdict, however. My home for the next four years was to be the Ridgeley Hotel. What the hell. It gives me something to look forward to. Besides, Steve Birnbaum, may he rest in peace in that great Disneyland in the sky, gave it four stars.

"At least we'll have great room service," I say to my disgruntled wife.

She makes a sour face, grits her teeth and says nothing. By this time we are almost to the hotel. It seems to be raining harder, if that's possible. The cheering crowd has thinned like an old man's hair.

"Not to mention, I hear there's a Chinese restaurant right up the street," I say. Things could be worse, I'm thinking. So what if I'm not the first Jew in the White House.

Yet.

On the grand marble stairway leading into the Ridgeley, as my first official duty as commander-in-chief, I am reviewing the troops as they march past. I am a bit uncomfortable in this role since I have never been in the service myself and I don't know if I am supposed to salute back when the troops salute me.

"Is it okay for me to salute?" I ask a sour looking general on my right. He is paunchy, rather short, with a ruddy complexion, and easily over sixty years old. Exactly the sort of person my ban on grays in the military, which I first proposed during the campaign, would ax. Critics, one of the loudest being Robert E. Lee Sanders, have said that forced retirement from the service at age 59 is grossly unfair. But I still maintain that the closer in age a general is to the young men and women he sends to die on the front lines, the more reluctant he will be to send them there in the first place. I mean, if you have some general who's pushing seventy, who figures he only has a few good years left at best, chances are he's going to think dying is no big deal. But a general at fifty, who maybe has a few decades left, might have an entirely different perspective on the value of life. Oliver Graham, chairman of Joint Chiefs, does not agree. Being in his sixties, I can understand why. He has said we should abide by the standard policy that applies to gays, which is Don't Ask, Don't Tell. Only trouble is, you can't hide your age as easily as your sexual orientation.

"It is appropriate, sir," says the general with a restrained sneer, "If your head is covered."

Fortunately, I still have my yarmulke in my pocket. "How's this? Better?"

This time the general's sneer is far less restrained.

⌒

After we "check in" to the Ridgeley, I ask Woody to see

about something to eat. There will be the Inaugural Ball later of course, but I need something to tide me over. "How about that Chinese place?" I say. "What's it called?"

"Tet Ching," says Woody.

"That's it," I say. "What say we give it a try?"

"Okay," says Woody. "I'll have the Secret Service take care of it. I'm sure they'll want to check for poison."

"Everybody needs to feel useful."

"Remember, no pork, Ron," says Sheila.

"I know, I know."

Woody still seems a little depressed but I don't pursue it. I have my own disappointments to deal with right now. Besides, he'll snap out of it. He always does. There's a slow but steady boil of optimism in Woody that hasn't diminished in the brief, albeit highly stressful, time I've known him. I suspect he gets it from his parents, a couple of 60s flower children, eventually becoming 70s weeds, who were heavily into Peace and Love. So heavily, in fact, that Woody was allegedly conceived on the tenth anniversary of the infamous Woodstock concert after his parents celebrated the occasion by twisting open a bottle of Boone's Farm and then getting stoned. Woodstock Stone. Two names that were definitely meant to be together.

"Don't let them forget the fortune cookies," I say.

"I won't," says Woody, and then he's gone.

Later, after we have our Chinese food and complain about our lousy fortunes, I look out the hotel window. Across the street there is a public garden and in the middle of the lawn, there is something that catches my eye. At first I think it's a bonfire, but as the flames die down I can see the charred remains of a wooden object that looks like an inverted rake. Then it hits me. It is not a rake at all. It's a menorah. Is it too late for one more recount? I wonder.

COOKIE STARTS
WITH C

I was not always the president. And I didn't always live in Washington.

I grew up in Worcester, a medium-sized city in the center of Massachusetts, the state I carried by fifty-four votes. When I attended Worcester Academy, then a poor man's prep school, not so anymore, the boarding students liked to say that Boston was the asshole of the nation and that Worcester was forty miles up. Tim Green had once suggested to me that Worcester promote tourism by adopting the advertising slogan, "GET AWAY FROM IT ALL. WE'VE GOT NOTHING."

Tim might have been onto something, because, in truth, the city was nothing to brag about. It was like a videocassette that had been recorded over, time and time again. New buildings went up where old ones were torn down. Tenements fallen into disrepair became vacant lots, burial grounds for stolen and stripped cars; vacant lots became subsidized housing; then most everything downtown eventually got leveled to make way for the miracle that was called Worcester Center, which, if you looked at it closely enough, you would recognize for what it really was: another shopping mall.

It wasn't all that long after that the anchor stores pulled out, causing the smaller ones to sink, leaving the Center an empty shell. Shoppers, it seemed, preferred the free parking of suburban malls, not to mention that getting to the Center wasn't half the fun, but certainly was twice the gas. So the Center soon got knocked to rubble, its dust coating the broken ground of a mixed-use development to be called City Square. Which so far has gone nowhere. And which I expect, if it ever does move forward, will share the fate of its checkered predecessor.

Clearly, Worcester was not a sentimental town. You could count the historic sites on the fingers of one hand. The Worcester Preservation Society consisted of one member, a high school librarian named Lillian Barrow, who was also the president of the Worcester chapter of the DAR and a member of the Worcester school committee. Busy though she was, Lillian Barrow was more than able to take care of the business of preserving on her weekends. It's funny, but now whenever I see those labels on food that say, "no preservatives added," I think of Worcester.

God help me, I still love that town, blemishes and all. If nothing else it had been home for nearly twenty years. I was born there. I took my first steps there; at ten and a half months, so family lore goes. I broke my arm in fifth grade there, sliding head first into third base during a game we ended up losing by twelve runs. (It may have actually been more runs. As time goes by, the margin of defeat gets smaller.) I was captain of our sixth grade basketball team there when we won the city championship in 1972. I fell in love, unrequitedly, for the first time there. My father and brother died there and are buried there. All my pets died and are buried there. And so on.

I am not certain what the current law is governing the burial of presidents, ex or otherwise, but if I am not required to be buried someplace else, Arlington or wherever, I'll probably end up in Worcester, too. That won't be too soon though. There is much to be done. In my journey of a thousand steps I have taken but one so far. There are still multitudes to be fed, governments to be overthrown, rain forests to replant, global warming to reverse, dry cleaning to be picked up. Fetch my tux, boys! We're going out tonight!

❧

I wonder if Hodgetts knows anything about the burning of the menorah. Or maybe the culprit is Robert E. Lee Sanders, his way of conceding perhaps. Or maybe it's just the KKK's way of saying, WELCOME, MR. PRESIDENT. Or maybe even Diya Bakir, giving me a taste of things to come. It's just hard to know these days who would be so thoughtful.

I am having trouble putting on my tux. I don't know why. It was one of three I had custom-made for me on Sheila's insistence immediately after I was elected. She said with all the formal affairs I'll be attending over the next four, hopefully eight, years it would be worthwhile for me to own a few. It's just all these darn parts. It's so damned confusing.

There is a knock at the door. "Yes?" I say.

"Only me, Mr. President," says Woody.

"Come on in, Woody," I say. "Almost ready."

Woody comes into the suite. "Very presidential, Mr. President," says Woody.

"Thanks," I say, strapping on my cummerbund.

"Is the First Lady ready?"

"Not quite. She thinks the egg roll didn't agree with her."

Woody checks his watch. "We still have time."

But we don't. "I'll check on her," I say.

I cross to the other side of the suite and enter the bedroom. I can hear Sheila in the bathroom. It's mostly dry heaves at this point. "Sheila? Honey?"

More retching. "Ron? That you?"

"It's almost time, sweetheart."

"I know, I know. I'll be ready."

"Maybe you shouldn't push it."

"I'll be ready." Retch. Silence. Flush. Silence. Moaning. Silence. "Oh, Ron, I feel so God awful."

"I think you should just rest," I say. "It's really okay."

More retching. "No, it's not. Just give me another minute."

"Okay." I go back to Woody.

"How's she doing?"

"She really took it on the chin," I say.

"Tet Ching," says Woody.

"More like Ret Ching," I say. Woody groans.

A moment later Sheila emerges from the bedroom. She is rigid and unsteady but the luminous pallor of her face, framed by her ebony hair, gives her the elegance of a Greek statue. I can tell immediately that there is no force on earth great enough to prevent her from fulfilling her duties as First Lady. Suddenly I feel an uncontrollable urge to kiss her.

"My God, Ron, not now," she says fanning her mouth with her hand. "I smell like a sewer."

"With my mind always in the gutter, Sheel, we make a hell of a pair."

❦

I mentioned falling in love, unrequitedly. The object of this ill-fated and undernourished emotion was the first Jewish girl I ever fell in love with. I did not know she was Jewish at first because her last name was Dunn and because she, like me, grew up in a non-Jewish neighborhood. Cookie's father was not a born Jew. He converted when he married Cookie's mom. Ironically, he turned out to be a much more devout Jew than Cookie's mother ever was, or either of my parents were, for that matter. He even served for two years as president of the Dunns' congregation.

In any case, Cookie's real name was Lorna Dunn. Which is why she became known as Cookie. Lorna Dunn, Lorna Doone, Cookie. I trust you can see the evolution.

Cookie Dunn was easily the most attractive girl in junior high school and everyone pretty much acknowledged it, except for Cookie herself who remained stubbornly humble through all the jealous affirmations of her unmatched beauty. Cookie was neither short nor tall, about 5'4", I'd say. She was slender and had the body of a dancer, though she denied that she ever took dance. Her hair was shoulder length, dark brown and wavy, with long bangs. Her eyes were sky blue, her lips and nose as delicate as a doll's. If she had ears, I never discovered any evidence of them.

At the year's end, we voted for the superlatives and Cookie was voted Most Likely To Get Married First, Second, Third and Fourth. Cookie was one of the few seventh grade girls to have the body of a woman. The fact that I never saw this exquisite creature in a bathing suit is still a source of great distress to me.

There's something else you should know. Cookie had a fetish. She always wore cashmere sweaters. She must have had a dozen different ones, mostly in pastel colors — lime, lemon, tangerine and so on. She never wore them over a blouse. We boys liked that she didn't, although personally I never admitted it to anyone, not wanting to risk humiliation by letting my classmates know how I really felt.

Cookie's sweaters became legendary around school and, I believe, were a major reason for the dramatic decline in school absences and tardiness. It was a black day for junior high school education when Cookie Dunn was permitted to graduate.

~

"Make sure you save a dance for me," I say to Sam, my youngest.

Sam giggles. When we dance she stands on my feet. "I will," she says. Sam is wearing a lacy white dress. She looks like an angel.

"You, too, Ray," I say.

"Okay, Daddy," she says. Ray no longer has to stand on my feet because she knows the steps. I wonder how many more years I have left before dancing with her father becomes embarrassing to her.

"You girls better not forget me either," Woody pipes in.

Both girls giggle. They're nuts about Woody. I wonder how long it will be before they really fall in love with him.

"Okay," says Sam.

Ray just smiles, suddenly too shy to utter one word.

The rain has stopped. The clouds are starting to disperse. "Think we'll get to see the moon tonight, ladies?" I say.

~

One day Cookie was having lunch by herself in the cafeteria. She often ate alone because her beauty was so intimidating. The fact that she was an all-A student didn't help to endear her to anyone either. So much for the bright and the beautiful being the most popular. Seeing Cookie sitting there all alone made me realize how stupid everyone was for thinking she was quiet. It's hard to be anything but quiet when you don't have anyone to talk to.

I often ate alone, too, so right away Cookie and I had something in common, the seed of a bond. Of course my solitude was not the result of my beauty, though looks-wise I suppose I was no slouch. My isolation came from intense shyness. How can someone whose mouth had always gotten him in so much trouble be so painfully shy? Frankly, I don't know. Ask Freud. Anyway, that day I wasn't alone. I was with my friend Tim Green, who was no prize either.

Tim was tall and skinny and always wore old clothes with slashes at the knees and gaping holes here, there and everywhere. He had no valid reason for this eccentricity. The grunge look was nearly two decades away. Nor was it because his parents were poor. The Greens lived in a six-bedroom gar-rison colonial in one of the ritzier parts of town. Worcester wasn't a totally depressed city.

Tim's mother was a dental hygienist. Tim's old man was a pediatrician, with a sub-specialty in allergies. I always thought giving kids shots was his way of taking revenge on them for being little brats when they were brought to him for routine pediatric care. I imagined him saying, "Mouth off, will ya? Hmmm, you look like a kid with allergies. Injections once a week for three years should do the trick!" The point is, Tim came from plenty of money. He just liked to dress trashy. That he now only wears $2,500 Italian suits is one of life's great ironies.

One other thing about Tim Green. He liked to pick fights with the toughest guys in school, which worried his dental hygienist mom to no end because she figured that eventually this proclivity would lead to the premature loss of his permanent teeth. Tim's feeling, however, was that none of these guys would dare hit him, for fear that he might break in half, and they'd end up doing serious time, or at least get expelled for a few days. The fact that Tim is alive today is, to me, unquestionable proof of the existence of a caring higher being.

Anyway, after Tim and I filled our trays with food, Tim suggested that we go keep Cookie company. Tim had the hots for Cookie, as did just about every other guy in school who was still breathing. Tim fancied himself a sort of charmer, though he was anything but. Tim's tongue had two left feet. And even when he managed to get the words right, he'd spoil everything with the delivery. But my opinion of his social graces aside, Tim plopped himself down next to Cookie. I sat down, too, but I left two empty chairs between myself and Tim, sort of like a firewall. After a while, one learned to give Tim Green plenty of room to make a fool of himself. "Is that a camel hair sweater?" Tim said to Cookie. The look on his face could only be called a leer.

"No," Cookie said, in the most bored sounding voice she could muster. She had no interest in Tim and his kind, or his stale jokes, refugees from a world and time that Tim's brother, thirteen years his senior, inhabited. Obviously she preferred me. I could tell by the way she was pretending that I didn't exist.

Tim was unfazed by Cookie's icy reaction. Her perfume was intoxicating, her rejection of him was the ultimate turn-on. Even when she glared at him she looked beautiful. "So how come the humps?" Tim said and then he howled. I blushed. Half the people in the cafeteria jerked their heads around to see what Tim Green had done this time. Meanwhile, Cookie calmly collected her tray, books and pocketbook, and got up and left.

Tim was out of the running for good.

❧

Even today I believe the best, the purest, kind of love is unrequited love. After all, what other kind of love lets you hang onto your illusions?

Though I still think about Cookie often, I have never told anyone how I really felt about her and how she felt about me.

❧

A few years back, when Sam and Ray still watched reruns of classic "Sesame Street" episodes, and I with them whenever I could, I used to cry when Cookie Monster sang his signature cookie song: "C is for cookie, that's good enough for me. C is for cookie, that's good enough for me. Oh, C is for cookie, that's good enough for me. Oh, cookie, cookie, cookie starts with C!" If my children ever read this, and I suspect someday they will, they'll find out why I cried.

❧

For the next several years I labored to make contact with Cookie. I wrote to her, pouring my guts out, endlessly quoting Shakespeare, Nietzsche, Kahlil Gibran, Rod McKuen, the Beatles, Sonny Bono, Charles Schulz and Karl von Clausewitz. I made feeble attempts to write my own love poems, like:

> *Roses are red.*
> *Ragweed is smelly.*
> *One look at you*
> *And I turn to jelly.*

And:

I may be a jerk.
I may be a slob.
But you are the shish
in my shish kabob!

I asked her out on dates, fearlessly putting my ego on the line. I even asked her to my senior prom, though I dreaded dancing with her, not exactly being Fred Astaire. I confess I was more like Fred Flintstone. But none of what I did mattered anyway. Cookie turned me down flat. Either she would have me all the time, or not at all — that was the message I extracted from her behavior. In time I learned to accept it. After all, Jews were born to suffer, were they not?

&

I almost forgot. Cookie and I did have one date back in seventh grade. We went to a movie. I had no idea what the movie was about, because I spent the entire time waiting for the right moment to slip my arm over Cookie's shoulder. I imagined the right moment coming in the form of a signal from Cookie that I did not totally nauseate her. All she had to do was subtly push her shoulder against mine, or tilt her head slightly in my direction so that her hair, that extraordinary hair, would gently touch my neck like a fine piece of silk. Or she could have reached for the bucket of popcorn at the same moment I did, accidentally coming in contact with my moist hand. But neither of these things, or any other signal, ever happened and, try as I did, I never had another date with Cookie. Tim later explained why. According to Cookie's friend Karen, who back then was considered a "reliable source," and whom I now think of as "Sore Throat" because her information was always bad, Cookie thought I was "nice," but too shy. Being nice in those days was the kiss of death. Nice guys in the movies were the ones who never got the girl. Cookie wanted a tiger. What she got that day at the movies was a pussycat.

～

I never had another date with Cookie and I haven't seen or talked to her since high school. Tim Green sees her from time to time though. His parents still live in Worcester and when he goes home to visit he usually gives Cookie a call. After the camel hair sweater incident, Tim decided that he would try to be Cookie's friend instead of her lover. I don't know what he said to her to patch things up. He never told me, but darned if it didn't work. All I can say is Cookie must have needed a friend awfully bad.

Cookie is now a freelance radio producer. Most recently she produced some commercials for a family planning clinic in Boston called Roe Your Own Boat, RYOB for short. Tim told me she used to work for RYOB as a counselor back in the early 1980s. One time she broke a pro-lifer's nose when he shoved a monkey fetus into the face of a fourteen-year-old girl Cookie was escorting into the clinic. The man threatened to sue, but then, for some unknown reason, backed down. Two weeks later, shots from a semi-automatic weapon ripped through the front windows of the clinic. Miraculously, no one was hurt and the perpetrator, a man wearing a black ski mask, driving what turned out to be a stolen van, was never caught.

I have always admired Cookie for the way she fights for what she believes in, even when her beliefs don't represent the popular choice. I remember when she was just twelve years old how proudly she displayed her McGovern '72 button. And how two years later, during the height of the Watergate fiasco, she went around school wearing Nixon's

1972 campaign button, "Nixon's the One," knowing full well that the parents of most of the kids voted for Tricky Dick. She just couldn't resist the role of gadfly. The amazing thing is, she never seemed to piss anybody off. She always knew what to say and when to say it. What a good political wife she would make! What am I saying? What a good president! Ashley Jones always tells me that in public life the package is always more important than what's inside. And I guess that was true as far as Cookie's various constituencies were concerned. Her manner was always calm and gentle, cloaked in an innocent sexiness. There was something truly hypnotic about her. God knows I've been under her spell for more than four decades now.

The last time Tim saw Cookie was about six months ago when he was back on Cape Cod for the summer. He said he ran into her in Chatham where both of their families have summer homes. He saw her at the beach, he said.

"Fifty-two years old," Tim said. "And damned if she doesn't still look sensational in a bikini."

"A bikini?"

"One that left very little to the imagination."

"Goddamn lech," I said.

"Hey, I'm her friend. It's purely platonic between us," Tim said.

"You're telling me you wouldn't try something if she gave you a little encouragement?"

"I'm not crazy, Ron," Tim said.

"You're something," I said. "Really something. I don't suppose she asked about me."

"No," Tim said. "Your name didn't come up."

"Guess it's no big deal having gone out with a guy who's now a U.S. Senator."

"You were just Ronnie Goldberg then," Tim said. "Plain old vanilla."

I said, "Yeah, that's the truth."

∽

Cookie got married right out of college. She has three kids now, two from her first marriage, and a stepchild, a boy, from her second. Her own kids are girls. They're older than Sam and Ray. I think they're probably seventeen and fourteen. The boy, like Ray, is twelve.

"So you finally managed to quit," I said to Tim, changing the subject. Tim was a three-pack-a-day man before his doctor told him a year ago, "Quit smoking, Mr. Green, or die." Tim doesn't believe in health insurance, never has, and never participated in the tobacco industry's coupon program, so an operation was out of the question for him. Now he chews gum, Wrigley's Spearmint, about two packs a day.

"Cold turkey," Tim said proudly.

I can remember the thing that bothered me most about Tim's smoking was when he ate and smoked at the same time, and then put his butts out on his plate, or in his water glass. "Good for you," I said. Exactly why Tim continues to work for the tobacco industry as a lobbyist I'll never know. Sure, he enjoys an almost god-like status because of it. But without the major perk, which he so oddly refused, it doesn't make much sense. "That coupon program is like cheating, Ronnie," he told me once. "You smoke the pipe. You pay the piper. Ask for favors, you have to give favors. I don't want to owe anybody anything." I guess, too, it's like an alcoholic becoming a bartender. You're not completely cured until you can confront it. Good for him, I thought. And then I said, "A bikini?"

∽

We are about midway through the Inaugural gala evening and I am running on pure adrenalin. We have attended so many white-tie dinner dances, I have lost count of them. Sometimes we have only stayed long enough for the one obligatory dance, which I have performed alternately with Sam, Ray and Sheila to give poor Sheila an occasional break from the spotlight. We are finally sitting down to eat and my feet are throbbing. But the incredible lightness I felt while taking the oath of office still swims happily throughout my body like a young country boy in his favorite pond. I only wish that Sheila were doing as well. As I look over at her I notice that she is starting to swoon. I slide my chair back from the table and get ready to catch her. "Honey, you okay? You don't look so good. Maybe you shouldn't have come after all."

She steadies herself with both palms planted firmly at the table. "Not come to my husband's Inaugural gala? Ron, you know that I —" She picks up her purse and drops it between herself and Bull Dozier. "— would never hear of it." Next thing I know she jackknifes under the table and begins puking.

I grab her around the shoulders to steady her. Then I begin to rub her back, stroke her hair. "Oh, Sheel. You poor kid." Briefly I look around for reactions, but no one has noticed a thing. The din of two hundred and fifty voices has drowned out any sound and the tablecloth hanging over the front of the table hides Sheila from everyone's view. Do they all think she just disappeared?

"Oh God, Ron, I just puked." Sheila says, sitting up straight again. She holds one hand over her mouth and one against her throat.

"I know," I say. "Don't worry about it." Poor, poor Sheila. She looks like hell, white as one of Fergus Preston Helms' sheets.

"All over Dozier's shoes," she adds. "It filled up all those itsy bitsy teeny weenie little holes in his wingtips." Sheila demonstrates the size of the holes with her thumb and index finger nearly touching. Then she bursts into laughter.

Fortunately the jovial hubbub all around us has absorbed that commotion as well. Few take any heed of her and those that do just smile emptily. All except Bull Dozier, who cocks his head suspiciously in our direction. I can tell I have to think of something to talk about fast. But what? The weather? Too light. The Iraqi plan to assassinate Solomon Dayan? Too heavy. Baseball, you fool, try baseball. That always works. Even in January. "Hey, Bull, how about those Red Sox?"

Bull grunts and turns away.

I turn to Sheila. "Hey, Sheel, how about those socks?" I blurt out while pointing under the table.

Sheila lets out a guffaw so loud that perhaps half the heads in the room turn toward her. When I burst out laughing, the rest of the heads turn toward us like dominoes. We have ignited a conflagration without any firewood because the whole room is soon shaking and swaying with laughter without having a clue why. Dom Perignon is a very wonderful thing. Bull, more disgusted than ever, suddenly gets a look of utter distress on his face and then bends down to look under the table. "Goddamn it!" he says. "Goddamn it to hell!

Sheila howls uncontrollably. Her body shakes with utter mad delight, her laughter piercing my heart like Cupid's fabled arrow. It's times like this that memory softens everything it touches, allowing the good times to eclipse the bad. It's times like this I know I really love her.

And George Bush thought puking all over his Japanese hosts was something spectacular.

Later that night in our suite at the Ridgeley, after I have tucked in the kids, I join Sheila in bed. On her bedside table is a glass of ginger ale. "Feeling better?" I say.

"I'll recover," she says. She takes a sip of her drink. "But I'm not so sure about Bull Dozier."

We both begin to howl and shake again, eventually falling against one another for support. We look into each other's eyes and embrace. Then we kiss. Gently, lovingly, the way we used to. A moment goes by. "My mouth aches from all that goddamn smiling," I say.

"Poor baby," Sheila says. "Come to mama."

Come to mama is what Sheila says as a green light to making love. "Are you serious?" I say.

Suddenly Sheila is up out of bed and racing into the bathroom.

~

My first official order of business as President of the United States is to have a mezuzah put on the front doorpost of the Ridgeley. It shall be a sign of my devotion to God — "May God protect my going out and coming in, now and forever" — but also a sign of what is to come. I have no intention of keeping who I am or what I am hidden from view, no matter what the cost. I will not take a back seat. I shall carve my own way. I shall be the sole author of my failures. I shall not make excuses. Such are the privileges of first-class citizenship. As the legendary lawyer Alan Dershowitz once wrote, "Many in my generation no longer feel like guests in anyone's else's land." And neither do I. In the shower this morning I was not surprised when I started humming "This land is your land, this land is my land...this land was made for you and me."

Day 1, 7:58 a.m. I am in my office, also in the Ridgeley

instead of the White House, reading *The Washington Post.*
Next I will read *The Washington Times.* At 8:45, I will have
my first staff meeting with Woody Stone, Ashley Jones, Phil
Hurley and Calvin Foxx. At 10:00, I will meet in the Situation Room with Candace Rowe, Oliver Graham and their
various deputies to discuss the Iraqi affair. Tanya Gregson,
my assistant on national security affairs and Bull Dozier,
my ex-running mate, will be joining us for that. As will CIA
Director Warren Gates, probably the most paranoid person
I have ever met, and Milton Buck, who is the first Amish
secretary of defense. At 11:00, I am scheduled to meet with
congressional leaders. Then at noon, I am to have lunch with
Max Berger and Abe Rubin. In the afternoon, I will have my
first cabinet meeting. I do not see them noted anywhere on
the agenda, but I am hopeful that my scheduling secretary
has allocated enough time for a couple of potty breaks.

I pick up the phone. "Rosalee, get me Fleming Hodgetts."

A moment later I have Fleming on the line. "Fleming," I
say. "You were absolutely right. The Ridgeley is going to be
worlds better than Blair House ever would have been. Thank
you so much."

"We aim to please, Mr. President."

"But there are a few things I need to ask you about."

"Of course, Mr. President," says Fleming graciously.
"Nothing would please me more than to be of further assis-
tance to you."

"It's about all that stuff you had moved out of the White
House. For one thing, I'd love to borrow that portrait of
Washington, the one above the mantel in the library. And
Sheel really has her heart set on a few of those Duncan
Phyfe pieces from The Green Room. And since I'm such a
big James Fenimore Cooper fan, well, I'd really love to put
that chandelier from the library, the one that used to belong

to his family, in our private dining room. You think you can arrange all that?"

"I'm sorry to say, Mr. President, I can't. All of those items are already in storage."

"You can't get them out?"

"I suppose I could try."

"It would be much appreciated, Flem."

"Just don't count on it. You know, sir, how the bureaucracy works around here. Course not everything has been tucked away yet. There's still a cabinet full of various gifts from Middle Eastern leaders."

"Oh?"

"Yes, sir. One of which is an exquisite wine goblet given to President Whitney's wife by Nobel laureate Yasser Arafat."

"Now there's a treasure. What a nice *Kiddush* cup that would make."

"A what?"

"Never mind. I think I'll pass on that one, Flem. But see what you can do about the other things."

"Your wish is my command, Mr. President. But no promises."

∼

Once, in couples' therapy, in between the births of Ray and Sam, our therapist asked Sheila and me to make separate lists of the things we each thought were more satisfying with two people. On the top of my list was sex. Big surprise. But on Sheila's list, sex ranked fifth. What were the other conjugal activities Sheila felt were better with two? In order, making the bed, unloading the dishwasher, yard work and hugging. Kind of redefines foreplay, doesn't it?

THE JEWISH TENANT

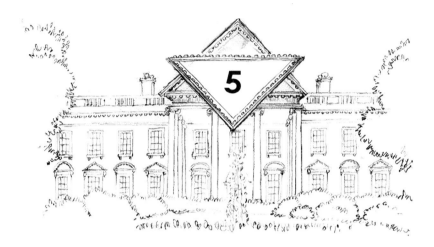

Uncle Leo is driving the Secret Service crazy. He keeps an apartment in New York City in what used to be, forgive the expression, a nice Jewish neighborhood, but what is now a battle zone, overrun by street gangs, denim and leather-clad trolls who would just as soon kill you as look at you. Every year, come February, Uncle Leo, who is actually my mother's uncle, goes to stay in his apartment for a couple of weeks. He says it's to make sure that the pipes haven't frozen. Uncle Leo is a plumber by trade, long since retired, but he still maintains a nostalgic interest in plumbing. He has lifetime subscriptions to *American Plumber* and *Pipe Dreams*. Uncle Leo will be eighty-eight on his next birthday, if he makes it. I think it must be unusual to see a black limousine pull up in front of his apartment and dump Uncle Leo and his Secret Service entourage on what's left of the debris-covered sidewalk.

Woody tells me that Uncle Leo will have to give up his apartment, or give up the Secret Service protection. I tell Woody that Uncle Leo will never give up his apartment because it is rent-controlled and, therefore, one heck of deal. I also tell Woody that Uncle Leo never requested the protection in the first place. "What's to protect?" he said to me. "My virginity?" Uncle Leo's first and only wife died nearly sixty years ago. They had only been married for three years and she had two miscarriages. I am the closest thing Uncle Leo has to a son.

I had promised Uncle Leo a job at the White House but, thanks to Fleming Hodgetts, I have become a liar. I thought being a tour guide would have suited Uncle Leo fine. When he served in World War II — enlisting in 1943 at the impressionable age of 18 — he got hooked on uniforms and when I told him I had a job for him where he could once again don a uniform, he became quite excited. It wounded me deeply to disappoint him.

"So how about putting him in the Smithsonian?" Woody says.

"He's not that old," I say.

"I mean as a guard. Maybe the National Air and Space Museum."

"Would he get to wear a uniform?"

"Of course."

"Sold," I say.

~

Okay, so Sheila's connubial priorities are a bit different from mine. Unfortunately, knowing that doesn't assuage my frustration when a little thing like vomiting takes precedence over a long awaited, eagerly anticipated rock and roll in the hay.

It was not always this way. Not long ago we made love three, four, sometimes five times a week. But then something happened. She seemed to get bored with it. When I spoke to her about it, or more accurately about my need to have a physical release, she said to me, "Oh, for goodness sake, Ron, what do you think God gave you a right hand for?"

Didn't Woody Allen once say that masturbation was sex with someone you love? The real problem is, I love Sheila more than I love my right hand.

∾

Speaking of apartments and renting, I just had a funny thought. Ever since I can remember, Jews, in disproportionate numbers, have been landlords. We have gotten something of a bad rap for this. But that aside, I think it's kind of funny to think that now the country's chief executive, a Jew, is a tenant.

The American people, they are the landlords, my land-lords, and if I slip up, it's eviction time, goodbye Charlie. It's out on the street with old Myron S. Goldberg.

∾

The sad truth is, even if it weren't for Hodgetts and his bill, I wouldn't be the first Jew in the White House. The first Jewish president, but not the first Jew.

The first Jew in the White House was actually Moshe Polchuk. Moshe Polchuk, as you may remember, was mar-ried to Lena Harrison, my great-grandmother. That would make Moshe my great-grandfather. Lena and Moshe had four children, named Jacob, Bertram, Ruth and Adolf, the latter being quite a popular Jewish name until, for a reason that should be obvious, it plummeted from favor. Ruth, the third, who would eventually hobble into her nineties, was a sickly child. She was born in 1898 and suffered from a childhood disease, which could not be mentioned by name because it was believed that that would make it spread to the boys. Nevertheless, she did become healthy and virile enough to sire four children of her own, the second of whom was my father, Alfred, who was born in 1935.

Anyway, back to great-grandfather Moshe. Born in 1845, he left his native Poland for America in 1860, the year he became orphaned. He had heard that America was the promised land and that America wanted to become the greatest nation on earth, so it was sending out an invitation to freedom-loving people all over the world, to special people like Moshe Polchuk, asking them to come and be Americans, to join hands in this glorious experiment. Emma Lazarus may have written, "Bring me your tired, your poor, your huddled masses yearning to breathe free, the wretched refuse of your teeming shore," et cetera, et cetera, et cetera, but what America really wanted was not the world's "tempest-tossed," not the world's sickly castoffs, not the scabs that had fallen off some national wound — poverty, famine, whatever. No indeed. What America wanted was the world's best factory seconds. During this period, from 1820 to 1870, known as the second great wave of immigration to America, states actually sent recruiters to Europe to attract settlers. Railroad companies did the same thing. Could this latter instance of friendly coercion have given rise to the popular expression "I was railroaded?" Perhaps. In any case, great-grandfather Moshe caught and rode that huge wave at its crest and soon found himself cast upon the teeming shore of the land of opportunity, just as this great country of ours was about to come apart at the seams.

But Moshe had more working against him than bad

timing. When his ship docked in Richmond — a storm had kept it from entering New York Harbor — he spoke not one word of English. In fact, hapless Moshe nearly got himself sold into slavery shortly after his arrival because of his ignorance. Wandering off by himself, he came across a sign that said SLAVES. Thinking that SLAVES was simply the plural form of SLAV, Moshe followed it. Moshe's face was almost black from not having bathed for so long, so he was easily mistaken for what was then called a Negro. Only when he hollered in protest on the auction block did the crowd realize something was amiss. The auctioneer took a long hard look at Moshe and then, with his spit-moistened shirtsleeve, rubbed some of the dirt off the lad's face. "Why this here's a white boy," he said. There was a blast of laughter from the crowd.

Moshe had no idea what the auctioneer was saying, but he knew he would no longer follow any signs that said SLAVES. In just a few months Moshe was speaking English almost like an American.

∽

How did Moshe Polchuk, a mere lad of fifteen, become the first Jew in the White House? Quite by accident, actually. Moshe was alone, yes; Moshe was an orphan, yes; but he had an older brother, Josef, who had come to America two years before him. Josef did not know that his parents were dead and Moshe thought that he should know.

After his narrow escape from slavery, Moshe decided the safest thing for him to do was to head north. Several weeks later he ended up in Washington. Half starved and still without a bath (except for having stood out in the rain twice), he staggered into town. Everything looked strange to him. There were no familiar sights, no familiar faces and his English was not perfect yet.

Moshe wandered down Pennsylvania Avenue and came to a stop in front of what he surmised was the nicest house in town. Moshe thought this: If anybody knows where I can find my brother Josef, the people who live here will. He walked up the stoop and knocked on the door.

In a moment the door opened and there in the doorway was a very tall, very thin, very ugly man. He had a huge wart on his face that Moshe was ashamed to be caught staring at. For all his outward ugliness though, the man had a gentleness about him. What Moshe didn't know was that he was standing on the doorstep of the White House and that standing before him was none other than Abraham Lincoln, the sixteenth president of the United States. "Yes?" Lincoln said.

"I am trying to find brother," Moshe said. He fumbled with his cap as he slipped it off his head.

Lincoln smiled and said nothing.

"His name Josef. Josef Polchuk," Moshe said.

"Don't know anyone by that name, son. Maybe Mary does." Lincoln turned back into the house and hollered, "Mary! Mary! Damn, where is that woman? Off to buy more gloves, no doubt. Why, you'd think she had a hundr'd hands!" The tall man guffawed.

"He's butcher, too," Moshe said.

"Too?"

"Yes. I, too, am butcher," said Moshe proudly. He made a motion with his hand as if he were slitting his throat.

"You, too, butcher," said Lincoln. "Hmmm."

"Yes."

Suddenly Lincoln got a very peculiar look on his face. With one hand he stroked the chin where his famous beard resided. "A butcher, eh? Follow me, Polchuk. I have something that needs killing."

Moshe Polchuk, Polish Jew, hat in hand, dutifully followed Abraham Lincoln into the White House.

~

The thing that needed killing, by the way, was a chicken. That very morning, Lincoln's cook, who normally did all the slaughtering of fowl, had quit over an argument with one of the maids. Moshe showed up before Lincoln had time to place an ad in the paper to find a new cook.

Of course, as it turned out, Moshe could kill but not cook, so Lincoln had to replace the old cook after all. And since the new cook would also be required to kill a fowl now and then, there was no continuing need for the services of young Moshe Polchuk.

A few years later Moshe opened a butcher shop in Washington. And it was there that he met and fell in love with and ultimately married one of his customers, Lena Harrison.

Moshe never found his brother. As near as he could ascertain, when the Civil War broke out in 1861, Josef joined up with the Union Army and was later killed at Gettysburg. Josef was strong and agile and brave and probably made very good cannon fodder.

~

Jack Frost has just called to tell me that I am still rising in the polls. According to the latest Gallup Poll, which will appear in the *Post* tomorrow morning, 61% of the American people rate my job performance as "favorable." What's more, 65% thought my inaugural speech was the best one ever made. And 3% think *"Ein Keiloheinu"* should be made our new national anthem. When I mention my favorability rating to Woody, he says, "Mazel tov, Mr. President."

"Now if only Diya Bakir thought so highly of me," I say.

"Oh, I'm sure he does," says Candace Rowe.

"Yeah, right," says CIA Director Gates. With his black hair slicked back and his leathery skin, Gates appears serpentine.

"Now, Warren, I'm sure it's not quite as bad as you think." It's fun to tease a man as humorless as Gates, but he does have a point. He always says that in his business it's far safer to think everyone's your enemy than to believe the opposite. And I have to admit I agree.

"Mr. President, we have reason to believe that Bakir's threats are not idle. The threat on Solomon Dayan is very real. As is the threat against yourself."

"So what do we do? Blow the guy up?"

"Not a bad thought," says Oliver Graham.

Oliver looks different today, but I can't figure out why. Then it hits me. "Grecian formula?"

"Mr. President, can we please stick to the issue at hand?"

"That's it, isn't it?"

"Yes, that's it. So what?"

"Mr. President," says Candace Rowe. "What we need here is something more than a few well-placed smart bombs. Even if we blow out the Iraqi intelligence headquarters again, you know as well as I do they'll just rebuild it somewhere else. What we need is something bigger. Much bigger."

"Like what?"

"I don't know."

"She doesn't know," says Warren Gates, derisively. Candace shoots him a look that by all rights should have killed him. Gates sneers, shakes his head, looks away. He has a good jab but he also has a glass jaw.

"Well, whatever it is," says Tanya Gregson, "it sure as hell better not involve a whole lot of ground troops." Tanya, a sleek forty-five-year-old African American, has a tone that's always above the fray though her words are invariably in the thick of it. She has been highly critical of the disproportionate representation of minorities in the front lines. That's not what equal opportunity is supposed to be about, she once said.

"Well, whatever we come up with, it damn well better be ironclad. Fool proof. I'm sick and tired of hearing nothing but goddamn SWAGs." SWAG is the Pentagon acronym for scientific wild-assed guess. It has long been a favorite euphemism of the newly brunette Oliver Graham.

"Now hold on there, Mr. President," says Graham, his dander up.

"No, General, you hold on there. I want a plan that isn't piecemeal. I want a plan that's going to rid us of these cancers once and for all." I recall the words of Ashley Jones and, thinking now's the time to get any potential blunders out of the way, I add, "And I want it soon."

~

There are now about ten minutes left in my first day as president. I look over at Sheila. She is sleeping, curled up in a fetal position, her beautiful black hair across her face like a tattered curtain. When she wears no expression it is easy for me to imagine that passionate woman she was such a short while ago. When I am frustrated by her rebuffs of my swollen passions, or when she is engrossed reading God-knows-what in bed, I am not so imaginative.

Oh, honey, please. Not tonight.

Headache again?

Not yet. But soon.

I know this is a bit unfair of me, since in so many other ways Sheila is a warm and wonderful woman. Not to mention that the moment her libido went into hibernation does seem to correspond more or less to the announcement of our exile to the Ridgeley. Nevertheless I do have a body to think of, too. The *Talmud* says the greater the man, the greater his sexual appetite. I do not know if I really believe this — or even if I fit into this category — but I do know that lately I have had a much stronger urge to eat between meals.

I am now in the bathroom, the thrown room. As I am standing here urinating, I suddenly get this burning sensation. When I am done, it stops. Odd.

ᗧ

The next morning, after breakfast, I am brushing my teeth. I am humming a song that, to me, sounds very familiar but has a name that escapes me. I keep humming after I have rinsed. I wipe my mouth, check my gritting, lipless smile in the mirror, and go back into the bedroom. Sam is sitting on the edge of the bed.

"C is for cookie," she sings.

"Oh, cookie, cookie, cookie starts with C," I sing back. Then I hug her hard and we both laugh. I hug her longer than usual because I don't want her to see my eyes.

WHAT'S IN A NAME?

My full name, as you know, is not Ron Goldberg. It's Myron S. Goldberg. How did a baby born in 1960 come to be named, of all things, Myron, an obvious throwback to another era? The answer is my mother, Ethel. She named me after her father, a cobbler from Hungary, who died a year before I was born. Grandfather Myron was one of the many eager Myrons who were herded like so much livestock through Ellis Island during the late nineteenth and early twentieth centuries.

Myron Bromberg came to this country in 1917. It was the year he turned twenty-one as well as the year the United States entered World War I. Hostility toward foreigners ran high. So high in fact that America, in its zeal to keep its national bloodstream pure — though it had already been polluted by Irish, Germans, Danes, Norwegians, Swedes, Poles, eastern European Jews, Austrians, Czechs, Slovaks,

Italians, not to mention other Hungarians — passed a law that required adult immigrants to demonstrate that they could read and write. *See Spot. See Spot run. See Spot run after the dog that doesn't have a spot.* Fortunately, Myron could read and write, which could not be said for tens of thousands of those who already enjoyed American citizenship.

When he got on the boat headed for America, Myron's head was rich with dreams about the good life he would soon enjoy, but he did not have a penny in his pocket. Being a cobbler, however, he had the nicest pair of shoes of anyone in steerage. His shoes were his pride and joy. In fact, he wore them while he slept because he was afraid that someone would steal them.

Myron had come to America, in part, because of a lie told to him by a friend. The friend told him that half the people in America had to go barefoot because of a shoe shortage. If Ireland could have potato famines, his friend contended, why couldn't America have a shoe famine? Young Myron saw only joy in America's presumed adversity. His dream was to see his shoes on the feet of every man, woman and child in America. Dreams loom large when their fulfillment is four thousand miles away.

Of course they stole his shoes anyway. They cut right through the laces and yanked them off while Myron snored like an old sot through the whole ordeal. "I was fortunate they left me my feet," he later said. An eyewitness, an old and nearly toothless woman, said, "Serves you right, boy, wearing shoes like that in front of people like them."

It could have been worse. My name, I mean. 1960 was also the fortieth anniversary of the mandating of Palestine to Great Britain by the League of Nations, thereby planting the seeds of the Jewish state, though the oil-loving Brits, afraid to stir up Arab hostility, refused to water them. Immigration limits for Jews were quickly put in place. Nevertheless, it was a start. So, to commemorate this day of mixed blessing, my mother seriously considered calling me Israel. Israel Goldberg? Izzy Goldberg? No thank you. I'd rather be called Mandy, after mandate. In any case, Myron was bad enough.

In all fairness, Mother did speak to me about the dangers that lay ahead for me when I encountered all those acceptable, but undistinguished, Daniels, Davids, Samuels, Marks and so on, and sprung my anachronistic name on them. Nevertheless, her love for her shoemaking father outweighed what she surely believed would be insignificant troubles for me down the road. I think she secretly thought that any difficulty I encountered would toughen me up, and toughening up was something that every little Jewish boy could benefit from, particularly one growing up in a non-Jewish neighborhood as I did.

Mother also gave me an out. She said that if I became the subject of too much ridicule and got too many bloody noses, I could always start using my middle name. What was my middle name that, according to my mother, would spare me future grief? I don't know for sure. She told me that it was either Shippe or Solomon, and that I could pick the one I liked best.

These names originally belonged to Harry S. Truman, the 33rd President of the United States. Truman, who took over the reins of power upon the death of Franklin D. Roosevelt in 1945, was elected in his own right in 1948 by defeating New York Governor Thomas E. Dewey, to the surprise of almost everyone, including, no doubt, Truman himself. A framed copy of the famous photo showing a beaming HST holding up *The Chicago Tribune* with the headline, DEWEY DEFEATS TRUMAN, still hangs, on a wall all its own, in the den of my parents' house. The photo used to belong to my grandparents, on my mother's side, to whom Truman was a god-like figure. I suspect that one day I will inherit this heirloom. And, frankly, I will be proud to have it.

Truman, like me, did not know for sure what his middle name was and apparently had no interest in starting a feud between the families of his two grandfathers.

One can just imagine the verbal tennis that went on.

"The S is for Shippe!" said Grandfather Shippe's side of the family.

"The S is for Solomon!" said Grandfather Solomon's side of the family.

"Shippe!"

"Solomon!"

"Shippe!"

"Solomon!"

"Shippe!"

"Solomon!"

And so on.

To appease both sides, Truman did the diplomatic thing: he only used the initial S.

I eventually did that, too, though I had no one not to offend. But rather than choose to avoid ridicule by having people call me Shippe or Solomon, I opted for the truncated form of Myron: Ron. How American can you get?

I sometimes wonder what my middle name would have been if I had been born in 1956. Adlai perhaps? Or in 1945. Winston? Dwight? Yalta? Hiroshima? And if I first had seen the light of day in late 1941? "What does the 'P' stand for, dear?" "Why Pearl, of course."

Lest you think I exaggerate my mother's chameleon tendencies, consider this: On a warm November day in 1966 my mother, feeling the recent loss of a close childhood friend taken unexpectedly by cancer, came home with a mangy calico cat that she had fallen in love with and saved from the city pound. For the first two weeks we had the cat, it gagged continuously and spat up stringy gray phlegm all over the rugs and furniture. Things got so bad, Mother had buy plastic slipcovers to try to salvage what was left of the sofas and stuffed chairs. The vet called it kennel cough. I called it disgusting.

The point is my mother was a baseball fan. Fan, in her case, being short for Fanatic with a capital "F". This was explainable. Mother grew up in Brooklyn, and you couldn't grow up in Brooklyn in the 40s without being a Dodgers fan. If you ignored or, worse, berated the Dodgers in any way, shape or manner, you were either shipped off to Bellevue, or beaten senseless on the spot. My mother never stopped loving the Dodgers, even when they deserted her for the sunnier skies and deeper pockets of Los Angeles. But she never forgave them either. Some things you never forgive.

Anyway, back to the cat. At the time of its arrival, Mother had become particularly enamored with a handsome young fastballer who had won the Cy Young award three times. He had the lowest ERA in the National League from 1962 to 1966. He had pitched four no-hitters and one perfect game. And as if that weren't enough, he was also Jewish. Talk about a son of God!

So what did my mother name her rescued feline? Koufax. What else?

❦

My mother never stopped suggesting or creating names for people and pets according to the way the wind was blowing. In 1973 she bought a goldfish, which she named

Watergate. In 1976 she came home from the pound with yet another stray cat. This one she named JC, after Jimmy Carter, not the other famous JC. When Elvis Presley eventually self-destructed in 1977, mother honored him by naming one of the squirrels that regularly raided her bird feeder, Elvis. The squirrel was terribly fat, so the name did fit, I have to admit. When Rachel was born in 2000, Mother wanted Sheila and me to name her Israella, since 2000 happened to be the eightieth anniversary of the Palestine mandate. Sheila thought that as a middle name, it wasn't so bad. I said, "One Myron in the family is enough."

∽

If you don't mind, I would like to jump backwards to my childhood for a moment. It won't take long. I promise. For me, it has always been a short trip. Besides, it may help to shed some light on my current state of mind. You see, as flip and nonchalant as I am about not being able to live in the White House, or even Blair House, it really does grate on me. I'll never forgive Hodgetts for it, not that he's hanging on absolution from me, but it's not even that so much. This situation cannot be characterized as a personal vendetta. It is a breach of trust. I put my faith in the country and, so it seemed, the country put its faith in me. So how do you explain that I have had to take up residence in the Ridgeley Hotel, which isn't all that bad a hotel really?

What I remember from my childhood as the Devil Dog incident is, I think, instructive here. A Devil Dog, as you probably know, is not a fiendish canine. Nor is it, in this context anyway, a member of the United States Marine Corps. It is instead a rather tasty, cream-filled chocolate cake, made in the shape of a hot dog. Which, I venture to guess, is how it came to be called Devil Dog. In any case, next to Hostess

Twinkies, Devil Dogs were my favorite snack, and my love for them was well known among my friends.

I mentioned earlier that I grew up in a non-Jewish neighborhood in Worcester, Massachusetts. My parents were the first Jews that many people in the neighborhood had seen, not counting pictures of Holocaust victims in magazines. Younger children stared at them with intense curiosity, I was told, on the day my parents moved in. It was as if they were looking for some deformity, horns perhaps, anything to reassure them that these Christ-killers, these demons who supposedly made matzo with the blood of sweet young Christian children (though, somehow magically, the matzo was never red), were in no way similar to themselves. The hostility was never open. It always remained politely beneath the surface.

Because the hostility was never open, I didn't take my parents all that seriously when they told me that it existed. Their generation was very good at believing in things you couldn't see; my generation was more of the "show me" variety. We needed our golden calves, our stereos, our sports cars. Besides, I was so un-Jewish looking, I could venture out among the gentiles incognito. An underground Jew, so to speak. What did I have to fear?

Nevertheless, as a precaution, I pushed myself to excel in every way that I could, thinking that by excelling, by being better than everyone else, I might be considered their equal. I became an all-A student. I became a darn good athlete, too. I was especially proud of this, because the perception of Jews among non-Jews seemed to be that, as a people, we were smart, but klutzy when it came to athletics. Sandy Koufax aside, we were not expected to excel on the baseball field, on the gridiron, on the basketball court. And so on.

The day I was named captain of my grammar school basketball team, the team that later went on to win the city championship, I thought I was going to burst with pride. I couldn't wait to get home to tell my parents. I knew that they were most proud of my academic achievements, but my mother, being the baseball nut that she was, and my father, having adopted the Boston Celtics as his own (They once had a Jewish coach, didn't they?), would be thrilled that I had also managed to excel in sports.

After practice I ran home as fast as I could. Practices lasted about an hour and a half, and were usually quite exhausting, but on this day, I felt not the least bit tired. I got home at four-thirty. It would be another hour before my father arrived and, since it was Tuesday, my mother's market day, she probably wouldn't get home until five. I had no idea where my brother was, and didn't care.

I ran down our long driveway. It was clear that no one was home yet. It was dark inside the house. The windows reflected the trees, the lawn, the driveway, me. I stopped about halfway down the driveway to catch my breath. I leaned forward and braced myself with my hands on my knees. I was breathing hard, and I started to feel fatigue for the first time since the announcement of my captaincy at the beginning of practice. When I caught my breath, I straightened up, and that's when I first saw it. Written on the picture window of our house, in huge letters, were the words, FUCK YOU, SUPER JEW.

At first, I didn't know what to do. I didn't move for what might have only been minutes but seemed like hours. Then I went to the garage, got a rag and wiped the words off the window as best I could. I expected to be grossed out by the material used to write the words. I thought it was something mostly fecal in nature, cut perhaps by shaving cream. Imagine my surprise when I realized that the writing instrument had been a Devil Dog. So much for the power of the pen.

～

When my mother got home, I was still cleaning the window, though by then the words were gone. I had used up half a bottle of Windex and three rags. When I told her what had happened she said nothing. She just looked sad and shook her head. Later that day, after dinner, I heard her say to my father, "Maybe we shouldn't have come here. Maybe we should move."

"It's just kids," my father said.

I thought back to the basketball practice. When it ended, I saw Pete Dawson and Charlie Clark get into Pete's mother's car. Pete and Charlie lived in my neighborhood and frequently gave me a ride home after practice. Pete was a starting forward. Charlie was a second string guard. I was a guard, too, so Charlie and I were often paired off against one another for scrimmages. Today, they didn't look for me after practice. They just got in the car and left.

～

You probably think that my love for Devil Dogs went away after the Devil Dog incident. To my surprise, it didn't. In fact to this day, I still love them. After all, you can't blame the Devil Dogs for what happened, any more than you could blame fire for the burning of a menorah. Devils Dogs don't kill friendships. People kill friendships. So I have Woody or Phil pick me up a box or two now and then. I don't think there is any harm in this. I don't feel like I'm compromising my principles, losing my integrity, taking in too many empty calories, dangerously bumping up my cholesterol. I just don't eat them in front of my mother anymore. You have to make some concessions.

～

My father had his own version of how I got my name. He claimed that it had absolutely nothing to do with Harry S. Truman and that, for the record, my father's record, my middle name was really Saul, after no one but the ancient king. He said the reason I am named Myron Saul Goldberg is because he wanted my initials to be MSG, which, as anyone who has ever gone to a Chinese restaurant knows, stands for monosodium glutamate, a flavor enhancer. My father loved Chinese food with an enduring passion. Many Jews do. There is no logical reason for this. It just is. Like God just is, I suppose.

One thing my father really liked to do in a Chinese restaurant was pick up the soy sauce at the beginning of every single meal and say to me, "You know what this stuff is, Ronnie?"

My job was to say, "It's soy sauce, Pop. The Chinese use it in place of salt."

"That's right," he'd say in a drawn out voice, with a facetious smile.

My mother was never amused. She was not so crazy about Chinese food. She claimed, as many people do, that MSG gave her headaches. "MSG gives me headaches," she would always say whenever my father announced his intentions to dine Chinese. I think now when she says that, she means me.

～

It is about three a.m. and Sheila hasn't had to make a trip to the bathroom for several hours. She is sleeping, uneasily though, so I am trying not to squirm about too much. If I wake her, she'll never get back to sleep and it'll be hell to pay. I wonder if Ret Ching is still open. I wonder, too, after all these years, if the Chinese really use soy sauce in place of salt, why do they also put salt shakers on the tables?

ANYTHING FOR A SMOKE

I t is now about a month after my inauguration and they still say I never would have won the election had it not been for Israel. My Republican opponent, Robert E. Lee Sanders, is the biggest proponent of this theory. But Fleming T. Hodgetts isn't all that far behind. For every three tirades Sanders delivers on the subject, Hodgetts averages two. Their remarks have been a thorn in my side, but not a serious one. The polls show that I'm still holding my own. So let the chips fall where they may. They'll not easily dislodge old Myron S. Goldberg from the Ridgeley.

Of course, they are right, you know. I wouldn't have won without Israel. On the night of the election, when NBC projected that I had lost both New Hampshire and Maine, a projection, Woody told me, that was quickly adopted by CBS and ABC as well, the importance of Israel loomed large indeed. I had visions of the DEWEY DEFEATS TRUMAN headline in my head, only this time it meant SANDERS DEFEATS GOLDBERG. Nevertheless, when the votes were all tallied, Sanders could only lay claim to 273 electoral votes; I had 275.

Vermont	3	Electoral Votes
New York	36	" "
Massachusetts	13	" "
Rhode Island	4	" "
Connecticut	8	" "
New Jersey	16	" "
Pennsylvania	25	" "
Maryland	10	" "
Ohio	23	" "
Indiana	12	" "
Illinois	24	" "
Michigan	20	" "
Wisconsin	11	" "
Minnesota	10	" "
Florida	21	" "
Texas	29	" "
Israel	10	" "
	275	

The last results to come in were from Israel. This was because the polls there had been ordered, by congressional decree, to stay open until 7 a.m. Israeli time on Wednesday, November 8, which was 9 p.m. Tuesday on the west coast, one hour after the polls there closed. It was the fear of many a member of Congress that, should the Israeli polls close at 8 p.m. Israeli time on Election Day, seven hours before mainland America's east coast polls closed and ten hours before the west coast polls closed, the results might have a domino effect on the rest of the nation. "As Israel goes, so the nation might go," Fleming Hodgetts, his fist pounding the podium, warned his Senate colleagues. As it turned out, Fleming's words proved prophetic. I carried Israel with 88% of the vote, the highest winning percentage in the history of the state, and it was her electoral votes that nudged me over the top.

~

When I first suggested to my Senate colleagues back in 2008 that we make Israel a state, the idea was met with considerable resistance. Many a senator saw the annexation as a serious drain on our national resources, citing endless examples of how the Arabs and Palestinians in the occupied territories would end up on the already overburdened welfare rolls. The military brass felt equally threatened. They claimed that the incessantly battle-tempered Israeli soldiers would become an elite corps within the armed forces, thereby undermining the traditional power base. In a few words, they feared for their jobs and lobbied vigorously against the Israeli proposal in order to save them. Of course, on the other side of the world, there was resistance as well. Why, after struggling to maintain their independence, indeed their very existence, for sixty years, should the sovereign state of Israel suddenly become a subservient state of the United States of America? Why give up our autonomy? In exchange for what? Protection? We can do that better ourselves, they argued. But the sad truth was, Israel was in dire straits economically. The country had nearly been torn apart by triple-digit inflation. Military expenditures were saving them from aggressors, but they were killing Israel internally. Israel needed help, a way to shift the burden. Statehood could provide the solution, I argued. But I knew that pulling it off would be no picnic.

The person who really began to turn the tide in the debate was Thomas "Bull" Dozier, who is now my Vice President. Dozier, a jowly, balding Texan and former Reagan Democrat, served in the House from 1982 to 1994 and in the Senate since 1994. He first received national attention in June of 1980 when, as one of the American hostages held by Iran, he was videotaped by his captors wearing a Reagan for President button, reading a statement that denounced Jimmy Carter for providing political asylum, not to mention medical care, for the deposed shah, whom the Iranians wanted back in exchange for the hostages. "This ain't brain surgery, Mr. President. Just a simple swap." Dozier said. "The shah's gonna be dead in a month or two anyway. And all of us here sure as hell got a lot more days in us than that." He was right of course. The shah died a month later. And since a dead shah wasn't much of a bargaining chip, the imprisonment of the hostages continued. Dozier never forgave Carter for that and, although he was a loyal Democrat, he hitched himself to Reagan's wagon in 1982 and was elected by a landslide. He was thirty-five.

Prior to being elected to the House, Dozier worked for the CIA, often posing, as it became well known, as an embassy employee. He was no stranger to covert action. For most of his life, he played his cards close to his vest, a trait, I am told, he inherited from his wheeler-dealer father, a Texas oil man whose company, in the early 90s, had gone belly up. Bull Dozier had no love for foreign oil. And while he had no great love for Israel either, he saw statehood as a way of building an American launch pad from which military action, covert and otherwise, could be taken to secure Arab oil fields. OPEC to Bull Dozier was the devil incarnate, and had no right to wield such enormous power over the Western world, the only decent God-fearing nations on this Earth. Bull called for the support of Israel's annexation and said that it was the patriotic duty of every American to lend his or her support to the notion. Though he was alternately crude and rude, Dozier had the respect of his Senate colleagues. He would not have been able to become the Senate majority leader had Senate opinion been otherwise. So having Dozier behind the cause really got things moving. The fight for Israeli statehood became known unofficially as the Dozier-Goldberg proposal. Suddenly supporters seemed to drop down from the most unlikely of places.

One of the truly surprising supporters of the measure was both the one-time chairman of the Senate Foreign Relations Committee and now the Senate minority leader, Fleming T. Hodgetts.

Now, initially, Hodgetts saw no reason whatsoever to support Israeli statehood. He had continually denounced Israel for her "inhumane" treatment of the Palestinians in the occupied territories, and he had stated repeatedly that Israel should give back the land that she stole and return to her original boundaries. His opinions were by no means radical. Many shared them. The surprise was that he decided to support Israeli statehood in spite of his feelings. And surely he had not forgotten that it was Myron S. Goldberg, the "wide-eyed liberal" senator from Massachusetts, who engineered what he called a "vicious sniper attack" upon the "unimpeachable character and the fine, fine record of public service" of Supreme Court nominee Clement T. Bosworth, an avowed white supremacist, back in 2006. The Senate subsequently rejected Bosworth's confirmation by a mere four votes. It was Hodgetts' firm belief that, without my "meddling," his man would today be sitting pretty on the Supreme Court. So why the sudden change of heart?

Well, Hodgetts is a crafty old bird. He never misses a trick, and he wasn't about to miss a chance to turn what seemed to him a negative situation into a positive one. First off, he knew that this time, I could not get what I wanted without his support. And with that in mind he did what every sensible human being would do: He told me what his support was going to cost me.

Hodgetts loved his home state of North Carolina. He loved the sylvan countryside, he loved the spunk of the cities. But most of all, he loved the sight and smell of tobacco. To say that he was a friend to the tobacco industry would have been a gross understatement. He was more like a patron saint. He despised the fact that tobacco had fallen so much out of favor in the 1990s, thanks to all this "cancer scare nonsense," as he called it. He grieved for months when the government forced the cigarette companies to place warnings on their packages like, CIGARETTE SMOKING HAS BEEN SHOWN TO PRODUCE BIRTH DEFECTS, CIGARETTE SMOKE CONTAINS NOXIOUS CARBON MONOXIDE, CIGARETTE SMOKE CAUSES PROSTATE CANCER, and so on. He nearly got an ulcer during the secondhand smoke controversy, downing a family-size bottle of Maalox every day for six months. And when a Charlotte restaurant banned smoking totally, it was rumored that Hodgetts was personally responsible for the restaurant being firebombed just two weeks later.

Of course, all these bad things being said by the surgeon general about the proud American institution of smoking quickly became history when Fleming T. Hodgetts told me what his support would cost. Certain concessions, he said, would have to be made to the tobacco industry. Then, and only then, would he lend his support.

I am not proud of the bargain I struck with Fleming, even though the new status of smoking tells me I should be. But I can honestly say I no longer lose any sleep over it, though I did for the first few months after I agreed to his terms. Sometimes the end does justify the means, that's all I can say. People have to make up their own minds. I am not naive enough to think that a warning about carcinogens on a package of cigarettes, no matter how explicit, is going to change someone's mind one iota about lighting up, particularly now. There's probably a fair amount of rationalization in that statement, but this fact remains: Israel, in 2008, on her sixtieth birthday, became the fifty-first state in the union.

⁓

There was one other part of Fleming Hodgetts' proposal I did not back down on. At this time, there was the beginning of a groundswell of support for a bill that would make the birthday of Ronald Reagan, our 40th president, a national holiday. The bill was to take effect on February 6th, 2011, which would have been the Reagan's 100th birthday. Fleming, having ridden to election on Reagan coattails as I mentioned earlier, always had a soft spot for the man they called "The Great Communicator" as indeed the American people on the whole did, though I confess I was not a member of this fan club. Mr. Reagan may have been a sometime friend to Israel, but he was no friend of the Jewish people. Still, I was prepared to deal. One must always be prepared to deal. So what I told Fleming was this. I would support the bill under one condition. As a way of resolving recent trade policy and tariff disputes with Germany, I suggested that we have Reagan's body moved from its current resting place in California to the military cemetery in Bitburg, Germany, a town where Reagan is still revered. Reagan went to Bitburg in 1985 and, along with General Matthew Ridgeway — who was 90 years old at the time and the last living four-star general involved in the European Theater of Operations — placed a wreath on the ground where German foot soldiers were buried. A public outcry erupted, mostly from Jews, when plans for this event had been announced because this part of the cemetery was contiguous to the section where 49 Waffen SS, the guards who ran the Nazi death camps, were buried. The whole thing was billed as a ceremony of healing, but it was about as effective in achieving that as holding a Texas-style barbecue at the American embassy in New Delhi would be in patching up our differences with India. Coincidentally, the cemetery visit followed an important economic conference with what was then still West Germany. "You've got to love the symmetry, Fleming," I said.

"Symmetry my ass," growled Fleming Hodgetts. "You goddamn people just can't let it go, can you?"

"Let go of what?"

"The fucking past. It's not like most of those people would still be alive today anyway."

"Fleming," I said. "There's an amazing concept you should know about. It's called children. The only problem is, dead people can't have them."

Fleming scowled, his eyes firing daggers at me. He knew Mr. Reagan would have wait for his holiday.

❧

What I agreed to, by the way, was to see that all of the "alarmist" warnings, as Fleming called them, were promptly removed from cigarette packages.

"They simply have no purpose anymore, Mr. President," Hodgetts said. "Haven't for some time. Why they're like a tail on a human being. Vestigial poppycock."

He was right, of course. Ever since the cure for lung cancer and other smoking-related diseases had been found, there was no reason to badmouth tobacco companies anymore; particularly when you considered that it was all those vast profits from overseas markets, coupled with the total redirection of advertising dollars, that funded the research that lead to the cures for these deadly diseases in the first place.

"People will still get sick, Fleming," I pointed out. "You have to admit that."

"Well, of course I do, Mr. President. We ain't denyin' that anymore. We'll even concede that secondhand nonsense. It's just that now we got the cure. Not to mention, sir, the means for people to pay for it. Like that new ad says, 'A pack a day and the surgeon we'll pay.'"

I couldn't deny that either. All a smoker had to do was collect 10,000 coupons — one came with every pack — and he or she would then be entitled to a free lung replacement, or whatever other treatment was required to restore them to health. Nevertheless, I had to tell Fleming that I could not, in good conscience, lend my support to the wholesale withdrawal of all warnings. "People will still get sick, Fleming," I repeated.

"Can't get the cure, senator, until you get the disease," Fleming chirped.

"No, I guess not," I said. I was cornered and we both knew it. Besides, there was Israel to think about.

So what words of caution did Fleming suggest?

WARNING: THE SURGEON GENERAL HAS DETERMINED THAT CIGARETTE SMOKING CAN YELLOW TEETH AND CAUSE BAD BREATH.

Like I said, I am not proud of my hand in this.

～

Two weeks after Israeli statehood became a reality, there was a Gallup Poll printed in the *Post*. The question put to the American people was this: WHAT DO YOU THINK THAT ISRAEL, AS AN AMERICAN STATE, SHOULD DO ABOUT THE HAMAS PRESENCE IN THE GAZA STRIP?

21% said that Israel should ban the use of Hamas on pita bread.

11% said that Israel should put up an invisible dog fence, although half of this group thought it would be difficult to get the Palestinians to wear collars.

58% said that such places encouraged immoral behavior and should be closed.

10% had no opinion.

～

More than anything else, what held up Israel's admission to the most exclusive club in the world was the debate over the configuration of the new American flag. There would, of course, be fifty-one states to contend with now. This was no small problem. The current design of five rows of six stars, alternating with four rows of five stars, would obviously have to go, completely go. No satisfactory modification could be made. It was as if the country had planned to get to fifty states and stop. Little did the country know about the brainchild of Myron S. Goldberg.

The first suggestion was to make three rows of seventeen stars. This was followed by the suggestion to make seventeen rows of three stars. The inherent problem with both designs was that they totally destroyed the integrity of the red and white stripes. No one really wanted to see the size of the blue field change. Something had to remain the same, didn't it? "Besides" said Senator Drinkwater, Chairman of the Senate Flag Committee, "hostile states cruising the Mediterranean and the Persian Gulf might not recognize such a departure from the traditional stars and stripes. America would become dangerously vulnerable, for she would no longer be given the respect she had always commanded from friend and foe alike. This, my friends, we cannot tolerate. This, I cannot tolerate. This, I will not tolerate." The applause in the Senate chamber was deafening.

Senator Drinkwater suggested that the blue field be filled with circles of stars, ever diminishing, or ever increasing, depending upon your point of view. But again there was criticism. It is too radical a departure, critics said. Hostile nations will mistake New Glory for the Liberian flag or for the Malaysian flag, they insisted. Others wondered if the pattern meant that the country was in fact a collection of power circles, with the inner circles privy to more of what it takes to seize and maintain power. And if this were true, which states were represented by, say, the two innermost circles? The obviously divisive nature of such a design rendered its adoption unfeasible.

Finally, came the suggestion from the distinguished senator of North Carolina, Fleming T. Hodgetts, that we keep the circle idea, only this time, we create three interlocking circles of seventeen stars each. Most of the senators applauded this concept. First, because the blue field could remain the same size and, secondly, because of the attractive symbolism that could be found in the pattern. Three interlocking circles suggested that while our country was made up of different peoples, with different philosophies, we were nevertheless unified. It suggested a country that had no beginning and no end — something that some were quick to point out was only half true.

In any case, the measure passed by a vote of 96 to 4, with only the senators from Hawaii and Alaska voting against it. Forming a coalition, which they called the Alliance for Xenophobia (AX), they dared to ask the question, "Why should we allow a territory, so removed from the American mainland, to become a state?" The answer to this question, as I have just said, was "Why not?"

HITTING BELOW THE BELT

I was not circumcised. A bris had been scheduled, but then the mohel got sick and couldn't make it. A bug was going around. For months after his recovery, the mohel was tied up with other engagements and he could not come back to preside over a makeup circumcision any time soon. The mohel apologized profusely but remained unavailable. As time went by, my shortcoming, or rather epidermal dividend, became less important for my parents to fix. I suppose it was like when you buy a house. If you don't make changes when you first move in, you just get used to living with things the way they are. Besides, in our household, Jewish traditions and holidays, with the exception of Rosh Hashanah, Yom Kippur and Passover, received only token attention. My parents' passion, after all, was assimilation, not foreskin.

~

When I was nine years old, I was sent to the Temple Shalom summer day camp. Mother thought this would help me to overcome my shyness. She thought it would give me some much-needed confidence. Secretly, I think she dreamed that I'd become another Sandy Koufax.

The camp ran from late June to the end of August. This was the first time in my life that I had to undress in front of strangers; except for our family doctor, who really wasn't a stranger at all; he was Tim Green's father. Still, I wasn't nervous about undressing. I suppose this was because I didn't have a clue that there was anything different about me.

I picked up my camp t-shirt and shorts from the supply room and went to the locker room to change out of my street clothes. Because I had arrived late, they were out of t-shirts in my size. I had to take an extra large. In front of my locker was a long, wood bench mounted to the cement floor on two steel poles about a foot and a half high. I put my camp shirt and shorts on the bench and then stepped out of my pants and undershorts and hung them in my locker. I did this quickly because I didn't want anyone to see that my mother had sewn a nametag on my undershorts. Then I reached for my jock. I was about to put it on when a boy next to me said, "My God, what the hell happened to you?"

"Huh? What do you mean?" I said, frightened. I could see nothing wrong with myself, nothing I had not seen a thousand times before.

The other boy got undressed quickly, leaving his clothes in a pile on the floor. "This is the way it's supposed to look," he said.

I gulped. My heart started pounding. I thought, my God, was this what cancer looked like? Other boys began to circle around me. Each one was naked. Each one had a penis that was disturbingly different from mine. Each of theirs had a prominent bald crown; mine wore a shriveled up raincoat yanked over its head.

I felt like dying and I was afraid that I wouldn't. The other boys started to point at my penis and laugh. I said nothing. I was not prepared to defend myself. That I was a freak was obvious. I got dressed and left and never went back to the day camp. In my haste, I decided to keep the t-shirt but not the shorts. I could always use an extra t-shirt, I thought, and though it was far too large, I would soon grow into it. In the meantime, I figured it would make a good nightshirt. It would also remind me of my first lesson in prejudice. That it came at the hands of my fellow Jews is still a source of much heartache for me.

~

About five years later, in April, we had our usual Passover Seder. Passover is the holiday that celebrates our deliverance from slavery in Egypt and, to help us remember all that we should, everything we do and everything we eat has some symbolic meaning. For me personally, and I suspect for many of my Jewish brothers and sisters, it is also a night to remember that worldwide freedom for Jews has not yet been achieved. Not even in America.

The Passover story begins approximately 1300 B.C.E., back when God was much more of a hands-on sort of Guy. Around this time, God paid a visit to Moses in the land of Midian where he had fled after killing an Egyptian overseer who had beaten a Jew senseless. God appeared to Moses in the form of a burning bush, a fire that burned unconsumed, which frankly in the Middle East, where oil fires can burn for decades, was no big deal. Nevertheless, the phenomenon was new and fresh then, so Moses was duly impressed. He quickly obeyed the voice of God that emanated from the bush, which told him to return to Egypt to free our people from the bitter slavery they had endured for more than 400 years. Leaving his wife Zipporah behind and collecting his brother Aaron on the way, Moses went to Egypt and demanded that the Pharaoh let our people go. Unfortunately, the Pharaoh, who didn't believe in unions or child labor laws, responded by making things even harder for the Jews. This angered Moses and he said, "Let my people go. Or else —"

"Or else what?" said the intransigent Pharaoh.

"Or else my God will rain ten plagues on all of Egypt, the likes of which you've never seen."

"You people, you really have this thing about the number ten, don't you?" the Pharaoh snickered. "Next thing you know, you'll be jabbering about ten commandments." The others of Pharaoh's court joined in the snickering.

"This is no laughing matter."

"Indeed," the Pharaoh said skeptically. "Then why, Moses, do you tell such outlandish jokes?"

"Ten plagues! And here is the first. Watch, oh Great One, as all your water turns to blood!"

"If this your God can do, then blood we shall drink," said the Pharaoh with a sneer.

But then the water did turn to blood.

"Now will you let my people go?"

"Because of some cheap trick? I think not," said the Pharaoh. He picked up his goblet and drank. "Hmmm. This stuff isn't half bad. A little Tabasco and some vodka and I think we'll really have something. I think I'll call it a Bloody Phary."

And so it went on. Moses pleading, the Pharaoh refusing, the plagues descending. Next frogs, then lice, wild beasts, cattle disease, skin disease, hail, locusts, darkness and, finally, most horrible of all, the killing of the first-born Egyptians.

And only then, with the deaths of the first-born, did the Pharaoh give in. But though he let the Jews go, he would try one more time to annihilate us, only to fail once again as the Red Sea, which had parted to let the Jews escape, crashed down on the Pharaoh's troops once the Jews were safe.

So on this night we celebrate freedom. But we do not celebrate the deaths of our oppressors, tempting though it may be.

∾

At the beginning of the Seder the afikomon, a broken off piece of matzo, is hidden either by the leader of the Seder or by one of the children. In our family it had become the tradition to let the children hide the afikomon and to have my parents find it. This year it was again my turn to hide the afikomon since my brother had done it last year.

No Seder can end until the afikomon is found and eaten. But once this is done, the meal is over. Nothing else can be eaten. The idea is to teach us to live in the moment, to savor the moment, and not to attempt to freeze time with cryogenic devices like cameras. This art of savoring — of emotional and intellectual relish, of celebrating life to the fullest degree at every nanosecond in time — is especially important on this night of freedom. It is also vital to the path of personal growth and character refinement called Mussar.

William Blake once wrote, "He who bends to himself a joy/Does the winged life destroy/ But he who kisses the joy as it flies/Lives in eternity's sunrise." I suspect that Blake was a closet Jew since he understood this concept of savoring exceedingly well. The only problem this year was that by the time we got through the entire *Haggadah* — for the first time ever — I was so tired I had forgotten where I had hidden the afikomon, and my parents, as well as my brother, had been unable to find it. About two months later, a platoon of ants led us to the final crumbs. And so ended the world's longest Seder.

～

As part of the Seder, it is also traditional to have the youngest person present read the Four Questions. The Four Questions and their answers help to explain the meaning behind all the ritual. They are asked in hopes of answering the ultimate question about the Seder, which is: *Mah nishtanah halailah hazeh mikol haleilot?* Why is the night different from all other nights? Because, on this night, we celebrate our freedom from bondage and our subsequent exodus from Egypt.

Why on this night do we eat matzo? Because in their haste to get out of town before the Easter rush, the Jews could not wait for their bread to rise and removed it from the ovens while it was still flat as a pancake, and not nearly as tasty as bread should be. Matzo is unleavened bread.

Why on this night do we eat *maror*, bitter herbs? Because they remind us that life in Egypt was not all it was cracked up to be. Among other things, we had to pay retail.

Why on this night do we dip twice? The answer to this question, as you may have suspected, has nothing to do with dancing, frenzied or otherwise, but with the kind of dips we eat. First, we dip greens in salt water and then we dip *maror* in *charoset*. The salt water reminds us of all the tears we shed in bondage. The *charoset*, a mixture of mashed apples, nuts and sweet wine, reminds us of the mortar our ancestors used for erecting the buildings of the Pharaoh. This mortar was mixed with much of our blood and sweat which no doubt explains why so many ancient Egyptian structures have survived 'til this day. Clearly Jewish blood is rich in iron.

Finally, why on this night do we eat in a reclining position? A good question. Because in ancient times, only free men could recline while eating. (Women, of course, remained in bondage for another three thousand years or so.) Therefore, on this night of Passover we eat and recline simultaneously to demonstrate our freedom and hope that someone in the family remembers how to do the Heimlich maneuver.

"Sit up straight," my mother said.

"It's Passover," I said. "I get to recline."

"You'll choke to death. Look at this, the boy will choke to death."

"Freedom has its price," said the future president.

As she had during every one of our previous Seders, Mother called upon me, another year older but still the baby, to read the Four Questions. In the past I dutifully responded, reading them in perfect Hebrew from the highly authoritative Maxwell House Coffee edition of the *Haggadah*. But tonight I had something else in mind. What I said instead was this:

Mah nishtanah hazayin hazeh mikol hazaynim?

Which means this: "Why is this penis different from all other penises?"

∾

My mother tried to explain why the bris never came off as planned. She told me that the mohel had been very ill — that his body ached and his hands shook — and that she did not want to risk either my safety or her large investment in a blue wardrobe. She told me that the mohel had also been very busy for several months afterwards and was, therefore, unable to arrange an immediate rain date. The mohel suggested to my mother that she call back in December and they would try to reschedule then. I was born in late March. My bris had been planned for early April, eight days after my expulsion from the womb, in accordance with Jewish tradition. December was a long time to wait. A lot could happen.

"So why didn't you call back and set up another time?" I asked. Finally, I was going to find out the reason behind my humiliation, my deformity.

"I forgot," my mother said. "The whole thing just slipped my mind."

❧

It is now the spring of 2013. I am starting to feel more comfortable as president. I am not feeling more comfortable in every way, however.

I am sitting in the office of Washington's most prominent urologist, to whom I was referred by my good friend and personal physician, Bernie Cohen. The urologist's name does not matter. That he knows penises like the back of his hand matters immensely. I have been complaining about a nearly constant pain, a burning sensation, in the area of the prostate. Urologists, I am told, like to call this zone the land between the rain and the thunder. My pain — which varies in severity — is generally worse after urination.

I get undressed and sit down on the exam table and place a soft paper sheet over my private sector. When the doctor comes in, he says, "Hello, Mr. President," and then removes my protective covering. The doctor is wearing rubber gloves that fit his fingers like condoms. What is his first comment to me regarding my prostate pain? "I thought you were Jewish," he says.

❧

The urologist tells me that he wants to run a series of tests. He wants to do a urinalysis. "Just leave it on the sink," he says, handing me a plastic cup. On the cup, he has scrawled my name. "That sounds easy enough," I say. He wants to check my prostate. "Bend over," he says. This is not so easy. "No enlargement," he says. "Good," I say. He wants to do an IVP, which he tells me is a procedure where I would be intravenously injected with a dye and then X-rayed to see if there are any abnormalities in my renal system. He wants to do a voiding urethrogram. For this, I am told, I would be asked to drink as much liquid as I could without drowning and then lie on my back and try to urinate uphill, while three technicians take pictures. He wants to do a vasogram. This, I gather, is like a vasectomy minus the ectomy. He says I'll still be fertile, probably, after the procedure, but he is not making any guarantees. An incision will have to be made in the scrotum. "Do you want to have any more children?" he asks. "Maybe," I say. For a split second, I think of Cookie. He also wants to do a cystoscopy, which means that he wants to stick a long hollow tube up my penis while I am under general anesthesia. He can then look through the tube to see if there is anything inside my bladder or prostate or urethra that might be causing me pain. He seems to think that this procedure will be the most fun. He asks if I might like to hear a little joke about it. "I'm game," I say.

"Well, do you know what the definition of a cystoscope is, Mr. President?"

"I haven't a clue," I say. I am buttoning my shirt.

"It's an instrument that connects two pricks together," he says and then lets out a laugh so loud it startles us both. I guess his point is that urologists are not famous for their sensitivity.

❧

When I finish at the urologist's office, I go back to the

Ridgeley, the temporary White House. On the way, I order my driver to stop in front of the Washington Monument. The Secret Service objects, but that's too bad. I have to get a closer look. I am feeling quite low. The thought of all those tests, necessary or not, depresses me. My driver asks me if where he has stopped is close enough. "Plenty close, Tom. Thanks," I say.

I glance over at the monument with admiration and jealousy. And why not? To honor the father of our country, America has constructed the world's largest phallus. I imagine that Washington himself is lying beneath the ground and that the monument is his petrified, erect penis. It is an impressive and intimidating sight when you think of it in this way. It reminds me of when, as a boy of perhaps four, I first saw my father's penis. I knew on the spot my own penis would never be that big. (So much for worrying about filling the old man's shoes!) The news is not all bad though. I think that if this tribute to Washington's manhood and paternity has any basis in reality, however exaggerated, then George and I have something more in common that goes well beyond the accidental fact that we are both presidents of the greatest nation on the face of the earth. It is clear from this representation that he, too, had not been circumcised.

My brother, my only sibling, died tragically. He committed suicide at the age of thirty. I was twenty-seven at the time. There are two reasons why my brother did this. The first was that he had no sense of humor about himself. The second was that, when he was twenty-eight, he discovered that his penis was longer than our father's. Now a discovery like that could kill anybody and it was, for my already too fragile brother, the straw that broke the camel's back. I think that if my father hadn't started, at age sixty, parading around the house stark naked to prevent, as he explained, "spontaneous germatitis," my brother would still be alive today. I can say that now because my father is dead, too. And, fortunately, still hard of hearing. My father died from cancer, a tumor that ate his brain in polite little bites. He took nine months to die once he got started. My brother, as was his prerogative and preference, went quickly.

My brother left behind a suicide note, which I still have in our family safe deposit box, along with our house deed and our insurance policies. The note said, "I was going to shorten it, but I just didn't have the guts."

"Shorten what, I want to know?" my father said.

"His life, Pop, what else?" I said.

"But he *did* shorten it, didn't he? He *did* have the guts for that."

"Then I don't know what the hell he meant, Pop," I said, impatiently. "Does it matter?" I could see no purpose served by telling the truth.

◦◦◦

What relevance does a dead brother have to the presidency of Myron S. Goldberg? Well, to be honest, he would have had none at all were it not for a statement made by Senate Majority Leader Fleming T. Hodgetts. Flem despises what he calls my commie liberalism. He hates the fact that I hardly ever wear a pinstriped suit, the only kind he wears, but prefer blazers and tweeds. He hates that I am not particularly well-to-do, a reality that throws cold water on his theory that I am a member in good standing in the international conspiracy of Jewish bankers. Of course he hates the fact that I pushed for Israeli statehood and won, though he certainly made out all right when I had bargained for his support. Anyway, to make a long story short, Flem has hired people to follow me around the country, wherever I go to make a personal appearance, to try to rattle me. They hoot and holler obscenities and often carry placards that say things like, NO CHRIST KILLER IN THE WHITE HOUSE; GOD YES, JEWS NO; and STOP THAT HEATHEN FROM BREATHIN'. But the worst one I've seen by far is this one: IF WE KNEW YOU WERE COMIN', WE'D HAVE BAKED A KIKE. Flem has vociferously denied that he had anything to do with this despicable campaign. But it really doesn't matter. I have become quite thick skinned about such things. Fleming has no idea how Devil Dogs can build character. As far as my brother goes though, and he didn't go very far, Fleming T. Hodgetts has some interesting thoughts. In fact, the very day after I was elected, *The New York Times* quoted him as saying, "That's great, ain't it, boys? It's not enough the Russians are once again trying to wipe us off the face of the planet. Now we got a guy in the White House who'll probably kill himself." Apparently Fleming thinks that suicide runs in my family. I'm sure he lives for the day when he can finally say to the American public, "I told you so."

"Slipped your mind? Slipped your mind!"

My mother bit greedily into her roasted egg. This reminded her of the second offering brought to the Temple on Passover. "Slipped my mind," she said with her mouth full.

I stood up and threw my napkin on the table. The napkin was cloth. Why is this night different from all other nights? Because on this night we use cloth napkins instead of paper ones. We also use silver utensils instead of stainless steel.

"Do you have any idea what it was like for me in that locker room?"

"Myron, love of my life, this may come as a shock to you, but I had better things to think about than a little boy's penis."

I sighed and sank back onto my chair, feeling altogether defeated. Does any child ever really win an exchange with his or her mother? I looked over at my father who was eating bitter herbs he had dipped in salt water. The bitter herbs reminded him of the bitterness of slavery. The salt water reminded him of the tears we Jews shed in bondage. My father was a quiet man, a pensive man. He seldom showed even a flicker of a sense of humor. This made what he was about to do all the funnier. I looked at my father with pleading eyes. He looked back blankly, his forehead creased, and swallowed hard on the bitter herbs. "She has better things to think about than a grown man's penis, too," he said. I sprayed the water I was drinking across the entire length of the table.

If Fleming T. Hodgetts, or Robert E. Lee Sanders, finds out about my "prostate" problem, I fear they will have a field day with me, each one trying to outdo the other to bring me down with a definitive thud. I can just hear those sons-of-bitches now, their tongues running amok with slander, which the eager press will eat up, I have no doubt. It has just occurred to me that I forgot to ask my urologist if he is a Republican or a Democrat. I hope I do not live to regret this oversight.

I am sitting in the Oval Office of the Ridgeley with

Woody Stone, Ashley Jones, Phil Hurley and Calvin Foxx. The reason I call this room the "Oval Office" is not because it is oval, but because the conference table in the middle of it is oval. Freud would no doubt say that my giving the room this misnomer points to some repressed desire embedded deep within my psyche. But the truth of the matter is, there is nothing at all remotely repressed about it. I want to be in the goddamn White House!

I have just finished phone conversations with Candace Rowe, Al French and Abe Rubin. Candace had called to say that Diya Bakir may be behind the menorah burnings and that a short while ago six other large wooden menorahs were simultaneously set ablaze — one behind the Jefferson Memorial in East Potomac Park, one each on the northern and southern sections of West Potomac Park, one next to the Freer Gallery of Art and one on the Ellipse. She said the lines connecting the locations form two overlapping triangles. "You sure the culprits aren't Jewish?" I said. "I seriously doubt it," Candace replied. During the call from Candace I had to take — and quickly curtail — a diatribe by Al French about the EPA relaxing pollution control standards. As for Abe Rubin, he's still fuming about the Christian right dubbing him the "secretary of usury." He wants me to look into revoking their tax-exempt status. He also told me that a reliable source told him that the rank and file of the Secret Service isn't too happy about their director getting fired. I hope this displeasure doesn't translate into sub-standard job performance.

I am drumming my fingers on the table and I can tell that this is particularly irritating to Ashley, because she is not looking at me. Finally, she reaches out and places her hand over mine, snuffing out the noise. "You're going to be great," she says. "Just remember." She kisses the air.

I kiss the air back. "Right."

"Just be yourself," Woody says.

"I can't very well be someone else, can I?"

Isn't that right, Pop?

Don't talk to me now, Ronnie. Keep your eyes on the road.

"No, I suppose not," says Woody.

"It'll be a piece of cake," says Ashley.

Her apparent confidence bolsters me. "Still the honeymoon?" I say.

"Exactly," she says. "Trust me, Mr. President. They'll keep it light. Later, they'll bring out the artillery. But not this time."

"Wouldn't be kosher, would it?"

"No, it wouldn't."

I adjust my tie. "How do I look?"

"Like a president," Calvin Foxx says. In his gray suit, with his full head of gray wavy hair neatly combed, one can easily see why he's known as the Silver Foxx. "And if they do happen to press you on fulfilling your campaign promises, just remember which president in the last five decades kept the most promises."

"Who?"

"Jimmy Carter."

"So I should lie my ass off then."

Calvin shrugs. "At this stage it couldn't hurt."

"Ashley?"

"At this stage? You can say anything you want."

"Within reason," says pollster Jack Frost. "Let's see if we can keep those numbers climbing."

"Jack, for you, anything."

I am starting to feel much better about the whole thing. I can feel a rush of confidence flood through my body. Suddenly everything seems to be falling into place. I am in command. There is no force more formidable than the one I am about to face and if I can win them over I know that all will be well for the presidency of Myron S. Goldberg. Suddenly I begin to relive those post election, pre-inaugural glory days, when throngs of people cheered and waved as my motorcade passed them by. I imagine myself soaring above the crowd like a bird and yet I feel like I am one of them, a man of the people. I can see now why people speak of power trips. Power is not static. Power is motion. Power is taking control constantly, a dynamic, endless process. I feel like I have to move. I want to get this show on the road. Bring on the questions. Test me. Ask me anything. I will not stumble. I will not buckle. I get up and start to walk about the room. Woody remains seated but his eyes follow me.

"Sir," Woody says insistently. He taps his watch.

"Let's do it."

"You want these?" Phil Hurley asks. He hands me some notes I had been making.

"No," I say.

"You sure?"

"I'm sure. No net for Myron S. Goldberg tonight, Phil."

I walk out the door and into the corridor that leads to the briefing room where the press conference will take place. Secret Service agents line my path. They say nothing to me. They don't even acknowledge me. They just cling to their posts like an oil slick to a rock. As I make my way down the corridor, I can hear the door to the Oval Office close. As the briefing room, podium and crowd of reporters come into sight, I picture Ashley's beautiful lips.

Ashley told me to expect questions mostly of a personal nature, questions that should be easy for me to field. As it turns out, she has been right. I have been asked to confirm how old my children are and what they think of being part of the first family. I have been asked whether or not my wife plans to get involved in any social causes, the way Mrs. Roosevelt and Mrs. Clinton did. I have been asked what I like to eat for breakfast, what I like to eat for lunch, dinner and so on. I have been asked if I will send my children to public school in the fall as I had promised to do.

I have told the press that Sam and Ray, in spite of their new restrictions, seem to be adjusting quite well to, indeed they seem to be relishing, their revamped existences. I have told them that Sam, my youngest, is something of a baseball nut and that she is looking forward to joining me when I travel to Fenway Park in Boston next month to throw out the first ball of the season. The moment that I said Sam was a big baseball fan, all conversation seemed to stop, and pens and pencils took notes furiously. There was considerably less enthusiasm displayed when I told them that Sam's other passion was rearranging furniture. You just can't figure the press out sometimes. Of course they did perk up again when I mentioned that Ray would be turning thirteen this year. One reporter, from *The St. Louis Post-Dispatch*, wanted to know if I planned to arrange for Ray to meet the fifteen-year-old son of Alexi Brezniski during my fall summit with the Russian leader. When I said that this was entirely possible, there was again a flurry of writing. As for my wife following in the footsteps of Eleanor Roosevelt or Hillary Clinton, I was deliberately vague. Sheila, though passionate about causes, has never been a political activist. I always suspected that she was just along for the ride. Going to pro-choice rallies during the late 80s, for example, was, for her, like going to a movie. She approached movies and rallies with the same detachment. Sheila has always been more of a hands-on person. She has no patience with bureaucracy. She believes the only way to have an impact on the world is one person at a time. "You'll have to ask the First Lady herself about that, I'm afraid," I said, thinking nothing of the remark. Nevertheless, a woman reporter from the *Post*, who was known for her feminist bias, seemed positively elated by my reply. I can only conclude that she thought my letting Sheila speak for herself was somehow indicative of my deep and widely publicized support for feminist causes.

The questions have gone on for about half an hour and already I feel exhausted. It's a darn good thing Robert E. Lee Sanders is not among the press corps, because if he was, I am certain he would love to call me on the stamina issue again.

I look over at Ashley, who is now in the wings, and manage to catch her eye. I nod slightly, our prearranged signal that I have had enough. The nod is so slight I am certain that only Ashley can interpret it for what it is. Ashley takes a few steps forward, making herself visible to the entire gathering. She raises one finger in the air. Immediately a hundred or so arms pop up, each reporter hoping that his or her question can be the last one of this historic event. I wonder if this is the one that'll hang me, if this is the one that will end the honeymoon prematurely, destroy my standing in the polls, banish me to the Ridgeley forever. I look about the room for the most sympathetic face I can find and spot Fred Siegel, a moon-faced reporter in his late forties who writes for *The New York Times*. "Fred?" I say.

"Mr. President," Mr. Siegel begins, "in the past, the press has given, I think, an inordinate amount of attention to the pressures placed upon women in public life. Women are constantly being hounded with the question, 'How, Ms. Politician, do you manage to strike a balance between your public and private persona?', as if both were full-time careers, which indeed they might well be. My point, Mr. President, is this: as a dedicated father and husband — and as a clearly dedicated public servant — you must feel the push and pull of private versus public obligations all the time as well, as much as any woman. I think, therefore, it would be a great disservice to men everywhere to assume that these pressures do not exist. With that in mind, sir, I ask you this: how do you balance your public and private life?"

"First of all, Fred, I'd like to thank you for your brevity," I say. A general wave of laughter laps against the walls of the room. "I guess I've never really viewed my two lives as being in conflict with one another, but more like two sides of the same coin. To adapt a statement one of my senate colleagues made many years ago, I have a brain and a penis, and I use them both." I was not asked to qualify how much I use either.

∽

"You were," says Ashley, pausing to find just the right word, her face twisted with confused wonder, "incredible, Mr. President. No, beyond incredible. I'm absolutely certain there has never been a first press conference by a president quite like yours in the history of the country."

"Thank you," I beam.

"The temperature's definitely going to rise, Mr. President," says Jack.

"Let's hope," says Phil. He looks as if he just swallowed an entire lemon.

"I think you were superb," Calvin says. "Mazel tov."

"Yup, definitely a first, Mr. President," says Woody. He shakes my hand.

A first. Of that I am sure. I do not know what on earth possessed me to make that brain and penis remark. A political death wish, I imagine. Perhaps I was starting to get delirious because I had to urinate so badly. As it was, I barely made it to the toilet in time. "You really think so?"

Later, back in the presidential suite, Woody flops down on the living room couch and loosens his tie. We're the only ones there. The kids are in bed and I can hear Sheila in our bedroom talking to her appointment secretary about a speaking engagement with the ADL. "No question. You were a big hit, sir."

"You don't think they'll crucify me with that penis remark?"

"I think they loved it," says Woody. "I think they found it refreshing. I mean, could you imagine Sanders saying something like that? You were honest and straightforward with them, Mr. President. They eat that kind of stuff up."

"If you say so," I say.

"I do," says Woody. "And you heard what everyone else had to say."

I flop down in the big wing back chair to the left of the sofa. "I don't know, Woody. We'll just have to wait and see." I loosen my tie.

"Hungry?" says Woody. "I am."

"Sure. How about some Ret Ching?"

⁓

Sheila is next to me in bed, but she is fast asleep. I am about to turn off the light, but first I pick up and reread the fortune from the cookie I got tonight. Here is what it says: "You will perspire to greatness." I think that "You will aspire to greatness" is what they probably had in mind. But then I think back to the third Goldberg-Sanders debate and I realize just how appropriate this fortune really is. Maybe I really am being watched over by some benevolent Supreme

Being who also happens to have a rather warped sense of humor.

❧

When I get up in the morning, Sheila is snoring heavily in my ear. She has thrown the covers off herself — which is her habit, though I usually get blamed for it — and is curled up in a fetal position, cowering to keep warm. The room is cool. Sheila is wearing a cotton nightgown. It is blue and white with a red floral pattern. My daughters wear the identical nightgown. On them it looks cute. On Sheila it looks frumpy.

My mind is still fuzzy with sleep as I turn off the alarm. It is seven and I am not sure that what I have dreamed is a dream, or if it actually took place last night at the press conference. The dream involves my urologist. In it I see him standing next to a reporter whom I believe is Sidney Stockman from the *Post*. Sidney is a tall, lean man of fifty years with a receding hairline. He looks very much like a young version of my Republican opponent in last year's election, Robert E. Lee Sanders. Beyond appearances though, these men have nothing in common. Sidney is a sanguine fellow, quick to laugh, especially at himself; Sanders is a morose one, always with the gloom and doom, as quick to attack as Sidney is to laugh. Sidney, for all his pleasantness, however, has a reputation for being a gossip. And it is not without foundation. Sidney began his career as a cub reporter for *The National Enquirer*. Certainly that is where he developed an interest in fiction. In any case, it was his first job and he needed the money, so one can hardly hold it against him. All I hope is that the only place he talked to my urologist was in my dream.

LET'S PLAY BALL

Tuesday, April 9, 2013. It's a beautiful spring day in Washington. The cherry blossoms are in bloom. The natives and the tourists fill the parks and sidewalks. It is not so difficult to tell them apart and not simply because the former are dressed for business, the latter for pleasure. It is a curious thing, but I have noticed over my years in this city of lawyers that among the natives there is an uncanny adherence to pedestrian law. In fact, the only law I have not witnessed people here fold, bend, spindle, mutilate or break on a regular basis is the law against jaywalking. Indeed the culprits who ignore this law invariably are "foreigners", casually dressed, every third or fourth one of them with a camera slung over his or her shoulder, often with kids in tow, "Don't Walk" signals ignored as if they weren't even there, defiantly dodging cars and tour buses. But the locals, they respect the laws of the street. Patiently, they wait for "Walk" signs to light up, showing no indication of rage against their imprisonment, no cursing at the unfair impositions made upon their valuable time. Can this patience be explained by the fact that here everyone is always "on", always taking care of business, no matter where they are, so that no time is ever really lost or stolen? I think not. Other cities across the country are filled with Type A personalities, workaholics who are also notorious jaywalkers. So why then are Washington politicians so cautious about jaywalking? My own theory is this: they want to demonstrate as visibly as possible what law-abiding folks they really are.

Be that as it may, it's the tourists with whom I now feel more in synch. They all seem to be in a dreamy state, caught up in the weather, the happy victims of spring fever. From my balcony in the Ridgeley I watch them. I wish that I could walk among them like a normal person, but I cannot. I am the president, and presidents can't do that sort of thing — at least not without legions of Secret Service chaperones. Robert Mancini, Abe Rubin's new Secret Service head, has warned me repeatedly and angrily not to stand out on the balcony. Mancini is a short, stocky man, as tough on the inside as he is on the outside. His hair is thin and wispy. Because of all this, coupled with the fact that he has a habit of resting one hand inside his shirt, I call him Napoleon. I don't really think Mancini gives a rat's ass about my safety but, according to Abe Rubin, his reputation means everything to him. He'd die for his reputation, Abe told me. Which means he'd die for you. So be it. I never said the guy had to love me, too.

"Remember what happened to JFK and Martin Luther King," Mancini barked. I am only ten flights up and would be an easy target for even the most mediocre marksman. "Lee Harvey Oswald had to have a perfect aim," he continued. "But all some guy has to do today is buy himself a

Chinese semiautomatic assault weapon for a hundred bucks or so, spray a couple dozen rounds left to right, and we've got one very dead president." Perhaps it will be the death of me one of these days, but I have chosen to ignore the warnings. Besides it is not as if I stand out here at the same time every day. I just do it when the cabin fever gets too much for me to handle, which admittedly is a few times a week at the very least. The point is, for someone to accurately predict when I will venture out onto the balcony, he or she would have to be endowed with no small amount of psychic power.

At approximately ten o'clock this morning I will be boarding Air Force One to fly to Boston. I have taken pollster Jack Frost's advice and agreed to throw out the first ball for the season opener in Fenway Park. Jack has always insisted that showing up at major sporting events is the fifth best way for a president to boost his approval ratings. The first is getting assassinated, the second is orchestrating a successful military action, the third is negotiating the release of American hostages and the fourth is issuing a major tax cut. I have told Jack that I would prefer to start small and work my way up, if that's all right with him, although, frankly, I do have reservations about tax cuts.

My visit has been well publicized in the local press, so I suspect that security will have to be stepped up. I am to have lunch with the governor at the Ritz around twelve-thirty. From there we will head directly to the ballpark. Game time, I believe, is 2:30. If I decide to hold on to the ball for longer than I am expected to, game time could turn out to be a little later. I am feeling a bit mischievous today.

I have had my breakfast but I am still on the hungry side. It is probably just nerves. Returning to my home state, which I carried by only fifty-four votes, has put quite a strain on me. I have not been able to figure out why I carried the state with so few votes, when my margin of victory for both my House and Senate races had been substantial; I never got less than 56% of the vote, and in my last campaign for the Senate in 2010 I got 71% of the vote. Woody can't figure it out either. Nor can any of my other senior advisors. Jack's best guess was that the people of Massachusetts thought I made a damn good senator but just wasn't, in their eyes, presidential timber. It hurt to think that this might well be the case. I would rather believe that they simply wanted me all to themselves, that I was simply too much of a treasure to share. I would even prefer that they felt uncomfortable with the idea of a Jew in the White House. Prejudice I have learned to deal with reasonably well. At least on a personal level. But a lack of confidence in my ability to lead, to govern on a national basis, now that was something else again. That really hurt.

I suddenly start to feel cold standing out here on the balcony, unprotected on three sides. The wind has started to blow. There is still a goodly amount of winter in it. I push open the sliding glass door and go back into the living room. Woody is seated on the couch with his legs crossed. In front of him on the coffee table is his opened briefcase. He is flipping intently through a stack of papers. Seated next to Woody is my daughter, Ray. She is still wearing her night-gown. She apparently is in no hurry to get dressed because she will not be making the trip to Boston with me. Neither will Sheila, for that matter. Sam, however, is planning to go. As I mentioned at my first press conference, Sam is some-thing of a baseball nut. She collects baseball cards, new and old. Most of the older ones in her collection come from my mother. Sam has the cards of practically every player who ever played for the Dodgers. Every now and then I enjoy trying to stump her with Dodger trivia.

"Who won the home run crown in 1941?"

"Dolph Camilli."

"How many did he hit?"

"34."

"Who was the next Dodger to win the crown?"

"Duke Snider, 1956. 43 homers."

"How about the first Dodger to lead the league in RBIs?"

"Camilli again. 1941."

"The second?"

"Snider. In 19 —"

"56?"

"55."

"Can't catch you."

Yes, Sam knew them all. Every stat for every Dodger great — from Dolph Camilli to Jackie Robinson to Roy Campanella to Steve Garvey to Bobby Clifford. Lifetime batting averages, lifetime ERAs, titles; she can probably even tell you how many bases Maury Wills stole in the 1963 World Series when the expatriate Dodgers whipped their former crosstown rivals, the New York Yankees, four games to zip. But Sam's truest love was one that she inherited from my mother. Numero Uno on her all-time great list was the incomparable Sandy Koufax, the David of the Diamond. One entire wall in her room is covered with Sandy Koufax photos and newspaper clippings, which my mother collected over the years. In the center of it all is a life-size poster. In Sam, Mother got the son she always wanted. Much to Mother's dismay, basketball was my great love.

I sit down on the couch next to Ray and give her a little pat on the knee. "How's my big girl?" I say.

Ray is watching Woody as if he were doing something magical. Her infatuation with him is growing by leaps and bounds.

"Fine," Ray says evenly. She is trying very hard to act grown up. She is holding her glass of chocolate milk perfectly straight.

"Can I have a sip?" I say.

"Huh? Oh, sure," she says and hands me the glass.

I take a sip and hand it back to her. "Now that's chocolate," I say.

Ray smiles weakly and puts the glass on the coffee table. "One more," I say and pick up the glass.

"Finish it," Ray says. "I didn't really want it in the first place. Sam made it for me without asking."

"What a thoughtful kid," I say.

"She was making one for herself. It was no big deal to make another."

"Well, it was nice just the same," I say. I keep trying to do whatever I can to foster good feelings between Sam and Ray. The kids are a lot different now that Ray is about to turn thirteen. Ray is becoming a young woman, full of hopes, hormones and confusion. She is beginning to see men not as father figures, or brothers, or friends, but as companions, potential lovers. Sam is into baseball cards, double chocolate milk and rearranging furniture. Two years ago they liked the same movies, the same clothes, sometimes even the same rock groups, though they each had a favorite group member; but now, they couldn't be further apart. I wish things could be different. I wish there could be harmony. But I guess that's life. I pick up Ray's glass and down it.

A crew of Air Force men and women salute me as I make my way past them to board Air Force One. There is no pomp in this circumstance, strictly routine. I salute back, still not completely confident that I am doing it right, although I suspect I'm getting close. I am following Ronald Reagan's advice. Reagan once said the way to salute was to "bring your hand up like honey and shake it off like manure," and I figured that since he was a military hero, the veteran of more than a dozen World War II training films, he ought to have known.

During the second of our three televised debates, Robert E. Lee Sanders tried to make my lack of military service a central issue. How, he wondered, could a man, who never served his country in a truly patriotic fashion, be expected to competently handle his role as commander in chief of the armed forces? When I attempted to counter his argument by bringing up my record of service with the Peace Corps, Sanders said, "having served in that namby-pamby outfit, delivering granola bars to Zulus, hardly qualifies anyone to be a leader of men in times of crisis." I then pointed out that the true measure of leadership is not how many people you have exterminated, but how many people you have saved. My words drew a hefty and sustained round of applause from my supporters. And later my senior staffers said that with that counterpoint I had won the debate, although Sanders did manage to get in one parting shot off-camera. As we shook hands, he leaned forward and whispered into my ear, "Too bad Hitler missed a few of you. Guess it's up to me now." Then he put his arm over my shoulder and broke out that famous grandfatherly smile of his for the TV cameras. Jack Frost figured that conciliatory gesture was worth about a 5% bump in the polls for him. "Thank God that's all," I said. "If America heard what he whispered in my ear, I'm sure it would've been worth ten."

◦∾◦

From the sky, Washington looks magnificent. I look

down and see the Jefferson Memorial, the Lincoln Memorial, the Washington Monument. I see the Capitol, the Supreme Court Building, the Library of Congress. I see Blair House, the Treasury Building, the Department of Commerce. And of course I see the White House, though I choose not to look at it for more than a second or two. It is too painful to do so. When you cannot have what you desperately want, sometimes it is best to pretend that you really don't want it all that much. I can tell these little lies and some people will believe them. Unfortunately, I cannot count myself as part of this gullible group. I may not be able to see through every politician who crosses my path, but I can see through Myron S. Goldberg.

There is something magical about this city. There is the unrelenting sense that this is where it's happening. This is where the decisions are made that will affect the lives of every single American, and the lives of the seven and half billion other people who populate our shrinking planet. This sense of controlling mankind's destiny pervades everything and everyone in this city. It is no veneer. It runs deep as well as wide. And no one can escape it. Some can hide to greater degrees than others, but we're all caught up in its sticky web. It is easy to understand why people who come here become intoxicated with power. The city is like an open bar. Come, enjoy, be merry, be happy, drink, drink from the bottomless well. Come dash the hopes of millions with the wave of a pen. Put another colony on the moon. Feed the starving in Africa. Send more ammunition to the freedom fighters in Iran. Whatever you want, my friend, whatever you desire is yours. All you need do is ask. That is all there is to it. No reasonable request will be denied, and neither will many of the unreasonable ones. As the plane climbs higher, its gentle roar soothes me. I put my head back and close my eyes. I feel sleep coming on.

～

It is not as nice in Boston as it was in Washington. The sky is overcast. There is only an occasional break in the clouds. Ashley Jones tells me it's supposed to clear by afternoon, but she forgets that I come from around here and I know that the weather in New England will do exactly as it pleases whenever it pleases, regardless of any presidential edict.

At this moment my fifteen-car motorcade is zipping its way down Commonwealth Avenue. The street has been blocked off to regular traffic and the sidewalks have been cordoned off to keep people from getting too close to my limo as it passes by. The limo I am riding in has no top. Robert Mancini was, of course, dead set against my using such a vehicle.

"Mr. President, didn't we just have a conversation about JFK and Oswald the other day?" he said.

"These are very different times, Bob," I said. "Besides, this is my home state, not Texas."

"Oh, right, I forgot. Massachusetts, yes. The state you carried by, what, fifty votes?"

"Fifty-four."

"And of course you're as popular as ever here, aren't you, Mr. President?" Mancini no doubt knew that Jack Frost's own poll, taken a week ago, showed my approval rating actually declining in Massachusetts.

"After today, Bob, all that's going to change. Trust me. The people here were just feeling a little neglected, that's all. They're used to having my undivided attention."

Mancini then suggested that I would be safer in Texas because it was not only the home state of my vice president, but also a state I carried with 59% of the vote. That may well be, I said, but you can be sure that no one is going to take a shot at me with Governor Edwards at my side. The man is practically a saint here, as evidenced by his 78% winning margin in 2012. Finally, Mancini relented, but he refused to guarantee my safety. I did insist, by the way, that Sam ride in a staff limousine instead of mine. I was the only one going topless.

We make it to the Ritz without incident. There were not even any distasteful placards in the crowd this time; no ethnic slurs, nothing at all. At lunch the conversation centers on baseball. Governor Edwards says he has a good feeling about the Sox this year. "For once, they have pitching right down to the bullpen."

"Glad to hear it, Bill," I say. "Last year was a heart-breaker." Last year, the Reds managed to win another pennant but then went on to lose to the Cardinals in the World Series, four games to three.

"Like '86 all over again," Edwards says. Edwards is a slight man with furry black eyebrows and black hair, surgically cropped. What he lacks in charisma, he makes up for by being scrupulously honest. He is a friend to business and to the rank and file, a difficult balancing act to pull off, but pull it off in spades he does.

"So this year will be different," I say. "It's in the air." Actually what's in the air is the smell of an incredible filet mignon a waiter has just placed in front of Bill Edwards. I begin to salivate. I cannot wait to get mine. But when I look up, I see a foil TV dinner descending in front of me like an alien spaceship. I can identify peas, but I'm not too sure about the rest of it. Perhaps it's turkey and mashed potatoes. "What the hell is this?"

The waiter's face pales. "Kosher turkey," he says nervously. "Is there something wrong, sir?"

~

Fenway Park hasn't changed all that much since my mother dragged me there when I was a kid, Lord knows how many times. There is still the short left field, backed up by the Green Monster, the thirty-seven foot high, two hundred and fifty foot long wall that makes the park a paradise for right-handed power hitters. There are still the cheap seats in center field, where fans still claim they can see what's going on better than any second base umpire, and still seats behind poles along the left field and right field lines. There has been a lot of talk lately about building a new stadium for the Sox. The argument "for" says that if the Celtics can have a new sports arena, then the Red Sox should get a new Fenway Park. The argument "against" was much simpler: the Red Sox are not the Celtics. No one, except those center field fans, would argue with that.

Ashley was right. The clouds are breaking up. Patches of blue are pushing through. We are seated in a box behind the Red Sox dugout. The governor is on my right. Woody and Ashley are next to him. Sam is on my left. She is engrossed in her copy of the Red Sox Yearbook. No doubt she has already memorized the stats of the key players. The stands are a mass of bright spring colors. Some of the fans are wearing shorts. Some of the women are in halter tops. A handful of very brave, possibly very drunk, men have taken off their shirts. About a zillion people are wearing Red Sox caps. In the middle of all this is Myron S. Goldberg, the President of the United States, surrounded by his Secret Service entourage, all of them wearing dark suits. Viewed from the clouds, we must look like a black eye on the face of brainless joy.

Among those who occupy the presidential box are the sportswriters. A couple of them I already know, but most I have met for the first time today. There's Jack Kelly from *The New York Times* and Collins Nelson from *The Washington Post*. Those are the two I know. The ones I didn't know include Tom Meagan of *The Boston Herald*, a paunchy, middle-aged, red-faced Irishman who looks a little like Babe Ruth; Eddie Biggs, of *The Boston Globe*, a fortyish-looking fellow with a salt and pepper beard; and Red Trombley of *The Los Angeles Times*. Trombley is the oldest of the contingent. He is all of seventy. He has a long and narrow face, an ashen complexion and a neck like a rooster. Trombley is famous for two things: a searing column about Shaquille O'Neal's lackluster play in the 2000 playoffs, and bow ties. Today all he can talk about is the starting Red Sox pitcher, Harmon Wilson, a twenty-game winner for the Cubs last year who was acquired by the Sox just prior to spring training, a trade in which the Sox gave up Mike Pearson and Tom Billings, two three-hundred-plus hitters, and a 2015 first round draft pick. It was Trombley's belief that no pitcher, at least one not super sized with steroids, could have a successful career in Fenway Park. "Built for hitters," he says. "There's just no way. No way."

"Hell, this kid can strike out the side practically every time," says Collins Nelson. No matter what Trombley says, Nelson disagrees with it.

"You throw strikes all the time, sooner or later they're gonna figure you out," says Trombley. Trombley is wearing a seersucker suit that must have been bought about thirty pounds ago. I don't think that he could button the jacket if his life depended on it.

"Maybe. But not the Indians," Nelson says. "They've been in the cellar so long, they're starting to look like bottles of wine."

Some more bickering goes on between Nelson and Trombley but I cannot be bothered with it anymore. My moment is rapidly approaching. I can see Bucky Blake, the Sox catcher, finishing his warm-up with Harmon Wilson. He heads back to the dugout and disappears, but a moment later he reemerges. They have allowed a number of photographers onto the field and they begin to assemble in a giant huddle around Blake. Blake has taken off his mask and has wedged it into his armpit. In his right hand he is holding a brand new baseball, as white as the first snowball after a storm. He makes his way over to the presidential box and hands me the ball. I flash a big smile and wait until Blake backs up a few yards from the stands. Then I cock my arm back and get ready to throw him the ball. I don't throw the ball, however. Instead I turn to Sam and give her a little nudge with my elbow. Then I offer her the ball. She is shocked but takes the ball from me anyway. "Burn one in there, kiddo," I say. Sam breaks into big smile.

Sam takes a look at Bucky Blake, who is all buck teeth now, to make sure that he is ready. Bucky crouches and gives her a sign. Sam waves him off. Bucky gives her another sign. Sam waves him off again. Bucky, clearly getting a kick out of Sam, shrugs and gives her a third sign. This time Sam nods her approval, winds up and then lets fly a perfect strike. Cameras are clicking and popping all over the place. The crowd is cheering wildly. Harmon Wilson has one tough act to follow.

∽

Trombley was wrong about Harmon Wilson, and Collins Nelson was right. Harmon Wilson has pitched a shutout for eight innings, striking out fifteen, walking three and allowing only four hits, two of which barely made it out of the infield.

It is a superb first outing and the Red Sox must be pleased as hell. The unfortunate part about all this is that the Red Sox can't hit the broad side of a Green Monster. They've only managed to collect six hits themselves, no more than two in any inning. So after eight, the teams are deadlocked, zip to zip.

The ninth inning looks like a repeat of all the rest for Harmon Wilson. The first two batters he faces, he strikes out, one of them on three pitches. The crowd roars its approbation. The third batter is where the trouble comes in. Harmon gets behind him three and 0. His next pitch is a strike. But the batter, Ronnie Gibson, Cleveland's best hitter, has been given the green light. He takes hold of that strike and sends it not simply over the left field wall, but over the screen as well. Goodbye. One to zip. Harmon calms down, fixes his jockstrap, blows an enormous bubble with the wad of gum he's been chomping on and strikes out the next batter. Unfortunately, the damage has been done. However, in the bottom of the ninth, Frank Calzone lines a solo shot into the right field seats to tie it up. It is not time to go home yet.

～

Whatever bad stuff you could say about Sox pitching in the past, you can't get away with anymore. Harmon Wilson pitched nine nearly flawless innings, striking out eighteen. The three relievers who have followed him have pitched shutout ball. It is now the bottom of the nineteenth and we're still tied at one run apiece. I wanted to leave six innings ago, but how would that look? I could kiss my fifty-four-vote plurality goodbye in the 2016. Kiss the White House goodbye, too. So here I sit. I haven't been to the bathroom in six hours. Six hours! And how would it look if I went now? First off, I might miss the BIG PLAY. Secondly, there isn't a person in the park who wouldn't know where I had been when I came back to my box a few minutes later. I am stuck. It is prayer time.

My prayer is about to be answered. I feel it. Bucky "The Beaver" Blake is up. He's been hitless in eight trips, but he has, I overhear Trombley say, hit the ball well in six of those at bats. The count is now two and two. Blake has just taken a strike. Boos pour down onto the field like sludge. Blake steps out of the batter's box, drops his bat, rubs his hands in the dirt, spits, adjusts his jockstrap and spits again. He's ready now. He digs himself back into the batter's box. He twists his left foot into the ground. He is anchored. Yes, he is ready. The Cleveland reliever puts his foot on the rubber and looks in for the sign. He shrugs off the first two and then nods his approval to the third. In a second he lets the ball fly. Blake shifts his weight backwards and then swings. There is an incredible cracking sound. Blake is off and running and the ball is flying deep into the center field bleachers. The crowd is going absolutely bonkers. A fan makes a spectacular one-handed catch. Blake, watching, leaps high in the air and begins prancing like a gazelle. He raises his arms in triumph above his head. BUCKY! BUCKY! BUCKY! the crowd chants. Blake rounds third base and receives big pat on the back from the third base coach. Halfway between third and home he is mobbed by his teammates. He pushes through them and jumps, feet together, on home plate. My God, what a moment. At least now I can go to the bathroom.

∾

When I first started coming to Fenway Park with my mother, no individual urinals existed. Instead, as many as thirty men and boys simultaneously emptied their bladders into a single trough, a process that, to an uncircumcised and consequently overly self-conscious Jewish boy, seemed to go on — horrifyingly — forever. The trough was, I can see in hindsight, a veritable American melting potty, fiercely democratic, a field much more level than any man would ever dare admit. For better or worse, this nostalgic mix of male bonding and involuntary penile comparative research is gone now, replaced by partitioned urinals and electric eye flushers which, thanks to Bush 2, probably double as surveillance cameras. Bad for illegals I guess. But certainly a boon for every male American citizen, allowing him to pee in relative privacy, or if he happens to be the President of the United States, in complete privacy.

In fact, the Secret Service has blocked off the men's room so I can take a leak without being assassinated. I have told them that it is not necessary that I go in there completely unaccompanied. Woody has expressed a need to relieve himself as well, as have Trombley and Tom Meagan. I tell the Secret Service that it's all right for these other men to join me in this ceremonial draining of the male bladder, though not precisely in those words. The more the merrier.

Once inside the bathroom, Trombley gets into an argument with Meagan about the pitch that Bucky Blake sent sailing, which made this blissful moment possible. Trombley insists the pitch Blake hit was a split-fingered fastball; Meagan maintains it was a forkball.

"Lopez never threw a goddamn forkball in his life," says Trombley.

"There's a first time for everything," says Meagan.

Woody is standing in front of the urinal next to mine. I am still more than a little angry that this game took so damn long. "Woody, as far as I'm concerned," I say, "the only reason baseball was invented was to give guys something to talk about while they're taking a piss."

"That could be, Mr. President," says Woody. "That could be."

Suddenly it has become very quiet in here. You can almost here a dribble drop. Trombley and Meagan have stopped arguing. They are looking at me like I have just committed some terrible blasphemy. I hear their flies close like zippers on body bags.

~

It is twelve hours since I shocked a couple of sportswriters with my theory about the origin of America's favorite pastime. I am sipping coffee in the Oval Office, discussing the day's agenda with Woody Stone, Phil Hurley and Calvin Foxx when there's a knock at the door. "Come in," Woody says. It is Ashley Jones and Jack Frost. Their expressions are extremely grim. They are each carrying a stack of newspapers. The top one in Ashley's pile, *The Los Angeles Times*, is opened to the editorial page. "Read it," she says.

"Now?" I say.

Ashley nods with a pained expression. Phil grimaces. The others look at me expectantly.

I take the paper from Ashley and begin reading. At the top of the editorial column is the headline, STRIKE THREE, MR. PRESIDENT. What follows is this:

We Americans are a proud people. We Americans are a strong people. We take our commitments to our friends throughout the world very seriously. We take our commitments to our people at home with equal seriousness. As a people, we work hard, but we also play hard. We play hard as amateurs. We play hard as weekend athletes. But, above all, we play hard as professionals. Anyone who chooses to demean the contributions of our professional athletes to the

American spirit demeans all of us who love and honor sport in any way. Anyone who would dare trivialize these contributions indeed trivializes the very soul of America. We are not suggesting that the outcome of sporting events has any real or measurable impact on world peace, or on the search for cures for deadly diseases, or on the problems of world hunger and poverty. No, indeed. But what we are saying is that sport, in a very real sense, brings out the best in us, because to succeed in sports, and in life, we must always do our best.

The recent remarks of our chief executive during the opening of baseball season at Fenway Park go against the grain of America, the very fabric of our society. To say that America's favorite pastime, as our president did, "was conceived simply to give men something to talk about while urinating," is not only despicable, but darn poor taste. And this from a man who shares an ethnic heritage with that great Hall-of-Famer, Sandy Koufax. Shame one, shame two, shame three, Mr. President.

I put the paper down. Ashley immediately hands me another. This one is *The Boston Herald*, Tom Meagan's paper. Like *The LA Times*, this one is opened to the editorial page. I read the headline. It says, PREZ GETS BASE WITHOUT BALLS. This editorial likewise blasts my blasting of America's favorite pastime, but the gist of it is that I would never have the guts to make such an unthinkable remark in public. They are quite right about that. But what they call a lack of guts, I would call discretion. "No more, Ashley," I say. "I get the drift."

Ashley tosses the stack of papers on the floor next to my desk. There is a slapping thud of finality in the way they crash land. Jack bends down and puts his stack on top of

Ashley's as if he were placing a wreath on the grave of a dead soldier. "I can't take it back, can I?" I say.

"You can try," says Ashley.

"You better try," says Jack.

I start drumming my fingers on the coffee table. I wish, albeit briefly, that I were the Teflon president and not the tefilin one. My head feels like a house with every room on fire. Abe Rubin wants to defrock the tax-exempt status of the Christian right. The Republicans want a $350 billion tax cut, primarily to benefit hedge fund managers, as well as organized prayer on commuter flights. Fleming Hodgetts is demanding that I call off my economic summit with Alexi Brezniski in the fall. Warren Gates insists Brezniski is about to attack and reclaim Alaska. The Secret Service is still seething over the firing of Robert Mancini's predecessor. Al French wants me to take on the EPA. Candace Rowe wants me to take on the Iraqis. Oliver Graham wants me to rescind my proposal to eject grays from the military. The nuclear arms race, mostly fueled by second tier powers, is once again spinning out of control. My prostate, or whatever the hell it is, just keeps getting worse. As do my favorability ratings. And now this. What next, I wonder? What next?

∾

Sam is not speaking to me. When I knock on the door, she shouts, "Go away!"

"I need to talk to you, honey," I say.

"Go away!"

"Just open the door," I say. "I won't even come in. I promise. Just open up, so I can see you."

"Go away, Daddy! Go away!"

I can hear the sound of furniture being moved. I wonder if Sam is building a barricade, or if she is simply trying yet another new arrangement. I never knew that there could be so many different ways to arrange two twin beds, a desk, a bookshelf and a bureau. "Please, Samantha," I say.

"Go away!"

It is a losing battle. The irony of it all is that I don't even think she really understood the editorial in the *Times*. All she knows is that I did something bad and that whatever it was, it slung mud at her idol, Sandy Koufax. Couldn't the *Times* at least have had the decency to leave that remark out? I guess not. "C'mon, hun. I won't bite. I promise."

Sam says nothing. But something hits the door hard. A shoe perhaps, followed by several other objects of the same weight in rapid succession. Finally, the door opens and there's Sam, her face streaked with tears. "I hate you," she says.

"I don't believe that," I say.

"Believe it," she says defiantly. "'Cause it's true."

I step forward and put my hands on her shoulders. She stiffens. I pull her to me and hold her tight. "I'm really sorry, Sam. I really am."

Sam starts weeping and shaking again. I kiss the top of her head. Her blonde hair is a shade darker than usual because it is moist with perspiration. I look past Sam into her room. Everything — the beds, the bookcase, the desk, the bureau — is in a new place. This does not surprise me. What surprises me is that Sam's Sandy Koufax wall has been torn down and the life-size poster ripped into small pieces. "Oh, Sam," I say.

Sam puts her arms around my waist and hugs me back.

༺✿༻

As I return to the living room, my private line starts ringing. I move to it quickly and pick it up. "Hello," I say.

"Mr. President?" The voice sounds familiar. It also sounds shaky.

"Yes," I say. "This is the president."

"We have to talk, sir," says the voice.

"Paul?" I say. "That you?"

"Yeah."

"What's wrong? It sounds like something's wrong."

There is a pause. Pauses, I think, always accept responsibility for what follows them. "I think he knows," Paul says.

"Who knows what?" I say.

"Bull Dozier. The Arizona Project."

This time I hesitate. "You sure?"

"Pretty sure," says Paul. "What should I do? You want to abort?"

Abort. A dangerous word indeed. I think for a moment about the Christian right and I wonder if they are possibly taping this conversation. I remember the "Jew Bastard Baby Killer" signs they waved in front of me at so many campaign stops. Then I think, gee, too bad they're not listening. "Abort? Not on your life. Do not abort," I say emphatically. Got that, you SOBs? "The future of the world is hanging on this project. Do not abort."

"Just tell me what you want me to do," says Paul. For a man who has never served a day in any military capacity, Paul is a damn good soldier.

"Sit tight for now, Paul. I'll be in touch."

"What about Dozier?"

I say, "I'll handle Dozier. You've got enough on your mind."

"Okay," says Paul.

"Take care, Paul," I say. I hang up the phone. I wonder what Sandy Koufax would do in a spot like this. Pitch to him, I guess.

~

"I have a brief statement to make tonight, after which I regret to say there will be no questions." There is a murmur of disapproval from the audience. I hold up my palms to quell it. "Sorry, sorry," I add and, as the grumbling slowly fades, I spot Ashley Jones in the back of the briefing room. She gives me a low wattage smile and kisses the air. A reporter whose name I have forgotten looks at Ashley with astonishment and then at me. And then at Ashley. And then at me. He whispers something into the ear of another reporter seated next to him. Suddenly whispers spread like a flame along a fuse. "Ladies and gentlemen, please, if you let me proceed, I will only take a few moments of your time." The whispering intensifies the way drivers will often accelerate when a traffic light turns yellow, but then quickly ends. "You all know what took place at Fenway Park the other day. And I think you all know in your hearts that what I said was said not only off the record, but also in jest. Years ago, you may recall that President Reagan spoke into what he thought was a dead microphone, saying 'The bombing of Russia will start in five minutes.' And while I know that blaspheming the sacred institution of baseball is in many ways more serious than President Reagan's gaffe, I ask you to forgive me none-theless as the American people forgave Reagan back then." Once again I make eye contact with Ashley. She nods her approval and draws her index finger across her beautiful throat. "Thank you and good night."

~

Nearly two and a half decades have passed since The Great Communicator departed from the White House.

Though history hasn't been as kind to him as folklore, he is still a popular hero. In fact, one cannot go into a residential neighborhood anywhere in the country these days without seeing children laughing and playing intergalactic war games with their Ronald Ray-Guns. Somehow I doubt that I will enjoy such posthumous status. But one never knows.

THE ARIZONA PROJECT

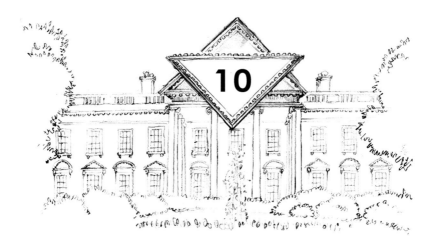

Somewhere in an obscure part of Nevada, not found on any map, a huge complex is being built. Construction began two months ago. At this complex, which is located far beneath the barren, tumbleweed-strewn landscape, a few hundred people work. These people are totally dedicated to the task before them. They arrive at six in the morning and do not leave until seven or eight at night. They see very little sunlight. Though they are permitted to leave the complex at lunchtime, few of them do, because the nearest town is nearly thirty miles away and the road that leads to it is little more than a cow path. They see very little of anyone except each other, not their families, not their friends. They seem content in this arrangement. They do not act bored or lonely nor do they complain. Some of them know each other from having worked together on other projects, similar in style if not in content to this one. Practically all of their names

149

are known to one another. This is because of the high level of competence they have each achieved in their respective fields. For their parts in the creation of this complex, they are extremely well compensated. The funds for the project, designated as "general research for strategic weaponry," come from a bottomless pit called the defense budget.

What these people are doing beneath the ruddy surface of the earth is something of great importance. It is top secret. Only a few dozen key personnel besides those working directly on the project know of its existence. Oliver C. Graham, the Chairman of the Joint Chiefs, and General Edward Black, Chief of Staff, Air Force, know about it, as do the other members of the Joint Chiefs. Senate Majority Leader Ed Drinkwater and Senate Minority Leader Fleming T. Hodgetts know about it. Speaker of the House Malcolm Rodgers knows about it. Secretary of State Candace Rowe and Secretary of Defense Milton Buck know about it. Attorney General Max Berger and Treasury Secretary Abe Rubin know about it. Woody Stone, Phil Hurley, Calvin Foxx, Tanya Gregson, Warren Gates, Jack Frost and Ashley Jones all know about it. I, Myron S. Goldberg, know about it. And, if I talk in my sleep, which I have been known to do from time to time, Sheila, my wife, is privy to it as well.

Beyond these chosen people though, there is only one other person who knows about it. His name is Paul Finkelstein. He is a film director, whose twelve films head the list of the twenty top-grossing films of all time. The films are considered modern classics. Indeed, Finkelstein's work has won twenty-four Academy Awards, including three for direction, eight for special effects, two for cinematography, five for sound and one for I forgot what — stunt costume design, I think. Paul Finkelstein is widely recognized as a creative genius. And he is only forty years old.

The denizens of this underground complex have all been recruited and brought here, under extreme secrecy, by Paul Finkelstein. Why have I enlisted Paul Finkelstein, the creator of the reluctant but always-rising-to-the-occasion hero, Arizona Smith, to help me save the world from itself and at the same time, if I am lucky, to help me get reelected? Time will tell.

∾

When I first spoke to Paul Finkelstein and told him what I had in mind, he was reluctant to volunteer. Like me, he had worked for the Peace Corps, his contribution being a year-long stint, right after he graduated from Berkeley, flying in supplies to yet another starving, disease-ridden dot on the map of Africa, his plane nearly crashing once into Mt. Elgon. But he had never done anything, he said, that was remotely related to what I was asking him to do. No kidding, Paul, I said. For a genius, he could be painfully slow at times.

"My specialty is not reality, Mr. President," the great director said to me. "My specialty is illusion."

"I know," I said. "And that's precisely why I want you."

"It is?"

"Frankly, Paul — may I call you Paul?"

"Certainly, Mr. President," said Paul.

"Ron," I said. "Please call me Ron."

"Okay — Ron," Paul said, saying my name as if it were the first word he had learned of a foreign language.

"Frankly, Paul," I continued, "I think that reality has been grossly overrated."

∾

Why would a secret project being carried out in the bowels

of the Nevada desert be called the Arizona Project? There are two good reasons for this. Reason number one: I want to throw anybody who discovers the name of the project off the trail until it's too late for them to do anything about it. Reason number two: Arizona Smith, Finkelstein's brainchild, is something of a hero to me. We have a lot in common. He is Jewish but WASP-y looking. His hair tends toward blonde, his eyes are blue. He is strong-willed and strong principled. He has a habit of putting his foot in his mouth. And he loves Chinese food. Of course, beyond these, the similarities become a little thin, tapering off to nonexistent. "Yes, I think he is circumcised," said Paul Finkelstein during one of my earlier tours of the nascent facility.

Sometimes I think Paul wonders about me.

⁓

Thomas "Bull" Dozier, my vice president, is one of the many people from whom I wish to keep any knowledge of the Arizona Project. Bull has never been quite comfortable with either the concept or the reality of my being president. He has always made it perfectly clear that, in his opinion, he was far better suited for the job. Why he finally agreed to place his name in a subordinate position to mine on all those banners, posters, pins and bumper stickers is still hard to fathom, although I think he believes, deep down in that thick skull of his, that someone will assassinate me and then he will finally have what was rightfully his all along. With Bull Dozier on the Democratic ticket, party bosses felt that I was a shoo-in in the South. Robert E. Lee Sanders had strength there, there was no denying that, but it was not overpowering strength, and with Bull on the ticket, the scales were supposed to tip my way. They did not. Though the races were close, I lost every single southern state, except Texas,

Bull's home turf. I did carry Florida as well, but I hesitate to call it "southern," since so many of the voters who now inhabit it have migrated from the North, especially from the Northeast. Anyway, it all makes me wonder why in the hell I needed Bull in the first place.

I don't know how Bull Dozier found out about the Arizona Project. I am certain that Paul Finkelstein didn't tell him about it. I suppose it is possible that Fleming Hodgetts told him, not that they are any better friends than Flem and I are. More likely, Bull used his CIA connections. During the late 1970s and into 1980, when Bull was participating in covert actions in Latin America and the Middle East, he made a lot of friends in low places, any one of whom could have uncovered something — which, I can only assume, they did. Still, Bull doesn't have enough to cause trouble. Not yet anyway.

"It wasn't you, was it?"

"No, Mr. President. It was not." Warren Gates and Bull Dozier go back a long way. In fact, Gates, like Bull Dozier, had been one of the CIA agents held hostage by Iran in 1980. What makes me inclined to believe Gates is his intense paranoia; he is reluctant to trust even his closest associates with sensitive information.

"Then who?"

"I have no idea."

"Well, let's just hope this leak doesn't become a flood."

"You mean like what happened at the Sox opener?"

I am only a hundred days or so into my presidency and I have experienced my first major plunge in the polls. According to Gallup, the impetus behind the tumble was the remark I made at Fenway Park on the opening day of baseball season. The good news is the poll was taken before I delivered my contrite statement to the Ridgeley press corps on national TV, so I still have a chance to rebound. The bad news is I now have a 38% favorability rating. Jack Frost tells me that the day after Nixon was implicated in the Watergate scandal, his favorability rating slipped to 42%. Apparently a nasty remark about baseball is far more unforgivable in the mind of the American people than using the Constitution for a pincushion. Suddenly, the White House seems like million miles and a hundred years away from the Ridgeley.

How did I get the inspiration for the Arizona Project? Actually it came to me in a dream. In the dream, I was sitting at the breakfast table in the house in which I grew up. My father was seated opposite me. I could not see his face because it was hidden behind his newspaper. There were always two things my father could never do without in the morning. One was his cup of coffee — a manly, unsweetened black — and the other was his newspaper. One of the many things my father could do without in the morning was talk, no matter how small, so in my dream, it struck me as being rather odd that he was talking to me.

Son, he said to me, *you're just pissing your life away. You're on a long slide to who knows where.*

I was about nine years old in my dream, so these words came not only as a shock to my prepubescent brain, they caused me considerable confusion. *To school, Pop,* I said. That was the only place where I knew for sure that I was going to.

Focus, Ronnie, he said. *I'm talking about focusing your life. You see, son, the mistake we all make is being too goddamn spread out. Look at me, Ronnie, a jack-of-all-trades and master of none. Is that how you want to end up?*

Yes, I said. For all his shortcomings, and he had a lot of them, I truly believed my father to be a great man. His penis, after all, was overwhelming to me.

Yes? What do you mean, yes? my father shouted. All this, mind you, was still shooting out from behind his newspaper. *For God's sake, Ronnie, listen to me. You can't thread a needle with a rope!*

Even at nine, I knew that this was true, though I had never personally tried to do it, or knew of anyone who had. I couldn't imagine why anyone would attempt something so utterly futile. *I guess not,* I said. Then I almost fainted from what I saw next. My father put down his newspaper and pushed himself away from the table. My mouth hung open dumbly. On my father's shoulders, in place of his head, was a giant sewing needle. The eye of the needle was facing me and when my father spoke, the needle's eye changed shape.

You can't thread a needle with a rope, he repeated.

Unless you have a big needle.

Don't get cute with me, Ronnie. You just remember what I tell you.

Yes, sir, I said. And then I woke up.

~

Since my inauguration several months ago, I have had this same dream at least a dozen times. It took that long and that many times for me to finally figure out what the hell it meant. I am certain now that I've got it straight. The irony, I suppose, is that I started to implement the advice I was given in the dream about two months before I consciously understood it. What it all comes down to is this: Because one cannot thread a needle with a rope, my mind gave birth to the Arizona Project, although I must admit that Fleming

Hodgetts inadvertently played a role in the creative process, too. But that's another story.

～

News item: Thanks to the press, specifically to Tom Meagan of *The Boston Herald*, I shall have some additional baggage to cart around with me wherever I may go from this day forth. Meagan, I am told by Ashley, was the author of a *Herald* front-page headline that appeared two days after my ill-fated visit to Fenway Park. The article that followed portrayed me as a buffoon, a man totally out of synch with the true spirit of America. I was vilified as the ringleader in a traveling circus. And, because I was such, my medium of transportation required a new designation.

What was the heinous headline that appeared on the front page of the *Herald* that day? It was this: PREZ TAKES AIR FARCE ONE ON THE ROAD. As I hear all this from Ashley, I think about the Arizona Project and I have to bite my tongue, metaphorically I mean. Even Tom Meagan will benefit from what I am about to do.

～

There is, I'm afraid, a much sadder postscript to the baseball fiasco. On the evening of the day Tom Meagan's column appeared in the *Herald*, one day after his paper ran its PREZ GETS BASE WITHOUT BALLS editorial, which I am certain he had something to do with, the B'nai B'rith cemetery in Worcester was vandalized. At least three dozen gravestones were overturned and spray-painted with black swastikas. Even worse, one grave was dug up, the casket crowbarred open, and the skeleton sprawled out on the ground. Into the skeleton's pelvis, approximately where his testicles would have been, two baseballs were placed. The baseballs, which bore the signature of Myron S. Goldberg, were drenched with urine. The signatures, of course, were not really mine. But the skeleton, in some respect, was; it belonged to my father. My heart sank when Ashley Jones gave me the news. But my first thought was, and my continual prayer is, that Sam and Ray never find out about this. Unfortunately, my mother already has. It has been her life-long habit to read the sports pages during baseball season, and since this was considered by the news media to be a sports-related event, a brief article appeared there as well. I am not certain, but I don't think my mother will be reading the sports pages anymore.

∽

I do not know when I will have my dream about my father again, but I suspect that it will be soon. As a rule, it happens once a week. Sometimes it upsets me so much Sheila has to wake me. She says that frequently I flail about as if I am trying to extricate myself from something. She says that my shouting is what really gets to her. Perhaps if I kept my voice under a little more control, she would be happier. She says she wishes the dreams would stop. She thinks that I should see someone. But the truth is, I like having these dreams. And I don't want them to stop. I think a son should try to have as much quality time as possible with his father. And seeing my dad more or less in the flesh is often more poignant than our disembodied conversations. What's more, because my father has been dead for so long, I sometimes find it difficult to picture him in my mind. That he now appears to me as a pinhead does not make it any easier to do so. But I am hoping he will soon return to his old form. In the meantime, I wonder if he has found out about the way his remains have been treated. I hope not.

∽

"Hello."

"Who's this?"

"Who's this?"

"This is the Vice President of the United States of America. Who the hell are you?"

'I regret that I am not at liberty to say."

"Whatta ya mean, you're not at liberty to say? What kind of answer is that?"

"It's the best I can do. Sorry."

"Look, whoever the hell you are, I know something is going on. I know he's up to no good. So you may as well come clean now."

"Excuse me, you know who is up to what?"

"Don't play dumb with me. You know exactly what I'm talking about."

"How'd you get this number anyway?"

"My job is to ask, you son of a bitch. Yours is to answer."

"With all due respect, Mr. Vice President, if that's who you really are, I think you're nuts."

"Oh, you do, do you?"

"I do, yes."

"Listen, you asshole, I don't know who you are or what you're up to, but I promise you, I'm going to find out, and when I do, there's going to be hell to pay."

"It's been very nice talking to you, too, sir."

"W—-"

As best he could remember, and he seems to have remembered pretty well, that was the conversation that Paul Finkelstein had with the Vice President of the United States, Thomas "Bull" Dozier, which rattled him so much and precipitated his phone call to me. Paul is very theatrical. He prefers acting things out, rather than providing an unadorned summary of an event. Prior to his becoming a director, Paul was an actor, a child star actually. His credits include a highly acclaimed TV sitcom called "Colorado Springs" about a small town that's entire existence depended on a mattress company. He also made five movies which were less successful, mainly because each new one was basically a remake of the last. Even to a child, they quickly became boring. So in 1985, at the ripe old age of twelve, Paul Finkelstein made a career move. He placed himself behind the camera instead of remaining in front of it. "That's where the real power is," Paul said.

About the call, Paul concluded, and I think rightfully so, that Bull had not dialed the wrong number. Somehow Bull, quite deliberately, had cracked the first line of defense surrounding the Arizona Project. It is time now, I think, to prepare countermeasures.

I wonder if it occurred to my clever vice president that the phone number for the Arizona Project has a Nevada area code?

~

In the morning I will fly to Nevada to visit with Paul Finkelstein and review the progress being made on the Arizona Project. It is my hope that the project can be finished by the fall, prior to my summit with Alexi Brezniski. It never hurts to have a few aces up your sleeve before the start of a summit and I want to be certain I have all that I can. The Arizona Project, in any manner of speaking, is my ace in the hole.

It is midnight. I am tired, but I cannot sleep. I get up out of bed, careful not to rouse Sheila, who is a light sleeper.

"What's wrong?" says Sheila.

I have made it to the doorway. "Nothing," I say. "Go back to sleep."

"Ugh," Sheila says. She rolls over and pulls the blanket over her head. She is gone before I am.

I tiptoe through the doorway and close the door behind me as gently as I can. Lights from the street make a mosaic of shadows on the walls and ceiling of the living room. I walk to the glass doors that lead to the balcony and draw back the curtain with one hand. I peek through at the city. What is it about this city at night that makes it so seductive? The way it shimmers like a sequined evening gown? My own loneliness perhaps. Sheila and I have not been together, as they say, for more than two weeks. My pain, meanwhile, is intensifying. Is there some connection between my priestly existence and my prostate pain? A limousine pulls up in front of the hotel. A uniformed Secret Service agent opens the limo door. A man and a woman, in their early thirties, step out. The man is Woody. The woman is no one I have ever seen before. She does not appear to be Woody's type. But what is Woody's type? Samantha? Ray? Ashley Jones? The woman is wearing a brown, white and black, presumably imitation, fur coat that looks as if it were made from remnants. The collar is turned up but the coat is unbuttoned. Under the coat she is wearing a black cocktail dress with a plunging neckline. On her feet she wears spike heels. When Woody and the woman disappear inside the Ridgeley, I wonder if I am dreaming. Ray would be crushed, I am thinking.

&

Tuesday, April 23, 8:30 a.m. On board Air Force One en route to Nevada. I am sitting quietly, reading the *Post* and sipping coffee. We have been in the air for about an hour. Calvin Foxx is talking quietly with Phil Hurley about the proposed Republican tax cut, or more accurately, how to scuttle it without costing the Democrats heavy losses in 2014. Candace Rowe, Tanya Gregson, Oliver Graham and Milton Buck are talking about Candace's new favorite subject — Diya Bakir. Milton, who, though Amish, concedes the need for his using modern transportation, is tightly gripping the arms of his seat, sipping on what could easily be a screwdriver though I suspect it's just orange juice. Every once in while I snatch a morsel from this buffet of discourse and respond to it with my usual clarity and wit. Meanwhile, Woody Stone is shuffling through a stack of papers, deleting this, adding that. He seems as chipper as ever, maybe more so. I think that he must have had a good night, but I decide against asking him about it at this time. Maybe later. There is always later. I put down the *Post* and take another sip of coffee. Then I unbuckle my seatbelt. I have to go to the bathroom. For the second time since we took off.

Inside the bathroom, after I am done urinating, I wash my hands. While I am doing this I look at myself in the mirror and I notice that I have a black hair sticking out of one nostril. I rinse my hands and try to remove the hair with a little yank. It will not come out without a fight. I will have to cut it off when I get back to the Ridgeley tonight.

Back in my seat, I write myself a note, TRIM NOSE HAIR, and as I do, I suddenly think back to the 1980 crash of a Japanese 747 just after it took off from Tokyo International Airport. I was only twenty years old then, but it was one of those events that immediately fused to your memory like Super Glue. It was one of the worst air disasters in history, but the main reason it received well above normal media attention was because of the incredibly brave way in which the doomed passengers died. Knowing that death was imminent, many of them had the presence of mind to write farewell notes to their wives, husbands, children, friends. One note that received particular attention, and so it should have, was one that was found clutched in the hand of a thirty-five-year-old Japanese businessman. The note was to the man's son. It said simply, BE A MAN, MY SON. I LOVE YOU. I cried when I read about that man and that note and that fatherless child. I thought, too, how proud this young boy must have been of his courageous father. And now here I am, winging my way to Nevada, perhaps the target of an airborne assassin, or bad weather, or bad luck, my future, my life, in the hands of a pilot I hardly know. I imagine the plane crashing. I picture the cleanup crew picking through the wreckage, stuffing what's left of my former self into a giant Glad bag. I can see them pry a piece of paper from my stiffened hand. The one who does the prying, however, is not senior enough to read what the president has written, but a man in a suit and tie, standing nearby, is. He takes the note, the soon to be famous last words of the President of the United States, unfolds it and reads, TRIM NOSE HAIR. At least I am wearing clean underwear.

∾

The plane touches down on the huge but well camou-flaged runway in the middle of the desert. The terrain is flat, uninviting. I can see the heat rising. The plane taxies to a spot where a group of a dozen or so men are standing. A few of them wear ties, but no jackets. All of them are wearing short-sleeved shirts. As the plane approaches, the men shield their eyes from the dust that's being stirred up. Finally, the engines are cut and there is a momentary silence, followed by the unbolting and opening of the plane's door. Before I can unbuckle my belt, the sunlight that has been pouring in the doorway is suddenly eclipsed by the body of a man whom some have described as nerdish.

"Good morning, Mr. President. Ron."

"Good morning, Paul," I say. "It's a perfect day for banana fish."

Paul looks at me quizzically.

"Salinger," I say.

"Of course," says Paul.

"Well, let's see what we've got here," I say.

Paul steps aside and lets me deplane first.

THE GRAND CANYON INCIDENT

11

Paul Finkelstein leads our entourage through the doorway of a large warehouse. Inside the warehouse are tractors, excavators and other sorts of earth-manipulating equipment. On one wall are floor-to-ceiling shelves loaded with supplies. I cannot tell what they are because they are all in boxes labeled by number only. I do not ask what they are. I have little interest in the means of what is being done here. I am concerned only with the results and how soon they can be achieved.

"Everything on schedule?" I say to Paul.

"So far," says Paul.

"Good, good," I say. "Let's keep it that way." We walk down the center of the warehouse through a corridor of large wooden crates. Inside are gray, boxlike items. Paul notices me giving them an extra long sideways glance.

"Air ducts," he says. "Ventilation."

"Army surplus?" Oliver Graham asks, knowingly.

"We try to save a buck wherever we can, sir."

"How damn un-American," says Tanya Gregson. Graham snarls at her.

"Okay, boys and girls," says Candace Rowe.

"Well, it looks like you got enough," I say.

"The farther down we go, the more we need."

"Going straight to hell," I mumble.

"What's that?" says Paul.

"Nothing," I say. "Let's keep moving."

We follow Paul to a manhole-sized opening cut in the floor. Pressed into the hole is a circular staircase made of steel tubing. It wobbles as Paul and I and the rest of our entourage make our tentative way down. After we circle down the poorly lit shaft for what seems like three or four stories, we suddenly come to a stop. The bottom of the staircase feeds into a short, narrow corridor. We follow Paul, single file, through the corridor. "Eventually, we'll make this wider, put in an elevator." Paul says.

"Either that or I'll have to lose some weight," I say.

The corridor takes us to an enormous room, perhaps three times the size of the warehouse that sits like a buoy above it.

"1500 feet by 1000 feet," Paul says proudly.

"Big enough for what we have in mind, eh, Woody?" I say.

"Looks like," says Woody.

"Magnificent," says Oliver.

"Probably nothing a few million moles couldn't do," says Candace.

"Eventually, we'll be able to remove these beams," Paul explains. There are a dozen of them, about forty feet high. "They're just temporary. Until we get the final support system in place. When that's done, the entire area will be usable space. Except for the little bit we'll lose around the perimeter to the air ducts."

"Gotta breathe," I say. My eyes wander about the immense room, thinking of what is to come. "You have all the materials you need to finish?"

"Everything's here," says Paul.

"Even the materials you need to build the ship?"

"Everything," Paul says.

"Good, good," I say. "Whatta ya think, folks?"

All heads nod their approval.

"Spectacular, Mr. President," says Oliver Graham. "Just spectacular."

I smile broadly. "That's entertainment, General," I say.

~

By six o'clock that evening I am back in Washington. I am having a dinner meeting tonight at the Ridgeley with Fleming Hodgetts to apprise him of the progress being made on the Arizona Project. Ed Drinkwater was supposed to be there, too, but one of his uncles unexpectedly passed away in the morning, so Ed was on his way back to Mississippi by noon. I will have to bring him up to speed when he returns.

I am seated at the table in my private dining room with Woody. So far we have the place to ourselves. In addition to Fleming, Tanya Gregson and Phil Hurley will be joining us. Woody, who is not much of a drinker, is sipping on his first Bacardi cocktail, clearly a non-drinker's drink. I am nursing my second Stolichnaya on the rocks, which is not a drink for the faint-livered. Usually I prefer to have it with tonic, but I am preparing for the fall summit with Alexi Brezniski. By then I hope I will have mastered it without even the benefit of ice.

"So, are you going to tell me who she is, or do I have to torture you to find out?" I say.

"Who who is?" says Woody.

"The bombshell."

"Bombshell?" says Woody. Obviously he is not familiar with this archaic term.

"The woman I saw you with last night. In front of the hotel. About midnight."

"Oh, her," says Woody. "No one, really."

"She looked like someone to me," I say, my voice doused with innuendo.

"No one you know, I mean."

"That's why I'm asking now." I take another swig of Stolichnaya. Good stuff. I could get to like this. "So?"

"Her name is Marcy Gillis."

"And?"

"What?"

"Who is she? What does she do?"

"Just someone I met," says Woody with uncharacteristic awkwardness. "She's in the entertainment field."

"No kidding. Have I seen her in anything?"

"Not yet," says Woody. "She's not exactly mainstream."

"No, I don't suspect she is, to look at her."

"Another?" Woody says, holding up his glass.

"Sure, why not?" I say.

Woody signals the waiter, then becomes very somber.

"Something wrong?" I say.

"No, nothing," he says. He takes a sip of his cocktail. "I hired her."

"Hired her? What for?"

"Ridgeley masseuse."

"Don't they already have one?"

"You don't understand. I hired her to be your personal

masseuse," he says. "You know, for that back problem of yours."

I do not have a back problem and Woody knows it. I have a prostate problem, but rather than announce that to the world, we have told the press that I have a "back problem." Hell, if JFK, good old Jack the Zipper, could have one, well damn it, so could I. The prostate thing was simply too hot an issue to handle, what with Robert E. Lee Sanders and Fleming Hodgetts constantly searching for a way to expose what they firmly believe is my diminutive masculinity. What Woody also knows is that my urologist suggested that my problem was being aggravated, and most likely was caused, by my lack of sexual activity. "Not chasing the old lady enough," the urologist had said. "Chasing isn't the problem," I countered. "Not catching enough, that's the problem." The doctor led me to believe that three or four good fucks a week would probably have me as good as new in no time. "Woody," I say, "God bless you. You found me a hooker?"

"Call girl," says Woody. "One of the best."

"What'd you say her name was?"

"Marcy. Marcy Gillis."

"You tempt me, Woody. You really tempt me."

"Your health, Mr. President, is a matter of national security." There is no smile on Woody's face and this absence surprises me.

"You're saying I should fuck her for the good of the country? I don't know. I think I should find out how Candace and Tanya feel about this first."

Not even the hint of a smile. "I know it sounds a bit crazy."

"More than bit. If anyone finds out, I'm done for. Remember what Ashley always says about keeping mistakes complicated and successes simple. Affairs people understand. They'll strap me to a goddamn anthill if this ever gets out."

"It won't. Besides, she really is a bona fide masseuse."

I am playing with the ice cubes in my glass, swirling them around with my finger. "I'll have to take the matter under advisement."

Woody grins. "Sleep on it, you mean."

"Yes. Sleep on it." Has there ever been a better cure for what ails you, I wonder?

❧

"Evening, Mr. President," says Hodgetts. Fleming has big, fleshy hands. When we shake hands, mine practically disappear in his. He is wearing a three-piece suit, navy blue. His shirt is too tight at the collar, so his fat neck spills over the top of it. Flem has just returned from a five-day trip to the Middle East. He spent most of that time touring our 51st state, but also managed to touch down in Egypt, Lebanon, Syria and Kuwait long enough to sample each country's hospitality. His ruddy complexion looks tanner than usual. Though he is not smoking, he smells of tobacco.

"Evening, Fleming," I say.

"Senator," Woody says and nods toward Fleming.

"Woody," says Fleming.

Tanya Gregson and Phil Hurley greet and shake hands with Hodgetts, too. Phil, deferentially. Tanya, warily.

"How was your trip?" I ask.

"My trip? Hell, my trip was nothing out of the ordinary. Ya see one Ay-rab, ya seen 'em all," Fleming says. "Now your trip, that's what I want to hear about."

"It was great," I say. "Things couldn't be progressing more smoothly."

"Well, that's mighty gratifying to hear. Mighty gratifying indeed. The fall deadline's no problem then?"

"Not in the least. In fact, they could well finish ahead of schedule."

Fleming laughs, his belly shakes. "Now, don't that beat all. A goddamn government project finishing ahead of schedule."

"Gotta be a first," says Tanya.

"They're not asking for more money, are they?" Fleming asks.

"Not a dime," I say. "We're on budget, too."

"Well, maybe we should keep these guys on the payroll permanently," Fleming says and laughs again. I have always wondered why redneck Southerners seem to think that everything is so darn funny. I imagine he was positively hysterical when he heard what they did to my father's bones.

"I hardly think that'll be necessary," I say. "Drink?"

"You buyin'?" says Fleming, laughing.

"Yeah."

"Bourbon. On the rocks."

The waiter, already hovering, takes drink orders from Tanya and Phil as well.

Fleming lights up a cigar. Tanya pushes back her chair and fans the air in front of her face with her hand. "You mind?"

"Hell, no, I don't mind. You?"

"Yes, I do."

Fleming drops the cigar in his water. "Better?"

"Much," says Tanya.

"You know, Mr. President, after all these years, I still don't trust 'em far as I can spit."

"Trust who?"

"Trust who? Why, those Russians. You're sure they're gonna go along with all this?"

"They have indicated a willingness to," I say.

"At the top?"

"According to our contacts," says Candace. "Brezniski will definitely play ball. No matter what comes out his mouth, he knows deep down how much he needs us."

"Piss on your contacts, Candy," says Fleming. He lifts his drink to his mouth. "If you ain't got it directly from the horse's mouth, you ain't got it."

"Well, we're sure getting plenty from the horse's ass, aren't we?" says Candace.

"Now, now. No need to get ugly."

Woody drains his glass. "We'll have Brezniski's word," he says.

"I have every confidence that Brezniski will fall in line," I add.

"I hope you're right," Fleming says. "I'm still not convinced this whole harebrained plan is gonna work. Depends too much on the good faith of some pretty slippery characters. It won't be the first time they pulled the wool over our eyes. Remember all that glasnost garbage? And they're still after Alaska."

"I've thought it through a thousand times, Fleming," I say. "I know it'll work just fine."

"It better," says Fleming. "Or we're all dead."

"You can't thread a needle with a rope," I say.

"No, Mr. President, I don't suppose you can."

∾

The next day I planned a visit to the office of Bull Dozier. Bull receives me right away. His calendar for the morning is light.

"You're leaving tomorrow?" I say, referring to his upcoming visit with the governor of Israel.

"That's right, Mr. President," Bull says.

"Good, good," I say. "Look, when you get there, Bull, you be certain to let the governor know, in no uncertain terms, that I'm behind him 100%."

"Will do, Mr. President."

"And that we'll be taking care of, you know, the whole Iraqi matter."

"I'll be sure to tell him that," says Bull. "But what are we doing?"

"Nothing you have to know about, Bull. Just tell him everything will be worked out."

"Will do."

"Good, good. Now, don't forget any of it."

"It's all written down right here," Bull says, tapping his head.

"I'm sure it is," I say. "Oh, and one other thing. That fishing trip with the governor still planned?"

"Yes, as far as I know."

"Good. Here's what I want you to do. You know that the governor and I go back a few years."

"Yes, I do."

"Well, we've had this bet whenever we went fishing together. If I caught the biggest fish, I'd win Israel. If he won, he'd get Rhode Island. Just a joke of course."

"Of course," Bull says warily. "But what do you want me to do?"

'I want you to take my place this time. Make the bet with him. Maintain the continuity, if you know what I mean."

"Consider it done," Bull says.

"One stipulation, though," I say. "It can only be a particular kind of fish."

"What kind?"

"Gefilte," I say and then I spell it for him.

"Gefilte, got it," says Bull slowly.

Leaving Bull's office, I drop a piece of paper on the floor. The paper comes from my personal note pad, bearing my initials. The sheets are small and, when folded in quarters, they are about the size of postage stamps. On the paper, I have written some notes, scribbles really. This is what they say: GRAND CANYON/ARIZ/ POSSIBLE LANDFILL/CONSIDER RENAMING — JAMES WATT NATIONAL PARK. When Bull leaves his office, he will not be able to miss seeing the paper on the floor. It is my hope that it will give him a lot to think about as he wings his way to Israel in search of the ultimate gefilte fish.

❧

The word *gefilte*, by the way, is Yiddish, meaning "stuffed." So literally, gefilte fish means "stuffed fish." Gefilte fish is fish cakes or fish loaf, made from various fishes, which are chopped or ground and mixed with eggs, salt, onions, carrots and matzo meal. Some people add sugar to this mishmash. Gefilte fish is the traditional Friday night fish, served at the Sabbath dinner. My mother loves gefilte fish, especially when served with horseradish. Like my father, I never developed a taste for it.

If my vice president is lucky enough to catch a gefilte fish, he will become a very famous man indeed — not only in Israel, but also in any part of the world where Jews can be found.

❧

My vice president is not speaking to me. He has locked himself in his office, changed his access code and will not come out. Ashley Jones tells me that the Israeli press had a field day with his challenging the governor to a gefilte fish fishing contest. I doubt that Bull will be paying any further visits to our 51st state in the very near future.

Bull has made no statement to the American press about the incident. On the day it occurred, the *Post* ran a brief article, mercifully placed on page 7, with the headline, THE GEFILTE FISH STORY — NOT A PEEP FROM THE VEEP.

Maybe I went too far. Woody and Calvin have reassured me that I did not. Jack agrees. As does Ashley. Max Berger and Abe Rubin didn't think I went far enough. The only dissenting voice in the Goldberg administration so far has come from Phil, who believes that a wounded Bull can very dangerous indeed. "Let's not forget what he did to Carter," Phil said. In any case, there is nothing I can do now to make the whole smelly mess go away. Nor is there anything I want to do. The truth is, I believe the more distracted I can keep Bull, the less likely he is to interfere with the Arizona Project. The more of a buffoon I can make him, the more the press will eat him up. Soon he will become such a liability to me that party leaders will compel me to replace him. Then it will be bye-bye, Bull Dozier, once and for all. He'll never be able to do me harm again.

No Sleep for the Veep

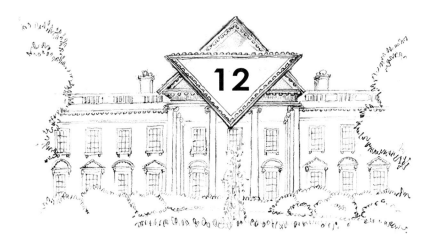

D ozier is a man of many talents. He has a gift for homespun oratory that can make even his most boorish
stories seem charming. At the same time, he has an
instinctive ability to insult broad swaths of the population.
Case in point: at a press conference immediately following
his announcement to seek the presidency in 2012, Bull,
when asked what he thought President Whitney's chances
of reelection were, replied that a fart had a better chance
of winning a perfume contest. (He was right, too, since
Whitney, plagued by rumors of corruption, didn't even survive the primaries.)

His frequent lapses into buffoonery aside, Bull Dozier
knows how to make himself be taken seriously among the
many who count. He has a penchant for back room negotiation that's second to none, most notably evidenced by his
key behind-the-scenes role in the successful fight for Israeli

statehood back in '08. A complementary skill is his ability
to uncover dirt in areas believed to have been swept clean.
But of all his many talents, the one in which he takes most
pride, is his poison expertise. When Bull worked for the CIA
during the Ford and Carter administrations, he became so
skilled with a variety of esoteric poisons that he could predict, almost to the second, the moment one of his victims
would terminate. In covert circles, Bull was so revered for
this talent, his colleagues nicknamed him "Sandman." If
someone needed to be "put to sleep," you could go to a lot
of people. But if you needed to virtually pinpoint the time of
death, you came to Thomas (Bull) "Sandman" Dozier.

Personally, Bull puts me to sleep without the aid of any
lethal substances. I am not trying to make light of the matter.
With very little effort I'm sure he could do me in, leaving no
pharmaceutical fingerprints whatsoever. He could no doubt
make my death look like an ordinary heart attack. I am over
fifty, after all, and though my health is generally good, it's
not perfect. Still, even so natural an exit from this life might
create suspicion. A more likely scenario would involve my
new outlet for an old passion. No, I am not talking about
making lust to Marcy Gillis, the courtesan whom Woody
has brought home for me to play with. I am speaking of Tet
Ching and my passion for food with names that were an
essential part of my Jewish upbringing — Moo Goo Gai Pan,
Char Shu Ding, Hon Shu Gai. God help me, I cannot stay
away from the place. Figuratively speaking, that is. I never
actually set foot in there, though a handwritten sign in the
window would like patrons and potential patrons to believe
otherwise. MSG SERVED HERE, it proudly proclaims.

In any case, if Bull Dozier or one of his cronies somehow
gained access to my takeout order, he could lace it with some
untraceable poison that I myself would probably never notice

until it was too late, my body writhing in pain, my mind mistakenly thinking that I had fallen victim to some common intestinal one night stand. No, Phil Hurley was right. What's more, Phil's caution, coupled with Warren Gates' paranoia, makes me think of an old joke. When Hitler came to power, there were two types of Jews in Germany — pessimists and optimists. The pessimists fled the country. The optimists went to the gas chambers.

∾

Since his return from his fishing trip with Solomon Dayan — the governor of Israel, who is, by the way, no relation to the legendary Moshe Dayan (though the fact that many people believed that he was never hurt his electability) — Bull Dozier has been a changed man. There is a far off, brooding quality about him now. He definitely seems to be plotting something.

Other peculiarities in Bull's behavior have manifested themselves. Granted, it may be my imagination, but I could swear that Bull's Texas accent has been getting significantly stronger lately. When I first met him in 2001, when he was the seasoned Washington insider and I was the naive, idealistic, freshman congressman, I remember my surprise in discovering that, for a good ol' boy, who was a Texan to boot, Bull had almost no Southern accent. However, by the time I was elected to the Senate in 2004, his soupy accent slowly, almost imperceptibly, had begun to congeal. Still, by 2008, with his first failed campaign to grab the party's nomination for president, his accent, though stronger, betrayed no serious viral inflection. It wasn't until 2012, when he campaigned against me, yet another presidential aspirant from the too blue state of Massachusetts, that he suddenly started speaking in a nearly unintelligible drawl. It seemed quite clear that he was doing it all for show, attempting to differentiate himself from me in yet another superficial way. I think it irked the hell out of Bull that we were so close on so many issues, and that the major point of difference between us was one of sex appeal, where I must say, in all modesty, I have the advantage. Bull, all things considered, is a good man, if not a cosmetically appealing one. That he probably wants to kill me at this point in time does not alter this fact. Is it better to die at the hand of a friend or an enemy? I am not sure.

❧

It is Monday, April 29, 2013. Three weeks have now passed since the baseball fiasco. I have rebounded slightly in the polls, thanks in part to my plea for forgiveness, although I cannot attribute this rise in my approval rating, a blip really, simply to that. My guess is that the American people have taken pity on me because I am stuck, for the present, with Thomas Dozier, the famed gefilte fisherman, for my vice president. (I think Americans have always had a soft spot in their heads for innocent victims.) Wait until Bull spills the beans about the Arizona Project. Then you'll see some real activity in the polls. I only hope the direction is upward. Everything will depend upon the public's reaction to Bull's accusation and to my subsequent denial of any wrongdoing. I wonder if I should dignify Bull's accusation by responding to it myself. Perhaps it would be wiser not to. Presidents, and Danish queens, must not protest too much. On the other hand, if I do not protest enough, people will view my silence as an admission of guilt. Have I, by demeaning baseball, already given America permission to believe the worst about me?

It is getting late, near midnight, close enough so that I can comfortably call the chicken chow mein I am eating a midnight snack. Am I worried that Bull Dozier has tampered with my order? Not really. Because I know for a fact that tonight Bull Dozier sleeps in Detroit. Tomorrow at breakfast he is giving a speech to the UAW. I was scheduled to do it, but I was not completely at ease with the idea. The UAW has never forgiven me for buying a Honda Civic in 2007.

In any case, Bull cannot possibly do me any harm tonight. Although I have to admit, the duck sauce does look a little funny.

~

Just a case of food poisoning, Bernie Cohen said, albeit a somewhat vicious one. Odd, but I don't remember them taking me to the hospital. My last recollection was that of clutching my abdomen and picking up the phone. After that it was fade to black.

Nurse Ratched wants to know how we are feeling this morning.

We are feeling just dandy, chipper in fact, I tell her. Actually my stomach feels like a toxic waste dump.

Drink this, Nurse Ratched says. She hands me a glass of milky liquid. I eye the glass suspiciously. Go ahead now, the nurse says, it will make you feel better.

How the hell does she know what will make me feel better? A new vice president would make me feel better. A constitutional amendment banning baseball would make me feel better. Some good old-fashioned copulating would make me feel better. I take the glass from her and drink. When the liquid is gone, so is Nurse Ratched. Just like magic. And with her gone I do indeed feel suddenly on the mend.

Sitting in a chair at the foot of the bed is Woody Stone. He is wearing a charcoal gray suit, a blue shirt and a club tie. This must seem like déjà vu to him, for it certainly does to me. He is reading a copy of the *Post*. When the nurse disappears, Woody looks up from his newspaper. "Tough night," he says.

"Me too," I say.

"I meant you," says Woody.

"I know," I say. "Just trying to be adorable."

"You're adorable all right, sir."

Nurse Ratched returns with young Doctor Kildare. So we're doing better, I hear, says the young, well-buffed, handsome doctor. He pushes his blonde hair off his brow in a slow, fluid motion.

Word travels fast around here, I say.

Took your medicine. Good.

Yummy, I say.

He asks me what I had to eat last night.

Chicken Ptomaine, I say.

The good doctor laughs indulgently. Nurse Ratched looks as humorless as ever. She appears to suppress a smile. She is doing her darnedest to tolerate me, God bless her.

To go, I add.

Clearly, says the suntanned healer. It is my turn to chuckle.

Before he leaves, the doctor tells me that I should be as good as new in a few days. While I had hoped to be better than that, this is the best news I have had in quite some time.

❧

Bull Dozier's press conference, Ashley Jones tells me, will take place this afternoon, shortly after his return from Detroit. He will be preempting the soaps, a brave thing to do, though he was given little choice. None of the networks would carry his press conference during prime time, as he had requested that they do.

For this bit of good fortune I have Ashley to thank. She put a bug in the ear of Francis Hackbaum, my good friend and chairman of the FCC. He in turn casually mentioned to the heads of the various networks that, should they grant Bull a prime time slot, the FCC might be forced to eliminate ratings for news shows, which happen to be the networks' big money-makers. And what a sorry situation that would be since, without ratings, the networks couldn't charge their advertisers big bucks. It's so nice to see the news media, whose power over us mere mortals is surpassed only by God's, act so reasonably.

Nurse Ratched is checking my pulse and taking my temperature while a crew of technicians sets up six TV monitors in my room, one for each major network, plus The Comedy Channel and MTV. I suspect there is a warm and sensuous woman hiding behind Nurse Ratched's severe mask of clinical efficiency. She is handsome woman, not what you would call pretty. She is unpretentious. She wears no makeup. Her face has not one wrinkle, though I would guess she is hovering somewhere in her mid forties. She is well proportioned, clearly a woman who takes care of her body — no doubt in much the same disciplined way she takes care of her patients. She runs a tight ship, Nurse Ratched does, inside and out.

I think I have misjudged Nurse Ratched. I think I have confused her dedication with autocracy. I could even be wrong about her party affiliation. Perhaps she is a Democrat. As I reflect, I realize that she has given me no reasonable cause to think otherwise. I wonder if she likes me. I wonder if she is afraid to show me that she is interested, for fear of rejection. Most of all, I wonder if what I am going through now is the real thing or simply another case of the Florence Nightingale syndrome.

It never ceases to amaze me what a prisoner of my sexual desires I can be. Alas, my kingdom for a vagina!

◦∽◦

The time has come for Bull Dozier's press conference. Ashley, Woody, Phil, Calvin, Jack and Tanya have surrounded my bed with their chairs. My six TVs have been primed with titillating chatter from various anchor people and are ready to go.

Though MTV did a great job of getting out the under-21 vote in 2012, a segment of the population I carried with 63%, my eyes linger on ABC. I have always been partial to ABC. And they to me. Even during those agonizing days that immediately followed the baseball fiasco, they took it easy on me. While other networks devoted major segments to the story on four consecutive nights, ABC had the decency to carry it just once — and even then, almost as a footnote. And not only that, they made a point of saying what a good father I was because I let Sam throw out the first ball. The other networks completely ignored this act of selfless love; they had nothing good at all to say about my conduct that day, although I am grateful again to MTV for setting the whole mess to a catchy and upbeat piece of music by Blud In The Gutter, one of Sam's favorite groups.

Bull Dozier is holding his press conference in the lobby of the Ridgeley. He apparently would like to look as presidential as possible. Good luck to him. I gave my blessing to his choice of location to indicate that I do not feel even the slightest bit threatened by what he will say.

Peter Taylor, the anchor for ABC Nightly News, has just returned to my TV screen after a brief commercial break. He says that in a moment, he will be taking us to the lobby of the Ridgeley Hotel, the temporary White House, for live coverage of Vice President Thomas Dozier's press conference. He says the subject of the press conference has been a "closely guarded secret."

"Yeah, right," I mutter and the high-powered assemblage in my room laughs through their tension.

"And here we go," says Peter Taylor. All six TV sets cut to Bull Dozier at the podium looking as if he means business. Suddenly my stomach is filled with butterflies. Or perhaps they are moths.

THE LANDFILL

13

"**M**ah fellah Amuricans," Sandman Dozier begins soberly, "Ah come to ya with a heavy haht. Ah bring to ya news that Ah fear will shock ya. But shock ya, mah fellah Amuricans, Ah must. It is the God-given role of the Vahce President of the Yoo-nited States to be loyal to the chief executive. But it is also his duty, his most sacred duty, to fulfill his oath to the people of this great and pahrful land. Sometimes there are tahmes when the vahce president cannot do both. (A PREGNANT PAUSE.) This, mah fellah Amuricans, is one of those tahmes. (CLEARS THROAT AND GLANCES AT NOTES.) Ah have become inadvertently privy to a plot to destroy one of ah national treasures. A treasure that has taken the good Lahd millions of yee-ahs to create. A thing of unparalleled beauty to which countless Amuricans have made their pilgrimages for cen-turies. An ahh-inspirin' sight of which we can ahl be proud, because it lahs on ah sacred Amurican soil. I speak, mah fellah Amuricans, of the Grand Canyon, and of a dastardly plot to turn this national treasure into a landfill! A landfill for garbage! For plastic bottles and cans! For rancid food scraps! For Bahbie dolls without heads! For a zillion kinds of trash! A refuge for teeming refuse! And who, might you ask, is behahnd this despicable plot? What mannah of man, what godless un-Christian creature, could turn ah beloved Grand Canyon into a vast wasteland, and then have the utter gahl to rename it — and this, Ah am ashamed to say, is also true — the James Watt National Park? It pains me to say this, mah fellah Amuricans, but this man, this low lahf, this apple-bearing serpent, is none othah than the President of these Yoo-nited States."

Following a brief summary of the veep's statement, Peter Taylor cuts to his colleague Stan Cooper, who is standing on the steps of the Columbia University library with Dr. William B. Kettle, a noted archeologist, specializing in twentieth century civilizations, and the world's foremost authority on landfills. Dr. Kettle has been called "the father of garbology."

"Dr. Kettle," Stan Cooper begins deferentially, "assuming for a moment that there is some validity to the vice president's statement, what are the real implications of such a proposal?"

Dr. Kettle rakes his fingers through wild mane of gray hair and purses his lips. "Stan, if you're asking me would the Grand Canyon make a hell of a landfill, the answer is unquestionably yes. If you're asking me what affect this would have on tourism, I think I'll have to defer to someone who knows more about that sort of thing than I do."

"Satisfy my curiosity, doctor. Just how long would it take, in your estimation, to fill the Grand Canyon with refuse?"

"Well, given that we still bury 51% of our municipal

refuse and given that the Grand Canyon covers over a million square acres, is up to eighteen miles wide, one mile deep and 277 miles long, with an approximate volume of —" Dr. Kettle pulls a pad out of his breast pocket, a pencil from behind his ear and does a few quick calculations. "Phew! Now that's a hole!" Dr. Kettle shakes his head in amazement.

"Dr. Kettle?"

"Ah, yes, I would say we'd be in pretty good shape for at least a hundred and fifty years."

"That's it? A century and half?"

"Don't blame me, Stan. I keep saying, 'recycle, recycle,' but does anyone listen? Still, a century and a half for one landfill would be unprecedented in modern times."

"Indeed. Although it would be a shame, wouldn't it, Dr. Kettle, to erase something it took Mother Nature a million years to make?"

"Six million years, Stan, to be exact. But, hey, nothing lasts forever."

"Six million years," says Stan Cooper, mentally ruminating on the wonder of it all.

"Yup, six million, Stan. Give or take a hundred thousand."

෴

From the moment Bull Dozier completed his vile statement, the temporary switchboard right outside my hospital room, capably handled by Rosalee Wilson and five of her subordinates, has been ringing like the phones on the Home Shopping Network when a $50 zircon ring goes on sale. Rosalee and the others have been transferring some of the more official calls to my room, where four extensions have been installed. Woody and Ashley have fielded most of these calls, but occasionally Phil and Calvin have jumped into the fray. Jack Frost and Tanya Gregson had to leave due to other commitments, but I'm sure they would have been equally helpful had they been able to stay. Sometimes I pick up a line myself and tell the caller, with sincere regret, that they have gotten the wrong number.

The bottom line is that the reaction from Congress, members of my own administration, the American people and the press has not been even faintly positive. Indeed it has been hostile. "If Goldberg wants the perfect hole, why doesn't he try his own asshole?" one caller suggested. However, the most frequently and most respectfully asked question has been, "Is he out of his goddamn mind?" The first time Woody fielded this one, he said, "Dozier?" The unidentified drawler barked a few obscenities and hung up. Others want to know if I have lost my sense of perspective, my sense of judgment. Do I really think the country's solid waste problem is at such a critical point that it warrants such a drastic measure as turning the Grand Canyon into a land-fill? Can't we give recycling a few more decades to work first? And can't we, in the meantime, look into alternate landfill sites — the Carlsbad Caverns in New Mexico, for example, or the Luray Caverns in Virginia? Neither of these places is nearly as popular as the Grand Canyon and both have the added advantage of being underground. Who would notice?

After a few hours, things quiet down. Rosalee and her staff have been told not to transfer any more calls, but, as is our policy, to keep a tally of pros and cons. We are all frazzled and ragged. I am in bed, hands behind my head, propped up on a few pillows, half dozing, half staring at the ceiling. Woody is sitting on a chair at the foot of my bed sipping coffee from a Styrofoam cup, watching CNN with the sound turned off. Calvin Foxx has gone to a midnight meeting with Tanya Gregson and Candace Rowe. Phil Hurley is pacing along the side of my bed, muttering every so often about "major raisins in the pudding." He has put in a call to Jack Frost and has said he will give my pollster until 1 a.m. to return it before he quits for the night. In the meantime I have dispatched Ashley to meet with various network heads to make sure that they haven't forgotten their recent conversations with Francis Hackbaum. Of all of us, Phil looks the worst. He is becoming so tightly wound, I fear that he might explode at any moment.

"The gefilte fisherman has taken the bait," I say.

"Bait?" says Phil Hurley. "What bait?"

Woody, arching his eyebrows, looks my way. "Yeah, what bait?"

Suddenly I feel alone, cornered. *Pop, you there?* Phil and Woody are staring at me so intently I must be getting eyeball dents. "I guess I forgot to tell you guys," I say. "I planted the seed for Bull's press conference in his office the day he left for Israel. I accidentally dropped a note on his floor about the alleged landfill. I'd say it turned out pretty much the way I thought it would. I can always count on that Bull."

"Mr. President, what the hell were you thinking?" says Woody. The unflappable Woodstock Stone is now flapped. He finishes his coffee with one gulp, crushes the cup in his hand and tosses it in the basket.

"The son of bitch was getting too close. We needed a diversion."

"There had to be a better way."

"Trust me, Woody, everything will be okay."

"Define 'okay.' Promise me, Mr. President, that the next time you leap, we'll look first. Damn it, that's what I'm here for, isn't it?"

"Of course it is. And, sure, we'll look." I refuse to say that looking will have any effect on my decisions once they are already made.

Phil continues to pace like a bobcat in a cage. His tie is askew. His eyes are glazed. "Mr. President, this whole thing is crazy. The press is going to crucify us."

"They don't do that to Jews anymore," I say. "Besides, Ashley is making sure that they won't."

Woody is once again watching the news without sound. I have done this myself sometimes and, I have to admit, it does make everything go down a bit easier. "Let's hope she's successful."

"Well, even if she isn't, which I know she will be, it's not like the baseball mess. All we're talking about here is a big hole in the ground, for chrissake."

"But it's like the man said, Mr. President," Phil says, "It's a national treasure."

"Phil, Phil, who's going to take this nonsense seriously?"

"Bert French, for one."

"What're you talking about?" Albert French is my secretary of the interior.

"I just got off the phone with him a few minutes ago. Says you'll have his resignation on your desk in the morning"

"That's absurd. I can't believe he would take Bull's accusation seriously."

Albert French is not a man I would like to lose. As secretary of the interior, he has done more to preserve, protect and defend the beauty of America than any man ever has. When he served in the same capacity from 2009 to 2013, under President Whitney, he added 32,752,631 acres to our national parks, an increase of nearly 50%. His nickname was "Bert Parks." He is a tough-minded man with strong principles. His departure would indeed call into question the moral character of this administration.

"It's what he said. And you know darn well, when Bert says something, he means it."

"I know it all too well," I say.

"Of course, a few well-chosen words from you, Mr. President, might turn him around."

"Get him back on the line, Phil. Better nip this sucker in the bud."

&

The best-laid plans — well, it certainly seemed like a good idea at the time. And Bull could not have done a better job. He did exactly what I hoped he would do, what I was convinced he would do. How was I to know that so many intelligent people would believe him?

"Bert? It's Ron."

"Hello, Mr. President," says Bert French. Bert is a friendly, outgoing person who seems happy even when you know he is not. I have never heard him sound so subdued.

"Bert, I know what you're thinking, but I can explain. The whole thing was just a hoax. A joke. Albeit a bad one. But a joke nonetheless."

Albert French, a man who is always quick to laugh, is not laughing.

"Bert, you there?"

"I'm here," Bert says.

"Listen, Bert, I can tell you're upset about this whole thing. Who wouldn't be? But if you'd just come to my office tomorrow morning I can straighten everything out."

"My integrity is on the line here, too, Mr. President."

"Come on, Bert, you don't really think that the American people would believe that Bert Parks would allow the Grand Canyon to be turned into a landfill, do you?"

"You can't fool all of the people all of the time," says Bert.

"I'm not trying to fool anyone, Bert. Least of all you."

"I don't know," says Bert woefully. "I just don't know."

"Just give me until tomorrow," I say. "If you don't like what I have to say, I'll accept your resignation."

Bert is silent.

"Come on, Bert. Whatta ya say? For old times' sake."

"All right," says Bert. "Tomorrow morning."

"At nine," I say. "Okay?"

"Okay," says Bert.

We say goodbye and then I hang up. I wonder what I am going to have to tell Albert French to keep him from resigning.

～

The next day at 7:56 a.m., Ashley Jones bombs my desk with a copy of the *Herald*. The headline reads: JEW WANTS TO ERASE SIX MILLION. The gist of the article is that it has become one of my key goals in life to destroy what it took nature — and of course "the good Lahd" — six million years, give or take a hundred thousand, to create. The article also suggests that I want to do this as revenge for what I believe to be "the collusion of the civilized countries of the world, including the United States, in the death of six million Jews, give or take a hundred thousand, at the hands of the Nazis during World War II." One year's work destroyed for every Jew murdered. Now, while I admire the *Herald*'s imagination, I have to say quite honestly that this thought had never occurred to me.

～

Going through my morning correspondence, I find a sealed envelope that simply says, Mr. President, Confidential. I open it quickly. If Albert French has changed his mind about seeing me, and this is his resignation, then by all means, let's get it over with. I grab the letter opener and disembowel the envelope. Here is what the handwritten note says:

Dear Mr. President:
It pains me to have to do this, but in all good conscience I simply cannot continue my duties as Vice President of the United States. Therefore, for reasons of which I am sure you are well aware, I do hereby resign as your second in command. May the good Lord bring you all the comfort you deserve during the stormy days that will follow sure as rain.
Respectfully Yours,
Thomas Dozier

"For reasons of which I am sure you are well aware" — there is no doubt about that, Bull. I put the resignation down on my desk and breathe a sigh of relief. At least part of my plan could not be working better. Thomas Dozier will soon be out of my hair. I shall ask Woody to talk with the Secret Service about beefing up security to make sure that Bull stays out of my food as well. I shall also check with Ashley to make sure that, whatever new security measures we take, we keep them out of the newspapers. I have no desire to screw with the first amendment, but we are talking about my life here, damn it.

But what to do about Albert French? That is the question. I can tell him about my plan to humiliate Bull Dozier and to force him into political oblivion. I can tell him about the note I dropped for Bull to find. But what if he asks why I chose this particular means to destroy Bull? Why suggest that the Grand Canyon be made into a landfill? Why not suggest any number of ludicrous alternatives? Like turning the Statue of Liberty into luxury condominiums. Or the Lincoln Memorial into a McDonald's. Or selling off Jerusalem to Disney so they could turn it into a theme park. Why, of all things, the Grand Canyon? Is there some geological significance in this? Some economic significance? Perhaps some geographical significance. When questioned about the information he had gathered about the landfill, Bull mentioned that the code name for the project was "Arizona." If that is true, why is it true? Surely the name had not been plucked from thin air.

But how much of what I am really up to can I spill to Albert French? Mr. French has always been a strong opponent of nuclear power. He has also spoken out against the proliferation of the arms race that occurred under President Whitney, the very man for whom he was working. How would Albert French react to a project with the expressed purpose of "general research for strategic weaponry"? Not with enthusiasm, I suspect.

At 8:48 a.m., Rosalee Wilson, reinstalled at her post outside my Ridgeley office, calls me on the intercom. "Mr. French to see you, sir. Shall I send him in?"

Albert French is early for our appointment, but I have no intention of keeping him waiting. It is clear that he is anxious to settle this matter. "Yes, Rosalee. Thanks."

I stand up when French enters the room, but I remain behind my desk. It is a large oak desk, curved in the front, and it has power written all over it. Today I will need all the help I can get. "Thanks for coming, Bert," I say, and I offer my hand to him. He takes it firmly in his. We're off to a good start.

"Mr. President," says Bert. He sits down on a chair to the right of my desk. I have been advised by my media consultants to always try to seat people to my right in one-on-one situations. They told me that my three-quarters profile viewed from the right is much more authoritative than the one viewed from the left. I listen to every word my media people say. Look at what their brethren did for Nixon and Reagan.

"Believe me, Bert, I know the pressure you must be feeling. To have such a fiasco associated with your good name is unthinkable, a travesty."

"It's very upsetting, Mr. President," Bert says calmly. Albert French is very tall and very thin. He is a man of merged extremes. He is, on one hand, aristocratic. But there is also a homespun honesty about him that I would guess emanates from his Midwestern roots. He has curly, gray hair, which is never combed. When he is upset, his shoulders sag as if the weight of the world is upon them. In all of Washington, Albert French has not one enemy that I know of, which is a neat trick to pull off for such a principled, outspoken politician.

"Oh, I know it goes well beyond that, Bert. I've wounded you. Quite unintentionally. But I did it. It's always dangerous, isn't it, Bert, firing into a crowd?" I have to stop for a moment to collect my thoughts. In my head I see Ashley Jones blowing me a kiss. "Bert, I don't want you to think I'm patronizing you, but I have to say, and I mean this with all my heart, you're one of the best people I've got. Adding the name of Bert French to my cabinet instantly elevated my whole administration. In this game, Bert, you are what the people around you are. And I'm telling you, in all sincerity, that I'm proud to have you on my team."

"I've been proud to serve you, Mr. President," says Bert.

"Well, I hope you'll continue to serve me, and to be proud to do it."

"We have a small matter to resolve first, don't we?"

"Listen, Bert, I'm going to let you in on something that only a handful of others know about. I think once you hear about it, you'll understand." As I am about to tell Albert

French the true nature of the Arizona Project, I begin thinking about my recurring dream about my father. You can't thread a needle with a rope, I am thinking.

~

"So you see, Bert, it really has nothing at all to do with a landfill. The whole thing was just a diversion to get Bull Dozier off my case."

"It all makes perfect sense," says Bert. "But the fact still remains that you cannot, at this time, go public with this information. And until you do, my integrity will remain in question. Under the circumstances, it seems I have no choice but to resign."

"Damn it, Bert, all our actions can't be popular ones," I say, walking that fine line between command and request. "Please reconsider."

Bert takes a deep breath and folds his scarecrow arms across his chest. "I'll give you my final word by the end of the week." He gets up to leave. "By the way, how's the stomach?"

"Better, thanks," I say. I wish it were true. In a moment Albert French is out the door.

Woody enters immediately. Apparently he has been waiting in the wings. "So how'd it go?"

"It went," I say.

"You don't sound very encouraged."

"The man's got integrity by the truckload, Woody. I can't blame him for not wanting to compromise it. Had I known this was going to blow up in my face, I would have alerted him beforehand. As it is, he not only feels humiliated, he feels betrayed. A double whammy."

"So he's out?"

"Not officially. Maybe not at all. He's going to let me know by the end of the week."

"You think there's anything else we can do?" says Woody.

"I don't think so. We just have to let him make up his own mind at this point. And be prepared for the worst."

"Perhaps we should prepare your rebuttal."

"Rebuttal?" I feel a twinge in my lower gut.

"To Dozier's statement," says Woody.

"Oh. Yes, of course. The sooner the better. The more time we take, the worse it'll look for us. If we're telling the truth, we shouldn't need time to prepare a statement. Only liars need time to figure out what they're going to say. Let's have something ready for tonight. Tomorrow morning at the latest."

"I'll round up Phil and Calvin," Woody says.

"Ashley, too. I want to know how she made out with the networks."

∼

I did not tell Albert French everything about the Arizona Project. This is partly because we have not worked out all the details yet. I did, however, tell him as much as any of the other insiders know. So he now knows who is involved. He knows where the money is coming from. And he knows that, in spite of the hawkish appearance of the project, what I am really orchestrating here is a peace mission. I have given Albert French every assurance I can that what I am doing involves no increase in our nuclear arsenal. Hell, we already have enough megatons to obliterate half a million Hiroshimas, enough to blow up the entire planet many times over. I have also assured Bert that the facility itself is neither harmful to the surrounding ecology, nor even to the land upon which, or rather under which, it is being built.

Albert French knows that we are in a race against time. The Arizona Project must be completed by the fall, in order for it to be available as a bargaining chip during my October summit with Alexi Brezniski. If our countries are to make further progress toward disarmament, I will need all the ammunition I can get. After all, though Alexi can be a warm and charming man, I do not trust him as far as I can throw him. Behind his broad smile and sparkling eyes, there resides the mind of a cool, calculating pragmatist, indeed a ruthless man willing to do anything to achieve his ends. Alexi is a complicated man, extremely hard to peg. On one hand, he is all smiles and glasnost, eager to forge new and expanded alliances with American businesses. On the other hand, he seems cut from the same cloth as the infamous Vladimir Zhirinovsky, calling for the restoration of the Russian empire, blaming the Jews for starting two world wars and demanding the return of Alaska, Finland and Poland to Russia. Nor has Alexi had kinds words for Israel or Solomon Dayan, comparing Israel to South Africa before the end of apartheid and Solomon Dayan to a demonic plantation owner who treats Israeli Arabs like slaves.

With all that is at stake, this is not the best of times for my revered secretary of the interior to resign.

~

Sheila and I are having dinner in our private dining room at the Ridgeley. Sheila looks very lovely tonight. She is wearing a red cocktail dress. I have always loved Sheila in red. The night I fell in love with her, if my memory serves me correctly, she was wearing a red dress very similar to the one she has on now. That dress back then had the same effect on me that this one is having on me tonight. I am experiencing a hardening of the artery. "You look beautiful tonight," I say.

Sheila puts down her fork and picks up her glass of wine.

"You're looking pretty dashing yourself, Mr. President," she says.

I shake my head. "Sometimes I think it was all a mistake, coming here. I don't know what I thought I could accomplish."

"You haven't given yourself much of a chance," Sheila says.

"Have you seen the latest polls? Christ, Johnson was probably more popular than I am now. Andrew Johnson."

"You're too hard on yourself, Ron," Sheila says. I am a little shocked by the sympathy in her voice. Usually she has a low tolerance for self-pity. Could she be getting used to room service after all? Does she no longer regret not being in the White House? In Blair House? Does she no longer care about those Duncan Phyfe pieces from the Green Room? Will we make love tonight?

"Not half as hard as the sports press has been on me," I say.

"The sports press have their heads up their asses," Sheila says.

"Not everybody thinks so."

"Not everybody matters."

"I love you, Sheel."

"Your soup is getting warm."

I am eating vichyssoise. "Who cares?" I take Sheila's hand in mine and kiss it.

"Mr. President," says Sheila, feigning modesty.

A waiter comes by with a Waterford pitcher and fills our water glasses. His coal black hair is pushed back, his complexion is olive, his expression is serene. His movements are so fluid it would be more appropriate for the water to flow like a fountain from the sleeve of his blue blazer. "Did I tell you Bert French might resign?"

"I don't recall," Sheila says.

"I saw him this morning. This whole Bull Dozier thing's got him all in a huff. He says he can't allow something like this to tarnish his reputation. I told him I didn't blame him."

"Bert French is a pompous asshole," Sheila says. "He thinks he's Joan of Arc."

"The country loves him. He's a goddamn folk hero."

"Hero shmero. The whole country is full of assholes, too," Sheila says.

The waiter returns. He leans down in front of me and starts to reach for my half-full soup bowl. "Finished, Mr. President?"

"Yes, thanks," I say.

To Sheila, the waiter says, "Ma'am?"

"I'm done," says Sheila, and the waiter removes her bowl of French onion soup.

"Anyway it won't look good if he resigns. I'm off to a rocky enough start without something like this happening," I say.

"The public has a short memory. Reagan and Senator North proved that. By the time the summit starts in the fall, everyone will have forgotten all about Bull's press conference. And if Saint Bert is gone, they'll have forgotten all about him, too."

"I'm not so sure," I say.

The waiter places a slab of roast beef in front of Sheila and sole almandine in front of me.

"Looks good," I say.

Sheila is already cutting her meat. She takes a bite and begins to chew sensuously. "Is good," she says. "Look, Ron, you have to try not to worry so much. You've got all kinds of people around you who are being paid to do that."

"The buck stops here," I say.

Back in our room, I unzip Sheila's dress for her. She turns to me when I am done and kisses me passionately. Her lips are wet and slippery. I wrap my arms her and kiss her with equal fervor. She unloosens my tie. I slip her dress off her shoulders. It cascades to the floor. I unfasten her bra. She unbuckles my belt. We continue to caress and kiss. "One second," I say. All the wine I had for dinner is pounding on the door of my bladder, trying to get out. I break away from Sheila and go to the bathroom. I have to wait a few minutes for my erection to thaw before I can go. When I am done, I flush the toilet and wash my hands. I consider brushing my teeth, but since Sheila has not brushed hers, I decide against it.

When I come out of the bathroom, the room is dark. I leave the bathroom light on so I can see where I am going. Sheila, naked, is spread out on the bed, her pose Goya-esque, her eyes closed. I am as hard as a rock again. The Washington Monument has nothing on me. I pull off my tie and quickly unbutton my shirt. My pants are already undone, so I step out of them easily. By now my penis is so erect I feel like I can fuck Sheila from the next county. I climb into bed beside her. I kiss her forehead, her cheek, her marshmallow mouth. She smiles dreamily, but doesn't move. Her eyes stay closed. "Sheila?" I say. "Sheel?" She grumbles and rolls onto her side, away from me. I take hold of her shoulder and rock her gently.

There is more grumbling, sensual, but grumbling nonetheless.

"Goddamn it!" I mutter. I spring out of bed and storm back into the bathroom. I make the shower as cold as I can stand it.

◦

At around midnight I call Woody and tell him to arrange a meeting between myself and Marcy Gillis tomorrow evening, sometime before dinner. I can really use a good massage. I ache in places I have never ached in so intensely before. What with the food poisoning and Bull Dozier's press conference and Bert French's threat of resignation and Sheila's passing out on me, I am not at all surprised I feel this way. I anxiously await the miracle only a trained female hand can perform.

"How's seven sound?" says Woody.

"Seven sounds fine," I say.

"Good. I'll set it up," says Woody.

I feel a little depressed about putting my future in someone else's hands, but I also feel there is nothing I can do about it. I am going to burst otherwise, which would simply not be good for the country.

FRENCH KISSING

I told Rosalee Wilson to send Bert French the most spectacular arrangement of flowers that our Ridgeley florist could create. Bert is a horticultural nut. His home is surrounded by English gardens. When he finds free time, he loves to work in them. His truly great love is topiary. The perimeter of his property is protected by an array of fanciful creatures — dragons, unicorns, sea serpents. More than any other man I know, Bert French will appreciate getting flowers.

The flowers should arrive by Thursday. Bert has said he will get back to me on Friday and I know Bert to be a man of his word. I know it is silly to think that flowers can turn him around, should he be leaning toward resignation, but they can't hurt.

It is 6:32 a.m. and I have already been in the Oval Office for an hour. The older I get, the less sleep I seem to need.

Still I feel drained. Drained and plugged up at the same time. Interesting.

I am wondering if I will need to tell Bert any more than I have already to keep him on board. It is certainly clear that I cannot be totally up front with him. There is simply too much at stake to let the true nature of the Arizona Project fall upon his pacifist ears. How can I tell him that I fully expect my summit with Alexi Brezniski to fail? How can I tell him that it really doesn't matter? I have firmly believed for many years now that the nuclear destruction of our planet, should it ever come, will not be precipitated by one of the super powers, but by some tiny, insignificant speck of a country that has finally achieved the price of entry into the nuclear poker game. Any country with a leader with a small brain and a short fuse could precipitate a nuclear Armageddon. If we are to achieve any degree of security in this insane world, we must somehow, some way, bring these nuclear dwarfs into line. Jack Kennedy knew how to apply force and win. He got the Russians to back down. But when you're dealing with lunatics, conventional displays of force just don't carry any weight. The only way to counteract lunacy is with an equal, but not opposite, force. Lunatic threats require lunatic solutions. No, there is definitely a limit to how much a man like Bert French can know.

At approximately 7:00 a.m., there is a firm knock on my door. It is too early to be Rosalee, who generally arrives at 8:00, and too early to be Woody Stone. Woody is not an early riser. The earliest I ever expect him is 8:15 or so. Perhaps it is Ashley with news that the network chiefs have decided not to cooperate after all. Or maybe Phil Hurley with more bad news about Republican shenanigans on Capitol Hill. Or Candace with the latest menorah burning report or more details about Diya Bakir's plan to assassinate me.

Or Jack Frost with another dismal favorability poll. "Come in," I say.

The door swings open and there, darkening my doorstep much to my surprise, is the man I thought for sure I was rid of forever. "Hello, Bull," I say.

"Mr. President," says Bull.

"Sit," I say.

"No thanks," says Bull as if I had tried to bribe him. "I'll just take a minute of your time."

"What can I do for you?" I say.

"I think it's more like what I can do for you, Mr. President," says Bull.

"You've already done everything I wanted you to do. I couldn't possibly ask for anything more. Wouldn't dream of it." I feel like a kid on Chanukah. I pull the envelope containing Bull Dozier's resignation out of my desk. "This, Bull, was the ultimate gift," I say. "Thank you so much."

Bull apparently recognizes the envelope. "That's what I wanted to talk to you about."

"I can't imagine why. Seems like you already said everything that needed to be said. That, and a little bit more."

"I don't think so," says Bull. "You see, Mr. President, I've changed my mind. I'm not ready to throw in the towel."

I shake my head. "Well, Bull, that's really very sweet of you, to have such a change of heart. But I truly believe your instincts were right. Go with them. We're no more a team than Hitler and Chamberlain were. We're a joke, Bull, and everyone knows it. No, you did the right thing, resigning. Trust me."

"That may seem like the case to you," Bull says, "but from where I sit, stand, it looks a whole lot different. You're a dangerous man, Ron Goldberg. I've known it from day one. You and your quaint New England morality. Your asinine sense of mission. Someone like you needs to be on a leash. A very short leash. So I've made up my mind. I'm staying."

"It's a little late for that, isn't it?" I say, waving the envelope in the air.

"I don't think so," says Bull.

"Oh?"

"No, I don't. You see, there never was a resignation."

"Then what would you call this?"

"Scrap paper," says Bull.

I open the envelope and prepare to read Bull's pompous words back to him. Only when I unfold the letter do I realize that I have been tricked. "I should've known," I said. "I should've known I couldn't get rid of a virus like you so easily."

"Yes, I suppose you should have," says Bull. He turns and walks out the door.

∾

"He got me," I say. "I fell for it hook, line and sinker."

"He's not as dumb as he looks," says Woody. "He couldn't be, could he?"

"I should have suspected from the start. Who writes an official resignation in his own handwriting?"

"Trust is not a luxury a president can afford," says Phil Hurley.

"So maybe we shouldn't trust you either," says Woody.

Phil gets ruffled and snarls, "Maybe not."

"Maybe not," Woody echoes.

Phil waves his hand at Woody in disgust and leaves.

"I knew it was too goddamn good to be true, Woody."

Woody shrugs. His face has "I told you so written" all over it. As well it should. In less than two days, the ink that Bull Dozier had used to write his resignation had disappeared.

How did the son of a bitch know I wouldn't bother to have copies of it made right away? At least he still thinks the Arizona Project is a landfill. Even if he gets to Paul Finkelstein again, he won't find out what it's really about, because not even Paul knows that. "So, am I all set for tonight?"

"I don't think it's been confirmed yet. I'll have to check it out with Ashley."

"I don't mean the rebuttal to Bull's statement. I mean the massage."

"Oh that," says Woody. "Sure, that's all set. I'll be by around quarter to seven. I'll introduce you myself."

Being brought to the brink of ecstasy by Sheila and then abandoned has only added to my pain. Sometimes it feels like I have a hot poker up my urethra. "Good," I say. "That's good. Now, what about this statement I have to make?"

☙

Later in the day, Ashley tells me that the networks have agreed to carry my response to Bull's accusation at 7:00 p.m., so I have to push back my massage until eight. I could have made it for 7:30, but I figured I'd need a little time to unwind first.

Standing at the podium, I survey the room for friendly faces, but I find few. Even those reporters whose sympathies have been with me since the moment I declared my candidacy look apprehensive, as if I will not be able to successfully rebut the accusations Bull has leveled against me. So be it. I look at the teleprompter, shake my head and then step around to the side of the podium. Ashley Jones, stationed in the rear of the room, looks horrified. She whispers something to Calvin Foxx who whispers something back while Woody and Phil Hurley lean into the conversation.

"Ladies and gentlemen of the press, my fellow Americans,

206

I come here to you tonight not with hat in hand, nor with my finger pointing. I come here simply to say that there is absolutely, positively no way I could ever do what my vice president has suggested I would do. No way could I ever initiate or support a plan to turn the Grand Canyon into a landfill. Nevertheless, in denying these fanciful accusations, let me be the first to express my admiration for the man who has made them. For his courage to speak out against me, when he firmly believed that I was up to something that spit in the face of the national interest. Dissension is the essence of a free society. Without it, we are but slaves. So, yes, I respect Thomas Dozier and I sincerely hope he will remain my vice president, in spite of the hard feelings he apparently harbors toward me. Should you believe me? Should you believe Vice President Dozier? That I cannot answer for you. All I can offer is this: in matters where the truth is in dispute, always consider the source. And always consider the motive. Personally, I believe that unscrupulous members of the intelligence community have duped the vice president and I have already ordered an investigation of the whole incident. It is also true that he and I have had our differences. But I think that's why we make such a good team. We keep each other honest. Thank you very much and good night."

A flurry of hands spring into the air, but I wave them off. "The truth, my friends," I say, "requires no commentary. And it is the truth that I have spoken here tonight." As I turn to leave, a murmur rises up against my back like an incoming tide.

⁊

Moments later, back in my office, my troops enter and greet me with smiles and congratulations. Jack is beaming.

Phil can't spot a raisin anywhere. Woody offers me a pat on the back, Ashley a hug.

"They all bought it, Mr. President," says Ashley. "You had me worried when you ditched the teleprompter. But it couldn't have turned out better."

"A piece of cake."

"Yeah, right. Just don't ever do it again."

"Trust me."

Ashley puckers and tells me the best comment yet has come from Peter Taylor of ABC who said that it was nice to know that we have such a class act in the Ridgeley. "The president's denial, if you can actually call it that, was clean, crisp and straightforward," Taylor had said. He further pointed out that neither did I attack the character of Bull Dozier, nor cast doubt upon his ability to be my vice president.

Yes, praise is a wonderful thing. But I can only take so much of it. Besides, sex is better. By 7:25 I grow tired of being gracious and excuse myself for the evening. I am back in my suite now, preparing for my massage. The first thing I have to do is vomit.

~

At seven forty-five, Woody knocks on my door and then lets himself in. "Mr. President?" he says.

"Be right there," I say. I am brushing my teeth for the third time in ten minutes. I fear my breath smells like a land-fill. "Have a seat."

"Take your time," Woody says. "Hey, Ray, how ya doin'?"

Rachel apparently heard Woody come in. "Fine," says Ray flatly.

"You don't sound fine," says Woody. "Something wrong?"

"Nothing," says Ray.

"It doesn't sound like nothing."

"Hi, Ray," I say. "How's my big girl?"

"I'm not your big girl," says Ray. "I'm a woman."

Ray is almost thirteen. If womanhood truly begins with the first shedding of the uterine lining, then Ray has been a woman since she was eleven. I smile at her and give her a little kiss on the forehead. "I know that, hun," I say. "But you'll always be my big girl just the same."

Ray frowns and leaves the room.

"Tough age," I say to Woody. "She's torn between teddy bears and boys." I don't feel like telling Woody that I'm quite certain Ray has a crush on him.

"I guess," says Woody. "You ready?"

"Ready as I'll ever be," I say.

As we're about to go out the door, the phone rings. "Don't answer it," I say.

"It might be something important," Woody says.

"A pain in the ass is more likely."

Woody goes to get the phone. "Hello...oh, hello, Bert..." Woody gestures to me to take the phone.

I gesture to Woody that I don't want to take the call. I'll have trouble enough getting a hard-on tonight without more bad news.

Woody waves me to the phone again. "Mr. President? No, he's right here, Bert..." Woody cups his hand over the phone. "Mr. President! C'mon, c'mon," he whispers.

With a disgusted look I grab the phone from him. "Bert, hi. It's good to hear from you...no, no bother at all... you're not? Oh, great, that's terrific news...of course nothing's changed...I'm glad you are, too, Bert. And thanks for calling...goodbye, Bert." I hang up the phone and breathe a sigh of relief. "We still have a secretary of the interior, Woody. Thank God for small miracles."

In a few moments we are standing outside the door of Marcy Gillis' room.

~

"I'm starting to have second thoughts about this," I say.

"About getting a massage?" says Woody.

"Right," I say sarcastically.

"Just take it easy. No one's going to know."

"Three people are going to know," I say.

"And that's as far as it'll ever go. I promise."

"You're absolutely certain she can be trusted?"

"Absolutely," says Woody.

"If this ever gets out, I'm finished for sure. And I don't mean with Sheila either."

"Relax, Mr. President. It'll be okay."

I truly thought that I would be better at this than I am turning out to be. You start out being so angry at your wife for having denied you for so long, you think nothing, no splatter of conscience, nothing, is going to keep you from getting what you so desperately need. But then when you actually set out to do it, everything changes. You start to think, well, maybe it isn't so bad after all. You think, maybe a little of the blame does rest on your shoulders. Like the other night. Sheila's motor was in fourth gear. She would have fucked me standing on her head. But then I have to go and spoil it by taking a leak. I mean, what did I expect? You think passion can be turned on and off like a faucet?

Woody shakes my shoulder. "Mr. President? MR. PRESI-DENT? You all right?"

"Yeah, I'm fine. Just a little nervous. I never had an affair before."

"Don't think of it that way. Think of it as medical treatment."

"You never cease to amaze me, Woodstock Stone. I could blow Moscow off the face of the earth, be crucified in the press as a butcher, and you'd tell everyone to relax, take it easy on poor old Ron, he's just having a bad day."

"You want to knock? Or should I?"

"You're the matchmaker," I say.

Woody knocks on the door. A moment later it opens. "Hi," says the extraordinarily beautiful woman I first saw from my balcony. She couldn't be much more than twenty-five years old. She is wearing a baggy, gray sweatshirt, skin-tight dungarees and tennis shoes. Even with the sweatshirt on, I can see that she has substantial breasts. Her eyes are a dazzling blue. Her hair is a rich ebony, shaped into a tightly woven perm that spills over her shoulders and appears to have been formed by placing her finger in a wall socket. "Come on in," she says. I can only think about one thing.

"Marcy," says Woody, "I'd like you to meet the President of the United States."

Marcy reaches out to shake my hand. I take her hand in mine. It is very warm. Mine is cold as ice. "Nice to meet you, Mr. President."

I am nervous as a schoolboy, and I can't seem to shake the feeling. I smile awkwardly. "Nice to fuck you, too," I say.

∾

Marcy Gillis did not bat an eye at my faux pas. She acted as if I had said what I meant to say and directed Woody and me into the living room to sit down. "Woody tells me you've been under a lot of strain lately."

"Goes with the territory, I'm afraid," I say.

"You should learn to relax," Marcy says. She sits down next to me on the couch. Woody balances himself on the arm of the easy chair. It is obvious he does not plan to stay long.

"Massage isn't just a great relaxer, you know," Marcy says. "It's a great healer, too."

"I always suspected that was the case," I say.

"Look, I'd like to stay, but I have a few things I have to take care of," says Woody. "I'll see you two later."

"Good night, Woody," I say. "Thanks." It seems odd to me to have my chief of staff refer to Marcy and me as "you two". I just met the girl five minutes ago. It's not like we're a couple.

"Good night," says Woody.

"See ya, hun," says Marcy. She closes the door behind him. The President of the United States is now alone with his masseuse.

In the next hour, I discovered that Marcy Gillis is not your average masseuse. She confided in me her two great desires. The first was to go back to school to get her college degree. The second was to be a contestant on "Jeopardy!" She seemed like an intelligent young woman to me, so I told her I thought she could do anything she set her mind to.

Marcy Gillis quit college in her freshman year to pursue a modeling career. She was lured by the money and by the assurances of various agents that she had what it takes to become not only a great model, but also a great actress. It turned out that these agents were only interested in taking Marcy to bed. After a few one-sided relationships, she decided to give school another shot. This second attempt failed, or at least was about to fail when she was "discovered" by a film-maker named Skip Flamingo. Flamingo put her in what he called "art films." He paid her well, too. But they weren't the kind of films you took your mother to. They weren't even the kind of films you could see in a theater. Marcy wanted out, but Flamingo threatened to send copies of her films to her parents, a couple of religious fundamentalists, if she tried to break her "contract." Marcy split anyway and Flamingo, sleaze that he was, made good on his threat. Marcy hasn't been home since.

"This is something I'm really good at," she says. "I enjoy my work."

"But you can't go home again, can you?"

"No, I can't." Marcy's eyes begin to tear up.

"Hey, I'm sorry. That was a stupid thing to say."

"It's all right," says Marcy. "Besides, it happens to be true."

Suddenly I am filled with a need to save another human being, to pluck a life from the jaws of decadence. "Maybe there's something that can be done," I say.

Marcy sniffles. "Like what?"

"I don't know," I say. "I'll work on it." I don't have the faintest idea how I am going to help this young woman. I am not a rich man, so charity is out of the question.

"Come 'ere," says Marcy.

I move closer to her. "What?" I say.

Marcy kisses me, and as she does, she lifts up my hand, slips it under her sweatshirt and places it on her breast. She is not wearing a bra.

Ten minutes later, we are in Marcy's bed. We are both naked. Marcy is even more beautiful than I imagined she would be. But still there is something missing. I do not love this woman. I do not even know this woman. I have listened to a synopsis of her life, that's true. But is that enough to be intimate with her? I back my head away from hers and when I do, she senses something is wrong. Her eyes open wide, those big blue eyes.

"What is it?" she says. "Did I do something wrong?"

"No, no, you're wonderful. It's just that —"

"What?"

I feel embarrassed but there is nothing I can do about it. I have to say what's on my mind. "Look, you mind if I call you Cookie?" I say.

"Hun, if you can do for me what you say you can, you can call me Bill."

We make incredible love.

∾

I wake up in Marcy's arms at three in the morning. Surprisingly, I am not the least bit disoriented. I know exactly where I am and who I am with. I am surprised, too, that I am not filled with a sense of panic. Surely, Sheila must wonder where I am. I left our suite at seven.

Go ahead and lynch me if you must, but I do not feel any remorse for what I have done. I deserve this kind of treatment. My prostate deserves this kind of treatment. It is for the good of the country, just like my astute chief of staff has said. Indeed the good of the country does not hang in the balance, but in my scrotum.

I have to urinate. As I disentangle myself from Marcy's soft and sticky web, she makes a few mumbling sounds, but does not wake up. I roll on my side, sit up and get out of bed. I do not turn on the light in the bathroom. It is dark but I can see enough of my target to know what I am doing. Turning on the light would be too much for my weary eyes to withstand.

I begin to urinate but strangely I do not hear the familiar sound of my stream hitting the water in the toilet bowl. I look down to see what's wrong. All I can think of, in this post-coital penumbra, is that I have missed the bowl entirely. But this is not the case. What is happening instead is that my penis is blowing up like a balloon. I am overcome with panic. My heart starts to pound. "Oh, my God! Oh, my God!" I scream.

~

By the time Marcy gets to the bathroom and yanks open the door, I have been reduced to a lump on the floor.

"My God, Mr. President. What happened?" Marcy takes a wet cloth and rubs my brow with it.

"I'm all right," I say. "I'll clean it up."

Marcy suddenly realizes that the bathroom floor is soaked with urine. "My God," she says again.

"I forgot to take the condom off," I say sheepishly. "I thought my penis was going to explode."

Cupping her hands over her mouth, Marcy looks like she is going to cry, but then bursts into wild laughter. I feel a little hurt at first that she could laugh at so pathetic a thing as a urine-soaked president, but then I burst into laughter, too. She crouches down next to me and we collapse against one another, unable to speak. We gasp for air. We howl. I find it hard to believe that no one hears our howling. I feel a slight swelling of panic inside me, but it only makes me laugh louder.

Eventually we regain our composure. After we clean up and shower together, we go back to bed and make love again. At four, I go back to my suite. I hope that Sheila has not locked me out.

~

Sheila has locked me out, so I have to wake up Woody to let me in. "What the hell am I going to tell her?" I say.

"Don't worry about a thing," Woody says. "I told her we'd be working late. Something to do with the summit."

"Woody, you're a saint. An absolute saint."

"I know," says Woody.

"I want you to contact Tim Green for me this morning," I say.

"The tobacco lobbyist?"

"Yes. Set up an appointment with him. Have him come here for lunch."

"Should I tell him what it's about?"

"No. Just tell him to come. Tim won't need a reason to pay a visit to his old pal Ron Goldberg."

Sheila is asleep when I climb into bed next to her. I reach over to get my alarm clock — to reset it for 8:00 a.m. — but I knock it on the floor instead.

"Ron?" Sheila says.

"Go back to sleep," I say.

"What time is it?"

"Four-thirty," I say.

"You poor dear," she says. "Woody said you'd be late, but I didn't think it would be this late. Here," she says, pulling me toward her. "Come to mama." I nuzzle my head into her neck. She places one arm over my shoulder and with the other she reaches deep down beneath the covers and begins stroking my penis.

"My God, Sheila," I say. "I'm exhausted. I can't."

"Nonsense. Of course you can."

Sheila is right. In a few seconds I am as hard as a monument.

THE GREEN THUMB

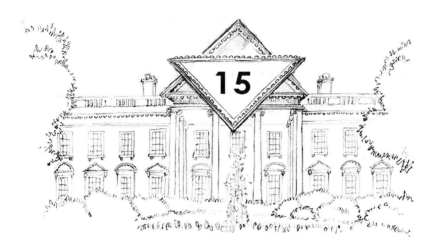

By the time I get to my office it is 8:40 a.m. I feel guilty for coming in so late, but I was working on behalf of the country last night, was I not? A healthy president is a more effective president. My prostate pain level has been greatly diminished as a result of my nocturnal activities. So where's the harm? Who's the victim? Even Sheila is satisfied. And will be for, who knows, another month or so.

There is more good news. Jack Frost tells me the Gallup Poll in the *Post* this morning revealed that I now have a 62% favorability rating. "Keep it up, Mr. President," he says. "And don't forget, we gain one seat in the House every time your approval rating goes up one point."

"I remember, Jack," I say. "But the mid-term elections are still more than a year away."

"No reason why we can't start building a foundation now."

"Sure, Jack, sure." Although he makes his living measuring and evaluating public opinion, deep down I suspect Jack doesn't think very highly of the intelligence of the American voter. In fact, during the 2010 mid-term elections, when President Whitney was starting to slip in the polls, and Republican incumbents looked like sitting ducks, Jack was still cautiously optimistic about Democratic chances for picking up seats. "The good news, Senator," he told me back then, "is that 96% of Americans hate their congressman. The bad news is that 98% don't know who the hell their congressman is."

In any case, I can't help but be pleased with my ascending approval rating. What's more, only 28% of the voters think I am doing a less than satisfactory job, and that figure is roughly the same percentage of voters in the country who profess to be Republicans, so I think I can discount it a bit. 10% still think it's "too early to tell" if I'm doing a good job or not, but there will probably be 10% of the voters who feel this way three years from now, when I'm up for reelection. I mean, who needs them?

 ∾

I wish it were cause for celebration all around. There is trouble in Israel. Solomon Dayan has said to the Israeli press that he feels that I am letting Israel down. He says that I made campaign promises to send more weapons, but to date have not sent one measly megaton. The truth is, I haven't sent one plane, or one rifle, or even one firecracker, for that matter. I wish that Solomon could understand the not-so-kosher pickle I am in. This isn't like the old days, when we could willy-nilly send Israel whatever she wanted. Israel was just an ally then. Now she is part of the family. She must eat from the same table we all eat from. True, she is in a combat zone, and should receive some special treatment. But how can I demonstrate to the world that I am a peace-loving man, and then turn around and send Israel enough firepower to blow up half the Arab world? Maybe things will change after the fall summit. But for now, I have to be on my best dovish behavior.

My rating among voters in Israel is a sad reversal of my rekindled popularity on the mainland. Only 37% of my Israeli constituents think I am doing a good job, while 63% rate my performance unsatisfactory. 0% are undecided, but that is no surprise. I have not yet met a Jew or an Arab who didn't possess an opinion.

$$\sim$$

At 8:53 a.m., five of the six lights on my phone begin flashing in unison. A split second later, Rosalee Wilson is on the intercom. "Good morning, Mr. President. You got Woody on one, Candace Rowe on two, Calvin Foxx on three, Tanya Gregson on four and Solomon Dayan on five."

"Put Solomon through first," I say. "It won't take long. Tell Candace, Cal and Tanya I'll get back to them. Tell Woody to hang on a minute." I pick up the phone. I push the last in the row of the flashing buttons. "Solomon, not a word, okay? We've been over this before. There's just nothing I can do now. And nothing I can do until after the Arizona Project comes to fruition. And, yes, yes, everything is on schedule. Okay? Solomon? You there?"

The line goes dead and the light flickers out like a candle in the wind. It is then that I realize that I had picked up line six and not line five. I quickly push line five. "Solomon?"

"Mr. President, we need to talk."

"Oops," I say inaudibly. And then at normal volume I add, "I know. I only wish we had talked even sooner."

When I am finished with Solomon and Woody, and have returned calls to Calvin, Candace and Tanya, I call Rosalee.

"Yes, Mr. President."

"Hey, Roz. Who'd you say that was on line six before?"

"Line six?"

"Yeah, when I was talking to Solomon."

"There wasn't anyone on six."

"You sure?"

"Sure, I'm sure. Why?"

"No reason. I just thought — never mind." I hang up the phone. Maybe there were only five lines flashing.

&

Uncle Leo is back in town after spending a few days at his apartment in New York. He is quite thrilled with his job as a guard at the Air and Space Museum. He tells me he likes to wear his uniform even when he is not working. I tell him that I don't think anyone will mind.

I called Uncle Leo this morning just to say hello and to see how things were going. He said the crowds at the museum are large, but they seem to come in waves, so he gets a breather every so often. I made him promise me that, if the job gets to be too much for him, he will quit or at least cut down on his hours. He told me he will do this, but I know Uncle Leo. He'd rather be dipped in honey and tied to an anthill than admit that he was too old to do something.

Five years ago, Uncle Leo had to have his prostate removed. Knock on wood, his cancer has not returned, but I think it is safe to assume that Uncle Leo has not had an erection since the operation. He knows that I know this, though I don't recall ever having discussed it with him. Uncle Leo's joking about his "girlfriends" is his way of hanging on to his masculinity. Now, more than ever before, I realize what a difficult thing this is to do.

❧

At noon, Tim Green struts through my office doorway without knocking, without having been announced. If I don't like it, and sometimes I admit I don't, it's my own damn fault. I have given instructions to let Tim come and go as he pleases. He is, after all, not a major security risk. Tim's access to the president drives other members of my staff and cabinet, whom I make jump through the usual hoops, a bit crazy. Too bad. Who's in charge here anyway? "Ron, you old son of a bitch, how the hell are ya?" he says.

"Tim!" I say. I get up and walk briskly toward him. We hug and clap each other on the back. "Boy, it's good to see a friendly face."

"Tough going lately?"

"It's always something."

"Woody told me about Bert French."

"That was a close one," I say.

"But, hey, you're still alive and kicking. That's all that counts."

"Yeah, that's all that counts," I say. I ask Tim to have a seat. He sits down in the chair to the left of my desk. As I go to sit down, I am thinking about what my media consultants have always told me about my authoritative right profile. I guess it's okay for Tim Green to see my left side.

"So," says Tim.

"I'm really glad you could make it on such short notice," I say. "I have some inkling what it's like to be a lobbyist."

"For you, Ron, anything. You know that."

"All the same, Tim, I appreciate it. I want you to know that."

"Enough said," says Tim. He reaches into the inside pocket of his sport coat and pulls out a pack of cigarettes.

"Tim," I say, reprovingly.

Tim looks deadly serious. He opens the package and offers it to me.

"No thanks," I say.

"Candy," says Tim. He pulls one of the cigarettes out of the pack and starts sucking on it. "You sure?"

"You son of a bitch. I thought you fell off the wagon again."

"You think I'm crazy?"

Of course I think Tim's crazy. I have always thought that. "Gimme one," I say. Now, aren't we a picture? The President of the United States and a tobaccoholic tobacco lobbyist sucking on candy cigarettes.

"Only two packs a day," says Tim, stuffing the package back into his pocket. "They last longer this way." Tim makes a slurping sound. "Helluva lot cheaper, too."

Tim and I reminisced about our schoolboy days. We talked about ringing doorbells and running like hell before someone could come to the door and then watching the confused, angry victim from behind a bush or tree, trying hard not to giggle away our position. We talked about making prank phone calls, asking people if their refrigerators were running and, if they were, telling them they had better go catch them. Or asking if they had Prince Albert in a can and, if they did, saying they had better let him out. We talked about cherry bombs and how incredibly impressed we were with anything that could explode under water; they were like miniature depth charges, and when we used them, we were making the world safe for democracy — even back then we had a strong sense of national pride. We talked about the summer we got our driver's licenses, and about my ancient

Austin Healey Sprite and Tim's equally ancient MG Midget. We weren't Tim Green and Ronnie Goldberg that summer; we were Indy legends Stirling Green and A. J. Goldberg. How we survived the insane chances we took that summer — the turns on two wheels, driving at speeds near 100 mph (downhill was the only way our underpowered cars could do it), passing each other on blind curves — is a minor miracle. We talked about our friends who OD'd, now and always with a little envy for all those tears that were shed in their honor by some very foxy girls. But mostly we talked about Cookie Dunn. And about Marcy Gillis, my Cookie surrogate, my Cookie without the calories.

"I needed a woman," I say to Tim. "It was either that or jerk off. Funny, with Sheila lately it's been like jerking off anyway."

Tim and I have picked up our conversation and carried it with us to my private dining room. "I'm sorry," says Tim.

Why is it that people feel the need to apologize for something that isn't even remotely their fault? "There's nothing to be sorry about," I say.

"Does Sheila know?"

"Know?"

"About the masseuse."

"Oh, sure, she knows about her. She just doesn't know I'm fucking her."

"What're you gonna do?"

"I don't know. That's not why I asked you to come here today anyway. I need you to do something for me."

"Name it," says Tim.

"I want you to contact Cookie for me. I want to see her."

"I'll do what I can. She's married, you know."

"Jesus, Tim, I just want to talk with her," I say.

"Okay, okay," says Tim.

"I called her Cookie," I say reflectively.

"What?"

"The masseuse. I called her Cookie. It was the only way I could go through with it."

When we're through eating, Tim offers me another candy cigarette. "No, thanks," I say. "I'm trying to cut down."

"Mind if I do?" says Tim.

"It's your life," I say. "Just remember you don't have any coupons for that lung transplant."

"Yeah, right." Tim looks at his watch. It is nearly two. "I have to be getting back," he says. We both stand.

"Thanks for coming, Tim."

"My pleasure, Ron. I'll be in touch."

As Tim Green walks out of the dining room, my mind is already at work, planning the arrival of Cookie Dunn at the Ridgeley.

～

A week has passed and I have no word yet from Tim Green. I understand that he has other things to do besides play nursemaid to my adolescent requests, but knowing this does not make waiting any easier. I have been seeing Marcy every night, sometimes before dinner, sometimes after. (She is a delicious appetizer, an even better dessert, but I know she'll never be a main course for me.) Either Sheila suspects nothing, or she doesn't care. Her mood lately has been playful and amorous. I cannot really explain it, but it's as if I am the sun and she is a planet moving around me in an elliptical orbit; sometimes we're closer than we are at other times, though I suspect we'll never return to the level of our Big Bang. But what a universe we have spawned!

～

Solomon Dayan is making more trouble for me. Now he has gone and told the *Post* that he is deeply disturbed by my lack of response to his response concerning my initial lack of response to what he claims were my campaign promises. It is true that I said I would never abandon Israel, never throw her defenseless into a pack of Arab wolves, and especially not into the bloody hands of Diya Bakir, but I do not regard my current inaction as sidestepping this commitment. I am biding my time, is all.

Solomon says the he is prepared to take drastic measures to get what he wants. When he was asked what these measures might be, he said, "Secession, for one." At the very least, he threatened to withdraw his support for me in the 2016 elections. Considering that it was Israel that put me over the top, such an action could spell disaster for me.

It is beginning to look like Governor Dayan might benefit from a tour of the Arizona Project.

∾

"Tim boy! Any news yet?"

"Negative, Ron. She's a tough one to track down."

"How tough could it be? You know where she lives."

"Gone, Ronnie. No forwarding address. No Facebook account. No other social networking sites either."

"Gone?"

"Poof," says Tim.

"Well, keep trying. And keep me posted."

"Will do."

"And if you get stuck, let me know. I can pull a few strings."

"I'll be in touch, Ronnie."

We fall silent for a moment. "Tim?"

"Yeah."

"I really need for this to happen. I know it may sound crazy. But I do."

"I understand, Ronnie. I'll find her."

"Tim?"

"Yeah."

"No one should know. It's just between you and me."

"Of course."

"And Woody. Woody knows, too."

"I'll check back with you in a couple of days."

"Either way."

"Either way," says Tim. "Goodbye, Ronnie." Tim hangs up.

Sometimes I think that if death has any sound at all, it's a dial tone.

I am sitting in the Situation Room of the Ridgeley. With me are Candace Rowe, Milton Buck, Warren Gates, Tanya Gregson and Woody. There is a tension in the air. There always is when Warren and Candace are in the same room, even if the occasion is social. Candace, her arms stretched forward with her palms on the conference table, looks as though she is ready to pounce. Gates looks as if he attending a funeral. In fact, with that greased-back black hair of his and that awful pallid complexion, it looks as if he's attending his own.

"Mr. President, we now have confirmation that Bakir plans to assassinate Solomon Dayan," Gates says.

"Where and when?" I ask.

"That we don't know yet."

"Isn't it your job to know?" Candace kicks in.

Gates snarls. "I don't need you to tell me what my job is, Ms. Rowe."

Candace snarls back. "Oh, I'm quite sure you know what it is, sir. I'm just not so sure you know how to do it."

Gates lets out a snort. "And you do?"

"Okay, let's not let personalities get in the way here," I say. "Let's just determine that the threat is real and, if so, take appropriate action."

"As I have just said, Mr. President," Gates says slowly, his contents clearly under pressure, "the threat is real. As is the Iraqi nuclear arsenal once again."

Frankly, I have no doubt of this on either count. In spite of my occasional attempts to treat the Iraqi situation with levity, I know full well that Diya Bakir is a man to be taken very seriously. After all, he has accomplished in Iraq what no one there, or anywhere else in the world, for that matter, would have thought possible. He wheeled, dealed, and manipulated his way to the top of the Iraqi food chain and along the way engineered the downfall Saddam Hussein, an event that was greeted with universal approbation not only by Israel and her allies, but by most Arab nations as well. Bakir's rise to power began the way weeds take over a yard, scarcely being noticed at first. In an attempt to appease the increasingly populous and vocal Kurds, Saddam Hussein, in 2004, insisted the Baath Party give permission to several Kurds to run for the National Assembly. One of these Kurds, Diya Bakir, was elected. Shortly after his election, Bakir became one of the assembly's staunchest anti-American members. A handsome man and an eloquent speaker, Bakir rode this proven tactic to stardom practically overnight. The irony is that the more powerful he became, the less anti-American he appeared to be. Cultivating relationships at every turn, especially within the Baath party, Bakir soon became one of the ten members of the RCC, the Revolutionary Command Council, which elected the Iraqi president to an indefinite term. While on the council, Bakir, with Machiavellian prowess, managed to institute free elections for president. He even won Hussein's support for this measure, telling the dictator that the way to play the game of international politics and to win the support, the military aid and the investment dollars of the West was to appear to be a democracy. He even invited, in a most conciliatory way, a group of Americans to oversee the elections. In the meantime he assured Hussein that he, Hussein, would win reelection by a commanding margin and that he, Bakir, had only put his own name on the ballot for show. In the end Bakir showed, and then some. He won the election with 57% of the vote, capturing the votes of nearly all the Kurds, who now made up 38% of the country's population, largely due to the waves of immigration from Iran, Syria and Turkey created by Bakir's celebrity.

As his first presidential act, Bakir disbanded the RCC and forced Hussein into exile in Iran where he was last seen being enthusiastically welcomed by Shiite militiamen, although no one really knows for sure if that was the real Hussein or one of his three look-alikes. At least two of the other Husseins faced equally unhappy final chapters. One was hung three years into the Iraq War by American sympathizers for his undeniable masterminding of 9/11. Another committed suicide, bleeding to death after shooting himself in the foot. A third, still at large, is believed to hiding at one of Iraq's nuclear weapons plants, all so well hidden that none has been found to this day.

Bakir, meanwhile, began to show his old stripes, delivering one hateful tirade after another against Israel, most of them directed toward the "devil incarnate" Solomon Dayan whom Bakir said was responsible for the destruction of three "nuclear power plants" and the taking of "countless" Iraqi lives. He was not totally inaccurate here. Solomon did order the bombing of the Iraqi nuclear plants in 2005, three years before Israel's American statehood, but this was because Iraq would not allow inspections of these plants, even though the presence of nuclear waste had been confirmed by Israeli intelligence. It was Solomon's belief, therefore, and one shared by the U.S., that these were not in fact power plants, as Iraq had claimed, but weapons plants. It should also be noted that, in addition to ignoring inspection requests, the Iraqis chose to ignore Solomon's humane handling of the bombing. In a move that angered the Israeli military command, who were demanding a "more robust target set," Solomon insisted on a far narrower plan of attack which certainly minimized casualties. This gesture, however, meant little to a grief-stricken Bakir, who lost two camels and one brother in the attacks.

"So let's do something about it," I say. "Now."

"The trick, Mr. President," Gates says, "is to be as discreet as possible. Otherwise we give Bakir a reason to come after you."

"You mean he doesn't have a reason already?"

〜

Hey, Pop, I always wanted to know one thing about being dead. Once you're gone, do you get to choose what age you're going to be for all eternity?

Ronnie, Ronnie, somebody finds out I tell you that, I'll catch hell. Worse, they'll probably send me there.

I promise I won't ever ask another thing about it.

Well, then, just this one question I'll answer.

I appreciate it, Pop. Your going out on a limb and all.

Yeah, yeah, sure. Look, Ronnie, it's like this: where I am, there is no age. There is no time. Everything just is. You're as young as you ever were and as old as you'll ever be.

That's it?

That's it, boy. The whole megillah.

"As young as you ever were and as old as you'll ever be?" That's a tough concept, Pop. I'm not sure I get it.

You will.

But —

No buts, Ronnie. This press conference is over.

DEFENSE MECHANISMS

Solomon Dayan is a small man, not quite five feet tall, though he claims to be five feet two and probably is most of the time because all his shoes have thick soles and heels. Solomon has the look and personality of a toy poodle. He has the densest curly gray hair that I have ever seen on a man. It is the kind of hair you feel compelled to run your fingers through, so when you talk to him, you often find yourself locking your arms across your chest to prevent yourself from indulging your innocent obsession. Solomon's hair turned gray when he was in his early twenties. He has always worried too much. He is also a notorious overachiever. And a brilliant one at that. I can only guess what his IQ might be. He finished high school by the age of sixteen, and graduated from Harvard three years later in 1979. He had planned to do graduate work in history, but when Israel and Egypt signed their famous peace treaty just two months before his graduation, Solomon decided to seek his destiny in Israel. He knew the treaty would mean more bloodshed and he wanted to do what he could to prevent it.

Solomon has agreed not to make any more public statements about our rift, until he has toured the Arizona Project. If, after the tour, he still feels that I am not justified in asking him to wait for military aid, then he can say whatever he wants, to whomever he wants. Secession, however, I have told him, is not acceptable under any circumstances; there has already been enough bloodshed, political and otherwise, over Israeli statehood.

෬

Air Force One touches down on the landing strip in the Nevada desert. The landing is surprisingly smooth, considering the terrain. "This is it," I say to Solomon.

When we come to a stop, Solomon is the first to click out of his seatbelt. "Looks like Israel out there," he says.

"Only on the surface," I say.

Solomon laughs. "I'll bet," he says.

We are led from the plane into the warehouse that sits atop the project. The air inside is as dry and hot as the air outside. I think about how much money I have saved the American people by not allowing air conditioning.

"It's like a goddamn oven in here," Solomon says.

"The further down we go, the cooler it'll get," I say.

"Now that's a paradox, isn't it?" says Solomon.

We make our way to the elevators and enter. With little sense of motion we descend for a few moments and then stop. The doors open. We enter the main room of the Arizona Project. "Wait here, please," our escort says. He is a young man, about twenty-five, who looks as if he has spent too much time under ground. His voice is crisp and sounds official. "I'll get Mr. Finkelstein."

"Finkelstein?" says Solomon.

"The movie director," I say. "You know, Arizona Smith."

Solomon Dayan surveys the enormous room. I am happy to see that considerable progress has been made here since my last visit. The ducts are all in place and the temporary wooden ceiling supports have been removed. It is possible now to feel the entire size of the room. It is like being inside a hanger built to house several 747s. Only it is empty. "What the hell is this, Mr. President? And what's Finkelstein got to do with it?"

"We're going to build a spaceship here, Solly," I say. "The likes of which no one has ever seen before."

"A real spaceship?"

"Of course, real. What do you mean?"

"I mean real. Will it fly?"

"Is that so necessary?"

"Well, I suppose that would depend on what you're trying to accomplish."

"Bingo."

∾

Later, back on Air Force One, the conversation continues.

"You're meshugge," Solomon Dayan says to me, after I tell him more about the spaceship that I have commissioned. "You think you can fool the world with video games and special effects?"

"It's been done before," I say.

"And Brezniski? He's willing to go along with all this?"

"Time will tell."

"You mean you haven't discussed it with him yet?"

"Not in so many words, Solly. Good God, I have to leave

some subjects untouched. Otherwise, come October, we'll have nothing to talk about but the weather."

"It's madness, Mr. President. How can you have a plan that hinges upon what the Soviets will do?"

"I think Alexi can be trusted," I say. "He owns a Lincoln Continental now, you know."

"But he also wants Alaska back."

"The SOB can suck on my pipeline."

"What about Ollie Graham? What's he got to say about all this?"

"I promised Mr. Clairol I'd ease up on the grays in the military issue for now. That and give him a ten percent increase in the defense budget. I might even let him wage a limited war somewhere. He tells me one decent war every decade is essential for our military fitness."

"What kind of answer is that?"

"Solly, relax. Ollie's part of the team. Diet Pepsi?" I offer a can of soda to Solomon, but he sneers and pushes it away.

"And Hodgetts. I suppose he loves the plan?"

"Have you been reading the warning labels on cigarette packages lately? Fleming and I are like that," I say, crossing my middle and index fingers.

"I don't know, Mr. President. It just seems so crazy."

"Crazy is what works these days, Solly." Good host that I am, I try once more to get Solomon to take a Diet Pepsi. Again he pushes it away. "You sure?"

Solomon grabs the Diet Pepsi out of my hand, pops it open and drinks the whole thing without taking a breath. "I don't suppose you can spare a few tanks in that 10% you promised Graham," he says.

"Come October, Solly. That's when it will all change. In the meantime, my friend, keep your eyes open for Diya Bakir."

"I never close them anymore," Solomon says.

On the horizon I can make out the Washington Monument. I check to make sure my seatbelt is securely fastened.

❧

My spaceship, I explained to Solomon Dayan, will be billed as an intergalactic Noah's Ark. In the event of a nuclear gunfight between the super powers, the ship will transport the leaders of all the peace-loving nations of the world to safety, to start anew. Besides their immediate families, each leader can select one couple to be their country's Adam and Eve in their new Eden, wherever it may be. Think of the possibilities, I tell Solomon, the opportunity to take a giant step up the human evolutionary ladder! But, take heed, we must select only the best of our species — the smartest, the strongest, the kindest. Go now, Solomon. Make your selections. The day of Armageddon draws near.

❧

It has been a long day. I am looking forward to a massage. When I get back to my suite, I shower to wash off the dust from the Nevada desert. Then Sheila and I have dinner in our private dining room. Neither one of us speaks, except when one of us needs the salt or the butter or another roll. We are not angry at one another. We are just tired. Sheila was up all last night with Sam; it was some sort of gastrointestinal invasion.

During dessert, I break the ice. "Sam okay now?"

"Better," says Sheila.

"She was asleep when I got back."

"She's been asleep most of the day."

"Poor kid."

"She's tough," says Sheila.

"Takes after her mother."

Sheila smiles. "So, how'd it go today?"

"How'd what go?" I say.

"Didn't you meet with Solomon Dayan?"

"Oh, that. Yes, I did. Good, I guess."

"You guess?"

"Well, he didn't exactly say he was going to behave."

"Ray was asking about you," Sheila says.

"Oh?"

"She thought you might be mad at her."

"Mad at her? Why on earth would I be mad at her?"

"She didn't say. It sounded to me like a father-daughter thing. I didn't want to get in the middle of it."

"I'll talk to her," I say. But by the time I get back to the suite after dinner, Ray is asleep. Her teddy bear is under her arm. I kiss them both.

&

At about ten o'clock I find myself standing in front of Marcy's apartment. The extra wine I had tonight makes me anxious for my next treatment. I tap gently on the door.

The door cracks open. The chain lock is still in place. "Oh, Mr. President, I didn't expect you," Marcy says.

"I'm sorry," I say. "I should've called first."

Marcy is wearing her uniform — dungarees, sweatshirt and tennis shoes. "Can you come back later?"

"I don't think so. It's been a long day. Can I come in for just a moment?"

"Well —"

I can hear someone moving about inside. "Company?" I say.

"Yes. Sort of," says Marcy.

"Oh. Look, I'm sorry to have bothered you. We'll do it again some other time."

A voice from inside says, "Where y'all keep the tonic water, hun?"

"Be right there," Marcy says. She turns back to me apologetically. "Gotta go." She gives me a peck on the cheek.

"No problem," I say. I grab the doorknob and close the door. As I walk away, I am thinking about two things. The first is that Sheila will wonder why I'm back so soon this time. The second is that I'm quite certain the voice I heard coming from inside Marcy's apartment belonged to Thomas "Bull" Dozier.

❧

The next night Marcy is free. But when I go to see her, I don't have on my mind what I usually have on my mind. At least I don't have on my mind what I usually have on my mind to the exclusion of everything else. "It was him last night, wasn't it?" I say.

"Him?"

"Bull Dozier." I am trying hard not to sound angry. Sounding hurt's okay, but not angry.

"Yes," Marcy says. "He just showed up at the door and introduced himself and said that he wanted a massage. I didn't know what else to do. It is my job, you know. Giving massages."

"I know," I say. "I know."

"He seemed nice enough."

"It's just a front."

"I'll know better the next time."

"What did he want?"

"A massage. I told you."

"That's all? He didn't ask you about anything else?"

"Well, he did ask if you ever came by for a massage."

"And you told him I did?"

"I didn't see any harm in it."

"Let's hope there isn't any."

"He seemed so nice though."

"That's how he sucks you in. That, and throwing his money around. I suppose he gave you a nice fat tip."

"No."

"Well, he will," I say. "You can count on it."

Marcy and I make love. It is quick, dry, abrasive. I think while it is happening that I am with Sheila.

~

The next morning at around 10:00, Woody slips quietly into a meeting I am having with the key members of the Department of Health and Human Services. James Rivera, the director of the Centers for Disease Control and Prevention, one of two Latinos I have appointed to key HHS positions, has been talking about a nascent health crisis involving a lethal AIDS-like virus that is apparently infecting only white men over fifty, predominantly from the Southern states. The disease, says Rivera, has been given the name WAIDS — white acquired immune deficiency syndrome. In all symptomatic respects — except for its highly discriminating nature and a bright red, band-shaped rash appearing around the neck — it mimics AIDS. The baffling thing about it is the way that it's transmitted. While this seems to be accomplished by exchanging bodily fluids or by sharing needles with an infected person, it is also done in as yet unknown ways, since many people, possibly a majority of the victims, who have neither exchanged bodily fluids nor shared needles with an infected person, have exhibited symptoms. That mystery aside, Rivera expressed serious doubts about the chances of the Goldberg administration winning funding to find a cure for this dreaded new menace, given the fact that medical research appropriations by Congress this fiscal year have already reached record levels.

"Jimmy, Jimmy, Jimmy," I say. "Did I hear you say this WAIDS thing is infecting only white men over fifty? Predominantly from the South?"

"That's right, Mr. President."

"And did I also hear you say that these men are gay?"

"No, sir, you did not. These men are all heterosexual."

"Predominantly Southern white heterosexual men over fifty, Jimmy?" I smile wryly.

"That's correct."

"Definitely no gays?"

"No sir. Not a single documented case."

"And you're worried about getting funding?"

Donna Carter, my FDA commissioner, an elegant black woman scooped out of the Maya Angelou mold, erudite but quick to laugh when confronted by emperors not wearing clothes, dissolves into hysteria. A chain reaction of guffaws and hoots and howls fills the room. Rivera's palomino complexion turns crimson. He fumbles with his pencil and smiles sheepishly. "I guess not, Mr. President."

As the laughter begins to subside, Woody puts his hand on my shoulder. "A moment, Mr. President."

"Excuse me for a minute," I say. I get up and exit the room, Woody in tow.

"What is it?" I say once we're alone.

"There's been an incident, Mr. President."

"The Iraqis again?"

"No. Here. In D.C. At the Air and Space Museum."

I can feel my heart begin to race. "Uncle Leo?"

Woody nods. "Yeah, Uncle Leo."

"Assemble the troops," I say.

THE SPIRIT OF UNCLE LEO

By the time I get to the National Air and Space Museum, nearly half an hour has elapsed. This isn't too bad, considering my movement is severely restricted these days by the perpetual leash that binds me to my ever-changing but always large and unwieldy entourage. My limo and the two behind it pull around to the Independence Avenue entrance of the building to avoid the crowd and tour buses blocking the Mall entrance. No doubt the Secret Service feels this maneuver will make us inconspicuous. It doesn't. As soon we step from the car, reporters descend on us like flies buzzing around a pile of shit. That "an incident" has occurred is frighteningly obvious.

As a wedge of Secret Service people hustles me into the museum and past the frozen-in-time exhibits, I have a terrible thought. I have never been here before. And I don't mean behind the scenes where I will end up; I have never been here, period. I have never seen the Mercury capsule, Friendship 7, which shuttled John Glenn into aeronautic immortality and political mediocrity. Or seen the first lunar roving vehicle to drive across the starkly beautiful face of the moon. I have never seen or touched a rock from the moon or walked through a Skylab space station. I haven't even seen the six iron used by Apollo 14 astronaut Captain Alan B. Shepard, Jr. to drive a golf ball 400 yards across the surface of the moon. Nor have I been to any other Smithsonian museum. I haven't seen Alexander Graham Bell's first telephone. I haven't seen Elias Howe's first sewing machine. Or Samuel Morse's first telegraph. Nor have I seen the desk at which Thomas Jefferson wrote the first version of the Declaration of Independence. Or the chair where Archie Bunker sat to watch TV. My God, I wonder. What kind of American am I? What kind of father am I? What kind of nephew am I? And what kind of political damage will I suffer if the Republicans ever find out about all this?

Eventually we come to a large glassed-in office. It is filled with somber men in dark suits. Some are standing. Others are seated atop steel desks, which are arranged in three even rows, stretching from one end of the room to the other. On either side of the doorway to the office is a uniformed cop. Also in the crowd are a few people wearing another type of uniform — one with which I am now intimately acquainted. It is the proud uniform of a Smithsonian guard.

I enter the office and the two dozen or so people there immediately stand and turn to face me. They all look as if their best friend has just died. I am thinking that one of my best friends really has. But while I am thinking this, I notice a thick cloud of smoke rising from behind the people huddled at the far end of the room. It is the smoke of cheap cigars, the kind Uncle Leo smokes.

"Uncle Leo!" I shout. "You're alive!"

Uncle Leo stands up and arthritically slices his way through the crowd toward me. "Of course I'm alive," says Uncle Leo.

Another guard intercepts us. "Baker, sir," he says, extending his hand to me. "David Baker. I'm the one who talked to your chief of staff."

"You?" I say angrily. "For chrissake, you idiot, you scared us half to death. I thought Uncle Leo here was —"

"He didn't let me finish, sir," Baker says.

One of the suits jumps in. "Sgt. Hall, Mr. President. D.C. Police."

"What the hell's happening here, Hall?" Suddenly I feel like I've been transformed into an alliterative fool, into a nattering nabob of nonsense, into Spiro Agnew.

"Your uncle has attacked a child," says Hall. "Bit him right on the ankle."

"What?" I say.

Uncle Leo eyes fill with watered-down venom. "The little meshuggeneh!" he says. "He was trying to yank one of the controls off the Spirit of St. Louis."

"How is that possible? I thought the damn plane was hanging from the ceiling."

"Not for over a year, Ronnie," says Uncle Leo. It seems that upon the 75th anniversary of the Amelia Earhart's disappearance in 2012, a year when I was preoccupied with other things, several women's groups demanded that Earhart's Vega, the plane in which she became the first woman to fly solo across the Atlantic, switch places with the Spirit of St. Louis, thus making Lindbergh's plane more readily available for vandalism.

"The mother has filed an official complaint."

"Uncle Leo, Uncle Leo," I say. "What am I going to do with you?"

"Is there something that has to be done?" Uncle Leo asks.

"We have a witness, Mr. President, to corroborate the mother's story," says Sgt. Hall.

"Uncle Leo, Uncle Leo," I say, shaking my head. Uncle Leo's tail now drops between his legs. "Does he have to go to the station?" I ask Sgt. Hall.

"I'm afraid so," says the cop.

"You'll have to go with Sgt. Hall, Uncle Leo," I say. "I'll send someone for you later."

As Uncle Leo is led away, he stops momentarily and turns back to me. His cigar has gone out, but he's still clenching it between his teeth. "Do you s'pose they'll mind if I keep the uniform?" Uncle Leo asks me.

❧

The next morning the news of the biting incident hits the streets. Not since Jimmy Carter was in the Ridgeley — I mean, in the White House — has a member of the President's family caused such a furor. The press has overwhelmingly sided with the eight-year-old boy and his mother. In fact, the only paper that took an opposite point of view was, ironically, the *Herald*, from my home state. The *Herald* had never supported me or my family before, but this time they had nothing but praise for the way Uncle Leo "gallantly protected, without fear of reprisal or repercussion, one of our most sacred national icons." The front-page article, which bore the huge headline, PREZ UNK TAKES CHUNK OUT OF PUNK, went on to say that Uncle Leo should be handed a medal instead of being slapped with a fine. I suppose the sad truth of it all is that, had Uncle Leo known what an anti-Semite Charles Lindbergh was, he would probably have given the child a sledgehammer and told him to club the damn old plane to death.

∽

One theory gaining momentum regarding the spread of the WAIDS virus is that it is also transmitted during sexual intercourse between humans and farm animals. To date there are at least a dozen cases where such acts have been conclusively determined to be the only possible means of viral transfer. In response to this sad news, a bipartisan coalition of Southern congressmen, headed up by my good friend Fleming Hodgetts, has won funding for an aggressive educational ad campaign advising Southern white males to use condoms when engaging in such activities. Unfortunately, while the message seems to be getting through to the target audience, it is apparently having virtually no impact since most of these men believe that wearing a condom is a sin.

∽

Uncle Leo could not be released on his own recognizance. Somehow this did not surprise me. How could the courts give special treatment to a member of the First Family? How would it look? Especially in the wake of all the charges of nepotism leveled against me when I secured Uncle Leo his post at the Air and Space Museum in the first place. (JFK didn't get such slanderous treatment, even when he made brother Bobby his attorney general. How times have changed!) Clearly, my supporters and critics would view any favoritism on the court's part very dimly. It makes a mockery of justice, they would say. They would say Uncle Leo has had his dance; now he must pay the piper. Still, I think setting the bail at one hundred thousand dollars was a bit excessive, though, as I reflect, it could have been a lot worse. Had Uncle Leo been a dog, I would surely have been ordered to put him to sleep.

Woody says the report from the hospital is not good. Uncle Leo's teeth broke the boy's skin. As a precaution, the boy was given a tetanus shot. Fortunately, no stitches were required to close the wound. If that had been the case, I suspect Uncle Leo would be dangling from the branch of a cherry tree by now. Or nailed to a giant wooden menorah.

The boy's mother has not reacted well to the incident. Apparently, she keeps screaming hysterically, "Animal! ANIMAL!" She has refused tranquilizers. "Oh, no you don't," she was reported to have said. "You're not going to fuck with my head! I'm staying alert for this." Sgt. Hall had told me that, after the woman learned who Uncle Leo was, she demanded to see me on the spot, which was the reason I was so hastily summoned to the museum. The arrival of an ambulance to take her son to the hospital moments before I arrived was the only thing that prevented an ugly scene. Sometimes there are advantages to traveling around in a vehicle that has the maneuverability of an oil tanker.

Be that as it may, at Phil Hurley's insistence, which I in no way oppose, I have asked Woody to get the woman on the phone. I am under what could well be the mistaken belief that I can reason with her. When Woody finally gets the woman on the line, he says, "Please hold for the president, Mrs. Kent."

Woody hands me the phone as if he were passing me a container of nitroglycerin. "Mrs. Kent, hello. This is Ron Goldberg."

"I know who you are," says Mrs. Kent. "And, by the way, I voted for Sanders." Her voice is husky and raspy and breathless. I picture her as an overweight smoker. I hope she is saving her coupons.

"Look, I know how upset you must be," I say.

"Upset doesn't begin to describe how I feel, Ron," she says.

I find her informality with me encouraging. "I'm not trying to trivialize what happened, Mrs. Kent. I can assure you of that."

"It's a wee bit late for assurances," says Mrs. Kent.

"I certainly hope not," I say. "You have to understand, Mrs. Kent, my Uncle Leo meant no harm." Even I realize as I say this how ludicrous it must sound. Of course he meant harm — he bit the little twerp in cold blood!

"No harm! NO HARM!"

"I guess what I mean is, he didn't plan to bite your child. He just lost his head."

"An animal like that should not be around children. Not around people, period! It's just the sort thing I'd expect from you people."

"You people?"

"Yeah, you know."

I do not pursue it. "Look, Mrs. Kent, he's a very old man," I say. "I hope you can find it in your heart to forgive him."

"Forgive him! FORGIVE HIM! Why on earth should I do that?"

"No one gets any pleasure from this sort of thing," I say. "There are only victims."

"How much?" says Mrs. Kent.

"Excuse me?" I say.

"That's what this is all about, isn't it? Paying me off, so I'll drop the charges. So I'll stop talking to the press."

"I wouldn't say, 'paying off'," I say. "Making a settlement would be more accurate."

"So like I said, how much?"

"I haven't really thought about it," I say.

"C'mon, Ron, you're the goddamn president. You expect me to believe you don't have a figure in mind?"

"Well...how's ten thousand sound, then?" I say. I have to be cautious. It's coming out of my own pocket this time.

"A little low," says Mrs. Kent.

"Fifteen?"

"I was thinking more like fifty."

"Twenty-five," I say.

"Fifty. Take it or leave it. That's my final offer."

"Well, then, fifty it is," I say. My only hope is that Alexi Brezniski won't be so intransigent.

❧

Much to my surprise, a Gallup Poll published in the *Post* two days later reveals that the great majority of Americans believe that Uncle Leo acted properly and appropriately and well within his authority as a Smithsonian guard. Gallup concludes that the American public is, by and large, fed up with the permissiveness so pervasive today. The consensus seems to be that our children need more discipline and, if the situation dictates, we must confront them with a tempered yet convincing show of force. Specifically, here is what the poll showed:

86%	Favored the biting of the child
8%	Opposed the biting
4%	Favored spanking
*%	Favored taking TV out of the child's room
*%	Favored taking away the child's cell phone
*%	Favored taking away the child's laptop

*% Favored taking away the child's home entertainment center
*% Favored limiting the hours the child plays home video games to four hours per day
*% Favored public caning

(*Contains less than 1% of these opinions.)

Had I known all this before I entered negotiations with the obdurate Mrs. Kent, the result might have been quite different. Thank God for the Arizona Project!

              ∾

I am worried about Uncle Leo. He has not been the same since he was hauled off to jail. He told me he was treated like a common criminal. He was frisked. He was fingerprinted. He had a mug shot taken. The whole megillah. Before they put him in a cell, they took away his shoelaces and his belt.

For nearly eight hours he was confined to his cell, where his only roommate was a middle-aged pickpocket. He spent most of that time bunched up in a corner, drinking weak coffee, and avoiding conversation. For lunch he was given only a sandwich — a single slice of bologna, slightly dry around the edges, on white bread, no mustard. For dinner he was given soup; he thought it might be vegetable. (He gave it to the pickpocket, so he couldn't be certain.) In the back of the cell, there was a sink. There was no soap or towel, and the water ran cold and orange from both faucets. Against one wall was a bucket where Uncle Leo and his roommate could urinate. During his incarceration, Uncle Leo urinated five times. The pickpocket urinated twice. The pickpocket also used the sink once for a bowel movement. If Uncle Leo was ever in danger of turning to a life of crime, he was now cured.

I tried to cheer up Uncle Leo as best I could, but nothing seemed to work.

∽

"They're not going to fire you," I say to Uncle Leo regarding his employment at the National Air and Space Museum. "I fixed it for you."

"You're sure?" says Uncle Leo. His joy is childlike – bewitched, singsong, trusting. His bloodshot watery eyes twinkle like puddles in the moonlight.

"Positive," I say.

"Ronnie, you're amazing. Truly amazing," says Uncle Leo.

"There is one catch, though," I say. "They won't let you have your old job back."

Uncle Leo frowns and says, "I knew it."

"It's not that bad," I say. "You just won't be on the front lines anymore."

"Yeah, so I won't be tempted to bite anyone," says Uncle Leo. "Believe me, Ronnie, he didn't taste all that good."

"C'mon. What say, Unk?"

"I'll have to think about it," says Uncle Leo. But it is quite apparent to me that he has already made up his mind.

TELL ME WHERE IT HURTS

18

I have an appointment today with my urologist. I do not want to go. When I was young, I felt that way about going to Hebrew school, but at Hebrew school they didn't shove a cystoscope up my penis, so going to my urologist is something to look forward to even less. I have asked Sheila to accompany me, because I want her to hear firsthand about the importance of sexual activity to my well peeing. Frankly, this liaison with Marcy Gillis worries me, although what man my age wouldn't love to have the body of a twenty-five-year-old? Sooner or later, someone is going to find out that I am not really seeing her to have my back and neck rubbed. It is my darkest fear that the person most likely to debunk me is Bull Dozier. He's already hot on my trail, and God knows how much Marcy has already told him, her denials aside. It would be much easier if Sheila would make her precious vagina periodically available to my penis, a vacancy for this weary traveler. But whoever said life had to be easy? Sheila has declined to join me. "I think you have the situation well in hand," she said.

～

After I get dressed, the urologist says, "Everybody's got a target organ, Mr. President. For me, it's my nose. I get stressed out, my sinuses clog up like the Lincoln Tunnel at rush hour. I can't breathe, headache. Awful. For you, it's your prostate."

"You're telling me I picked the place I wanted my pain to go, and that's the spot I picked!"

"Stress is going to rear its ugly head somewhere."

"I'd much rather have a sinus problem," I say.

"You have to be less preoccupied. That, and have regular sex."

"Otherwise, I'm stuck with this?"

"Well, you could always have an operation," says the urologist. "But I'm against it. There's no real need for it at your age. No significant enlargement. Besides, you have it, and you can forget about intercourse after that."

"Jesus," I say. "I can do without that. Do without the operation I mean. If that's what it entails."

"Let's just see how things progress over the next few months," says the urologist. "You can always change your mind later."

"Thanks," I say, and then I shake the doctor's hand. On the way back to the Ridgeley, we pass in front of the Washington Monument. I wonder, I am ashamed to say, what Marcy Gillis would feel like having that between her legs.

～

I remember Sheila told me that something is bugging Ray. When I get back to the Ridgeley, it is about three o'clock. Ray apparently beat me back. She has left her schoolbooks on the coffee table in the living room. I call out to her, but she doesn't answer. I go to her room and there, lying on the bed, her hands folded behind her head, is Ray. She is staring at the ceiling. "Hi, hun," I say. "How'd it go today?"

"All right," says Ray.

"Anything special happen?"

"No."

Good communicators will always tell you never to ask questions that can be answered with one word. I suspect that a majority of these good communicators do not have children. "Your mom said you had something on your mind. You want to talk about it?"

"I don't know. Maybe."

"I'll listen." I go to the bed and sit down. I put my hand on Ray's knee. Her eyes are teary.

"It's nothing," says Ray.

"So let's talk about nothing then," I say.

"It's stupid," says Ray.

It is clear to me that she's hoping that I will tell her that no problem of hers, especially this one, could be stupid. "No problems are stupid," I say. "What's stupid is how we handle them sometimes."

"I can't believe them!" Ray blurts out.

"Can't believe who?"

"Them," she says. "This dumb magazine." Ray has a magazine facedown on her night table. She grabs it and hands it to me.

"*Faces*?" I say. "What's wrong with *Faces*?" But I'm afraid I already know. Ashley Jones had slipped me a copy of the most recent issue a few days ago, saying, "Here's your copy of '*FECES*', Mr. President." What's more, she had found out two months ago that they were going to do a piece on Ray. I had forgotten to warn my daughter.

"What's wrong is this." Ray points to one of the lead stories featured on the cover. It says, RED ROSES FOR A BLUE LADY? Next to the title are two small photos. One shows Ray, her face wearing a frown. The other shows Raskolnikov Brezniski, the son of the Russian president, holding a bouquet of roses. I suspect the roses are the result of some very good retouching.

"Hmmm, what's this all about?" I say. I start thumbing through the magazine, trying to find the article. I am pretty good at feigning surprise and thick-headedness, having had years of practice, publicly and privately.

"Don't bother," says Ray.

I locate the article and begin reading anyway. The gist of it is that everyone in the world is wondering if romance will bloom between thirteen-year-old Ray and sixteen-year-old Raskolnikov when the boy accompanies his father to the fall summit. "A mishegoss," I say.

"Bullshit is what it is," says Ray.

"Rachel!"

"Well, it is."

"That may be, but I don't like to hear you talk that way."

"You talk that way to Mom."

She's got you there, Mr. President. "That's different. We're adults."

"Oh" says Ray. "It's like sex. When I'm an adult, it'll be okay."

Only between two consenting species, I think. "Just don't let your mother hear you talk like that," I say. "It would upset her."

"Bullshit," says Ray. "I learned it from her."

"Look, Ray, you just have to try to get used to this sort of nonsense. Like it or not, you're a public figure now."

"I don't like it," says Ray.

"So in a few years, you can go back to being a private citizen. But for now, there's nothing you can do about it."

"He only likes classical music. Yuck."

"Who?"

"Him. Raskolni-cough, cough." Rays coughs into her hand.

"It says that in here?"

"Yeah."

"It says you're going to fall in love with him, too. Is that true?"

Ray smirks. "He doesn't even wear jeans."

"That's in here, too?"

"Yeah," says Ray. She is staring at the ceiling again. Her arms are folded across her chest.

"Honey, as far as I'm concerned, you don't even have to like him. All I ask is that you be polite."

Ray sighs. "I guess I could do that."

"Besides, if something like this ever really happened, Woody would be crushed."

"Woody? What's Woody got to do with it?"

Could it be I have made up Ray's crush on Woody as a way of preparing myself for the real and inevitable betrayal that every daughter visits upon her father? "Never mind," I say. I lean over and kiss Ray on the forehead, pleased to know that, at this moment at least, I am still the most important man in her life.

~

The next morning Tim Green comes to see me. He looks a bit under the weather, but Tim frequently looks that way, so I think nothing of it. Tim is not dressed in his lobbyist attire. He is wearing chino pants and a light blue dress shirt, brown penny loafers, no socks, no pennies. The pants are somewhat worn at the knees. The shirt is torn at one elbow and frayed at both cuffs. Tim is chewing gum. I estimate that he has at least three pieces in his mouth. The exaggerated churning of his jaw makes him look like a cow. He better not plan any trips down south until he can bring this new habit under control.

"What's this?" I say. "Day off?"

"The whole week," says Tim. "Tracking down Cookie Dunn's a full-time job."

"For chrissake," I say. "You don't have to do that."

"I know how badly you want to find her," says Tim.

"Shows, huh?"

"Yeah, it shows," says Tim. He sits down on the chair to the left of my desk. I sit down on top of my desk, facing him.

"Well?" I say.

"Well," says Tim. "I've got some good news and some bad news. The good news is, Cookie's divorced again. A free woman."

"No such thing as a free woman," I say. "What's the bad news?"

"She split, left town. Neighbors said she was a wreck over the divorce. I guess it got pretty ugly. Lots of big league screaming, dishes flying, doors slamming. They said she and the kids went to stay with her sister in Chicago."

"Got the address?"

"Not yet. But I can get it from her parents. Turns out they're finally back from some Elderhostel jaunt to Antarctica."

"Do it then," I say.

"Ronnie, would I let you down?" Tim takes the wad of gum from his mouth and pulls a Kleenex out of his shirt pocket. He presses the gum into the tissue and then surveys the top of my desk. "Ashtray?"

"Got rid of 'em," I say. "They were mostly for you. Here, gimme that." I extend a hand toward Tim and he obediently places the tissue-clad gumball in my palm. I lean back and throw it in the wastebasket under my desk.

"Thanks, Dad," says Tim.

"I don't know, Tim," I say. "I don't know what it is. But I really need to see that woman. My marriage to Sheila is — I don't know. Anyway I'm just not comfortable fooling around. I'm too old for it."

"So what'd you have in mind with Cookie?"

"I don't know. Maybe something will be there. Hell, there never was. Not really. But maybe now will be different. It isn't fooling around when two people genuinely care for one another, is it?"

"Nice rationalization."

"Thank you. I thought so, too. So?"

"Ronnie, relax. I promise you I'll find her. And when I do, I'll bring her here."

"Thanks, old friend," I say.

Tim and I have breakfast in my private dining room. Tim has the cholesterol special — eggs, bacon, toast and butter, washed down by several cups of black coffee. Then he has seconds on the eggs. All I can eat is an English muffin. Since Tim has quit smoking, he has gone back to his old eating habits. He eats enough food to satisfy a man twice his size. Sooner or later, I think it will catch up with him and Tim will be as big as a pregnant elephant. That he isn't already attests to his incredible metabolism.

∾

Later that afternoon, I learn that Tim Green has been

in an accident on the New Jersey Turnpike. A tractor-trailer truck wiped out his Austin Healey 3000 from behind. The hospital maintains that if Tim were not double jointed, he would have broken every bone in his body, instead of the dozen or so that he did break. They tell me he'll survive, with no permanent damage, but he could be in the hospital for a month. God forgive my weak flesh, but all I can think about is that this means one more month without Cookie Dunn.

❧

After relating to Bernie Cohen that I was not very pleased with my visit to the urologist, he recommended that I go to see an acupuncturist. Bernie is a firm believer in alternative medicine. The acupuncturist's name was Dr. Chan. He was born in Hong Kong, and trained in both Eastern and Western medicine. He spoke English like he had lived in the U.S. all his life, which was only half true.

Dr. Chan put needles in my legs, feet, wrists, head, mouth and ears. Whenever he hit a spot that gave me a little jolt, he said, "Ah, good, good." All the points he needled allegedly corresponded to my prostate and perineum. He said the points in the ear, which I was surprised to learn were mapped by the French, were particularly effective. So, in order to prolong the effect of the treatment, Dr. Chan recommended putting four tiny needles in my ears, which I was to remove in three days. He also taped one tiny metal ball in each ear on top of a key pressure point. Several times a day I am to apply pressure to these balls to help control my pain. I am somewhat concerned, what with all I have on my mind these days, that I will forget to do what Dr. Chan has asked me to do. To remedy this situation, I have written myself a note: *Remove pins on Sunday. Squeeze balls gently every few hours.*

❧

The menorah burnings, which had stopped for a couple of months, have started up again. Sam saw one the other day in the park across from the Ridgeley and asked me why someone would burn something that looked like a menorah, particularly with Chanukah so far away. I told her that it wasn't a menorah at all, but a large wooden rake, and that the people who were burning it were protesting the use of grass-catchers by the Ridgeley maintenance crew. I told her the people were laid-off employees of a large rake manufacturer, and that they held me directly responsible for their predicament. What did Sam have to say about my explanation?

"I still think it looked like a menorah," she said.

❧

It is now around nine in the evening. Sheila and I have had an early dinner with Bull Dozier and his wife Philly, who, Bull is fond of saying, is named after the cream cheese, not the philodendron, despite the fact her sisters are named Petunia and Rose. Bull drank heavily and, thus fueled, told off-color jokes throughout the whole meal, scarcely letting anyone get a word in edgewise. Philly Dozier is a round woman, about medium height, with short, curly brown hair, and a face as flat as Kansas. I like Philly a lot. She's soft-spoken and good-natured and never has a bad word to say about anyone, which is neat trick in this town of cutthroats and bandits. Because she has stayed married to Bull for more than twenty-five years, I figure Bull can't be all that bad.

I kiss Sheila good night. She is already in her nightgown and in bed. She is reading a romance novel called *Passion On The Potomac*, but I can tell she will not be able to do that for very long. She is yawning profusely. I tell Sheila I have some work to do in my office. "Don't wait up for me," I say, knowing full well there isn't one chance in a million that she would.

"Don't be too late," she says. "You're driving yourself too hard."

It is true that I've only been getting by on three or four hours of sleep. "I'm just doing what I have to do," I say. Before I leave, I look in on Sam and Ray. They have separate bedrooms; Ray has a double bed and Sam has two twins. Tonight Ray is sleeping in one of Sam's twins, something she hardly ever does. Ray has her teddy bear in an affectionate headlock.

When I kiss my daughters good night, only Sam wakes up. "What time is it?" she says.

"It's late," I say. "Nearly ten. Go back to sleep, sweet-heart." Sam rolls over and instantly falls back to sleep. She won't remember that we spoke and will laugh when I tell her that we did. I check my watch as I leave. Actually it's about 9:15. Time to head down the hall for some therapeutic hanky panky.

⌒

In my diary I sometimes call Marcy Gillis Dr. Masseuse. During lovemaking, I often call her Cookie. I am keeping a diary so that when my term in the Ridgeley is over, I can write a book about it. The book will be different from the one I am writing now, because by then I will have a his-torical perspective. Right now I have no perspective at all. And whenever I try to stand back for a better look at things, things only get blurrier.

⌒

I have knocked on Marcy's door three times. No answer. Granted, I did not tell her exactly when I would be coming, but I did say it would be between nine and ten. It is now 9:25. I have the fidgets. I am a pendulum swinging from fear to anger, anger to fear, fear to anger. I knock once more and then, without waiting any longer, I turn and head down the hall. In a few minutes, I find myself sitting at my desk. I do not know how I got here. I had thought the feeling of levitation that had characterized the day of my inauguration and its immediate aftermath were over.

I pick up the phone and dial Marcy's number. I hang up before it rings twice. I put the phone down and pick it up again immediately. I dial Marcy's number quickly, poking angrily at the keys. This time I let it ring a dozen times or so. No answer. I hang up, dropping the phone onto its cradle like an airplane releasing a bomb. The bitch. She's got a lot of nerve. This isn't some ordinary John she's standing up. It's the President of the United States of America! But then I think, big deal. If I'm so great, what the hell am I doing in the Ridgeley?

First anger. Now self-deprecation. What next? Panic, that's what. I begin to think that something has happened, that Marcy has been kidnapped by the FBI and, at this very moment, is being interrogated under a beam of harsh light by Thomas Dozier himself. What exactly do you do for the president, Miss Gillis? Massage his back, you say? Is that all? You don't do any more than that? On the contrary, young lady, I think you know exactly what I mean. I think you also should know that if you do not cooperate fully with this investigation, you will be in very serious trouble indeed. What's that? You say you'll talk? A wise decision, Miss Gillis. Very wise indeed.

Before I leave my office, I reach for the wall switch by the door to turn off the light, but when I flip the switch, the light goes on, not off. Until then, I did not realize that I had been sitting in the dark.

A Ridgeley guard passes me in the hallway. "Good evening, Mr. President," he says. He looks about sixteen years old — neatly cropped hair, well scrubbed, Midwestern. No dirt under those nails, no sir. His black shoes are shined to a deep, blinding gloss.

"Good evening, son," I say.

It is now half past ten. I decide to knock on Marcy's door once more. This time the door opens immediately. "Hi," says Marcy. "Where've you been? I thought you'd be here an hour ago."

"I was," I say. "Knocked three hundred and one times, too."

"Oh, dear," says Marcy. She smiles apologetically. "I must've been in the shower. Sorry."

Some shower, I'm thinking. We are standing in the middle of the living room, Marcy in her robe, I in my gray suit. "No harm done," I say. I take a Kleenex from my pocket and wipe my brow.

∾

As it turns out, Marcy was with Bull Dozier from nine to ten. He stopped by to drop off some of her old movies that he had come across, and to discuss a business arrangement. In exchange for any information leading to the humiliation of the president, Marcy would receive $100,000 annually, Black & Blue Cross Master Health Plus, dental and disability insurance, $500,000 in term life insurance, a new car, an expense account, a lifetime membership to the Body Beautique Health Spa, plus the assurance that her movies would not be redistributed. Marcy's salary as my masseuse

— technically, she's my "physical therapist" — is $65,000 per year and while her parents and thousands of horny and inebriated, prenuptial bachelors have already seen her films, she is a little nervous over the possibility of new and broader exposure. I share her feelings. The only person I know who would benefit from the re-release of these films is Bull Dozier.

"The way it stands, he can't prove a thing about us," I say. "And you can always deny it's you in those films." Most of the time you can only see Marcy's mouth, breasts or vagina. At least that's what she told me. I have never seen the films myself. Nor do I want to. Why would I? I have the real McCoy.

"He seems so determined though," says Marcy. "I'm afraid."

"He's a buffoon," I say. "A gefilte fisherman."

"A what?"

"It's a long story," I say. And rather than tell it, Marcy and I make love. It is as good as it ever has been. My fantasy machine was in high gear. Oh, Cookie, Cookie, Cookie starts with C.

I leave around midnight. Sheila is asleep when I get back, as I knew she would be. I get undressed and climb into bed. I do not even brush my teeth and, contrary to what my mother always told me, my teeth do not fall out.

Mercifully, I sleep like a rock. I have no dreams, not even the fragment of one. In the morning I feel refreshed, rejuvenated. My appetite has returned from its hiatus. For breakfast, I eat eggs, bacon and an English muffin. I feel fueled and ready to go.

When I get to my office, I find a brown envelope on my desk. I am apprehensive about what might be inside, but a childish anticipation, a bubbly sense of discovery, overtakes me. I quickly rip open the envelope. Inside is a DVD. There is a note attached to it. The note, large block letters written with a thick felt tip pen, says only this: ENJOY! It is signed by Bull Dozier. I put the DVD in my player, and push 'play'.

∽

Bull's first venture into the dark and vulgar side of the world of Paul Finkelstein was a dandy. I don't know how he did it, but I guess I'm not all that surprised that he did. I should have suspected that painting in Marcy's bedroom, considering that it was, she told me, a gift from Bull. The Trojan painting, that's what it turned out to be, a realistic portrait of a man in his twenties taking a photograph, presumably of the unseen painter, with a Nikon camera. I never stopped to think that the painted lens might actually be the real lens of a video camera, operated by someone on the other side of decency — that is, behind the wall to the right of the bed in which Marcy and I have made contorted, moaning, slippery love. Marcy, who likes being on top, is mostly a head of hair, undulating breasts, bobbing ass. But my profile — yes, the one to which the cameras are always kindest! — is unmistakable, even in dim light. My expression for most of the ten-minute film was carved with ecstasy, but my mood now has sunk to a new low. It's one thing to be outwitted by a nemesis that in some odd way you respect. But to be outwitted by the likes of Bull Dozier, it's unthinkable!

As I sit here in my office, with the taste of recycled breakfast on my tongue, I wonder when the other shoe will drop. My pain is so intense I have to squeeze my balls.

∽

At 10:30, Woody Stone and Ashley Jones enter my office. Woody's forehead and upper lip are beaded with sweat. He does not do well in the summer heat. But then, in Washington, who does? Ashley, apparently. As always, she looks as cool as a cucumber.

"He's gone," Woody says. He is visibly upset.

"Who?" I say.

"Uncle Leo," Ashley clarifies.

"Uncle Leo? What do you mean gone?" My heart begins to pound. For a moment I picture Uncle Leo dead and I wonder if those irresponsible blockheads at the police station finally gave him his shoelaces back.

"Cleared out," says Woody. "Here, he left this. It's for you." Woody hands me a short note scrawled by Uncle Leo's shaky hand on a sheet of Ridgeley stationery.

I read the note aloud. "Ronnie: I know you meant well. But, let's face it, Ronnie, Hitler meant well too, didn't he? I'll be in New York, if you want me. Love, Uncle Leo." Paper clipped to the note is a dry cleaning receipt for one Smithsonian uniform.

"I don't get it," I say. "How could this happen? How could he sneak out of here without anyone noticing?"

"We're still investigating it," says Ashley.

"Nobody seems to know for sure," says Woody.

"But one of the busboys claims someone took his uniform, " Ashley adds.

"Uncle Leo and his goddamn uniforms!" I say. I crumple up Uncle Leo's note and toss it in the wastebasket. Then I start to laugh hysterically.

"What's so funny?" Woody asks. I can see that he desperately wants to laugh, too, but he's afraid to do it without just cause.

I shake my head. "Uncle Leo and his goddamn uniforms."

Woody still cannot manage a laugh. Neither can the ever-cool Ashley, who grabs my hand and holds on tight.

SMILE, YOU'RE ON CANDID CAMERA

Wednesday, August 21, 2013. A week and a day have passed since Bull Dozier dropped the DVD of Marcy and me on my desk. It is also a week and a day since Uncle Leo surreptitiously departed from the Ridgeley, dressed, presumably, as a busboy. I have not yet heard again from either one of them, but at least Uncle Leo's name has not yet appeared in the obituary section of the *Times*. I do not expect to hear from Uncle Leo any time soon.

I call Woody and tell him to come to my office. It took me nearly an hour to track him down. It turned out he was getting a massage. I could be wrong, but it seems as if Woody is getting a lot of massages lately. Either he's very tense, or he has something cooking with Dr. Masseuse. Marcy has said nothing to me about Woody's visits and this, as I reflect, makes me more suspicious. It's not that I feel Woody is betraying me in some way. It's just that I think that two people who know each other as well as Woody and I do should not be dipping their pens in the same inkwell.

"I want you to send someone to New York to check up on Uncle Leo," I say to Woody.

"Who?" Woody says.

"You want names from me? I don't know names. Just have Mancini pick two of his best people and put them on it ASAP!"

"The taxpayers won't be happy about this. Neither will Mancini, for that matter."

"Fuck Mancini. And the taxpayers won't know. That's what I have you and Ashley for," I say. "Besides, Uncle Leo has become something of a cult hero since this biting thing. Rosalee says he gets a stack of fan mail every day. A bunch of loony tunes have even started an organization to promote the values that Uncle Leo stands for. What a great country this is." The group formed to spread the gospel according to Uncle Leo is called the New Order of Citizens Rallying Against Permissiveness (NO CRAP). Uncle Leo — and I suspect he doesn't know it yet — is NO CRAP's honorary chairperson.

Woody relents. "Okay, I'll take care of it," he says.

"Something wrong, Woody?"

"No. Why?"

"You seem a little irritated."

"I'm not irritated, damn it," says Woody. "I said I'd take care of it."

Woody is like a son to me, so I forgive him his minor outbursts. He has them so infrequently. "So you did," I say. "Thanks. I'll sleep better knowing Uncle Leo is okay."

Woody leaves. A moment later my phone rings. It is Bull Dozier.

~

"One more week," says Bull. "If I don't get what I want by then, I take this DVD to your wife."

My first thought is, go ahead. My marriage probably isn't worth saving anyway. But then I think, if I go through an ugly divorce now, I can kiss the White House goodbye forever. Granted, the election is three years away and, as Jack Frost and Ashley Jones both like to remind me, American voters have short memories. But the other side of that equation is the Republicans. And their memory, appropriately enough, is like that of an elephant. "All right, all right," I say. What Bull wants is the real story behind the Arizona Project. "Come to my office in a week. We'll talk about it then."

"No funny business, Mr. President," says Bull.

"No funny business," I say. "Goodbye, Bull."

~

The next day the Arizona Project makes front page news. The article claims that the President of the United States is engaged in unsanctioned, and possibly illegal, activities that may involve a "strategic defense system," and not, as previously reported, a landfill. At several points in the article, the vice president is quoted. "This is nothing so innocuous as a landfill," said the veep. "We have every reason to believe that the president's secret project poses a real and deliberate threat to national security." When asked to elaborate, or to reveal the source of his information, Bull declined. "I have been out of the loop. I have not been privy to the intimate functions of this clandestine operation. I can assure you, if I had been, I would have come forward much sooner than this." As to when the veep might have evidence of a more incriminating nature, he said, "I am presently leveraging what information I do have to secure further details of the project. In a week, I should know more."

What Bull neglected to say was that this "leveraging" of information was blackmail. But that aside, he has started the water in the pot boiling. The question now is, can I keep a lid on it for another two months?

~

New revelations about the Arizona Project aside, Jack Frost has come to me with a surprising bit of information. "Good news, Mr. President. I don't think we have to worry about that landfill thing hurting us anymore," he says.

"We don't?" I say. "What about all those environmentalists out there who were ready to crucify me?"

Frost, deadpan, looks me in the eye. "Mr. President, considering all the noise the American people are making in favor of using the Grand Canyon for a landfill, I wouldn't give the tree lovers another thought."

"What?"

"68% of the people say, "Do it." Especially the city people. Hell, they're choking in waste. They want us to start filling that sucker up now."

"What about Congress?"

Frost guffaws. "Are you kidding? The American public says 'jump,' they all ask 'how high?' Hodgetts is already drafting a bill to put your plan into action. He says the RGNP is already ten times what it was just five years ago and we need to act pronto."

"RGNP?"

"Really Gross National Product. I think Fleming made that one up himself."

"Clever bastard."

"There will come a day, Mr. President," says Frost, "when you'll wish you'd thought of it." He is dead serious.

"It'll be a cold day in hell, Jack." I wonder if Bert French owns a gun. I hope not.

∾

Ashley Jones has fielded calls from the *Times* and the *Post* and all the major news services. To each one she has denied the existence of any secret project, and went on record calling Bull Dozier "an outright liar, trying to seize the office he always thought was rightfully his, but never had the guts or the ability to win legitimately." Will the president be demanding the veep's resignation? "That's for the president to answer," said Ashley, inadvertently creating a need for me to hold an immediate press conference. "But I suspect, if I know the president at all, that he will regard the matter as a family squabble." Ashley went on to say that the press would be wise to question the credibility of a man who would spend an afternoon attempting to catch a gefilte fish.

A press conference in the Ridgeley has been scheduled for eight this evening. Everyone who has been acquainted with the Arizona Project has taken the time to call me and wish me well and to tell me, in no uncertain terms, what a blockhead I am for allowing Bull Dozier to jeopardize the operation. Fleming Hodgetts was probably the angriest of all, cursing about this and that, not even taking the time to thank me for the latest opportunity I have given him to be adored by the public. How could I be so careless as to let an idiot like Bull Dozier discover even a hint of what we've been up to? I don't know, Fleming, I don't know. A lot of people are involved in this thing. That's a lot of chances for a leak. Bull has his goons out everywhere. They could have gotten to someone. And speaking of leaks, when I went to the bathroom a few minutes ago, it hurt like hell. Still does. Maybe I should have that damn operation, end my pain once and for all, give up sex, become a Republican.

Ashley has instructed me to wear one of my three navy blue pinstriped suits to the press conference. She wants me to look as presidential as possible, to rise as far above rumor and innuendo as I can. She tells me that the town is buzzing about the *Post* story. Not since the early 70s has the word "cover-up" been bandied about so much. In the hour before I head for the Ridgeley lobby for my exoneration or my execution, I have to urinate three times. The third time hardly anything came out at all, but when I was shaking myself, a drop of urine spotted my pants. I had to hide in the bathroom for a couple of minutes while it dried. "Everything all right in there?" Sheila says.

"Yeah, everything's fine," I say. "I'm just wetting my pants."

"Oh, for Pete's sake, Ron, you're making such a big deal about this. Everyone knows what a jerk Bull Dozier is."

"Even the village idiot must have his day," I say.

The press corps stands to greet me when I arrive at the Ridgeley lobby. Everyone seems cordial to me; I sense little or no hostility. Perhaps Sheila is right. Perhaps I have already been exonerated. Perhaps the real criminal here is that rumor mill, Bull Dozier. What was it we used to say as kids? He who smelt it, dealt it?

Good evening, I say. Good evening. Thanks for coming. Good to see you. Charlie, how's that terrific wife of yours? Jane, hi, good to see you, elbow still giving you trouble? Peter Taylor, what brings you here? This must be important. (Peter smiles appreciatively.) Bob, I hear congratulations are in order. Ashley tells me your Deborah got into Yale. A full scholarship? Mazel tov. I only hope Ray and Sam are so lucky.

Good to see you, good to see you, good to see you. I weave and bob like Muhammad Ali in his prime. Ben, lost a little weight I see. Thirty pounds? (Ben's twisted smile suggests that I overestimated a bit.) Gee, you look terrific though. Good to see you, good to see you, thanks for coming, good to see you. I take my place behind the podium. I wish that it were bigger and that I were smaller. I feel vulnerable, nervous. I can't remember if I put on any antiperspirant today. I can't believe that I did, because my underarms are dripping like leaky faucets. "Ladies and gentlemen," I say. "Thank you all for coming. Thanks for giving me the opportunity to respond to the accusations leveled against me by a member of my team. I have no prepared statement, except to say that I have done nothing that is not in the best interest of our nation, nor will I ever do anything that is not in the best interest of our nation." I point to a raised hand. "Yes?"

"Mr. President, is it, or is it not, true that you have initiated a secret defense project?"

"Well, you don't beat around the bush, do you, Bob?"

There is general laughter.

"No, Mr. President, I do not."

"Well, neither do I. So I'll tell you, unequivocally, that I did not implement any secret defense project."

"Mr. President?"

"Yes."

"Are you saying, sir, that there is no secret project, or that you simply did not implement one?"

"What I am saying, Mr. Churchill, is that if there truly were a secret project, and that I chose to discuss it publicly, then it would no longer be secret, now would it?"

"But are you actually denying the existence of a secret project?"

"I've always believed, Mr. Churchill, that my job is to

inform, not to interpret. And I think — you can correct me if I'm wrong — that the interpretation of what I say is your job, sir. Is it not?"

More laughter. Churchill attempts a follow-up, but I point to Barbara Llewellyn instead. "Yes?"

"Mr. President, assuming for a moment that a secret project doesn't exist, how would you explain the accusation made by Mr. Dozier?"

"I'm afraid, Barbara, that's one question I can't answer. I know that Mr. Dozier has been under a great deal of strain lately. Perhaps he would be the best person to answer your question. Yes, Peter?"

"Mr. President, may I digress for a moment?" says Peter Taylor.

"You won't get an argument from me, Peter," I say.

There is, once again, general laughter.

"During the upcoming summit with Alexi Brezniski, what is it you hope to accomplish?"

"I think everyone here knows that our ultimate goal is meaningful disarmament. But short of that, I would be happy if Mr. Brezniski agreed to throw away his personal arsenal."

Peter Taylor and a few others laugh. On the evening news a few nights ago, Peter reported that Alexi Brezniski — imitating one of his American heroes, General George Patton — frequently carried a revolver. There was also an unconfirmed report that he recently challenged an opposition leader to a duel when the man accused him of being soft on democracy.

"Mr. President?"

"Mr. President?"

"Mr. President?"

"Mr. President?"

During the next twenty minutes or so, I field questions about a variety of issues. Where do I stand on the WAIDS crisis? Will I support more funding for research? How much? Do I favor the distribution of condoms at square dances? At rodeos? On overnight cattle drives? At KKK rallies? What do I actually plan to do about the Really Gross National Product? Do I truly believe that turning the Grand Canyon into a landfill is the answer? Does Bert French support this proposal? So many questions, so few good answers. I do my best to equivocate, to straddle the fence. Yes, I support WAIDS funding and widespread condom distribution, but I am also sympathetic to the agenda of animal rights activists. No, I do not really want to see a national treasure like the Grand Canyon destroyed, but how can I oppose the landfill proposal now that it has received such overwhelming support from the American people? Besides, by the time the canyon is only half filled with refuse, all the people who could remember what it once was like will be dead. Will their children and grandchildren care about its ultimate demise? I doubt it. In fact, they'll probably find it ineffably more fascinating as the world's largest landfill and flock to it in far bigger numbers than any unimproved hole in the ground could ever attract.

Soon Ashley Jones joins me on the podium and, with one hand raised like a traffic cop's, she signals the end of the press conference. "Thank you all for coming," she says. I wave and slip out the back. "The president had asked me to interrupt him at 8:30. He has to tuck in Sam and Ray."

I can hear muffled laughter as I pass through the corridor behind the podium. When I meet with Woody in my suite fifteen minutes later, the first thing he says to me is, "You were great, Mr. President. First class."

"I only hope it bought us some time, Woody. Say, how about some Chinese food?"

Way back in the days when Spiro Agnew was showing no mercy for the "nattering nabobs of negativism," specifically the Vietnam War protesters and the liberal press, "Rowan & Martin's Laugh-In" frequently poked fun at this man who, in his own lame way, did whatever he could to destroy the First Amendment. The time I remember best — actually my recollection is a secondhand one, emanating from my father who was a big "Laugh-In" fan — was when Dick Martin looked eruditely into the camera and said, "How much news would an Agnew choose, if an Agnew could choose news?"

Tonight I am wondering, how much flak would a Goldberg hack, if a Goldberg could hack flak? I hope to God I never have to find out.

I say good night to Sam and Ray. Ray is back in her room and seems a bit miffed. "What is it, hun?" I say. "More gossip columns?"

"Did she have to make that stupid remark about tucking us in? I'm thirteen years old, Daddy. I don't need tucking in anymore."

"I'm sorry, sweetie. But don't blame Ashley. It was Woody's idea. And, to tell you the truth, I kind of liked it."

"Well, tell him I hated it," says Ray. She buries her head in her pillow.

I guess the romance with Woody is off. That's good news for you know who.

Question: Why is a Gallup Poll like a Jewish president taking a leak? Answer: Because, in both cases, I'm holding my own. Jack Frost gave me the good news at this morning's staff meeting. Apparently my press conference was a big hit with the American public, if not with every member of the press.

Unfortunately this has not stopped some members of Congress from chattering about impeachment. Nor has it stopped the venerable Robert E. Lee Sanders from putting in his two cents. "A presidency that is not totally up front with the Congress and the people will eventually choke to death on its own smoke screens," my illustrious opponent told reporters on the Capitol steps. I don't know about that, but I do know that as long as I have the American people behind me, I couldn't care less about the half-assed attempts of envious pea brains like Sanders to extract me from the Ridgeley.

❧

I have been trying to figure out what information I should pass on to Bull about the Arizona Project. He will not be easily pacified. But pacify him I must. I don't think I can resort to trickery again either. I think that Bull has tripped over my feet for the last time. Does this mean that I must finally level with the SOB? I think it does. There is little doubt in my mind what Bull will do if I cross him again. He will either send the DVD of Marcy and me to Sheila, or he'll make it public. Of course if he does the latter, he will automatically be doing the former as well. And why would a man with Bull's ambition stop at ruining my private life when he can simultaneously sabotage my presidency?

Bull is a sporting man, however. Though he despises losing, particularly presidential primaries to northeastern liberals with the initials MSG, he hates to win by default, or when the odds are disproportionately in his favor. He is a clandestine man, too. He may be very public about his political ambitions, but he is quite the opposite when it comes to his emotions. Besides, when he has tried to embarrass me publicly, he has failed, failed miserably. He may not want to risk having something backfire on him again. Even more likely, he may want to enjoy watching me squirm all by himself for a while, a lion toying with his very own Christian.

The irony of all this is that if I told Bull that what I am really up to is little more than theater, he would not believe me. Theater. Yes, theater. Perhaps I have stumbled onto something here.

～

I can remember a few years back, when Ray and Sam shared a room, Ray was constantly worried that her little sister would read her diary. I suggested that she hide it, but Ray thought that Sam would find it no matter where she put it. Then Ray came up with a brilliant idea. She would hide her diary in the last place Sam would ever think to look for it — under Sam's mattress. There's nothing so disarming as the obvious, is there?

～

I have been looking through some brochures about digital video cameras. I am not a camera buff by any means, though my father certainly was. My father owned three cameras: one for movies, one for prints and slides, and one for instant pictures. My father took thousands of photographs and miles of movies of my brother and me from the time we were born until the end of our middle teenage years. I have no doubt that we have the most visually documented childhoods of anyone who ever lived, with the possible exception of Shirley Temple.

Why am I now, at age fifty-three, considering the purchase
of a video camera? Certainly not to provide Ray and Sam
with piles of DVDs of what's left of their rapidly shrinking
childhoods; discs that, as adults, they can dust off and bore
their future families with once every six months or so. No, I
have something else in mind. Lights! Camera! Action!

~

"Mr. Rivera on four," says Rosalee. "He says it's important."

"When is it not?" I say. I tell Phil Hurley I'll have to call
him back and press line four. "Jimmy, what's up?"

"Something big, Mr. President. About WAIDS."

"What is it?"

"We've just found out that a certain anti-depressant
apparently stops the advance of the disease. The drug is
called Quaxil. It's a derivative of Paxil."

"That's great news, Jimmy. Fleming Hodgetts will be
thrilled." I picture Fleming on the Capitol steps, surrounded
by microphones, a hundred reporters hanging on his every
word, No, no, ladies and gentlemen, as instrumental as I have
been in the search for a WAIDS cure, I do sincerely believe
that there are other people who deserve more credit than I.
He will of course decline to name any and then dismiss the
eager troops with a self-effacing smile and the words, That's
Hodgetts with two T's, folks.

"Mr. President?"

"Sorry, Jimmy. I was thinking that, on second thought,
maybe we should keep this thing under wraps for a while."

"Why?

In spite of my recent pledge, I have been considering a
cut in WAIDS funding as a way to gain an advantage over
Fleming Hodgetts, an ace up my sleeve to make sure that
he does not withdraw his support for the Arizona Project.

However, if he finds out there is a readily available drug that halts the disease, he may not care so much about a funding cut. Bye-bye leverage. On the other hand, if Fleming's constituency starts taking anti-depressants to block the advance of WAIDS, they may, as a side effect, become happier and possibly more liberal and therefore more likely to support me in the next election. On the other hand, there is always the possibility that they might just become happier bigots. "I not sure," I say. "I just need some time to mull it over, to consider the implications."

"The implications, Mr. President," says Rivera with uncharacteristic boldness, "are that, without this drug, people will die."

I think about my fragile peace plan. "I know, Jimmy, but strange as it sounds, a lot more people may die if we give it to them now."

"The CDC & P can't keep this thing a secret forever."

"Don't worry, Jimmy, the amount of time I need is considerably less than that."

෴

The next morning, at precisely 9:28, Ashley bursts into my status meeting with Woody, Phil, Tanya and Calvin. Her face is ashen. The sight of her this way, a lack of composure I have never seen in her, sends a chill down my spine. "It's Abe, Mr. President," she says. She doesn't have to say anything else for me to understand her meaning. She walks the length of the conference table, stops in front of the TV and switches it on. After a laxative commercial, news anchor Harry Day Lodge appears.

"It was another first today for the Goldberg administration," Lodge begins in his revered baritone. "This one, tragic. Moments ago, on the steps of his Alexandria home, Secretary of the Treasury Abraham 'Honest Abe' Rubin was gunned down as he was leaving for work. The weapon used was a Rohm RG-14, a 22-caliber handgun, small but designed for accuracy. A Kurdish terrorist group, calling themselves the Holy Terrors, has claimed credit for the crime and has promised further reprisals against what they have called the 'international conspiracy of Jewish bankers.' For those of you out there who are trivia buffs, no secretary of the treasury had ever been assassinated, although the first secretary of the treasury, Alexander Hamilton, lost his life in a gun duel with Aaron Burr in 1804. For more on that, let's go to our political analyst at the Ridgeley, Jefferson Davis LaRoche. Jeff?"

"Harry, in talking to pundits throughout the country, I've learned that most believe the Hamilton shooting simply doesn't count in this context because Hamilton's term as secretary of the treasury had expired long before the time of his death."

"So Honest Abe Rubin is indeed the first sitting secretary of the treasury to be assassinated."

"Unequivocally, Harry."

"A real tragedy, Jeff. But, as you know, every cloud has a silver lining. Hamilton did end up on a twenty dollar bill."

"Indeed he did, Harry."

"Do you think that bodes well for Mr. Rubin? That we'll be seeing his stately visage on perhaps a lower denomination any time soon?"

"Probably not in our lifetime, Harry. Although who's to say?"

"Thanks, Jeff." Harry Day Lodge turns back to the camera. "For comment from the Hill, let's go to Mike Masters who is standing by with Senate Minority Leader Fleming Hodgetts. Mike? Mike?"

"Six million Jews Uncle Adolf zapped. Now I ask you, boy, who the hell is gonna miss one more?"

While the camera stays on Hodgetts and Mike Masters, we hear a shaken Harry Day Lodge say, "Ah, we seem to be having some audio difficulty. Mike? Can you hear us now? We've been hearing you just fine."

Mike Masters puts his hand on his earplug. The expression on his face changes from detachment to horror. "You what?" He whispers something to Hodgetts.

"Why, you SOB!" Hodgetts growls. "You were supposed to tell me when we were on the air. Damn it, boy. You from some goddamn high school radio station or something?"

Suddenly the picture goes dead. A few seconds later, a stunned Harry Day Lodge reappears. "We now return you to your regularly scheduled program," he says.

⌒

On the evening news, the lead story was no longer Abe Rubin's assassination. It was Fleming Hodgetts' declaration concerning the numbing effect of the Holocaust. In an interview with Harry Day Lodge, Hodgetts insisted that he had been misquoted. When Lodge pointed out to him that the words came directly out of his mouth, and that nobody had quoted him, mis- or otherwise, he accused Mike Masters of "an act of malicious ventriloquism." I suspect if anyone can make this accusation stick, it is Fleming Hodgetts. With two T's.

Move Over, Paul Finkelstein

20

The mile-long list of dignitaries and media people who will be invited to attend the unveiling of the Arizona Project is nearly complete. So, thank God, is the project itself, according to Paul Finkelstein. Paul reportedly had his troops working fourteen-hour days for the past month to stay on schedule.

I have asked Woody to send invitations not only to the leaders of those countries that already have nuclear arsenals, but to the leaders of the countries that claim to have one. I am, after all, taking some liberties with reality myself; others should be granted the same privilege. I have also insisted, over the strong objection of Candace Rowe, but with the strong endorsement of Warren Gates, that we invite the Iraqi president, Diya Bakir. Gates thinks I'm finally coming to my senses and that we should use this unique opportunity to kill the son of a bitch, accidentally of course. Candace thinks I may be losing my mind and that we should not be playing with fire in a place where there will be so much firewood. The truth is, I feel less threatened by an enemy I can see. Not to mention, I sincerely doubt that Bakir will show up.

In any case, the invitation will tell these world leaders that what they are about to see will have a profound and direct effect upon the future of mankind, not just on this planet, but throughout the universe. I am not talking small stakes here. Compared to what I am about to undertake from a strategic arms point of view, the Cuban Missile Crisis should be renamed the Cuban Firecracker Crisis. Compared to what I am going to propose from an exploration point of view, the 1969 moon landing was, at best, one baby step for mankind.

The unveiling ceremony is scheduled for Monday, November 4th, 2013, just a week and a half after my summit with Brezniski. That should give Ashley enough time to decide what suit I should wear — my navy blue or my gray one.

❧

Tim Green realized in high school that he was gay. He said he first knew something was up when he started seeing images of Robert Redford in his head whenever he was masturbating. Tim never told me about any of this until we were well into our thirties. By then he already had had a few relationships.

I never suspected a thing. Tim, not I, was the smooth talker with girls. He was always calm and in control during any tête-a-tit. I realize now that the reason for Tim's abnormal cool was the fact that nothing was at stake for him. The dating ritual was merely something he was good at, like I was good at basketball, but for Tim, there was a hollowness to it.

I am ashamed to say it, but I did not take Tim's revelation very well. (I almost called it a "confession," but that would hardly be accurate.) I felt as if my own masculinity were being questioned. Were my feelings of love for Tim homosexual? Were his feelings for me homosexual? I felt a sudden need to go out and fuck every woman I could get my hands on just to demonstrate how normal I was; I got so horny I probably would have fucked a keyhole. I only hope my feelings weren't transparent to Tim. Friends like him don't grow on trees and I'd never do anything to hurt him deliberately.

It doesn't bother me at all now, Tim being gay. In fact, we're probably better friends because of it. None of that divisive atavistic competition for female attention ever comes between us anymore. He can say things like, "I wouldn't mind finding Cookie's shoes under my bed," and I'd know right away that he was more interested in owning Cookie's shoes than making it with her. Considering this, it is a curious thing that I find myself a little jealous of Tim's relationship with Cookie.

❧

Sunday, September 22, 2013. It is midday and I have come back to my suite for a brief sabbatical from my daily routine. This morning I met with Fleming Hodgetts, who told me that he has heard rumblings that the *Post* is getting ready to publish another story about the Arizona Project. He did not know the details, but he warned me that I should be ready to respond, and said that any denials now of the project's existence would no longer hold water. "They're on to you, Mr. President," he said. I can remember when he used to say, "This thing of ours is an inspiration. A goddamn inspiration." Funny how credit is always plural, blame always singular.

Fleming and I did not speak about Mike Masters' "act of malicious ventriloquism." Nor did we talk about the newfound efficacy of Quaxil. There may never come a time for us to deal with the former. Truth is thicker and more substantial than mendacity, so there is little chance that Fleming's head will ever be porous enough to absorb it. As for the latter, it is still too soon to play my hand.

Fleming was not my only appointment this morning; he was just the only one who showed. Bert French was supposed to come, but canceled at the last minute, due to an "unexpected conflict." I was also to get together with Woody at ten, but at 9:30 he telephoned to ask if he could go for a massage instead. "I must have slept funny," he told me. "Neck's sore as hell." Other than that, my morning was uneventful, except for one thing. Rosalee told me that I received a call from an old friend of mine. She said the friend left no name, but did leave a number. When I called the number, you can imagine my surprise when the voice at the other end turned out to be Robert E. Lee Sanders. More about this later. I suddenly have to urinate.

～

Good news, bad news. The good news is that while I was urinating my penis did not blow up like a balloon. The bad news is I have to started piss blood. I know this requires immediate attention, but I am not inclined to return to the same urologist I went to before. Not after what just happened.

～

They have done a urinalysis. They say there is nothing to worry about, that it's a minor infection. Very common, nothing contagious, nothing life threatening. Here, take one of these three times a day, after meals, and you'll be as good as new in no time. Just be sure to use up the whole prescription. A lot of people start to feel okay again after a few days and think they're all better and stop taking the antibiotic and, wham!, before they know it, the infection's back again, sometimes angrier than before. You don't have to worry about me, I say. The sight of a toilet bowl turning red is motivation enough.

～

Marcy Gillis is taking a night course in genetic engineering at George Washington University. The course is being taught by a research scientist who used to work for a breeder of laboratory animals in my home state. "It's to improve my mind," Marcy said. I admire her spunk, but I can't help thinking — and I know this is unfair — that poor Marcy doesn't have any idea what she has gotten herself into. My guess is that she thinks she's going to be studying methods of birth control. In a sense, I guess she is.

The point is, the course is given on Wednesday nights, from seven to ten, and since this is Wednesday night, Marcy will not be available until late. I could wait for her, but instead I have decided to take advantage of my celibate status to rekindle an old flame.

"It's a digital video camera," I say to Sheila. It is mounted on a tripod to the right of the bed. It looks like an alien voyeur.

"What on earth?" says Sheila.

"I thought we could have a little fun with it," I say. "I thought, maybe, we could...well...make a movie."

"Of what?" says Sheila.

"Of us, silly," I say. "Why do you think I set it up in here?"

"No idea," Sheila says.

"So?"

"So what?"

"You want to be a movie star?"

"Movie star? Who wouldn't? Why don't you come up and see me sometime, big boy?" Sheila says, sounding like Mae West. Then she does something that startles the hell out of me. She sheds her silk, turquoise Chinese robe, revealing black bikini panties and a bra that looks as if the cups were made out of black yarmulkes.

"Are those what I think they are?"

"One hundred percent real, baby. No artificial additives."

"I mean these," I say, clasping the cups between my index fingers and thumbs.

"Yes, they are. I made it myself. You like it?"

"I love it." Suddenly my penis goes from zero to six inches in about three seconds.

Sheila unfastens her yarmulke bra and it tosses it on the floor in a sweeping motion. "Ready when you are, Cecil B.," she says.

"Wait," I say, raising my hands in front of my chest, my palms facing Sheila. "Hold that thought. I have to turn the thing on." I jump out of bed and switch on the camera. I set the Start/Delay switch for two minutes. Then I hustle over to my dresser to get something I hid in the top drawer. I'm in such a hurry, not wanting to jeopardize the mood, that I stub my toe on the side of the bed. It hurts like hell, but I swallow my pain instead of screaming. "Shit, shit, shit," I mutter, mutter, mutter.

"What's the matter?" says Sheila, sitting up.

"Nothing, nothing," I say. "I'll be right there." I grab what I'm after and get back into bed, sitting shoulder to shoulder with Sheila. "Here," I say. "The finishing touch."

"This is ridiculous," she says. "You expect me to wear this thing?"

"Just let me see how you look. Please?"

Sheila puts on the wig. She looks like a dark-haired bride of Frankenstein. "I feel foolish," she says.

"You look fabulous," I say. I turn my body toward her. We embrace tenderly, kiss softly. The camera clicks on. My stomach taut, I lean backwards onto my elbows, then onto my back. I draw her on top of me. She mounts me like a Republican presidential candidate straddling a fence. She leans forward. Our lips splash together like molten magnets. I squeeze her buttocks and she starts to move up and down on me, ever so deliciously. My flesh dissolves into hers. I reach for her breasts and gently caress them. I am always surprised how much larger they seem from this angle. Talk about mountains' majesty. As I continue to stroke her breasts, she begins to moan lasciviously, like a chainsaw on Valium. Her nipples harden and protrude. I bend forward for a taste. No gumdrops were ever so sweet. I linger a moment, savoring, then lower my head back onto the pillow. I reach again for her nipples. I gently twirl my fingers around them as if seeking a new station and adjusting the volume of some temperamental, shortwave radio. *Come in, orgasm! Come in!* Sheila's volume soars and drops, soars and drops, the glorious anticipatory static of mindless, unfettered pleasure. I feel myself about to explode. All the while, I am thinking, I can't believe this is Sheila! I can't believe this is Sheila! I only hope that if Cookie ever finds out about this, she will understand.

Soft on Communism

Sheila, wide-awake after our cinematic lovemaking, has finally read herself to sleep with her dog-eared copy of *Passion on the Potomac*. I remove the book from atop her palpitating breasts, place it on her night table and turn off her light. I twist my light to its dimmest setting. The children have long since gone to bed. It is wonderfully quiet, still, peaceful. Sometimes I think the best time of the day is this bittersweet, reflective interlude just before I fall asleep. It makes me wonder if the best time of life comes the moment before death, a moment of unprecedented clarity, a final soft lightning bolt impaling the darkness to come. In a way, I hope that is the best time because then I'll always have something to look forward to.

I suppose now would be a good time to get back to the Sanders call. I do not anticipate any physiological interruptions, none immediately at any rate. Later, I am sure. I outpaced Sheila by one cocktail, so I'm a bit fuzzy myself. I suspect my pinhead father could show up at any moment, shouting, "You can't thread a needle with a rope, Ronnie! You can't thread a needle with a rope!" God, how he haunts me! Does he know yet what has happened to his remains? Would he tell me if he did?

Sanders, as it turns out, is a friend of Dr. Fletcher, my new urologist. And while Fletcher came highly recommended — "The top in his field," Phil Hurley had said, which Bernie Cohen later confirmed — he has apparently violated the sacred rule of patient confidentiality. Either that, or Sanders has used his friendship with the good doctor to gain access to my medical file. I would like to believe that the latter, not the former, is the truth. But one can never know. This is Washington.

"I heard you were having some problems," Sanders said.

"Problems?" I said.

"With your health."

"Oh, you did."

"Yes. And I was so worried you might die before the next election and deny me the pleasure of whipping your commie ass, I simply had to call."

"I appreciate your concern, Bob E. Lee," I said. "But as far as I know, sore backs are no longer terminal."

"That's not what I heard."

"You mean they are?"

"I mean, I heard it was your prostate. The Big C."

I could only assume that the C, in this case, did not stand for Cookie. Oh C is for cancer, that's good enough for me. "Now where'd you hear that pile of crap?" I said.

"From a friend. I wish I could tell you who, but then if I did, he probably wouldn't be my friend anymore."

289

"Well, I hate to break it to you, Bob E. Lee, but you've been misinformed. It's the back."

"I don't think so. Besides, I have proof."

"The word of a questionable friend?"

"Proof," Sanders said. "And I intend to nail you with it. A man in your delicate condition shouldn't be at the helm of this great nation of ours."

"Is that so?"

"We both know it is," said Sanders.

Two days later, on Thursday, September 12, Robert E. Lee Sanders spoke before the UAW. I do not wish to rehash all that he said. It is unnecessary. His fifteen-minute speech can be summed up briefly, in his own words in fact: "Ron Goldberg is soft on communism." As proof, he told the gathering that a reliable source had revealed to him that "the president is suffering from cancer of the prostate — which I firmly believe is negatively affecting his policy decisions. Especially those concerning the Russians and the Iraqis." Sanders called for my immediate resignation and for new elections this November. He said that it was for the good of the country. The stunned autoworkers rose to their feet and gave him a thunderous ovation.

Friday, September 13, 2013. I have drafted a statement, which I have instructed Ashley to read to the press. It has to do with the erroneous and inflammatory assertion about my health made by Robert E. Lee Sanders during his speech to the UAW. This is the text of my rebuttal:

The President of the United States is not suffering from prostate cancer. In fact, he is in perfect health. Regarding the accusation made to the contrary, the President has only this reply: consider the source. Thank you and good night.

The next morning I watched on television as a sober-faced Ashley Jones read this prepared statement to the press. When she was finished, a flurry of hands sprung into the air.

"Ms. Jones!"

"Ms. Jones!"

"Ms. Jones!"

Me, me, me!

"I'm sorry, ladies and gentlemen, we have nothing more to say at this time."

"What about the accusation, Ms. Jones, that the President is soft on communism?" shouted one reporter.

"No comment."

"Does the fact that you are not denying outright the charge mean that there is, in fact, some validity to it?" said another.

"No comment."

"Ms. Jones, can you tell us —"

"I'm sorry, we have nothing further to add at this time." Ashley then he turned her back on the press corps and walked away.

"When can we expect something further?" shouted one reporter.

"Yes, when?"

But Ashley was already out of earshot. Besides the press and one hundred and fifty million TV viewers, only I heard the question. And I was not about to answer it either.

~

In the waning days of the Watergate scandal, when the Nixon administration was coming apart at the seams, Nixon's campaign slogan — "Nixon's the One" — which served him so well in 1972, helping him win reelection by the largest electoral margin since Roosevelt drubbed Alf Landon in 1936, now bit the hand that fed it. Where it once meant that Nixon was the guy who could do it, it now meant that he was the guy who did it. Nixon quickly became known again as "Tricky Dick."

I mention this seemingly irrelevant snippet of history because Ashley told me she heard a similar epithet for me the other day. She hesitated to tell me about it right away, not wanting to upset me any more than I already was, but then she realized that I was going to hear about it sooner or later anyway and, given that, she felt it would be best for me to hear it from her. Perceptive woman, that Ashley Jones.

So what was this abhorrent name for the President of the United States that was being spread about town like so much fertilizer, giving rise to a bumper crop of guffaws and giggles and titters wherever it went? "Dead Dick." I'm not sure, but there could be a campaign slogan in there somewhere. Perhaps Dead Dick rises again?

Now, Sanders may have been the catalyst for this unfortunate name, but I am sure he was not the source. More than likely, it was Benny "The Bouncer" Blocker, the feisty president of the UAW. They say Benny is eighty-eight years old, and he is still active mentally and physically. Make no mistake, he is no figurehead.

Benny is a man with a deep, and apparently unending, sense of family. In fact, he fathered three of his six sons since reaching his sixtieth birthday. But oddly enough, Benny is a man without a well-documented past. Life appears to have begun for Benny at age fifty, when he took a job as a bouncer in a seedy Detroit nightclub. Nothing is known about him before that time and his age has not been conclusively documented. One theory is that Benny is actually Jimmy Hoffa, who allegedly was murdered back in 1975 and then buried in an unmarked grave. The story went that, one fine August morning, two weeks after Hoffa's disappearance, Benny showed up for his first day at work as a bouncer with an unusual amount of dirt under his fingernails.

∼

Over the past decade, several studies — some conducted by highly reputable groups, the most notable being the University of California at Berkeley — have attempted to prove that Benny "The Bouncer" Blocker is Jimmy Hoffa. Benny's and Hoffa's physiognomy have been compared in tedious detail. The broad faces, the large noses, the sagging chins, have been said to bear a striking similarity. Body types have also been compared and, though both men appear to have the same type of build — endomorphic — Benny is a good deal shorter than the infamous Teamster boss. Proponents of the Jimmy-Is-Benny theory dismiss this discrepancy, however, by pointing out that people do in fact shrink with age.

∼

At first, Benny Blocker seemed amused by all the claims that he was Hoffa, rising from the dead like Lazarus, but as more and more groups jumped into the act, he lost patience, denouncing the theories as "absurd flights of fancy by over-zealous children." My own opinion is that Benny is in fact Hoffa. But then I also believe that Elvis is still alive and that the Beatles, John Lennon and George Harrison included, are planning another reunion concert, this time in Yankee Stadium. Yesterday, my arthritis seemed so far away.

∼

When I greet my secretary this morning, she is reading a *Post* article about Robert E. Lee Sanders' "soft on communism" speech to the UAW.

"I'm sure there's an upside to all this, Rosalee," I say. "I just can't see it yet. What's your opinion, my most trusted advisor?"

Rosalee adjusts her bulk and puts the paper down on her desk. "Other than that, Mrs. Kennedy, how did you like Dallas?" she says.

❧

It is Saturday morning. I am sitting in my office, sipping a lukewarm cup of coffee. In five weeks I will be meeting with Alexi Brezniski. In five minutes it will be nine o'clock. When I left my suite this morning, Ray and Sheila were still asleep. Sam, I think, was awake, because I could see a strip of light at the bottom of her door. Sam often gets up as early as I do on weekends, but stays in her room for most of the morning rearranging her furniture. When I was Sam's age, I had the same fascination with furniture rearranging, though I never told Sam that I did until long after she started doing it. Somewhere in our family gene pool swims the soul of an interior decorator.

Although I have dozens of people developing a winning script for me so that I can give the performance of my life during my summit with Alexi — their fingers are no doubt happily dancing on their PC keys as if they were the graves of their worst enemies — I have been trying to jot down some notes of my own. I am failing miserably in this endeavor. I can't seem to keep my mind from wandering. I feel like a mental nomad trapped inside the bondage of distraction. Bondage indeed. What a glorious prison is this world I now inhabit! In part I sought the presidency to free myself and my fellow Jews from the monstrous tyranny of small and impervious minds, to elevate us to the status of, say, a typical WAIDS victim. And yet what have I become if not a prisoner myself? Me on the inside, my fellow Jews on the outside. Imprisoned by walls, imprisoned by blindness, by idolatry, by fear, by complicity, by invisible quotas, by false myth, by requests for Jewish doctors but refusals of Jewish blood, by kosher meals served in aluminum foil trays, by the rancor of unforgiving baseball fans. How much longer, I wonder, how much longer?

∽

A few minutes pass. Rosalee calls me on the intercom to say that a man is here to see me, but that he does not wish to be announced. When I ask her if the man looks familiar, she hesitates and then says, "No." She is acting oddly but she frequently does. I don't pursue it. Rosalee is entitled to some fun now and then at my expense.

"Does he look dangerous?"

"He barely looks alive," says Rosalee. I hear a laugh in the background.

"Okay, okay, what's the joke?"

"No joke."

"Well, send him in then," I say. I can't imagine why Rosalee is pulling my leg this time or who this mystery person might be because my calendar, except for a few staff meetings, is clear for the morning. Did Ashley consent to an interview she neglected to tell me about? Did Woody? Did Phil? I used to like surprises, but not nearly as much since I've been in the Ridgeley.

The door to my office swings open and there, through the doorway, hobbles an overly thin man, supporting himself with a cane. The man looks about eighty years old. His curly,

295

salt and pepper hair is tousled, as if he had recently been riding in a convertible.

"Ronnie, you old son of bitch," the man says.

"Tim!" I shout. "Jesus Christ, why didn't you tell me you were out?

"Wanted to surprise you." Tim smiles weakly, more like a grimace.

I rush around my desk and give him a hug. In doing so, he nearly loses his balance. "Whoa!" he says, steadying himself on my desk.

"Sorry," I say. "How long you been in town?"

"Got in last night," Tim says.

I slide a chair over to Tim. He turns stiffly and then sits down. "Son of a bitch," he says.

"Accident really did a number on you," I say.

"Oh, I'll live," says Tim.

To look at him, though, I'm not so sure. "Just don't try to do too much too fast."

"Like you, I suppose," says Tim, mockingly.

"Even I'm slowing down a notch," I lie.

"I don't believe that for one minute."

I laugh. "Okay, okay. So maybe I'm not. Yet."

Tim runs his bony hand through his hair. "I found her," he says.

"You did? Where?"

"Chicago."

"Chicago?" I say. "That's where she is now? With — who'd you say? — her sister?"

"No, she's not with her sister. Or in Chicago anymore, for that matter."

"The Cape? She's on the Cape?"

"Here," says Tim. "Cookie's in D.C. Drove her down myself."

"You're kidding."

Tim shakes his head. "As a matter of fact, Ronnie, she's right outside your door."

～

Why is it that when you finally get what you've been after for so many years, you begin to doubt that you really wanted it in the first place? Cookie is in Washington. Cookie is unattached, accessible. Maybe. And here I am having second thoughts about the whole sorry affair. Now, it could be that it's just my insecurities rearing their ugly little heads again. My relationship with Cookie Dunn over the years hasn't exactly been the stuff that romance novels are made of; more like the stuff a Woody Allen movie is made of, I think. Do I really want this woman? Does she want me? And does it really matter? I could be dead tomorrow without ever having made love to her, our two vastly and ridiculously different lives remaining only tangentially connected for eternity. A debate rages within me. Should I pursue her? Should I give her up? (How, I wonder, can I let go of something I've never possessed?) Should I take a chance, throw caution to the wind, leave myself wide open for rejection and humiliation? Why, after all these troubled years, should the end be anything but a disaster? Oh, C is for catastrophe, that's good enough for me. On the other hand, she has journeyed one thousand miles to see me. That has to count for something. Surely, you don't do that sort of thing merely to say hello to an old high school acquaintance. Something must be there. It must. "Here? You brought her here?"

"I thought that's what you wanted," says Tim. There is an edge to his voice, an impatience with my apparent ingratitude.

"No. Yes. Of course. I mean, sure, I want to see her. But not here. Not now."

"Ronnie, pull yourself together. This ain't junior high anymore."

"Maybe not," I say. "But it feels that way."

"It'll be fine," says Tim. "Just relax."

"Okay, okay. Check her in downstairs. And tell her I'll see her tonight. I'll come by, say, around seven."

Tim struggles to his feet and heads for the door. "You're a piece of work, Ronnie Goldberg. A real piece of work."

THE TWO FACES
OF RON

Bull Dozier has made himself scarce, but I can't say that his absence has made me completely happy. I prefer to have Bull out in the open where I can see him. When he retreats, I know that he is up to something.

Lately, there has been a deluge of ink about the alleged Arizona Project and I'm certain that Bull is leaking the lion's share of the information to the press. God knows Ashley Jones has nothing to do with it, although much to my chagrin, it has KISS marks all over it. (The American people will have no trouble at all understanding the concept of a strategic defense system that Bull has said, "poses a real and deliberate threat to national security.") Fortunately, everything has been reported as speculation and has not once been attributed to a "reliable source," which has to be getting under Bull's thick skin.

In any case, I have other things on my mind tonight. In

less than half an hour I will be face to face with Cookie Dunn for the first time in I don't know how many years. I have been sweating so much I have just taken my second shower of the day. It has done no more good than the first. I am already beginning to sweat again. I am not sure if I have put on deodorant, so I put some on, perhaps again. I start to get dressed. First, my underwear, then my socks, next my trousers and, finally, my shirt. Buttoning my shirt up halfway, I realize that my buttons and buttonholes are out of synch, so I have to start all over again. Sheila is half watching me, half reading. "You seem nervous," she says, clearly amused.

"It's nothing," I say.

"You're acting like it's your first date."

"Don't be silly. She's just an old friend from high school."

"Tim Green told me you were sweethearts."

"Tim exaggerates."

"Maybe," says Sheila. Her eyes still on her book, she turns a page. "When did you see Tim anyway?"

"He was coming out of the hotel when I was going in. To tell you the truth, I didn't even recognize him."

"That poor man, what he's been through."

"Damn near died."

"I remember."

I begin wrestling with my tie. On the sixth try I finally get the ends the length I want them, the inner about two inches shorter than the outer. Usually it only takes me three tries.

"Need some help," says Sheila. There is still a muffled amusement in her voice, a suppressed smile on her face.

"I got it. Thanks," I say. "Now where the hell's my belt?"

Sheila looks up from her book. "Isn't that it?"

I look down at my waist. "Christ, who the hell put it there?"

"Honestly, Ron," says Sheila, chuckling.

A few minutes later I'm out the door and headed for Cookie Dunn's room. Woody has booked her in a guest suite that is two doors down from Marcy's room. The room in the middle is currently unoccupied. It belongs to Uncle Leo, whom I haven't seen since he left the Ridgeley in the dead of night, allegedly clad in a busboy's outfit. Well, he may not be here, but he's still very much on my mind.

Question: What's a little something between girlfriends? Answer: Uncle Leo. How is Uncle Leo, I wonder? I wish that he would call.

I worry.

∾

When I get to Cookie's room, I dismiss my two-person Secret Service escort. They depart for opposite ends of the hall. I lift my hand to knock on the door, then I hesitate. Sheila was right. I am acting like this is a first date. But why? Why am I so nervous? Could it be because I am expecting more, hoping for more, than a casual reunion? I must admit this is so. I do want this woman. I have always wanted this woman. And yet I want her to want me more, because I desperately need the decision to have an affair, or not to have an affair, to rest with me. I was the victim of Cookie Dunn's indifference once before. This must not, shall not, happen again. In fact, I am much more confident than I have ever been when faced with such an opportunity. In years past I had allowed Sheila's iciness to shatter my fragile male ego. There was no way I could have seriously entertained an affair at that time. But now, with Sheila's sudden — albeit, perhaps temporary — thaw (not to mention my liaison with Marcy), my confidence has not only been restored, it has been pushed to new heights. So, it is largely Sheila's passion that has made it possible for me to confidently pursue other women. My God, what a splendid marriage we have!

It is now 7:05. I again lift my hand to knock and this time I allow it to do its job. The knock, I am pleased, is not fainthearted, but one of authority, presidential one could say, if one can assume that presidents, too, are obliged to knock on any doors other than those that belong to their daughters. Only a few seconds elapse before the door swings open. "Hello, Mr. President," says Cookie Dunn, playfully.

Cookie is wearing a black cocktail dress and a string of pearls. "Cookie," I say. "My God, you're just as beautiful as ever!" I take her hands in mine and lean forward to kiss her cheek. As I do this, Cookie turns her head and our lips meet instead. I pull back, surprised how quickly even innocent intimacy can bridge the years. "It's so good to see you. You have no idea."

"I've missed you," Cookie says.

"Me too," I say. "Missed you, I mean."

"You want to come in?" says Cookie.

"Sure, we have time. I thought we could get a bite to eat at 7:30." I look at my watch.

"Anything's fine with me."

I let go of Cookie's hands and walk past her into the room. She shuts the door behind us. I feel as though I have entered a time warp — of cashmere sweaters, of death by acne, of clumsy attempts at intimacy. "I can't get over how good you look," I say. "You haven't changed a bit."

Cookie smiles. "You have," she says.

"I have?"

"Oh, yes. Much more confident. More self-assured."

"Maybe a little bit," I say. I take her hands in mine again. "Let me look at you." Cookie looks back at me like a child hungry for approval. "You know, it's funny. I always thought your eyes were blue, not green. How could I have made a mistake like that?"

"They are blue," Cookie says. "I'm wearing contacts. When Bill and I got divorced, I literally wanted to change everything about myself."

"I'm sorry," I say. "I didn't mean to bring up a sore subject."

"It's all right," says Cookie. "That's in the past. All I want to talk about now is us."

"You think there is one?" I say. "An 'us'?"

Cookie kisses me gently, this time on the cheek. "I think there always was one," she says. "You just never realized it."

~

Cookie and I have dinner in my private dining room. Filipino stewards on loan from the White House mess serve us with quiet fluidity. In their gray slacks and blue blazers with the presidential seal on their left breast pockets, they exude an aristocratic subservience. Cookie has ordered the swordfish. I have ordered veal scaloppini. We share a bottle of white wine. Much of our conversation focuses on the past. It was not a particularly happy time for either of us, and yet we talk about it with a sense of loss and longing. Perhaps because it really was easier then. We had no responsibilities of any bulk, certainly not any compared to what we have now — running households, running governments, saving worlds. All we had to worry about then was getting pimples, and not saying or doing something stupid enough to cause us eternal embarrassment. We of course failed on every account. Our faces broke out. We suffered greatly due to poor tongue and brain coordination. The way we conducted our lives seemed to constantly piss off our parents. How could we stand all that again? The truth is, we couldn't. The only safe and sensible way to return was the way were doing it — through memories declawed by time and voluntary blindness.

About halfway through her dessert, a chocolate mousse, Cookie says, "I can't stay."

"What do you mean you can't stay? Of course you can stay. For as long as you like."

"It's an imposition, my being here."

"The hell it is."

"It's no use, Ron. I have to leave tomorrow."

"Tomorrow? But you just got here."

"I had only planned to spend the night."

I look Cookie in the eyes. She looks back for a moment, but then looks away. "I want you to stay," I say. "I need you to stay."

"What about your wife?"

"Sheila? I'm sure she'd want you to stay, too."

"You know what I mean."

"Sheila's fine about it. In fact, I think she's pretty darn amused by your being here."

"Oh really."

"Well, I've been acting a little funny since you got here. Kind of like a schoolboy about to go out on his first date. Sheila's gotten quite a kick out of it."

"Your wife has a strange sense of humor."

"To tell you the truth, I never knew she had one at all until recently." I reach across the table and place my hands on top of Cookie's. "Please."

"Well, maybe for another day or two. But no more."

I smile. "Hey, how about a little champagne?"

After dinner, I walk Cookie back to her room. It seems as though there are Secret Service agents everywhere now, eyeing us with disinterested intensity. I am tempted to say something to them, I don't know what, but I know they are not supposed to converse with me. I wonder if they suspect any percolating hanky panky. I wonder if they care. After all, what am I to them but a beating heart? An object for which they are responsible, no different from any other object under guard — at the Louvre, at the Smithsonian, at Attica. One president, under guard, with liberty for not much at all. Yes, an object. And a Jewish one at that. Do they know I feel like a prisoner? Would it make them laugh if they did? I wonder if they would lose their jobs if I were assassinated. Or would they simply be issued a reprimand and told not to let it happen again? I suspect, deep down, I care more about them than they do about me. I should think it would pain me to recognize this, but I am with Cookie Dunn now, and thus am reminded of the absolute power, the self-controlled misery, the virginal beauty of unrequited love.

All I have on my mind at this point is making love to this beautiful woman and all I am greeted with, over and over, is a politely indifferent GOOD EVENING, MR. PRESIDENT. It really is true what they say about guilt. The only person who can make you feel guilty is yourself. And yet what do I, Myron S. Goldberg, have to feel guilty about? Am I not doing a good job as president? (At least 31% of the American people seem to think so, according the latest polls.) Am I not about to embark on a course of action that will ensure world peace for decades, perhaps centuries, to come? What other president, barely nine months in office, has dared to take such bold steps as I? What other president has encountered such hostility for actions clearly not meant to harm, and in fact meant to benefit, those around him? Did I intend to blaspheme baseball, America's favorite pastime? Of course not. And look at what an innocent remark did to my once soaring popularity! Did I not have anything but the best intentions in mind when I secured Uncle Leo his post at the Smithsonian? And look how I was so quickly blasted by the press when the biting incident occurred! And what about the Grand Canyon incident? My God, even Albert French thought I fully intended to transform this national treasure into a landfill. Which of course, thanks to Fleming Hodgetts, I'll probably have to do after all, in order to get a handle on the runaway RGNP. I tell you, it's tough doing your best, only to be thanked with enmity and mistrust. Very tough indeed. In fact, sometimes I think everyone is out to get me. But maybe I'm just paranoid.

You're not paranoid, Ronnie.

Pop?

Who else? The Messiah?

So you think I'm not paranoid?

Of course you're not paranoid, Ronnie. You're Jewish.

"Want to come in for a nightcap?" Cookie says. She yawns into her curled hand. Ah, to be a breath exhaled into the balmy cavern of that exquisite hand! "Oh, Ron, I'm sorry."

Gotta go, Pop. Can we talk later?

I'm not as busy as you might think. You just say when.

Thanks, Pop. I will.

"Perhaps another time," I say to Cookie. "You seem pretty tired. All that traveling's catching up with you."

"I'm fine, really."

"I don't know. Tomorrow's another busy day. Got to be up with the chickens."

"The chickens can wait for once," says Cookie.

"Okay," I say. "But just one drink. Then I have to go."

We go inside.

∽

I didn't lie to Cookie. I did have to be in my office early

today. As a matter of fact, I'm overbooked with appointments and meetings. Not the least of which is a phone meeting with Paul Finkelstein to see how things are progressing at the Arizona Project. I'm also scheduled to talk with Alexi Brezniski to discuss a few points of business concerning our upcoming summit. It is now about 7:00 a.m. and I am just getting out of bed. Trying to stand, I catch my left leg in the bedding and nearly tumble onto the floor. I don't feel hung over — I didn't have that much to drink last night — but I feel as though I were drugged. My mind is cloudy. My limbs feel heavy and weak. I wonder if I am coming down with something. I manage to make it to the bathroom. I flip up the toilet seat and begin to urinate. My prostate pain cuts through my dreamy numbness and reminds me of my terrible fragility. Pain, I think, is the preview of things to come. Pain is the first stage of death. God, it feels good to be alive.

By the time I finish showering and shaving, it is about 7:45. I go to the kitchen to make some breakfast. The first thing I do is pour myself a glass of cranberry juice. I have been told that it's good for the type of problem I have, but I am not so sure. I probably drink a gallon of it daily and I can notice no change whatsoever in my condition, except that I have to urinate a lot more. Truthfully, the only thing that seems to ease my pain is sex. Thank God for Marcy Gillis. Thank God for Sheila.

While I am rinsing my glass in the sink, I hear a door open. A few seconds later, Ray walks into the kitchen. "Hi, Daddy," she says.

"Ray," I say, "what're you doing home?"

"Sore throat. Mom said I didn't have to go to school today."

I give Ray a hug and kiss her forehead. "No fever at least."

"It was 99.7 this morning when I got up. What're you doing home?"

"Mom said I could stay home today, too."

"Oh, Dad," Ray says.

"You eat?" I say.

"I had some plain toast. I was just going to get some juice."

"I'm making a bagel. You want one?"

"No thanks. I'm on a diet."

"Diet? What kind of mishegoss is that? What thirteen-year-old goes on a diet? No wonder you're sick all the time." Ray has allergies, so it's often difficult to tell where her allergies end and her colds begin. When I need to discipline her about poor health habits, her allergies come in darn handy.

"I'm not sick all the time and you know it!" Ray protests. "Besides, other kids go on diets. Jen's on a diet. So's Heather."

"Heather should be on a diet. She looks like a haystack with a head."

"Okay, okay. Make me half a bagel."

I put three halves in the toaster oven. "Margarine or cream cheese?"

"Margarine," says Ray. "Less calories."

～

Seeing Cookie again has filled me with a desire to atone for old sins in a way only Yom Kippur has been able to do. I have decided to let bygones by bygones as far as Red Trombley of *The Los Angeles Times* and Tom Meagan of *The Boston Herald* are concerned. To each of them I am sending an olive branch, along with this note:

> Dear Tom (Red):
> I hope you know by now just how troubled I was, and continue to be, over my blasphemous statement made about the "Church of Baseball," as Annie Savoy so aptly

characterized it in that wonderful old film classic, "Bull Durham." It was never my intent to hurt, insult, or otherwise malign the many millions of Americans who love and cherish this noble American institution. (I hesitate to call it a game, for as you know, it is much much more than that.) Nevertheless, I have committed, at the very least, a grave error in judgment, perhaps even a sin. And while the act of contrition is in itself a reward for the offender, it is merely a down payment to the offended. So, without your forgiveness I shall not feel totally absolved. Therefore I entreat you now to find it in your heart to forgive me. Please believe that this is no capricious request. Please believe, too, that you have my solemn word that I will never commit such slander again. Finally, to demonstrate how contrite I truly am, I am giving you the enclosed gift. It's a baseball, which you could say is something of a family heirloom. It first belonged to my father. And he then passed it on to me. For what it's worth, I have personally autographed it for you. Please forgive the appearance and the slight pungent odor of the ball. But I am certain you understand that these things do yellow and grow musty with age. In any case, I hope you will accept it in the true spirit in which it is given.

As always, your humble servant,
Myron Shippe Goldberg

~

I wanted to call Alexi before I left for my office so I could catch him before he left his. This turned out to be a mistake.

There are two phone lines coming into the suite, one for the kids, and one for Sheila and me. The problem is, the kids' phone is out of order, so Ray has been tying up mine. It seems her friend Jen was also stricken with a cold and forced to spend the day at home.

The only time I had access to the line, Alexi was not available. I have reason to believe, however, that he will return my call shortly. In the past, he has always responded with courteous speed. Perhaps he has tried to get through already. (It's hard to say, since only the kids' line has Call Waiting.) Ray knows that he has been trying to get through, but she has been less than sympathetic. I think that she is still bitter over the speculation in the media that she and Raskolnikov will become an item during the summit. Maybe this is her way of trying to prevent the summit from taking place. I don't know.

Anyway I hope Alexi keeps trying, although I suppose the truly sensible thing for me to do would be to make another call from my office. Of course, Bull Dozier probably has a bug on that line by now. Which is not necessarily a bad thing.

&

Later, in my office, I try Alexi again. The phone rings five or six times and then I hear a click, followed by a man talking stiffly.

"Hello, you have reached Alexi Brezniski, President of Russia, once again the most powerful nation on the face of the earth, winner of ninety-eight gold medals at the 2012 Summer Olympics. I cannot come to the phone right now, but if you leave your name, number, and a brief message after the beep, I will call you back as soon as possible. Thank you." This is followed by a beep, which is followed by another man talking stiffly.

"Hello, Alexi. Ron Goldberg, President of the United States of America. Please call me back when you get a chance. I wish to discuss a matter of some urgency."

∼

I did not sleep with Cookie Dunn last night. And I do not know why. Perhaps, subconsciously, I want to save myself for marriage. Or maybe I want to save the marriage I have. After all, it's not Sheila's fault she has a malfunctioning sexual thermostat. Besides, it's more like she has zone heat because she radiates warmth and affection in so many other ways. Be that as it may, I am getting so horny there isn't a keyhole in the Ridgeley that's safe.

"Paul?"

"Mr. President, hello."

"Everything okay?"

"Great, great. Couldn't be better. Another few weeks and we'll be operational."

"Terrific. You've done an absolutely outstanding job. You and your people are to be congratulated."

"Thank you, Mr. President."

"Ron."

"Ron," Paul repeats awkwardly.

"Look, Paul, if you get any more calls from Bull Dozier, let me know immediately."

"Will do. There's been nothing lately, though."

"Well, I'm sure he's up to something. He's been a little too quiet of late for my liking."

"I'll be on the alert," says Paul.

"Anything else to report?"

"There was one other call."

"From whom?"

"He said he was from the *Post*."

"The *Post*. Jesus Christ!"

"Don't worry. I didn't tell him a thing."

"What'd he want?"

"Actually, it's kind of funny. He said, 'What in the hell are you boys up to out there in Arizona?'"

I laugh. "That's great," I say. "Just great." The Arizona Project, as you will recall, is in Nevada. "I guess a secret project by any other name would still be a secret project in Nevada. Eh, Paul?"

"Guess that's true, Mr. President," says Paul Finkelstein, the world famous movie director.

"Ron," I say.

"Ron," says Paul.

I hang up. I still haven't heard from Alexi. Maybe he's been assassinated, or delayed in traffic. I hope not.

༄

"Tim," I say. "Did I wake you?"

"You gotta be kidding."

It is 6:30 Tuesday morning. Tim has always been a late riser. He usually doesn't get up until nine. He never likes to get to Capitol Hill before ten. "I just thought..."

"Ronnie, I've been up for hours. What's on your mind?"

"Cookie."

"So what else is new?"

"Tim, I need you to do me a favor. I want you to ask Cookie to stay in D.C. for a couple of weeks."

"I thought that's what she was doing."

"Is that what she told you? She told me she'd stay until Wednesday and that was it. She said she had to get back to the kids."

"That ain't what she told me. Besides, her kids are spending the month with her ex. He took a job with some

312

insurance company in Chicago. Bought a house not more than a mile away from Cookie's sister."

"She didn't tell me any of that."

"I'm sure she has her reasons."

I realize that Cookie could've stayed until the end of the month all along. Maybe she even planned to. "I'm sure," I say. Maybe she just needed to know that I wanted her to stay. Maybe she just wanted to be asked. Damn it, thirty-five years have gone by and we're still playing the same games.

"Look, Ronnie, I'd love to chat, but I really have to go. Got an appointment with an old buddy of yours."

"Oh? Who's that?"

"Fleming Hodgetts."

"No kidding."

"Yeah. Said he wanted to talk to me about this WAIDS thing. No idea why."

"I'm sure he'll tell you."

"No doubt."

"Well, you be sure to send him my regards."

"I will," says Tim. "Hey, you going to tell me what you wanted, or do I have to come over there and beat it out of you?"

"It's nothing," I say. Tim's forgetfulness worries me. Is it a residual affect of the accident? Or just the result of having been awakened too early?

"It didn't sound like nothing a few minutes ago."

"Time changes everything," I say.

"Ever the philosopher," says Tim.

"Sorry I woke you."

"You didn't wake me," says Tim. "I told you — "

"I know, I know, Fleming Hodgetts."

"Right."

"Okay, so I'll talk to you later."

"I'm worried about you, Ron. You don't sound so good."

"You're kidding. You're the one who almost died."

"Thanks for the reality check."

"Sorry," I say.

"It's all right," says Tim. "You take care now."

"Okay, Dad," I say. "Bye."

"Bye," says Tim.

As I hang up the phone, I can think of nothing but Cookie. I dial her room number, determined to let the phone ring a million times if necessary, just to hear her voice. On the tenth or eleventh ring, she picks up. "Hello," she says. My God, that voice! "Hello," she says again. I have the strangest urge to ask if she has Prince Albert in a can or if her refrigerator is running. "Hello? Is anybody there?" she says. I hang up the phone ever so gently, as gently as I used to put Sam and Ray in their cribs after having rocked them to sleep.

∾

It is September 30th. Woody is about to take Cookie to the airport for her morning flight back to Chicago. I will not be accompanying them. It would require an extraordinary amount of security. Not to mention, Ashley Jones has cautioned, all the publicity it would get. A mystery woman in the life of Myron S. Goldberg would not, at this point in his presidency, do his credibility any good. Cookie and I say our goodbyes at the Ridgeley.

"I'm really glad you could come," I say.

"Me too," says Cookie. Her eyes, now blue again, are watery. So are mine.

"I'll expect you back here in November," I say. Cookie, shortly after my conversation with Tim Green, confessed that she and her ex now share custody of their children, with physical possession changing from one parent to the next on a monthly basis. I didn't have to prod this information out of her. It just spilled out.

"I'll try," she says.

I kiss her on the lips, in full view of Woody and several Secret Service agents.

"Ron," she says. "Please. People will talk."

"People are already talking."

"Not about us."

"Don't be so sure."

Woody eyes his wristwatch. "We should get going," he says.

"Take care," I say. I squeeze Cookie's hand. It is cold, very cold.

"You too," she says.

Woody and Cookie board the elevator that will take them to the underground garage where their limo is waiting. Cookie and I stare at each other while the doors close. I watch the floor indicator light until the elevator reaches the garage level. Then I press the up button. In a moment the elevator doors open once again. This time the elevator is empty.

⁓

The next morning, a *Post* story breaks, as Fleming Hodgetts promised it would, about the alleged Arizona Project. This time, the *Post* says that "reliable sources" confirm that a secret military project in Arizona not only exists, but also is, in fact, nearing completion. Sources claim that the project represents a major, and unsanctioned, expenditure of government funds, siphoned surreptitiously from the defense budget by way of a laundering operation involving "several" foreign banks. It is believed that Israel may be involved in the laundering operation, but Solomon Dayan has been unavailable for comment. The Ridgeley, the story continues, denies all allegations, insisting that they are "unequivocally false and politically motivated." According to Press Secretary Ashley Jones, the president will hold a press conference in the "near future" in order "to clear the air" concerning this "unfortunate fabrication." Furthermore, another Ridgeley source — believed to be either Senior Advisor Phil Hurley, Chief of Staff Woodstock Stone or one of the members of their respective staffs — has indicated that the president is "deeply and visibly upset" over this matter and that he has allegedly responded to the charges by saying, "If I were going to hide the afikomon, which I am not saying I did, believe me it would stay hidden until it's time for dessert." This latter statement, the *Post* says, has neither been corroborated nor explained.

∾

The truth? I have no intention of holding a press conference in the future, near or otherwise, concerning the charges leveled against me by the *Post* and its underground of political misfits and malcontents, who are, I suspect, headed up by Bull Dozier himself. Surely they can't expect me to give credence to these charges by going to the trouble of denying them. The afikomon remark? Yes, I did say that and ordered Phil Hurley to leak it. What does it mean? Here's the short version: dessert is a dish best served after dinner.

I did make one other concession to the press. I have invited them to the unveiling of the "secret project" on November 5. I have not asked them to RSVP. I do not, under the circumstances, feel that it's necessary. Personally, I think that if I failed to invite them, they would suspect that I am trying to cover something up.

∾

Alexi finally returned my call in the evening.

Besides Solomon Dayan, Alexi Brezniski is the only world leader who knows the true nature of the Arizona Project. We have spoken of it often during its invisible germination. When I say, however, that Alexi has been privy to the project, this does not mean that he fully trusts me. On the contrary, he approaches me with the mistrust with which adversarial allies must approach one another and, though Alexi is charming and outgoing, I have learned to mistrust him as well. Can a relationship built on mutual mistrust work? I don't know. I hope so. There is a lot at stake.

My conversation with Alexi went something like this:

"Ron? Alexi."

"Alexi? Ron."

"Ron Goldberg? The leader of the free world?"

"The very same."

"And what is on your mind, my esteemed equal?"

"I just want to be certain all is well, and that you will be here for the summit as planned."

"*Da*," said the Russian leader. "I will be there with balls on."

"Bells, you mean."

"Balls, *da*."

"And what about that big Raskol of yours? Is he coming too?"

"Raskol? But of course. He looks forward to meeting the leader of the country where Billy Joel lives." Since his concert tour to the now disintegrated Soviet Union in the late 80s, Billy Joel has enjoyed enormous popularity there. Recent reports have in fact confirmed that Billy and Joel are currently the two most popular boys' names in the country, with Boris coming in a distant third.

"Excellent," I said. I felt, I confess, like the head of a

royal family arranging a marriage between his daughter and the heir to a foreign throne. If Ray finds out that I breathed so much as one word of encouragement of this liaison, she will kill me. "Ray's looking forward to meeting him, too."

"So, then, everything is settled," Alexi said.

"Everything," I said. But I couldn't help thinking, and still can't help thinking, that I, we, have left something out.

꩜

Jack Frost looks happier than usual, if that's possible. "I'm pleased to report, Mr. President, that the American people, for the most part, still support the concept of a Russian-American summit."

"That is good news," I say.

"Yeah, the polls are running about 60% 'for' and 30% 'against,' with the remaining 10% either undecided or in favor of implementing a first strike."

"That's great, Jack."

"Fleming's been an asset, too. Even Dozier is getting in line." Fleming Hodgetts, God bless him, has defended the summit, calling it "an important step." Bull Dozier has said that it is "of some value." However, Robert E. Lee Sanders, the President-in-Exile of the United States, has warned the country that a "weak president," presumably meaning Myron S. Goldberg, could very easily "give away the store." Furthermore, Sanders said, anyone who would "cover up a prostate problem" has, more than likely, something else even more serious to hide. When Peter Taylor, the ABC news anchor, called later and asked me to comment on the Sanders statement, I said, "Personally, Peter, I think a man should cover up his prostate — at least in public."

"May I quote you on that, Mr. President," said Taylor with that wry laugh of his.

"Indeed you may," I said. And, much to my surprise, he actually did quote me during the final segment of the evening news. At least no one can say I'm losing my sense of humor.

 ∾

Tim Green has always been fond of saying that there are only two things you should ever put in your mouth — your food and your elbow. In lieu of my elbow, I have frequently inserted my foot. Still, the public reaction to my most recent remark has been largely favorable. Emails supporting my position have been flowing into the Ridgeley at roughly a 2 to 1 margin. And, I am proud to say, unlike the telegrams sent to the White House in support of the Nixon and Reagan administrations during times of controversy, members of my staff did not create mine, nor, as in Nixon's case, were they financed by some secret fund.

What did Robert E. Lee Sanders have to say about my comment on his remark? He said, "That's just the sort of thing I'd expect someone in his deteriorating condition to say."

I wonder if the menorah burnings will start again? I hope not. Now that Sam knows what they're all about, they upset her.

 ∾

Wednesday, October 16, 2013. The summit is rapidly approaching and all I can think about is Cookie. I cannot remember the last time I saw Marcy Gillis. The novelty has worn off, I guess. Besides, Woody has taken more than a passing interest in her and I certainly haven't changed how I feel about dipping my pen in the same inkwell as somebody else — particularly a much younger, more virile somebody else. So be it. I have bigger gefilte fish to fry. My rendezvous is to be with history, not with the masseuse next door.

∾

Alone in my office for a moment, I pick up the phone and call Cookie in Chicago. Surprisingly, I get her, not her machine. "Cookie?"

"Ron?"

"Yeah."

"Is something wrong?

"No. Maybe. Yeah. I need you, Cookie. I need you now. Here."

"Oh, Ron. You know that's just not possible. The kids. I can't."

"I thought they were with your husband."

"Who told you that?"

"Tim."

"Tim was mistaken."

"So bring the kids, too."

"I can't."

"Then just you."

"I'll think about it. Arrangements need to be made."

"For the kids? What about your sister?"

"I'll see. I've got to go now. Goodbye, Ron."

"Bye, Cookie."

∾

Is it my imagination, or have I suddenly been thrust back in time? It seems like junior high school all over again, every detail meticulously and sadistically recreated, the eternal recurrence of even the smallest, as Nietzsche said, everything but the acne. Oh, C is for Cookie, that's good enough for me.

But am I good enough for Cookie Dunn? That is the question. Perhaps in a few months I shall be. My God, is that why I am really doing all this? To win Cookie's love once and for all? It could be so. After all, did I not marry Sheila to make Cookie jealous? Oh, Myron, Myron, Myron! Is there no end to what you would do to make the fair Cookie Dunn yours?

∽

I don't suppose I would be believed if I said that all Alexi Brezniski and I talked about was my daughter Ray and his son Raskolnikov, and whether or not he, Alexi, still planned on showing up for the summit. The truth is, we did have other points to cover, which I wish I were at liberty to discuss. What went on between Alexi and me must remain between Alexi and me, at for the time being. I haven't even told Woody, Phil, Candace, Cal, Tanya or Ashley some of the things we talked about, although each of them knows something the others don't. I have found there is some merit in keeping one's puzzle pieces in different drawers.

Speaking of puzzle pieces, I still haven't seen Bull Dozier lately. With so many people, it seems, out of sight is out of mind. But not with Bull. If anything, the opposite is true.

∽

I wasn't expecting Woody until 9 a.m. But what's fifteen minutes? Besides, he's not a morning person of course, and I should be happy that he's so prompt for once — particularly this early.

I open the door. "Woody, what a surprise," I say.

"So I'm a few minutes early," says Woody, like it happens all the time. "What's the big deal?"

My eye is caught by Woody's zipper. It is all the way down. "Stay with Marcy last night?" I say.

"Yeah. How'd you know?" says Woody, sounding a little indignant.

"It's pretty obvious," I say, and I point to his fly.

"For chrissake, Mr. President," Woody says.

"How's she doing anyway? Got her Ph.D. yet?" I meant that last remark to be endearing, but I think it came off as being condescending.

"She's a lot brighter than you think."

"I know, I know. I didn't mean that the way it sounded. I'm a bit on edge lately. I apologize."

"For what? Being on edge?"

"You know what I mean."

"I guess I do," says Woody, acting now like the dutiful son. "Apology accepted."

"You want to know something else, Woody?" I say. "I'm scared."

"Ron Goldberg scared? I don't believe it."

"I'm scared the whole foolish project will fail. I'm scared...I'm scared of dying."

"Dying? Hell, what's dying got to do with anything?"

"You know, Woody, sometimes I think my entire adult life has been devoted to one thing and one thing only. To prepare myself for dying. That's what drives people, Woody. That's why we're so damn obsessed with making something of ourselves. I suppose if we manage, by some miracle, to turn our pitiful selves into something of value, then we don't have to fear that final journey, now do we?"

"The First Lady's been playing hard to get again, huh?"

"Yeah," I say and I sigh heavily. "Yeah, I guess that's it." But that isn't it. Not really.

~

At 9:02 a.m. the plane carrying Russian President Alexi Brezniski touches down at Andrews Air Force Base. It is very cold for this time of year. The skies are overcast and it is drizzling. To the west, a few patches of blue have appeared. I, and those around me, take this as a good omen. As the plane taxies toward its final stop behind the receiving stand, I make one more trip to the men's room. Standing in front of the urinal, my stream flowing, I think that there is probably no other time when a man is more vulnerable to attack. Whoever, I think, could get an enemy's armed forces to urinate simultaneously could ultimately conquer the world! How could a man possibly protect himself, except to urinate on his assailant? And what sorry counterattack that would be! Perhaps I should mention this to Ollie Graham.

Woody pulls up from behind and parks himself in the urinal to my left. "How 'bout those Sox?" he says.

I laugh so hard I almost wet myself. The Boston Red Sox finished dead last this year. Apparently my remark about baseball unnerved their attempts to muster a serious pennant drive. "Woody, Woody, Woody," I say, "you ever think how vulnerable a guy is when he's pissing?"

"A very humbling experience, isn't it?" says Woody.

"Maybe we should start the damn summit in the men's room."

"Maybe," says Woody, with the caution one uses to address someone thought to be insane.

I give myself a shake and flush the urinal. A couple of seconds later, Woody flushes. "Hurts like hell today," I say. "Today of all days."

Woody tries to lighten my load by acknowledging it. "Your timing has always been impeccable," he says.

"Timing is everything," I say.

Woody tosses a paper towel in the basket and then holds the door for me. "Shall we?"

"Thank you, sir," I say. "Time to roll out the old red carpet."

"So to speak."

As we make our way through the terminal, I am thinking about Robert E. Lee Sanders' "soft on communism" speech. Not this time, I am thinking. Not a chance.

∾

Regarding the summit, there is little need to rehash what the press has been rehashing *ad nauseam* for the past week. Once again, the Strategic Defense Initiative has proven to be the Achilles heel of Russian-U.S. relations. Everything had been going so well up to that point. The conditions for a new, vastly expanded INF Treaty had all been hammered and sickled out. The Russians pledged to dismantle an unprecedented amount of nuclear warheads, although they remained intransigent regarding their right to initiate the use of any nuclear weapons that remained, and the U.S., speaking so eloquently through Secretary of State Candace Rowe, pledged to reduce its arsenal by a like amount, while also maintaining its right to throw the first punch. But then suddenly, SDI reared what the Russians perceive as its ugly head and negotiations promptly fell apart. The window of vulnerability once again supplanted the window of opportunity. Worst of all, however, was not the Russian split with America, but my personal split with Alexi Brezniski. You always know that you're in serious trouble when your enemy resorts to personal attacks, no matter how clichéd the language of assault. Alexi denounced me as a "madman," as a "megalomaniac," as a man "who made Stalin look like Little

Bo Peep." He said that I had all the warmth of a bowl of borscht.

"Was it SDI that precipitated your action?" The press asked Alexi.

"*Da*," he said. "And *nyet*."

"No?" said the press.

"There was more. Much more. So horrible you cannot imagine. I pray for you, America. I pray that you survive having this madman as your leader."

The summit, which was to last for three full days, lasted barely one and a half. Alexi Brezniski walked out on the morning of the second day before he could even finish his second Danish — prune, which I happen to know he loves. So much for photo opportunities.

My popularity with my once-loyal constituents has slid into an abyss. I am, however, doing extremely well at this moment with the far right. Even former Vice President Quayle, who was vacationing in Latin America at the time of the summit, had kind words for me. Happiest of all, though, is my daughter Ray. She has been walking around the Ridgeley with a huge grin on her face ever since Alexi's walkout. I suspect her joy stems from the fact that she didn't have to spend more than an hour and a half with Raskol Brezniski. It's good to see her so happy. Particularly when I am the reason for it.

Even with some skillful deflecting by Ashley Jones, I was not able to avoid the press for long. About twelve hours, I guess. I had thought that if I allowed some time to pass between the meltdown of the summit and my expected press conference, cooler heads would prevail. I was wrong. When I finally allowed the press to corner me, I could see the anger in their eyes. They were out to get me, there was no doubt about that.

"Mr. President, what did the Russian president mean when he said, and I quote, 'There is more. Much more. So horrible you cannot imagine'?"

"I think he was unhappy with the breakfast selections," I said.

There was a pocket of laughter — a contingent of right wing journalists, I suspect.

"Mr. President, please," the same reporter persisted. "What did Mr. Brezniski mean by his statement?"

"He was reacting to a remark that I can assure you was made in absolute jest."

"And what was that, sir?"

"Well, he was being awfully stubborn about SDI, you know, so I said to him, 'Damn it, Alexi, Sylvester Stallone was right about you guys!'"

~

It is Friday, November 1, and Phil Hurley has just handed me a package. It is small, not much bigger than a wallet, and it is wrapped in brown paper. There is no return address on it.

"Has this been checked out?" I ask.

"What do you think, Mr. President?" Phil says soberly. "Of course."

I surmise he's right. Why else would the Secret Service be conspicuously absent? They've taken cover somewhere, the bastards.

With a letter opener I cut through the brown skin. Inside is a small cardboard box. The lid is Scotch taped shut, but I cut through it quickly with the letter opener. I open the box. What I find looks like a TV remote control. There is a note attached to the back of it. This is what the note says:

> Mr. President:
> I thought you would like to have this, so you can practice using it. It is the activator for the flight simulator. I am sending you — separately — the operating instructions. Look for them in a day or so. All continues to be well.
>
> Paul

As promised, the instructions come a day later in a plain manila envelope, again with no return address. I slice open the envelope and take out the instructions. They look simple enough. It does not appear that I will need more time than it will take to fly to Nevada to master the simulator control. I put the control in the envelope and leave it on top of my desk. I have learned from Ray that the best place to hide something is frequently the most obvious one.

〜

The press has not left me alone. Every day there is something in the papers or on the news about my incompetent handling of the summit. They are all convinced that I have led the country to the brink of nuclear war. Armageddon, these 21st century Chicken Littles claim, is right around the corner. Even when I have issued statements to the contrary, the cynicism and pessimism of the press will not disperse. Finally, exhausted, I have Ashley Jones tell the press that, "for the next few days, President Goldberg will be vacationing on Cape Cod. All he wants is to be left in peace." What was the press's response to my not unreasonable request? "Ms. Jones," one reporter said, "if peace is what President

Goldberg is trying to achieve, wouldn't you agree he has a damn peculiar way of going about it?"

Well, in every cloud, they say, there is a silver lining. I just never expected one of the silver linings to be Robert E. Lee Sanders. He praised my handling of Alexi Brezniski, saying, "it is indeed gratifying to see that the president has finally come to his senses and called a Red a Red." Furthermore, I have received thousands of emails from Sanders supporters as well, telling me, "Good work, Mr. President," "Give 'em hell, Ronnie!" and so on. I suspect that all I will have to do now to gain the full support of the Sanders constituency is engineer the overturning of Brown vs. Board of Education.

Where the hell is Judge Clement T. Bosworth when I need him?

~

It is one day before I must leave for Nevada, one day before I must give my answer to the extortionist Bull Dozier. I am still hoping I won't have to resort to telling him the truth. After all, if I did and he didn't believe me, I will have accomplished nothing. Surely, I'm better off sticking with a dandy lie.

~

On Monday, at 6:02 a.m., the phone rings, loud and clear, magnified by the black silence. I am still in bed and even though I am half awake, the ring startles me. I pick up the phone. "Hello?"

"For you, Mr. President. A Lorna Dunn."

"Lorna Dunn? Put her through."

A brief pause.

"Ron? Hi! It's me."

"Cookie?"

"Oh, Ron, I woke you, didn't I? I'm so sorry."

"No, no, I was up. Where are you?"

"In the lobby."

"Here?"

"Of course, here. What lobby did you think I meant?"

"I don't know. I just thought you'd call first or something. Does Tim know you're back?"

"I think so. He's standing right next to me."

"I wish I'd known you were coming."

"So you could've baked a cake?"

"Yeah, something like that. Look, why don't you and Tim meet me for breakfast?"

"Sounds good," says Cookie.

I tell Cookie I'll alert my staff, so she and Tim won't have a problem getting into my private dining room. "Why don't you go ahead? Get some coffee. I won't be long."

"Okay," says Cookie. "I can't wait to see you."

"I'm glad you're back," I say. "I didn't think you were going to come."

"Silly boy," says Cookie. "Of course you knew."

"I didn't know," I say. "But I was hoping."

"So you got your wish. Here I am."

"Look, I'll shower and be right down."

"Okay. Bye-bye."

"Bye-bye," I say. Bye-bye? I never say bye-bye. My God, am I becoming cute? I don't think it's in my contract. I hang up the phone.

Sheila rolls over onto her stomach. Her eyes are turned toward me, but her mouth is still embedded in her pillow. "Who's that?" she mumbles.

"No one," I say, instantly ashamed for having said it.

"Was it your girlfriend? What's her name? Kookie?"

329

"Cookie," I say. "Yeah, it was. But she's not my girlfriend."

"Oh? Then why is she calling you?"

"She wants to see me, is all. She and Tim just popped in to the Ridgeley this morning."

"Kind of early for a surprise visit, isn't it?"

"I don't know. What's early?"

Sheila picks up her alarm clock. It is now 6:11. "This is early."

"So go back to sleep."

"I can't," Sheila says. "I'm up now."

"Sorry," I say. Then I get up and take my shower. By the time I'm finished and start to get dressed, Sheila has fallen back to sleep.

∽

"So what happened to Tim?"

"I don't know," says Cookie. "Business, I guess."

"So it's just you and me, kid."

"That's the way it should be," says Cookie.

I turn over my cup and the waiter immediately brings me my tea. "Thank you," I say. "You order anything?" I ask Cookie.

"I was waiting for you."

I smile and give Cookie a peck on the cheek. "Welcome back."

"Thanks," says Cookie. "You look great. I don't know how you do it. I've been reading all those horrible stories. I know what you've been through."

"It's nothing. Goes with the territory."

"You're a strong person, Ron. A lot stronger than I'll ever be."

"Please," I shrug. "What are you having?"

"Just toast will be fine."

I ask for three orders of toast. "I'm getting a divorce," I say.

"What?"

"I said, I'm getting a divorce."

"When did all this happen?"

"It hasn't. Yet. I just decided it right now. I want you, Cookie. I've always wanted you."

"I don't know what to say."

"Say you'll marry me."

Cookie's expression is somewhere between disbelief and amusement. "This is crazy, Ron. You can't mean it."

"Say you'll marry me, or I'll hold my breath 'til I turn blue."

"Ron, please," says Cookie. I am embarrassing her, even though, for the moment, two Secret Service agents and I are the only other people in the room.

The waiter arrives with our toast. "I have to go to Nevada today," I say. "When I get back, I'll expect your answer."

"What about your presidency? You'll be scandalized."

"After today, it won't matter. After today, only one thing will matter."

"What do you mean? What's happening today?"

"Today, I thread the needle."

Air Force One is scheduled to leave at 9:05 a.m. The tour of the project is to commence at 2:00 p.m. Mountain Time. It will be preceded by a luncheon for the world leaders and the press. In the invitation that was sent to the dignitaries and the press, it was said that they would be put up in Las Vegas the night before. Everyone was satisfied with this arrangement, except for Moammar Mustafa, who refused to stay in the same city where Wayne Newton was performing.

Mustafa also claimed that he had received several assassination threats from a group who identified themselves as the One-Armed Bandits. An investigation of the threats by the FBI turned up nothing and it was dismissed as a prank. Mustafa, however, could not be swayed. He had to be put up at Lake Tahoe instead. In order to further pacify him, he was given tickets to a Sunday night concert where the featured act was Saddam the Sham and the Pharaohs.

It is now about 8 a.m. and I am on my way to my office to get my notes for today's tour and, most importantly, to retrieve the remote control unit for the flight simulator. When I arrive at my office door, I notice that there is a note attached to it with Scotch tape. The note has been written in a child's hand. Here is what the note says:

> Daddy:
> I have a surprise for you. I hope you like it. You are the best daddy in the whole world. I love you tons.
>
> Sam

I take the note off the door, fold it in quarters and put it in my pocket. My eyes have filled up with water. What could bring more pleasure to a father than a child's love, I wonder? I close my eyes and tears run down my cheeks. I sigh and lean up against the door. Sam, Sam, Sam, how I love you! Finally, I collect myself and I enter the office.

What was Sam's surprise? She has rearranged my entire office. Desk, chairs, file cabinets, sofas, lamps — everything has been moved. I am totally disarmed, completely disoriented. The remote, I think. Where the hell is the remote?

At that moment the phone rings. I grab it angrily. "Yeah?" I bark.

"Mr. President?"

"Bull?"

"Yes. We need to talk."

"We do?"

"Don't by coy. It's your ass that's on the line here."

"I don't think so."

"You would if you were me."

"Every day I thank God that I'm not."

"Today's the day to change your tune. Your time's up."

"No, Bull. Your time's up. I have absolutely no intention of capitulating to you."

"I'm sorry you feel that way, Mr. President. I take it that means you don't have any more information for me about the Arizona Project.

"You take it right." So what if the press and the world leaders will learn most of the story today. I am determined to keep Bull out of the loop, to make sure he is the last person to know, to make sure he keeps playing the buffoon.

"Well, you just do what you have to do, and I'll do what I have to do," says Bull.

"Goodbye, Bull," I say. I hang up the phone. My God, I think. I have already broken the Ten Commandments. Not to mention one of Ashley's five. Keep your mistakes complicated and your successes simple. Affairs people understand. Affairs are made of mud and Super Glue.

～

The moment I hang up, the phone rings again. "Yeah. What now?"

"Mr. President?"

"Fleming?"

"Yes. We need to talk, sir." He sounds as if he's on slow boil.

"Can it wait?"

"No, it cannot. It's about this WAIDS thing."

"What about it?" Could Fleming have found out about the efficacy of Quaxil?

"Well, I just got off the phone with James Rivera."

"No kidding."

"Yeah. And you'll never believe what he told me."

LEARNING TO DANCE

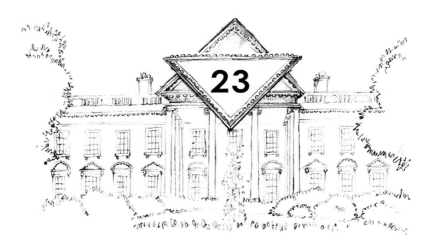

In a panic I begin to search my redecorated office. I move about awkwardly, bumping into things, unused to their new locations. The first place I look is on top of my desk. But where there were once several uneven stacks of paper, there is now a single neat one. And the envelope containing the remote is not a part of it.

After five minutes of rifling through drawers and file cabinets and shelves, it becomes clear to me that I am not going to find the remote without Sam's help. I rush back to my suite and run into Sam's bedroom. She is not there. I call out to her, but there is no reply. Meanwhile, Sheila enters the living room from the bedroom. She is still wearing her nightgown. "My goodness, Ron, what's all the commotion about?"

"I can't find Sam," I say. "Where the hell is she?"

"She's not in her room?"

"No, I looked."

"She must've gone to school then. What time is it?"

"8:20," I say.

"You have your breakfast?" says Sheila.

I do not reply. I pick up the phone and call Woody. I tell him to use whatever means necessary to track down Sam, including calling Robert Mancini and having the son of a bitch put every available Secret Service agent on the search immediately. I tell him to call Phil Hurley and Calvin Foxx to get them working on a way to stall for time, should we need to delay the tour of the project. I even tell him to call Tim Green, whose network of contacts rivals that of anyone I know. Then I remind Woody that we have to be en route to Nevada within the hour and he says he's well aware of that. Just find her, I say, and he tells me to relax for chrissake, not to worry, he'll take care of it.

Fifteen minutes later, Woody and I — along with Phil Hurley, Ashley Jones, Tanya Gregson and Arthur Epstein — board the helicopter that will take us to Andrews Air Force Base for our 9:05 flight to Nevada. Nobody has heard from Sam. "Apparently she didn't go to school," Woody says, but he assures me that every effort is being made to locate her and that it is only a matter of time before she is found.

"Didn't go to school?" says Arthur Epstein.

"Samantha," says Woody.

"Was she sick?" says Tanya Gregson.

"Not that we know of," says Woody.

"Look, nobody disappears in this city for too long," says Ashley Jones. "Isn't that right, Phil?"

Phil nods yes. He knows all too well that even the best-connected people in public service can't stay underground forever. Primarily because we couldn't stand it. It's always better to face the music than to never be able to hear it.

"I need that control," I say. "Nine months of preparation goes down the tube if I don't have it."

"Whatta you mean, down the tube?" says Epstein.

"We'll find her. And we'll find it."

"Find what?"

"I don't know. Woody?"

"Nothing. It's nothing."

"It doesn't sound like nothing to me."

"Or me."

"And it better be on time. These are not the kind of people you can keep waiting for very long."

"I've already made arrangements to have it flown in once we locate it. It'll be here on time. Trust me," says Woody.

"Famous last words," says Ashley.

~

So this is it, Pop.

You really think this will make a difference, Ronnie?

Absolutely. Jack Frost told me that I only have to perform one heroic act and my ratings will soar, my presidency will be saved.

That may be, my son. But didn't your cute little blonde tell you not to peak too soon?

Ashley? Well, yeah. She did. But sometimes, Pop, world peace has to take precedence over an election.

Not exactly spoken like a true politician.

I'm evolving, Pop. I'm now a statesman first, a president second.

I think you'll find, my son, that ultimately you can't be both.

~

I decide to break with my personal tradition and have a second morning cup of tea. It is 10:18 a.m. and we are winging our way through the skies toward Nevada. There is still no word from the FBI or the Secret Service as to Sam's whereabouts.

"It won't always be like this, Mr. President," says Woody.

"It'll be worse, probably," I say.

Woody shrugs. He can't think of an encouraging comeback.

"You know, Woody, it's like I've been learning to dance. Remember what it was like learning to dance?"

"Pretty humiliating."

"Not for me it wasn't. I spent the whole time staring at my feet. I was the last kid in the class to learn the fox trot. The last to learn the box step. Point is, Woody, because I spent the whole damn time watching my own feet, I didn't know that practically everyone was laughing at me. Didn't find out 'til much later. I don't think it's such a good idea, to watch your own feet."

⁓

At 10:32 Sheila calls to say that she has received a DVD by messenger. "It's from Bull Dozier," she says. "So I thought you'd want to know about it right away."

"You did the right thing, Sheel," I say. "Did you look at it?"

"Not yet," she says. "I'm just about to, though."

I can hear Sheila loading the DVD into the player. My heart is beginning to race. Suddenly there seems more at stake than my presidency. I want Cookie but I don't want to lose Sheila. Is it wrong to want them both? Is it wrong to have them both? "Sheel, you there?"

Sheila fumbles with the receiver. "Bombs away," she says.

As I listen for Sheila's reaction, I am covered by a shadow. It belongs to Candace Rowe. Her mood seems dark. "You're not going to believe this, sir."

"Try me," I say.

"It's Bakir. He's coming."

"You're joking."

"That's your department."

"Bakir? Coming? Boy, who'd've thought —?"

Over the phone I can hear erotic moaning. It isn't Sheila. "Look, Sheel, something's just come up. I gotta run. Sheel?" I sever the connection with the trivial effort of one finger. Candace is still in hold pattern, as if waiting for a new flight plan. "Is he coming alone, or is he bringing his camels?"

⁓

At 11:05, I learn that we have lost cell phone contact with the Ridgeley. Prior to that, there was still no word about Sam. How incredibly frustrating and ludicrous to have an object as small as a remote control precipitate such voluminous consequences!

"More tea, sir?" says Woody.

I hand Woody my cup, which still has the tea bag in it. "Just some hot water will do me fine," I say. What I don't need is the caffeine from a fresh tea bag. Get too much of an edge and you can stab yourself.

Woody returns and hands me the cup. "Here you go," he says.

"Thanks," I say.

Woody looks out the window. There isn't a cloud in the sky. "Great day to be alive," he says.

"I wouldn't know."

"We're going to find it."

"Have to find Sam first."

"We will."

"Ah, it was crazy for me to think this whole plan would work anyway."

"It'll work," says Woody.

"How do you know?"

"Listen, if you can win over Sanders, you can do anything."

"Good point," I say.

~

I can now see the landing strip of the Arizona Project. Nearby is a small, rectangular one-story cement building with slits for windows. The enormous storage facility that once stood above the project has been dismantled and carted away. What is left, this rather inconspicuous slab of concrete, is truly the tip of the iceberg.

We touch down smoothly and taxi toward the building. We kick up dust as we go. When the plane stops and the door is opened, the door of the building swings open as well. The first man to emerge is the great film director and the creator of the Arizona Project, the Assistant to the President for Special Effects, Paul Finkelstein. He puts his forearm in front of his face to shield his eyes from the dirt and dust. His hair is considerably longer than it was the last time I saw him, and even more unruly. When he lowers his arm, the sunlight bounces off his thick glasses. I exit the plane to greet him.

"It's good to see you, Mr. President," says Paul.

"It's good to see you, Paul," I say. We shake hands.

"Good trip?"

"Excellent," I say. Why tell Paul the remote is missing? The tour is still a couple hours away and surely it will arrive by then.

"Woody," says Paul, and he shakes the hand of the Ridgeley chief of staff.

"Paul," says Woody.

A whole lot of other shaking and nodding goes on as Paul greets the rest of my retinue.

We all walk toward the shed. "The others are expected when?" says Paul.

I look at my watch. It is 11:58. "They should start arriving in half an hour," I say.

"Well, everything's ready," says Paul proudly.

We enter the building. Inside there is nothing but a few sofas, a half dozen stuffed chairs and an elevator. Paul heads for the elevator, presses a button and the door opens. We get on and Paul presses the button marked "Level 4." The doors close and then I feel the sensation of downward movement. "I need to get to a phone," I say.

"You can use mine," says Paul. The elevator stops and opens into the vast belly of the Arizona Project. In the center of the room is a huge spaceship with a fuselage as massive as a Boeing 787, wings slightly larger than those of the latest Airbus and a nose that could skewer twenty Marines. In the tail section there's a honeycomb grouping of six exhaust ports, each one about ten feet in diameter.

My mouth hangs open. "It's magnificent, Paul. Absolutely magnificent."

"They did an incredible job," says Paul.

"Most of the credit certainly belongs to you, my friend," I say.

"Your brainchild, Mr. President. I am but thy humble servant."

"Bullshit," I say. "There's nothing humble or servile about you. What do you think, people?"

"It's beyond description," says Woody.

"Beyond description."

"Superb."

"Incredible. Just incredible."

"Magnificent."

"That's entertainment, eh Paul?" I say. "Now, about that phone."

～

"Hello. Agent Hunt here."

"Hunt, this is the president."

"Mr. President," says Hunt.

"Any word on my daughter yet?"

"As a matter of fact, yes."

"Well?"

"We found her at the Ridgeley, sir."

"At the Ridgeley? How could she have been at the Ridgeley?"

"She was with a Mr. Leopold Zigler."

"With Uncle Leo? Where?"

"They were having breakfast in Mr. Zigler's room."

"Breakfast! She was supposed to be in school." I cover the mouthpiece of the phone and say to Woody, "Uncle Leo. He's back."

"Thank God," says Woody. "What about Sam?"

"They were together." I take my hand off the mouthpiece. "Hunt, you there?"

"Right here, Mr. President."

"Did you get the envelope I was looking for?"

"Affirmative, sir."

"And it's on the way?"

"Affirmative."

"Good, good," I say. "When did you send it?"

"A couple of hours ago, sir. You should be receiving it any minute now. It was sent via military transport."

"Good work, Hunt."

"There is one other thing, sir."

"What's that?"

"Your daughter, Mr. President."

"My daughter? What's the matter with my daughter?"

"Nothing's the matter exactly," says Hunt.

"Well, what is it then? Stop being so damn cryptic, Hunt! Out with it, for chrissake."

"Your daughter insisted that she deliver the envelope to you herself."

"She what?"

"And your uncle, sir, Mr. Zigler, he wouldn't let her do it alone."

"You mean to tell me they're both coming here?"

"There didn't seem to be any other way," says Hunt. "Besides, Tim Green thought you might want the company."

"Tim Green?"

"Yes, sir. He was the one who actually found them."

"That Tim. He's something, isn't he?" I say to Woody. Then I say to Hunt, "Let me talk with him."

"Who?"

"Who do you think? Tim Green."

"Can't do, Mr. President. But you'll be able to talk to him in person soon."

"He's coming too?"

"He thought your daughter and your uncle shouldn't travel alone."

"Great. Anybody else?"

"Not that we know of, sir."

I hang up the phone. It's never easy, I'm thinking.

∽

At 12:29, the first world leaders arrive. Among them are Alexi Brezniski and Solomon Dayan. With Alexi I exchange a formal handshake. Solomon I embrace. Alexi is dressed like an American tourist traveling abroad. He has on a red sport shirt, khaki shorts and boat shoes, no socks. All that is missing is a camera slung around his beefy neck. Solomon Dayan is wearing a tan summer suit with a white shirt open at the collar, no tie. After we say our hellos, they make their way toward the elevator, guided along by Paul Finkelstein's crew.

By 1:00 all the dignitaries have arrived, except for Mustafa and, if his acceptance of my invitation is to be believed, Diya Bakir. There is some discussion between Woody and myself as to how long we should wait for them. "I'd give them 'til 1:15. No more," says Woody. "The others are getting restless already."

"I think you're right," I say.

"And hungry."

"So let's eat."

Woody tells a young man, one of Paul's people, to see about serving lunch. The young man tells Woody that Paul's regular caterer never showed up, so they ordered box lunches instead. The box lunches were expected to arrive in fifteen minutes. Moments later, I can see a dot in the eastern sky growing larger and larger, until it finally, embryonically, sprouts wings and a tail. I feel as though I have witnessed a birth. "Must be Sam and Uncle Leo," I say.

"Or Mustafa," says Woody.

"Or Bakir," says Candace Rowe.

"And who's behind door number three?" I say.

It turns out to be a U.S. plane. It lands in a cloud of dust and taxies to a stop. The door pops open. An Air Force captain is the first to exit. But immediately following him is Sam, and just in back of her are Uncle Leo and Tim Green. Sam hurries down the plane's steps, while Uncle Leo holds the rail and takes one cautious step after another, leading with his right foot each time. Tim doesn't look much more agile than Uncle Leo as he stiffly descends.

"Daddy! Daddy!" Sam shouts. "I got to fly the plane! He let me fly the plane!" The captain gives me a skeptical smile.

"You did?" I say. "That's terrific."

"I did the controls and everything. It was hyper-cool."

"Wow," I said. "Hyper-cool."

Sam gives me a big hug. By this time Uncle Leo and Tim have joined us. "Uncle Leo," I say. After Sam releases me, I throw my arms around him, pinning his arms to his sides. I smile at Tim. "Thanks," I say. Tim shrugs modestly.

"Careful, careful, you're gonna crush my cigars," says Uncle Leo.

"Still the same," I say. "It's good to see you, Uncle Leo."

"Good to see you, Ronnie," says Uncle Leo. "What's all this mishegoss anyway?"

"This? Business," I say. "Just business."

"Ah, you're up to something, Ronnie. You can't fool your Uncle Leo."

"So you're here. You'll see for yourself." I turn back to Sam. "Can I have the envelope, hun?"

"It's on the plane," says Sam. "I'll get it."

Sam runs back to the plane to get the envelope.

"She's a joy, Ronnie," says Uncle Leo.

"That she is," I say.

Uncle Leo notices that the man standing next to me is Woodstock Stone. "Woody," he says. "I didn't recognize you."

"It's been a few months," says Woody. "I'm much older now."

"Aren't we all," says Uncle Leo.

Aren't we all, I think.

Sam returns with the envelope in hand and gives it to me. I open it to make sure the remote is inside. It is. "Thanks, Sam," I say.

"Did you like your office, Daddy?" says Sam.

"My office? It was great," I say. "How in the world did you move all that stuff by yourself?"

Sam shrugs. "I don't know. I just did, I guess."

"Well, you did one helluva job, kiddo. One helluva job." I hug Sam again and kiss her on the top of her head. I suddenly feel guilty for having been so angry with her. "Come on, sweetie. I'll show you what Daddy built."

∾

While the world leaders and the press are eating their lunches, I give Sam, Uncle Leo and Tim a tour of the spaceship. They are very impressed. Sam asks me if she can work the controls. I tell her yes, but not this time. Uncle Leo asks me how many bathrooms the ship has and I confess that I do not know. Do you suppose he was looking for a job? Tim wants to know if it's a smoke-free ship, although I'm not certain why.

When I finish showing them around, I have one of Paul's people bring us our lunches. While we eat, I study the instructions for the remote — which I had planned to read on the flight. After a few minutes I feel I have the control mastered. Enough, at least, to convince the members of the press and the assembled dignitaries that I know what I am doing.

The remote, by the way, is not really a flight simulator control. I have referred to it as such, and have requested that Paul Finkelstein do the same, merely as a precaution. I felt that, should the control fall into inappropriate hands, it would be best for the owner to think that the control had an essentially benign purpose. In reality, I can say quite unequivocally that it does not.

∾

At 2:10 I tell Paul Finkelstein to start herding our guests into the spaceship. All but Mustafa, who finally showed up at 1:30, and Bakir, who waltzed in with a small army of bodyguards ten minutes later, have finished their lunches. Seeing everyone start to migrate toward the ship, Mustafa tosses his half-eaten turkey and Swiss into a refuse barrel. "I hate Syrian bread anyway," he grumbles. He grabs his chocolate chip cookie and follows the others. I have a funny feeling that a man like Mustafa, without a full stomach, is going to be a problem. Bakir, on the other hand, seems pleasant and tame. He is all smiles, enjoying the company of his new best friend, Alexi Brezniski.

～

Inside the ship, the guests are huddled in front of the control panel. There must be about two hundred people, split almost evenly between American press and foreign dignitaries. From the looks of the turnout, there aren't a lot of, if any, no-shows.

I make my way through the crowd, shaking hands as I go, smiling not happily but importantly. "Thank you for coming," I say. "Thank you for coming. Good to see you, good to see you." Most of my guests have looks of confused apprehension on their faces. There is only minimal interaction between them. Their attention is largely focused on me.

I take my place next to Paul Finkelstein behind the control panel. I whisper to him, "The moment of truth, eh Paul?" He smiles ironically. Is it the word "truth" that's making him do so, I wonder?

～

"Ladies and gentlemen, distinguished guests, Mr. Mustafa

and Mr. Bakir, it is a great honor for me to have you all assembled here for what I can assure you will be a demonstration of technology that you will not soon forget. The man to my right, some of you may know. Those of you who do not know him probably know his work. His name is Paul Finkelstein and he is the creator of the fictional hero Arizona Smith, the epitome of courage and integrity whose given name I have borrowed for this project. Thank you, Paul. Mr. Finkelstein's prodigious creative skills, combined with the unsurpassed technological expertise of NASA, have resulted in the craft in which you now stand. No ordinary craft, to be sure. No mere excursion vessel. No shuttle bus. But a space age Noah's Ark, capable of supporting, quite comfortably I might add, more than one thousand Adams and one thousand Eves, for an entire decade.

"But why, you ask, do I speak to you of Adams and Eves? Am I suggesting that we, the most powerful nations on the earth, should join together to colonize the universe? Am I suggesting that each of us here today should select the strongest, the wisest, the most peace-loving Adam and Eve we can find in our respective nations to participate in this colonization?" I pause here for effect. "Yes. Yes, my friends, that is exactly what I am doing. Imagine, if you will, not a world made up of petty warring nations, but a planet made up of one people; united in purpose, single-minded. Imagine not a nation whose boundary lines are constantly challenged, but a planet with no boundary line but the sky. My friends, we are, all of us, civilized people. But we are all so different. Lord knows we have tried to live together. But we have not succeeded, and never will. Our differences run too deep. Look at us! We are not different superficially. We are different to the core! Well, to each his own, I say. That is the only way. And that is what this ship is all about. I beg you, for the sake of the human race, to participate in this experiment of renewal, to participate in the creation of a thousand new Edens. My friends, it is all so very simple. From each of your countries, you shall choose one Adam and one Eve. One Adam and one Eve, who will board this very spacecraft and be flown to a new planet, a new Eden, where life can begin anew. Life in its purest form. Life without petty jealousies, life without conflict, life without Rush Limbaugh and Glenn Beck. Don't you see? There is no other way. And if you don't believe me, just look at yourselves. Every nation represented here today has, or will shortly have, a nuclear capability. And what, may I ask, are nuclear weapons? Deterrents? They are only if we all say they are. But who among you would swear on a stack of Bibles, or Qurans, or whatever, that under no circumstances would you initiate a first strike? I suspect very few of you. But even that will no longer matter. When every one of you has his very own planet, everything will be as it should be. The time has come for mankind to sow the seeds of peace elsewhere. I pray we do not let ourselves down."

With the exception of Paul, Uncle Leo, Sam and Tim, no one applauds. All the others appear stunned, frozen in the headlights of truth.

"That's a wonderful theory, Mr. President," shouts Otto Erhard, the Chancellor of Germany. "But how do you propose to implement it?"

"Great steps can never be taken without great effort, Chancellor Erhard. But I am certain that if we work together, we shall succeed."

"This spacecraft of yours," says Mustafa. "How do we know that it can do what you say it can do?"

"That, sir, is why you are here," I say. "If you would kindly take your seats and fasten your seatbelts, you shall see."

There is a general grumbling among the crowd. "Ladies

and gentlemen, please," I say. "I can assure you that everything is perfectly safe. You are in no danger."

"What are you proposing to do?" says Ravi Venkatamaran, the Prime Minister of India.

"We shall travel around Saturn and back."

"That will take months," says a disembodied voice.

"On the contrary," I say. "At the speeds at which this craft travels, it will take little more than half an hour."

Mustafa takes a bite of his chocolate chip cookie and says, "I don't like it."

"Don't like what?" I say. "The cookie? It's a Famous Amos."

"The President of the United States would do well not to treat this matter so lightly," says Mustafa.

"I agree," chimes in Diya Bakir.

"And you are both right," I say. "I apologize. But I hope you will reconsider."

"I will go," says Alexi Brezniski.

"And I," says Solomon Dayan.

Suddenly there is a chain reaction of yeas. I look over to Paul. "Well, Paul, let's see what she can do."

∽

Four stories above the cavern that contains the miraculous whale in which we all sit, the electric drone of a massive door sliding open can be heard. Our spaceship arcs slowly backward, coming to rest when it salutes the sky. I am buckled in but instinct makes me grab the arms of my seat to keep from falling. Suddenly the engines ignite. The candle, as those Mercury astronauts of old were so fond of saying, has been lit. The adventure of a lifetime — for all the dignitaries present and for our planet itself — is about to begin. The deafening rumble of the engines below us grows even louder. Vibration runs through my body from head to toe, from side to side. I sense upward motion. I sense intensifying weight against my body, pushing me deeper and deeper into my seat. Gasps of astonishment and wonder escape into the air, bouncing off the cabin walls. As we accelerate, the gasps turn to cheers. We are on our way to peace. We are on our way to the utter weightlessness of peace.

God, I love show business!

◈

Moments after launch, the protective foreskin of the spacecraft is drawn back, uncovering a massive windshield. Even above the roar of the engines, I can hear the reaction of my guests. They are witnesses to an incredible sight — on one hand, humbling, on the other, elevating. They are seeing death and creation, red dwarfs, white dwarfs, quasars, black holes, the whole cosmic theater. No one says a word to anyone else, but almost everyone is speaking, thinking aloud, mumbling mantras. When we pass the rings of Saturn, however, even these expressions of delight and wonder fade away to mouth-gaping awe. No one who has seen what they have seen can remain unmoved, unchanged. They will be putty in my hands.

◈

Our journey over, my guests regain their ability to speak. "It proves nothing," says one. "A brief excursion does not guarantee survival in space for a decade, or for however long it would take to find suitable planets for colonization."

"Assuming that any or all of us wish to accept your plan in the first place," says another.

"Personally, I think it is a brilliant plan and a brilliant

piece of engineering," says Prime Minister Edwards of Great Britain. "Bravo, Mr. President."

"Yes, bravo!" says another.

Soon all but a handful of skeptics take up the call in praise of the great cosmic pioneer, Myron S. Goldberg.

"You are all a bunch of buffoons," shouts a man who, to many, is one of the biggest buffoons of modern times, Moammar Mustafa. "You really think that we should entrust the futures of our respective nations to one man and one woman, placed in an unfamiliar, perhaps even hostile, environment?"

"We will make every effort, Mr. Mustafa, to explore each potential Eden to the fullest. Our resources in this regard are mind-boggling. In a matter of hours, from distances that will astound you, we can determine the ability of a planet to sustain and foster human life."

"And what of weapons, Mr. President?" says Mustafa. "How will our people protect themselves?"

"They will do that with the one and only weapon they need. Their brains, Mr. Mustafa," I say.

"Brains? What good are brains against a charging elephant? What good are brains against an enemy spaceship? Guns, Mr. President, guns and nuclear weapons. Without them there can be no survival."

"On the contrary, sir, WITH them there can be no survival. Just bear with me a little longer. You will see what I mean."

～

"My friends, leaders of the world, there is not a soul among you who does not desire immortality for his people. But how can we achieve this goal? Surely not by destroying every life-giving seed. Surely not by engaging in perpetual war. But how, you ask, do we avoid this endless conflict? We must first look ourselves in the mirror and admit that we are animals at heart. Territorial animals that will stop at nothing to achieve our ends. And what makes us so? Differences. As I have said before, it is our differences that will forever threaten us, that will one day lead us to Armageddon. Homogeneous colonization is the only way to ensure the survival of our nations, indeed of our species. But — and Mr. Mustafa is perfectly correct to express concerns — there are many obstacles to ensuring our survival. Not the least of which is maintaining the purity of our experiment. What do I mean by this? I mean simply that whatever couple you choose to colonize your planet, they must be the only couple from your nation to do so — save one other, which I will discuss later. If this rule is not adhered to, the experiment will fail. But how, you ask, can we keep others from our country from colonizing? Once the experiment takes root, won't others infected with the pioneering spirit want to join up with that great wagon train in the sky and settle on our new planet? Well, of course, they will. It is human nature to want to follow where the grass has already been trampled. But what, my friends, would prevent these new settlers from bringing with them the old baggage of a corrupt world — disease, hatred, mistrust, nuclear weapons, aerosol sprays? And then where would we be? Right back where we started from, only magnified by one thousand. No, the bottom line is, we must not allow this emigration to happen." At this point, I pat the outside of my jacket pocket to make sure the remote is inside. "I alluded before to another couple who would be allowed to accompany each Adam and Eve to their new Eden. Well, ladies and gentlemen, the couple is you and your wife, you and your husband, you and your relationship. Ah, but we have countries to lead, you say. How can we possibly abandon our respective peoples? A good question. But one that has a very simple answer. In the very near future there will be no countries on Earth, no peoples — indeed there will be no Earth."

There is suddenly much grumbling among my guests. There are shouts of "madman!", "maniac!", "atheist!", "infidel!", "Jew!"

"My friends, my friends, hard as this news is to take, you must recognize the truth in it, the inevitable necessity of it. And what, after all, is truth if not necessity? My friends, it is only a matter of time before one of our fingers presses the button that will unleash ultimate destruction. You have seen for yourselves in recent weeks the first stages of our disintegration. You have witnessed, once again, a breakdown in relations between the two most powerful nations on Earth. Look at us." I look at Alexi and he looks at me. "We know in our hearts that the Cold War is not fully over. We have merely turned up the thermostat a bit. How long — how long! — can this balance of terror go on? How long can we deceive ourselves? Eliminating one type of nuclear warhead, only to replace it with another even more lethal one? You talk of madness. This is madness."

"I do not believe that the Russians will attack," says Diya Bakir. "They, like us, are a peace-loving nation."

"That's just the point," I say. "They are peace-loving. But what is 'peace-loving'? Is it something you are or something you achieve? I firmly believe, and there is much evidence to support me, that it is the latter. Peace-loving is what comes after war-loving."

"He's crazy, he makes no sense," says Moammar Mustafa. "How long must we listen to this insanity?"

"Mr. Mustafa, it is my sincere hope that today's meeting

not be reduced to name calling. You may think of me as you wish, but I must insist that we keep to the issue at hand."

"Yes, let him finish," says Alexi Brezniski.

The grumbling abates and I continue. "Thank you, Alexi," I say. "I do not stand before you to threaten you with nuclear attack. I am beyond such trivial threats. For nearly seventy years now, the world has lived in fear of nuclear annihilation. The Russians fear the Americans. The Americans fear the Russians. India fears Pakistan and vice versa. And so on. But even though we fear one another, there is probably not one of us who sincerely believes that our enemy, or enemies, will ever attack. In a nuclear war, we say, there can be no winners. Only losers. So we scoff at threats. But while we do, a thousand little wars continue all over the globe. One way or another, we are determined to kill each other. Well, there is only one way to stop it. We must start fresh. Ladies and gentlemen, beneath your feet is an arsenal of nuclear weapons, the destructive force of which is not even imaginable. During all those years when America was allegedly eliminating nuclear warheads, we were, in fact, doing the opposite. We were adding to our arsenal, while at the same time storing away, far from detection, the missiles we had promised to disarm. Do you have any idea how many megatons that is? Neither do I. But what I do know is this. America is no longer in danger of a nuclear attack, because America is going to detonate its own nuclear arsenal, blowing herself up and the entire Earth with her."

❧

Jewish teaching has it that, when the Messiah comes, there will be universal peace. To the Jews, therefore, Jesus was not the real Messiah, because he was unable to deliver on this promise. Jesus had a good concept, but it fell apart in execution. Had he been backed by the world's largest nuclear arsenal, he might have done much better.

Now I wonder. Could it be that I, Myron S. Goldberg, another prophetic Jew, am the real Messiah? We shall see, we shall see.

"My friends," I continue to address the stunned throng, "the best rulers are yardsticks. And I intend to be the best yardstick of them all. From this day forth, I shall be the standard against which all leadership is measured. To Charlemagne, Alexander the Great, George Washington, Abraham Lincoln, Vince Lombardi, it is time to bid a fond *adieu*, for they shall be touchstones no more. A man named Myron has taken their place. Above all, remember, that great achievement only comes at great cost."

Somebody mutters, "Jesus Christ." I bite my tongue.

⁓

At this time, I would like to take a moment to voice my gratitude to Fleming Hodgetts for providing me with the inspiration behind what I call my Suicide Plot. It was, after all, Hodgetts who pointed out to the American people during my campaign for the presidency that my brother had committed suicide and that I, therefore, must be prone to do the same. I truly believe that without Fleming's timely kindness and support, I would not have been able to come up with such a plan. So thanks, Fleming, wherever you may be. And whatever James Rivera told you, please know that I just wanted to be certain that Quaxil kept WAIDS in check before I gave it my support.

⁓

I cannot even begin to express the lack of respect shown

to the Presidency of the United States in the wake of my proposal. What started out as sporadic insults became a continuous chant that lasted for ten minutes or more before order could be restored. "MADMAN! MADMAN! MADMAN!" Gimme an M...gimme an A...gimme a D...

Finally, Alexi Brezniski was able to calm the gathering. "Comrades," he began. "I am sure you realize by now that this despicable proposal is what precipitated my walkout during the October Summit. I called it madness then. I call it madness now. It represents the worst type of aggression. Aggression without humanity. My God, Mr. President, when we point our missiles at the United States, do we not still maintain our respect for human life? *Da*. Of course we do. Our motive has always been to protect life. But to destroy the world by turning one's aggression inward, this is unspeakable."

"I suspect, Alexi," I say, "you're just angry because I have defused your threats of destruction. Go ahead, threaten us with nuclear annihilation. You think, under the circumstances, that it would do any good, that it would serve any purpose?"

"You are truly mad, Mr. President," says Alexi with subdued realization. "Who but a madman would not fear the power of Russia?"

There is an enormous murmur of support for the Russian leader.

"Then it must be true that I am mad," I say. "Because I do not fear Russia anymore. The enemy, Alexi, is ourselves. It has always been so." I take the remote out of my pocket. "Here, in my steady hand, is the savior of mankind. With this control, I can detonate the nuclear arsenal below us from a distance light years away. God willing, those of us assembled here shall all be gone by then. Safely tucked away in our new Edens."

"I do not believe that even you would do such a thing," says Moammar Mustafa. "You would destroy my people, that is certain. But you would also destroy your own."

"The time has come again, Mr. Mustafa, to throw out the baby with the bath water. The time has come for a nuclear flood. God has spoken to me and this is God's will. All that's left for you to do is to make your selections. Then I shall split the world into a zillion pieces and scatter it into eternity."

"I don't believe it," says Mustafa. "He's bluffing."

"Bluffing, he's bluffing," says Diya Bakir.

"I do not think so," says Alexi Brezniski. "I do not think that here is a man who knows how to bluff."

"It is nonsense. He is bluffing," says another.

"Perhaps," says Alexi. "But can we take a chance that he is not?"

"Listen to him," I say. "Old enemies know more about one another than old friends. I can, and will, blow up this sorry planet with you on it, or safely off it. The choice is yours."

I put the remote back into my pocket. "I will give you some time, ladies and gentlemen, to talk among yourselves. We shall reconvene in one hour. I urge you to carefully consider everything that I have said. Perhaps I am mad. But ask yourselves: Is it madness to want humankind to survive?" I head toward the exit with Woody, Ashley, Phil, Cal and Candace in tow. Paul Finkelstein and the others remain behind. I am feeling elated, triumphant, my great goal within reach. But then suddenly all is shattered by the blast of a handgun, three or four shots pumped into an overhead fluorescent light. Sparkling glass rains. Panic erupts. People are screaming, shouting, cowering, shielding themselves with their arms, scattering, diving for cover. Before I know it, I am swept up by a phalanx of Secret Service agents and carried by this potent human current out of the room. Hands push against my head, against my shoulders and back, some propelling me forward, some making me contract into a smaller target. My heart pounds. My vision blurs. Am I wounded? I wonder. As we race down the corridor, I feel as though I'm in the belly of a huge, frightened snake. My body tenses, awaiting the discharge of more gunshots. But no more come. Finally, we enter another room, the eye of the storm. The door slams shut, but I can still hear the voices of panic in the distance. Safe, I stand tall. My fear transforms to anger. "Who the fuck —"

"It's Bakir," someone says. "He's got Dayan."

"Not Solomon," I say. "My God, not Solomon."

A KURD HAS HIS WAY

W e now have confirmation. Bakir does indeed have Solomon Dayan, holding a gun to that lovely head of his. We have been told that Bakir plans to execute Solomon and the four other members of the Israeli entourage as revenge for Israel's bombing of Iraqi nuclear plants in 2005, which also took the life of Bakir's two favorite camels. Bakir has said that Dayan's release is non-negotiable.

"Everything is negotiable in this business, Candace," I say. "You of all people know that."

"There is always the exception to the rule." Candace doesn't look at all like her old self. Her face is streaked with worry, which I find very disturbing. This seriousness fits her like a poorly tailored suit.

We are all — Phil, Candace, Ashley, Woody, Cal and I — seated around a conference table in a room in the massive belly of my spaceship, my almost crowning glory. Such a strange feeling it is to be enjoying freedom while just a few doors away one of my dearest friends sits before the executioner's block, perhaps to be murdered at any second.

"I sent for Warren Gates," says Phil. "He should be here in a couple of hours."

Candace grimaces. "Why not send for Curly and Larry, too?" she says.

I shrug and sigh. "I doubt that we have a couple of hours," I say. I also doubt, although not to the extent that Candace Rowe does, that even Warren Gates, who rose through the ranks of the CIA in large part due to his formidable hostage negotiation skills, could win Solomon Dayan's release. I get up and, hand on chin, begin to pace slowly. I feel edgy, angry, weary, alone. Thoughts of failed hostage negotiations appear in my head, especially the half-assed and disinterested German attempt to secure the release of the Israeli weight lifting team from Arab terrorists during the 1972 Summer Olympic Games in Munich. Black September, black ski masks, black hearts, and then, ultimately, black everything.

I can still see them, Pop. Some of the strongest men in the world, powerless to save their own lives.

A terrible tragedy. I often talk with them about it.

"They're all gone," Jim McKay said. I could never get his words out of my head. I could never get his face, their faces, out of my head. I don't want to get them out of my head.

They are grateful that you and others will never forget.

But the carnage, Pop, it's got to stop somewhere. It's got to stop here and now. I cannot, I will not, sit idly by, no matter the risk.

I know, Ronnie, I know.

Then you know what I have to do?

Yes, I know. We all know. Sadat, Rabin, we all know.

So be it, Pop.

So be it, Ronnie.

I stop pacing and lower myself back into my chair. "I've got it, it's solved," I say. "I know how to win Solomon's release. Bring Diya Bakir to me. You'll see."

"Anything you want to share beforehand, Mr. President?" asks Phil Hurley.

"No, Phil, nothing. There's only time left for action. Bring me Bakir."

∽

Phil escorts Bakir into the room. Accompanying Bakir are two Iraqi soldiers in combat uniforms. Bakir is in his ceremonial military garb. He is a tall, well-proportioned man, olive complexion, with waves of thick black hair. His eyes are brown, deep-set. There is an otherworldly character to his stare, to his controlled malevolence. He is clean-shaven. I gesture to a chair opposite mine and Bakir, albeit with a mixture of mistrust and disdain, sits down.

"Thank you for coming, Mr. Bakir," I say.

"The pleasure is all yours."

"Perhaps. Perhaps not."

"You wish to negotiate?"

"Yes."

"Then I should tell you first that I do not negotiate."

"Everyone negotiates."

"I am not everyone."

"Of course not. But I ask that you listen."

"Listening I can do. But even in this I have my limits."

"Then I hope I will not test them. I don't think I will. You see, Mr. Bakir, what I am proposing here is a trade."

"What sort of trade?"

"A life for a life."

"Whose life could possibly be worth more to me than the life of a man who has stolen so many lives I held dear?"

"Mr. Dayan would be flattered that you value his life so highly."

Bakir's eyes narrow. "Whose life, Mr. President?"

I stare into the caves of his eyes until he blinks. "My life," I say.

"Mr. President!" a shocked Phil Hurley exclaims. "You can't possibly, this is absurd, out of the question."

"Sir, what the —" Woody begins. I stop him by raising my hand.

"It seems this trade is something only you knew about," says Diya Bakir with a wry smile. I can only guess, but I suspect he is amused that an American president can act as capriciously and unilaterally as an Iraqi one.

"So it would seem," I say. "But in spite of who I am and whom I represent, it's my life to do with as I think best."

"Then your offer is sincere?" Bakir says.

"As sincere an offer as you will ever hear," I reply.

"Indeed."

"And what is your response?"

"I need a moment to consider it. I shall return shortly." Bakir and his military guard leave the room.

❧

"Have you totally lost your mind?" Phil Hurley says.

I say nothing.

"You can't be serious," Woody says.

"I can, Woody. And I am. Now maybe you don't think this is a big deal, but I'm not exactly setting records in the polls. And you remember what Jack Frost said."

"Which time?"

"He said there are only two kinds of people Americans revere more than war heroes and celebrities. Americans held hostage by terrorists. And assassinated American presidents.

And the way I look it, this is an opportunity for me to end up in both categories."

"Good plan," says Candace.

"Besides, just think how much more effective I could be if I were dead. Look at the landmark legislation that whipped through Congress after Oswald got JFK. There's no question about it. JFK was a helluva lot more effective when he was dead."

Now you're catching on, Ronnie.

That you, Pop?

Who else?

So, it's not such a hare-brained idea?

I didn't say that. But you're absolutely right. Getting yourself killed could be your best shot at greatness. It certainly did the trick for JFK.

All the same, Pop, I think I'll see how the hostage thing goes first.

Why not? You can always change your mind later.

"Well, gee, Mr. President, you do have a point," Candace says.

Phil and Woody still can't believe what they're hearing. Woody looks as if he is about to speak, but then Solomon Dayan, his head attached to an Iraqi soldier by the barrel of a gun, is brought into the room. He sits down at the table opposite me. His guard remains standing. "Is it true what I've heard, Ronnie? I mean, Mr. President."

"What have you heard?"

"That you would trade your life for mine?"

"Yes, it's true."

"I cannot let you do it."

"You cannot stop me."

Solomon sighs. He knows well my resolve. "Why?"

"Like it says in the *Talmud*, Solly. Specifically, *Mishna San-*

hedrin 4:5. 'He who saves one life, it is as if he saved an entire world.' I can save you and your delegation. That's five."

"Five infinities are not worth more than one, my friend."

"Unless you're talking about cars."

"Always with the joke."

"Better to laugh than to cry."

"Still, I am right, aren't I?"

"Maybe. But the seeds of my infinities have already come to life. Your seeds haven't been sown yet. Besides, we both know Bakir would gladly take your life, but I doubt he'd take mine. It's the old game, Solly. He wants a bargaining chip to free terrorists from Israeli jails. And what am I if not the best bargaining chip he'd ever get?"

"I don't know," says Solomon Dayan somberly.

"Solly, come on, don't be so upset. Does the different number of years we spend on earth really matter when you consider that we'll all be dead for the same amount of time? It's my time to act, Solly. My time to die, if necessary."

Solomon shrugs. "For a crazy man, you make sense."

Diya Bakir, in the room where Solomon Dayan is being held, is going absolutely bonkers, screaming at the top of his charred and raspy lungs that the deal is off. He has just found out that this is a smoke-free spaceship and that, should he light up, he will provoke a deafening assault of smoke alarms. Throwing a chair against the wall, he then marches down the corridor and back into the conference room. "I do not give — how do you American's say it? — a rat's ass about the alarms, I'm going to light up." Unfortunately, when he asks if there is a cigarette in the house, no one seems to have one. Which, in spite of the once again noble status of the cigarette industry, is often the case these days. My God, I think, for want of a nail the war could be lost.

"Shut off the damn alarms and someone get him a cigarette," I say, and people scatter to fulfill my command.

Tension becomes palpable as the frantic search for a cigarette takes place. Sweaty minutes go by. I begin to pull at my ear lobe and discover one of the little balls fastened there by my acupuncturist. Squeeze balls to relieve pain. Hey, why not? I squeeze one and then the other. Bakir, I notice, has a more conventional way to relieve stress. Now seated at the conference table, he snaps pencils in half and grumbles. The situation does not look promising. But then a miracle happens. Tim Green walks into the room clutching a virgin pack of Marlboros. He hands them to Bakir who grunts his approval and immediately violates the seal. "You're welcome," Tim says. He looks at me and shrugs.

"I thought you quit, you old son of a bitch," I say.

"And aren't you glad I didn't."

❧

Blowing smoke rings, Diya Bakir no longer seems enraged, merely his arrogant old self again. In fact he almost appears rational. "You are a clever man, Mr. President. And although it was the Jewish dog, Solomon Dayan, who killed my loved ones, I can see now that a Jewish American president is worth more than a Jewish American governor."

"I am very glad to see that your great wisdom shines through the immeasurable sorrow of your losses, Mr. Bakir," I say.

"Then you will come with us?"

"I will," I say. I stand, make my way around the conference table and head toward the door. No one knows what to say anymore. There is a smell of defeat in the room but, contrary to what my trusted advisors believe, it is not coming from me.

At the doorway, Ashley Jones grabs my forearm and holds on tight and kisses my cheek. She looks as beautiful as ever, even sexier in her sad trepidation. "I'll say a prayer for you," she whispers. Tears cover her cheeks.

I give her forearm an affectionate squeeze and smile with resignation. "As long as it's not the *Kaddish*," I say.

WANTED: DEAD OR ALIVE?

25

In spite of what many have called my act of heroic self-sacrifice, the press has not been willing to forgive, nay even to briefly ignore, the cosmic colonization proposal I presented, undeniably with the best intentions, to the leaders of the world. The consensus thus far seems to be that I have really flipped, that the strain of the presidency prior to this latest debacle — my roller coaster ride in the polls, my male problem, the baseball fiasco, the WAIDS crisis, Abe Rubin's assassination, the summit failure, and so on — has finally gotten to me. Could be.

One reporter has already coined a term for the strategy I developed to induce world peace and disarmament. He wrote, "Mr. President, do you really believe that the only way you can ensure the survival of our admittedly flawed species is through Jim Jones Diplomacy?"

The infamous Jim Jones was a Protestant clergyman and

founder of a cult called the People's Temple. In the 1970s, Jones established a settlement in Guyana, which he called — in a vain attempt to feed his insatiable ego — Jonestown. Reports that cult members were being held against their will brought a U.S. representative and three journalists to Jonestown in 1978. For the troubles they endured traveling halfway across the world, cult members promptly killed the representative and the media people. Shortly after, Jones ordered the members of his cult to commit mass suicide by drinking poison Kool-Aid — cherry, I think. There is a better world than this one, Jones was saying.

All things considered, I couldn't disagree with that.

❧

To demonstrate how hospitable they can be, my kindly jailers have given me unlimited phone privileges. And while I am sure that my every word is being recorded, I use these privileges extensively. "It's a funny thing, isn't it?" I say to Woody.

"What's that?" says Woody.

"Nations building up their nuclear arsenals to protect themselves from nuclear attack, spending God knows how many trillions of dollars, and then someone comes along who says he's going to blow himself up and take everyone else with him."

"It's a funny thing, all right," says Woody.

"Not much of a defense against that, is there?" I say.

"Not much," says Woody.

"Of course it's all moot now, Woody. Me being here and Bull having taken over the reigns of power, at least for the time being."

"I guess," says Woody.

"Anyway, give my love to the girls and Sheila. And to Cookie."

"Will do."

◡

I just had a flashback to when I first arrived in Washington in 2001 as a congressman-elect. I remember worrying that, by the time I got my chance to run for the presidency, there would no longer be any serious problems in the world for me to solve. I remember praying for pain.

◡

I guess now I will never know if my disarmament plan would have reaped any benefit. So be it.

But I did get them to think, didn't I, Pop? That's got to count for something.

You did good, Ronnie. Real good. Finally, I have a son who knows how to thread a goddamn needle! I'm proud of you, boy. Real proud.

Thanks, Pop.

And this room, Pop, it isn't so bad, is it? Kind of like being under house arrest at a Holiday Inn.

You could have done worse.

Tell me about it.

◡

Given the chance, would I really blow up the world? A good question. And one that deserves a good answer. In the meantime, let me say that I firmly believe that, as long as a nation can dangle the threat of nuclear self-destruction over the world, we've got a good shot at a meaningful disarmament.

One other thing. Alexi Brezniski didn't really storm out of our summit meeting without finishing his prune Danish. He ate the whole thing. He even licked his finger repeatedly to pick up the crumbs from his plate.

～

I am eating breakfast — rice, dates, a cheese-filled sanbusak and black coffee, spiked, I think, with motor oil — when the phone rings. It's Phil Hurley.

"Good to hear your voice, Phil. Any news about securing my release? I can't seem to get anything out of anyone here, least of all Bakir." Bakir, who used to pay me a weekly visit, now only shows up once every two or three weeks.

"Nothing on our end either, I'm afraid. To tell you the truth, Mr. President, Bull Dozier thinks we should table all the negotiations for a while. And Fleming Hodgetts is backing him all the way."

"Not surprised about Bull. And I guess I knew Fleming would be cutting me loose. Can't hold that WAIDS thing over his head anymore, now that Rivera spilled the beans. I hope you fired Rivera's ass, by the way."

"Just like you said, sir. Only Bull hired him back."

"Figures."

"There is some good news though."

"Yeah. What's that?"

"You're doing great in the polls. 88% approval rating."

"Incredible. Maybe that'll put some pressure on Bull to get me the hell out of here."

"I wouldn't count on it, Mr. President."

"How's that?"

"Jack Frost has been advising Bull against it. Said your ratings would probably go to hell the minute you're released."

"He could be right. But I gotta be honest with you, Phil; at this point I'm willing to risk it. The election's three years away."

"I'll see what I can do."

As it turns out, Phil can't do shit. No one can. And no matter how many Arab terrorists Israel releases in exchange for my freedom, Bakir decides afterwards that it isn't enough. I fear I will be stuck here for a good long time.

∽

Sometime in April 2016. I can't believe I have been here in Iraq, in this same drab room, for two and a half years. Were it not for my continued and remarkable success in the polls — last month my approval rating climbed to a record-breaking 94% — I would think that I am now a forgotten man.

A man, perhaps thirty, enters with a dinner plate, presumably filled with food, covered by a white cloth embroidered with blue Hebrew letters. The man, his demeanor deferential, leaves the plate on the small dining table next the sliding glass doors, which lead to the balcony. The balcony, by design or through lack of funding, has no floor. I sink my hand into my pants pocket, pretending to dig for spare change. "Sorry," I say, shrugging.

The man laughs even though I've been going through this empty tipping routine with him for years. I do not know the man's name. Once every week or so I ask him, but he will not tell me. He says it is enough that he knows my name and, though I disagree, he still refuses to tell me who he is.

"Some day you will tell me your name," I say.

The man smiles again and heads for the door. "On the day you leave here, Mr. Goldberg, I will tell you my name."

"Will you ever tell me your name then?"

"That, I suspect, will be up to you, sir."

The man smiles enigmatically and exits, gently closing the door behind himself as if I were sleeping and he did not want to disturb my slumber. I go to the table and remove the cloth from atop the food. On the plate is a stack of matzo. Could it be Passover already?

∾

Hey Pop, you won't believe the weird dream I had last night.

Was I in it?

Sorry. No. Just me. At first anyway. I was in this terrible rat-infested prison here in Iraq.

Instead of these luxurious quarters?

Yeah, right. And suddenly this little old street vendor plods by, pushing a rickety wooden cart loaded with merchandise.

And what, my son, was this merchandise?

That's the funny part, Pop. He was selling belts and shoelaces.

That's not so funny.

Maybe not, but I took a belt just in case.

Just in case?

Just in case I lose so much weight my pants start to fall down.

∾

I think I am in Baghdad but I am not certain. The skyline is modern and anonymous, no doubt largely created after the Israeli bombing in 2005. In the foreground is a traffic circle with two arms, two legs and a long neck. The neck is lined with a hodgepodge of buildings, none higher than ten stories. My own building is clearly higher since I have been given a vantage point, for some curious reason, that is at least a few stories above anything else I can see.

Every day, beginning at about 9:00 a.m., a crowd of Iraqi men gathers in the park inside the traffic circle. Most of them are young and neatly dressed, some in suits, some in casual clothes. As they mingle, they form a single mass that alternately stiffens and relaxes like a muscle being flexed. Many of the men hold signs with my picture on it. Some hold signs with Solomon Dayan's. The men face a podium. The speakers have their backs to me. Whenever something that strikes a nerve is said, which is often, the crowd shakes, raises and lowers the pictures of Solomon and myself and shouts things, which I do not understand. Favorite chants and cadences repeat themselves. This sometimes goes on for hours without a break. At other times the crowd listens to a speaker at the podium in rapt silence. On the weekends the crowd swells and spills over into the street surrounding the circle as well as down the arms and legs and up the neck. I have been told by Bakir and by some of his cronies that every one of these men is hungry for my blood and the blood of Solomon Dayan. I have also been told that, if I am not a good boy, these men will get their wish, but also that I have nothing to worry about so long as I continue to cooperate. It is nice to be held hostage by such civilized people. It is also nice that, promptly at 5:00 p.m., the speeches end and the demonstrators and camera crews go home to their families.

～

My phone, my only constant link to the outside world, rings. The sound, unlike the insistent ring of my Ridgeley office phone, is muted. It always is. This time it is my esteemed Secretary of State and head of the NSC, Candace Rowe. Though I know I shouldn't allow myself to think it,

I feel as if she has some wonderful news for me. I often feel this way when a member of my staff calls.

"Candace, how nice to hear your voice."

"And it's wonderful to hear yours, too. You're doing well?"

"You're kidding. You wouldn't believe how I am pampered and spoiled. It's like being at Club Med."

"I'm sure."

"So what news do you have for me?"

"Only that we've tried again and failed. I'm sorry, sir. We had really hoped, it being Passover and all, that this would have been a great time to secure your release."

"Good thinking. It's just too bad the Iraqis aren't as amenable as the ancient Egyptians were."

"Yes, it is."

Candace assures me that, in spite of Bull Dozier's and Fleming Hodgetts' opposition, she will keep using every means available to her to get me out, which she says unfortunately does not include the authority to order the release of every Arab terrorist and political prisoner still held in Israel. I thank her and tell her I know that she will do all she can.

◆

My conversation with Candace has reminded of Passovers past, of crude skeletal Seders with my parents and brother, of questions never answered to my full satisfaction. *Mah nishtanah hazayin hazeh mikol hazaynim?* "Why is this penis different from all other penises?"

◆

My God! Why indeed? I think now I know. I think with a little bit of luck I will soon learn the name of the gentle man who brings me the food that sustains my life.

❧

There are two college degrees on the doctor's wall. A bachelor's degree from Columbia University and a medical degree from Harvard. It is nice to be in such competent hands. The doctor is a stocky man, perhaps in his early forties. His hair is bushy and black. His expression clinical. His manner detached. He wears gray slacks and a white medical coat. "And how long have you had this pain, Mr. Goldberg?"

"What year is it again?"

"2016."

"Five years. On and off."

"Stand up and bend forward, please. Rest your forearms on the table."

I obey and soon have a latex-coated finger tunneling up my ass, going this way and that way, bouncing off this wall and that wall, like a drunken worm trying to find its way in the dark.

"Feels fine. No enlargement. Stand and face me, please."

I again oblige. And as I do, a look of bewilderment appears on the doctor's face. "What's this?" he says. "I thought, I thought you were Jewish."

❧

Bakir has asked to see me alone. I take this as a good sign. With just the two of us he will not be distracted by his need to play to an audience. We can talk turkey immediately. Bakir enters my room wearing a shallow yet menacing smile. His deep-set eyes protrude uncharacteristically. I can see that he is seething underneath. I can only imagine the depth of the rage he flew into when he heard the urologist's report.

"The report. Is it true?"

"You want to see for yourself."

"So you are not a Jew."

"Is that what you think?"

"We have learned that your great-great-grandfather on your mother's side was Scottish. And a Catholic. Is that true?"

"I won't deny it."

"So why then would anyone in his right mind pretend to be a Jew?"

"To be popular?"

"You have made fools of us."

"You didn't need my help for that."

"I should kill you right now."

"And what would that get you? A dead Jew may be worth more than a live one. But a live non-Jewish president is worth much more than a dead non-Jewish president."

Bakir slips a revolver from his jacket pocket and presses the cold barrel against my forehead. "What can you give me now that I have not already gotten?"

"You'd be surprised, Mr. Bakir. Very surprised."

Bakir slowly withdraws the gun and returns it to his pocket. "We shall see," he says and he is gone.

Two hours later, my long-time companion and food giver brings me my lunch. "My name is Yasser," he says as he exits.

❧

I have been allowed to fly to Israel on El Al. When I arrive at Ben Gurion International Airport outside Tel Aviv, I am greeted by a crowd that must be twice as large as the one that attended my inauguration. They are cheering wildly, waving American and Israeli flags, holding babies aloft, dancing, laughing. I cannot believe what I am seeing. Tears of joy well up in my eyes. On the tarmac I am greeted and embraced

by Solomon Dayan. Behind him is a beautiful woman, in
her mid-thirties I would guess, with ebony hair and olive
complexion. She is holding a newborn. "This is Yael, sir. My
wife." The young woman hands the baby to Solomon. "And
this little mensch, this is Myron S. Dayan, my son."

"You named him after me?"

Solomon shrugs impishly. "We thought you were dead."

"Well, it's good to have been remembered."

The crowd chants "MSG! MSG! MSG!" and I wave to
acknowledge them. However, as I do, their chanting, now
much louder, switches to "SOLOMON! SOLOMON! SOL-
OMON! SOLOMON! SOLOMON! SOLOMON!" Solomon
Dayan reads the disappointment on my face. "It's not for
me, Mr. President. It's for you."

"For me?"

"Yes. Everyone is calling you the new Solomon. They say
that anyone who could negotiate his own release from the
hands of terrorists, without asking us to release more of their
venomous kind from our prisons, must have the wisdom of
King Solomon. It's for you. It's all for you. Bask in it. It is
well deserved."

Stunned, I wave to the throng with both hands. Their
cheering is now deafening. I wonder if it would be so if they
knew the ignominious deceit I perpetrated to secure my
release.

The days of celebration come too quickly to an end. On
the evening of day one, I had a tearful reunion in Tel Aviv
with Sheila, Sam and Ray. Since then I have been unable to
pry Sam from my side. The poor kid was under the impres-
sion that the whole business with the remote led to my incarceration. I think she is beginning to believe that this could

not be further from the truth, but I can see that it will probably take years of therapy to fully convince her. It is a good thing that Blue Cross has recently increased its mental health benefit to a generous yearly allowance of $750.

∾

Perhaps I should have listened to Jack Frost, stayed where I was, spent the rest of my life eating sanbusaks and dates. My glorification — dare I say "deification"? — in Israel aside, the mainland press is taking every opportunity to rehash the events that, until this untimely rehashing, had long since slipped from public consciousness. They have even gone so far as to portray Myron S. Goldberg as a Jewish-American Hitler. Imagine. A Jewish-American Hitler! My God, could that be any further from the truth? I'm Hitler's worst nightmare, God damn it! That monster of monsters, that failed extinguisher of the people who gave the world the word of God, is rolling over in his bunker if he knows that the most powerful man in the world is now a Jew. But who knows? Maybe I'm America's worst nightmare, too. The press seems to think so. Only a madman, they insisted, would sacrifice the lives of everyone on the planet to achieve what he had the chutzpah to call peace. "The president's plan," wrote the *Post*, "called for the annihilation of every man, woman and child in the United States, including members of his own family. Only he and his wife would have been spared and they, along with an American 'Adam and Eve,' were to have been flown to a still undesignated planet in hope of starting a new civilization."

Lies! Lies! Lies! I shout to an empty room when I finish reading this loathsome account of the greatest peace plan of all time. I had no intention of taking Sheila!

It's getting worse. Woody tells me that, thanks to the press dredging up old news, reopening old wounds, some members of Congress are talking impeachment.

"And I suppose Fleming Hodgetts is leading the charge?" I say.

"You bet. He and some retired general named Thomas Ridgeway. The guy's a WAIDS patient. In remission."

"Quaxil."

"Yeah."

"Well, they're a bunch of ungrateful SOBs, the whole lot of 'em," I say. "I mean, after all I've done for this country. Come on, Woody, who's done more to advance the cause of world peace than Myron S. Goldberg?"

Woody purses his lips and raises his eyebrows.

"And who was held hostage by terrorists for two and a half years? Boy, I'll tell you, being a hostage isn't worth diddly anymore. Wonder what Jack Frost would say about that?"

Not much, if Woody's expression means anything. "I guess it's the Jim Jones thing, sir," says Woody. "Some people apparently find mass suicide offensive."

"You couldn't prove it to me," I say defiantly. "This country has been trying to kill itself, one way or another, for decades! Hell, all I did was give the suicide thing a positive spin."

"Not everyone sees it that way."

"So, what now? Crucify the Jew! Is that what they want?"

Woody sighs. I guess that is what they want.

When I get back to my suite at the Ridgeley in the evening, I cannot believe the state that Sheila is in. I have never seen her so furious. Not even way back when I told her that the House and Senate had voted to redecorate the White House just prior to my taking office. "Why don't we discuss this over dinner?" I say.

"Dinner?" says Sheila. "Honestly, Ron, how can you think of eating at a time like this?"

"But I'm a hero. The new Solomon. They love me. In Israel anyway. C'mon, hun, let's celebrate."

"I'm sorry, Ron. But I've lost my appetite."

"So forget eating, we'll go have a drink," I say, and then I lower my voice. "I don't want Sam and Ray to hear all this."

"All right, all right," says Sheila. "Let's go."

We do not say another word to one another until after our cocktails are served. Sheila's is a vodka gimlet, straight up; mine is Stolichnaya on the rocks.

"He thought he could finish us off," Sheila finally says. "He told me that DVD was all the evidence he needed to prove you were fooling around with some floozy. A floozy? I know you better than that, Ron. I know you wouldn't embarrass me with some sordid affair. I know that if you ever did fool around it would be with someone classy. Like Ashley. Or Candace. Or that Cookie person. And how on earth did he get hold of that thing anyway?"

I think of Ashley sending me a KISS signal. I think of her full lips, the doorway to exquisite passion, pressed against mine. I think of her lithe and strong legs wrapped around my torso like two boa constrictors in heat. I think of Candace and the erotic, mind-blowing thrill of making love to a woman with a tongue that can speak seven languages fluently. But most of all I think of Cookie, clad in that skimpy bikini Tim Green had so heartlessly paraded in front of my imagination.

I think of her mouth-watering breasts, ripe with lust, shrink wrapped in pink cashmere. I think of making gyrating, slippery love to her, one blinding climax after another. "I don't know," I say. "His goons are everywhere. There's hardly a place in Washington he doesn't have round-the-clock access to. Including my office, I'm afraid."

"He's despicable. A common thief. A vicious slanderer. The chutzpah of the man, calling me a floozy."

"Must've been the wig," I say. "Sorry about that."

"Oh, Lord, it's not your fault, Ron."

"I should have known he'd stoop this low. I can't believe how naive I am sometimes."

"It's okay," Sheila says. "I know you meant well. You wanted us to have a little adventure. And we did. Boy, did we ever!"

"You're not mad then?" I say.

"Not at you."

"What do you want to do then?"

"About Bull?"

"Yeah."

"He said I was crazy for sticking up for an adulterer."

"And what did you say?"

"I told him that he was the one who was crazy and that if he ever tried anything like this again, I'd use him to make matzo."

"He must've appreciated that."

"He threatened to make the DVD public."

"Oh, God."

"I told him if he even thought about doing that again, I'd have him arrested for pornography peddling as well as breaking and entering. That shut the son of a bitch up."

"Sheel," I say. "You're amazing. Goddamn one in a million."

"I guess I am," Sheila says through a smile.

I signal our strapping young Filipino waiter. "Another round, Ferdinand," I say with a flourish. "On me."

So?

So what?

Am I the hero the Israelis think I am?

Son, no one is ever the hero others think he is.

Am I a hero at all?

You did what you had to do.

But did I betray our people? Myself? My religion? My God?

You'll have to speak to Her about that?

God's a She?

And a He. Stick to the point, Ronnie.

The point, Pop, is that I'm a pragmatist, not an ideologue. I use whatever means, whatever weapons, I have to achieve victory. The end justifies the means. Or in this case, the end was the means. You could say I always had the answer right on the tip of my —

Enough of that talk, Ronnie.

Sorry. But isn't it better, Pop, to live to fight again than to die without purpose?

Don't ask me. I died for love of latkes and rugulach. On a good day my cholesterol was 268.

Be serious, Pop. When I'm dead, what more can I really accomplish?

That will be up to you, Ronnie. You'll have a whole eternity.

On Earth I mean.

You're forgetting JFK and all he accomplished after he died.

JFK had a program waiting to be pushed through Congress. I only had a suicide plot.

I see your point. But at least you had chutzpah. Truman, he had chutzpah. And look what a great man he was!

I don't know, Pop. Chutzpah is one thing. Stupidity is another.

Well, you don't have to lecture me about that. Remember I was the one who told you not to do that Torah thing at your inauguration.

I know, Pop, but you still haven't answered me.

Answered what?

Am I a hero?

Is he a hero, he wants to know.

Yeah, Pop. Am I a hero?

Ronnie, to me you'll always be a hero.

~

The next morning, alone, in a corridor of the Ridgeley, I pass two Secret Service agents, one male, one female, one mind. Neither pays attention to me beyond issuing a perfunctory nod, a barely audible hello. I wonder, since a main function of the Secret Service is to detect counterfeiters, if they think I'm a counterfeit Jew. From all appearances they do not have a clue. I take this as a good sign.

THE CLIMAX

I have been avoiding Cookie Dunn since I have returned from Israel. I had planned to see her immediately, while I still had a buzz on from the mammoth fuss the Israelis had made over me. But then came the shrill cries of the press, accusing me of crimes against humanity, followed by calls for my impeachment in Congress. And suddenly I was no longer in the mood to face the possibility of any further rejection. If Cookie says that she will not marry me, I do not know what I will do. Tim Green says she keeps asking for me and begs him to let her see me. I have instructed Tim to tell her that I am in no condition to see anyone right now. Cookie tells him that that is precisely why she must see me. She would be good for me, she says. She will restore my shattered hopes. Does this sound like a woman who is not in love?

"Tell her I'll see her tonight," I say to Tim.

"Where and when?"

"Her room. Say about nine."

"Will do. You sure you're ready for this?"

"How bad could it be?" I say. "The woman is obviously nuts for me."

                        ~

At 4:30, Woody and Phil rush into my office. Woody is more animated than he has been in months. Phil, as usual, plays his cards close to the vest. "You're not going to believe this," Woody says.

"Believe what?" I say.

"Follow me," says Woody.

Phil and I follow Woody through the maze of corridors that leads back to my suite. "Open it," he says. He sounds like a child who has just given his father a very special present, and can't wait for his old man to see it and say how great it is, and how great he is for having thought of such a wonderful gift.

"What's going on here?" I say. I'm not real keen on surprises anymore.

"You'll see. You'll see," says Woody.

We pass through the doorway. "Out here," says Woody, gesturing to me to follow him onto the balcony.

"This better be good," I say.

Woody just smiles and smiles. "Come on, come on, hup hup hup."

When I step out onto the balcony, I see the most amazing sight that I have ever seen or will ever have the privilege of seeing. Even exceeding what I had so recently experienced in Israel. Across the street in the park is a crowd that must be a million strong. There are young people, old people, in-between people. There are black people, white people, yellow people, tan people and red people. There are men and there are women. And signs. My God, thousands of signs, proclaiming things like WE AGREE WITH MSG, MSG HAS MADE US FREE, and OUR MESSIAH AIN'T NO PARIAH. There are even signs with Fleming Hodgetts' face that say IMPEACH THE LEECH. And hundreds more that say, BOMB THE PRESS WITHOUT REDRESS. And thousands more I cannot even read. I move closer to the rail. And then, when the crowd recognizes that it is me standing on the balcony, they begin to chant, SOLOMON! SOLOMON! SOLOMON! SOLOMON! SOLOMON! SOLOMON! I wave both my arms above my head to acknowledge them and they cheer even louder. OUR MESSIAH AIN'T NO PARIAH! OUR MESSIAH AIN'T NO PARIAH! SOLOMON! SOLOMON! SOLOMON! SOLOMON! SOLOMON! SOLOMON! Et cetera, et cetera, et cetera.

"My God, Woody, who the hell are all these people?" I say.

"You don't know?"

SOLOMON! SOLOMON! SOLOMON! SOLOMON! SOLOMON! SOLOMON!

"No, I have no goddamn idea."

"It's NO CRAP," says Woody, laughing.

"It's who?"

"NO CRAP. The New Order of Citizens Rallying Against Permissiveness. They're your Uncle Leo's people."

"Uncle Leo's people?"

"Yes! Yes!" Woody shouts above the madding crowd. "Don't you see? Uncle Leo's behind the whole thing."

"Son of a bitch," I say. "Uncle Leo? Ha! Uncle Leo!"

MSG! MSG! MSG! HELL NO, EARTH WON'T BLOW! HELL NO, EARTH WON'T BLOW!

"They love you, sir," says Woody. "Just listen to that. Listen to that!"

I listen. Boy, do I listen. It is absolutely intoxicating. How can it get any better than this?

∾

It is 9:07 p.m. For the past two hours, I have had my suite to myself. Sheila has taken Sam and Ray to the Frenches' house for dinner. I had been invited, too, of course but I declined, saying I had a previous engagement, which is true, but even if I did not I don't think I could have faced another confrontation with Bert regarding the Really Gross National Product and the Grand Canyon landfill. Only Sheila knows what I am up to and she told me that if my whereabouts should come up in conversation, she'll simply say, "Oh, these things happen. You know how it is."

"Thanks, Sheel," I said. "I owe you one."

"You owe me a lot more than one," Sheila said.

I start to feel a little guilty about what I am planning to do. But this feeling quickly melts into self-pity and resentment. If Sheila had been more of a wife to me all along, perhaps I wouldn't have become so much less of a husband now. Anyway, does it really matter who is to blame for this sorry state of affairs? The truth is, Sheila always was my second choice. And as long as Cookie Dunn is in my life, she will remain so.

At 9:30 I find myself at Cookie's door. This time I do not walk past. This time I am not suffering from the nervousness that so often accompanies indecision. What I'm feeling now is pure relief. If death is the ultimate form of liberation, then the failure of a marriage must be a close second. I knock loudly.

Cookie opens the door without hesitation. "Ron!" she says, her excitement obvious though muted. "I was starting to think that you weren't coming. What time is it? Come in, come in."

"It's only 9:30," I say. "The demonstration outside the Ridgeley today, I'm running behind because of it."

"Oh isn't it wonderful!" Cookie says. "I was so happy for you. After all you've been through."

"Through," I say. "That's the word for the day, isn't it? It's certainly how I feel."

Cookie takes me by the arm and walks me inside her room. She is wearing a pink cashmere sweater that clings lovingly to her firm, youthful body. Could this woman really be fifty-three years old? "How can you be through?" she says. "My God, Ron, those people adore you."

"It's not enough," I say. "They're not enough. Oh, sure, things are starting to look up for the next election. But —"

"But what? There are people everywhere who love you."

"Sure, like the suicide cults. Now that's a kicker, isn't it?" I clear my throat comically. " 'Ah, Mr. President, we have some good news and some bad news. The good news, sir, is you're gaining supporters by the truckload every day. The bad news is they're all killing themselves.' It's perfect. Just perfect."

"Ron, please, you mustn't think that way. You've done your best. Exceeded expectations. One day, if not soon, you'll be recognized as the great man that you are. It's happening already. Surely you can see it. A man before his time. That's what Ron Goldberg is."

"A man before his time. God's gift, maybe."

"Maybe you are," Cookie says with affectionate defiance, the way a child might defend a crazy parent when no other human being or shred of evidence will. I can see in her glassy eyes that she truly believes what she has said. How I want to as well! But how can I? A Jew who would deny his sacred birthright merely to save his own skin. Wasn't I burdened, cursed, with too much skin already?

"God's gift," I mutter again. I manage a self-deprecating smile. "If this piece of clay called Ron Goldberg is God's gift, Cookie, why on earth didn't God could pick some better wrapping paper?"

"Ron," says Cookie, smiling weakly, laughing softly. I gently touch her supple cheek.

"Look, I didn't come here to cry on your shoulder, nice as it is," I say. "I know that's what it seems like. But that's not it."

"Why then?" says Cookie.

"You know," I say. "I want to know what your answer is."

Cookie sits down on the couch and puts her feet on the coffee table. I sit down next to her. "There's something you must tell me first," she says. "I have to know, you know — if you were really going to do it."

"Do what?" I say.

"Push the Doomsday Button, or whatever it is you call it?"

I shake my head. "Cookie, I can't," I say.

"Don't you see, Ron? It's my children. I just can't believe that you would do such a thing to my children. Or to yours, for that matter. Your own kids, Ron! How could you?"

"I can't answer that," I say flatly. "For the good of the country, I have to do more than keep the world leaders guessing. I have to keep everyone guessing. Even you, Cookie. Especially you."

Cookie's face turns disappointed, then sad, finally blank. "Then I can't stay," she says.

"I understand."

Cookie leans toward me and presses her soft warm lips

against my cheek. Then she gets up. She has never looked more beautiful. "You should go now," she says.

I nod. There is nothing left to say. Standing in the doorway facing Cookie, I reach out and take her hands in mine. Hers are warm, mine are cold. We look into each other's eyes, searching. Fruitfully? I do not know. How could I know? Cookie's lower lip begins to quiver. Her eyes, blue again, close, fracturing our visual link. She continues to let me hold her hands. Her eyes reopen, searching mine once more. I kiss her gently on the forehead. Her forehead is moist. She manages a weak smile. I cannot. I release her hands.

The next morning she is gone.

∿

I've said it before and I'll say it again. The purest kind of love is unrequited love because it lets you hold on to your illusions.

THE AFIKOMON

Tuesday, October 26, 2016. It is one week prior to the election and I have taken a commanding lead in the polls over hapless Fleming Hodgetts. However, like Richard Nixon in 1972, I am taking nothing for granted. I am not about to break the law, mind you. But I am not against pulling another rabbit out of my yarmulke.

Ashley Jones, tanned from a recent vacation to St. Martin, looking like a goddess in an elegant white suit with a lavender silk blouse, stands alone before the Ridgeley press corps. "I have a brief statement from the president to read to you today," she begins. "And I promise you that at some point in the near future you will have the opportunity to personally ask him any questions you would like regarding this most historic news. 'Yesterday afternoon, in Tel Aviv, an agreement between the Iraqi government and a major U.S. corporation was signed, bringing to fruition weeks of intense negotiations. In exchange for becoming the site of what we expect to be the most advanced theme park in the world, Iraq has agreed to end all hostilities toward the United States, more specifically toward Israel. The theme park, which will be called *Holy Land*, will feature Noah & the Great Flood, the world's largest water attraction; Burning Bush Gardens, 188 acres of thrill rides, Jonah & the Whale, a 72-hole miniature golf course designed by world-renowned scuba divers and Biblical scholars, and 20,000 Inches under the Dead Sea, a terrifying encounter with a giant shrimp that has gone berserk from high blood pressure caused by living in water nine times saltier than the ocean. Park revenues for the first full year in operation are expected to exceed those of Iraq's other tourist attractions combined.' Thank you and good day."

And my critics said I accomplished nothing of value during my two and a half years as the houseguest of Diya Bakir.

❧

I am still smarting from my circumcision. I may never forgive my mother for caring so little about a little boy's penis, for cutting me off from my people, albeit invisibly to almost everyone but God. "And the uncircumcised male who is not circumcised in the flesh of his foreskin, that soul shall be cut off from his people; he hath broken My [God's] covenant." (Genesis 17:14) On the other hand, where would I be now had it not been for her fortuitous and prolonged distraction? Dead as a doornail, most likely.

I am also not pleased that, when presenting a report of the procedure to the press, my team of mohels used a modest-sized diagram with a legend explaining that one foot equaled one inch. Any fool could see the entire chart was less than four feet high and five feet long and that my whole penis fit comfortably within the confines of its Lilliputian borders. And as if that were not embarrassing enough, Fleming Hodgetts, on the day after the procedure, introduced a bill to a full Senate chamber to have the name of the Washington Redskins changed to the Washington Foreskins. At his side for the first time, pledging their full support for the measure — and I certainly can't blame them, because the ignominious epithet Redskins should have been cast off long ago — were ten representatives from various Native American tribes.

〜

Tuesday, November 2, 2016. 11:43 p.m. Joy, elation, ecstasy! The election is mine, a stunning and convincing victory. Better still, with the renovations of the past four years now complete, the White House itself is finally mine as well. I can move in immediately. Move over, Fleming Hodgetts. Things are going to change around here.

〜

A miracle has happened on the south lawn. A menorah burns, but it is not consumed. Indeed, it is probably a miracle that a menorah burns on the south lawn at all. When I first announced that this would take place on Chanukah of this year, there was immediate and widespread protest, the most vitriolic of which came from the Christian right. Fortunately, I was prepared for this. And during my weekly internet address I had this to say: *My fellow Americans, religious freedom is a guaranteed constitutional right. An individual right. Therefore, this ceremony, this Festival of Lights, need not reflect the plurality of American society, but simply the religious persuasion of the First Family. Yes, I am well aware of the huge uproar about this, most notably from the Christian right, whose members have bellowed loudly about how I have defiled them, how I have tampered with what they so frequently proclaim on other occasions to be the tamper-resistant character of this great and God-fearing Christian country of ours. But I will not flinch. I will not back down. Nor will I shortchange them by simply turning one cheek in their direction. I will turn two, if you get my drift. I will also tell them to go read about tolerance. Where? In the New Testament, of course. 'Honor all men. Love the brotherhood.' I believe that's The First Epistle of Peter 2:17."*

∾

The next day — Sunday, cold, gray and raw — dampens my spirits. I sit alone in my White House office.

I failed, Pop, didn't I?

What do you mean failed? You won a by a landslide.

Not that, Pop. I mean I didn't save the world.

Maybe not the world, Ronnie.

I don't understand.

Maybe not the *world, but* a *world.*

Solomon Dayan?

Of course Solomon Dayan. You've already forgotten his little boy, your namesake?

No, Pop. I guess you're right. Thanks.

You're a good boy, Ronnie. But you worry too much.

∾

Monday, December 29, 2016. Though I didn't need it today, my mood just received an atomic blast of light, a sling-shot ride through the roof of ecstasy. And the reason behind this precipitous lift, this transcendental orgasm, was a wonderful note, handed to me a moment ago by Rosalee Wilson, from my good friend Red Trombley of *The Los Angeles Times*. Here is what it says:

> *Dear Mr. President:*
>
> *Although I am mainly writing to you about something that has been on my mind for some time, first let me offer my belated congratulations on your record landslide victory over Senator Hodgetts. No president in history has done more to earn such a vote of confidence and I can only imagine how gratifying all this must be, given the early stumbles of your administration and the unique hurdles you had to face. Indeed, sir, if guts, as Ernest Hemingway once wrote, is grace under pressure, then you are guts personified.*
>
> *But to the point. Because I failed to do so previously (and I sincerely apologize for this), I wish to tell you now that your kind gift has meant everything to me. I have fashioned a wooden pedestal for it with my own two hands, woodworking being an avocation of mine, and have placed the pedestal and baseball atop my living room mantel for all to see and admire. Since that time, you couldn't imagine how many of my friends and loved ones have told me that the tangy smell of that ball reminds them of the ballpark! So I thank you once again, sir, for this very special and thoughtful gift. I will treasure it always, as I treasure our friendship. At this juncture I would say onward and upward but, frankly, I have no idea how your next four years could possibly attain a higher level of achievement than your first four. God bless you, President Ron Goldberg, and God speed.*
>
>
>
> *Your friend always,*
> *Montgomery "Red" Trombley*
>
>

❧

I cannot begin to describe the tears of joy Red Trombley's note brings to my weary eyes, these eyes that have seen so little yet so much. My God, was there ever a Jew blessed with more serendipity than Myron Solomon Goldberg?